SHAE RUBY
SHOT FOR MERCY

Shot For Mercy Copyright © 2025 by Shae Ruby

All rights reserved.

No portion of this book may be reproduced in any form, or stored in a retrieval system, or transmitted in any form or by any means, electronic, mechanical, photocopying, recording or otherwise, without written permission from the publisher. It is illegal to copy this book, post it to a website, or distribute it by any others means without permission, except for the use of brief quotations in a book review.

This book is entirely a work of fiction. The names, characters, and incidents portrayed in it are the work of the author's imagination. Any resemblance to people, living or dead, and events is entirely coincidental.

ISBN: 979-8-9927049-1-4

Cover Design: Quirky Circe

Formatting by: Quirky Circe

Cover Photographer: Michelle Lancaster @lanefotograf

Edited by: The Cauldron Author Services

Lunar Rose Editing Services

SHAE RUBY
SHOT FOR MERCY

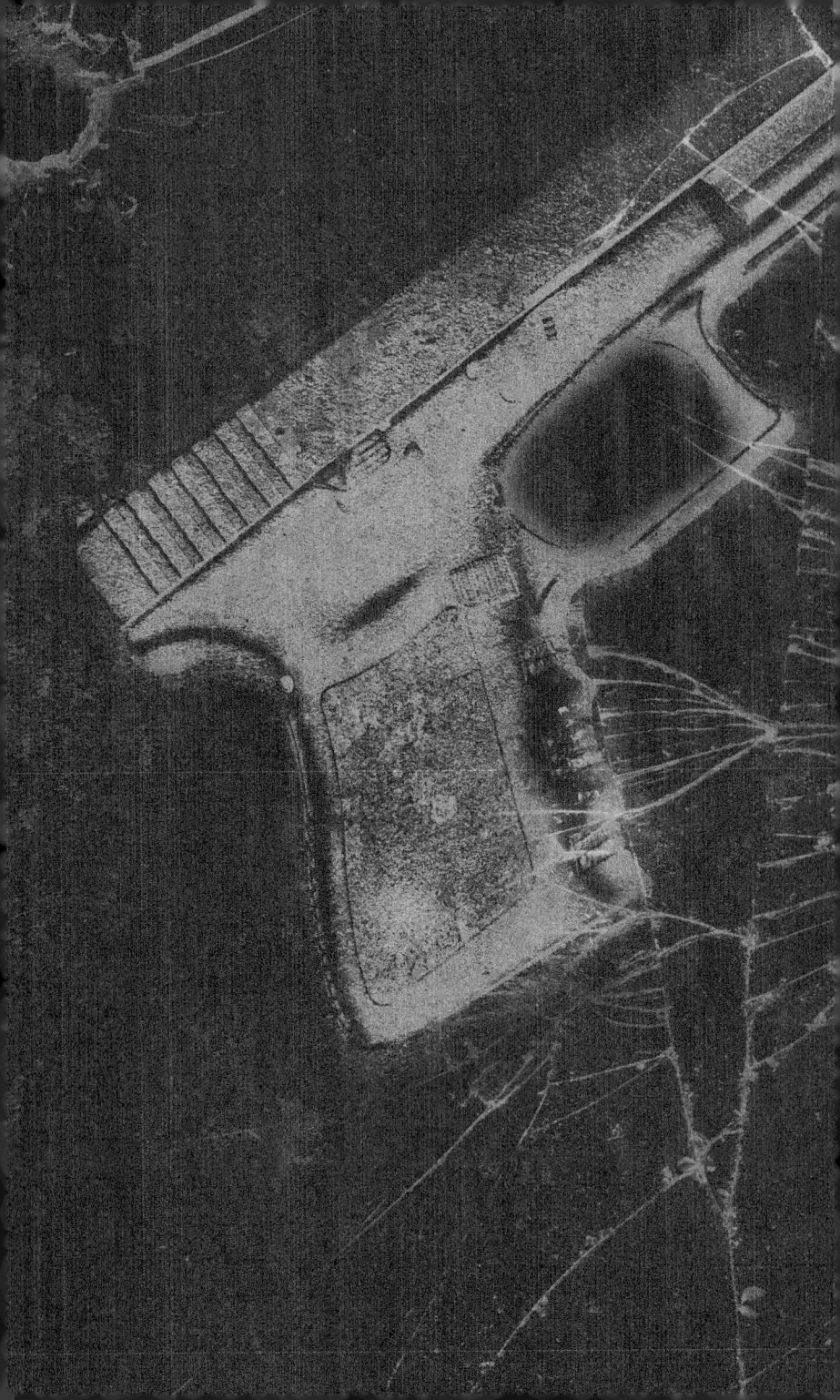

When love is love, nothing else matters. Not age. Not the meet cute. Not the trials and tribulations.

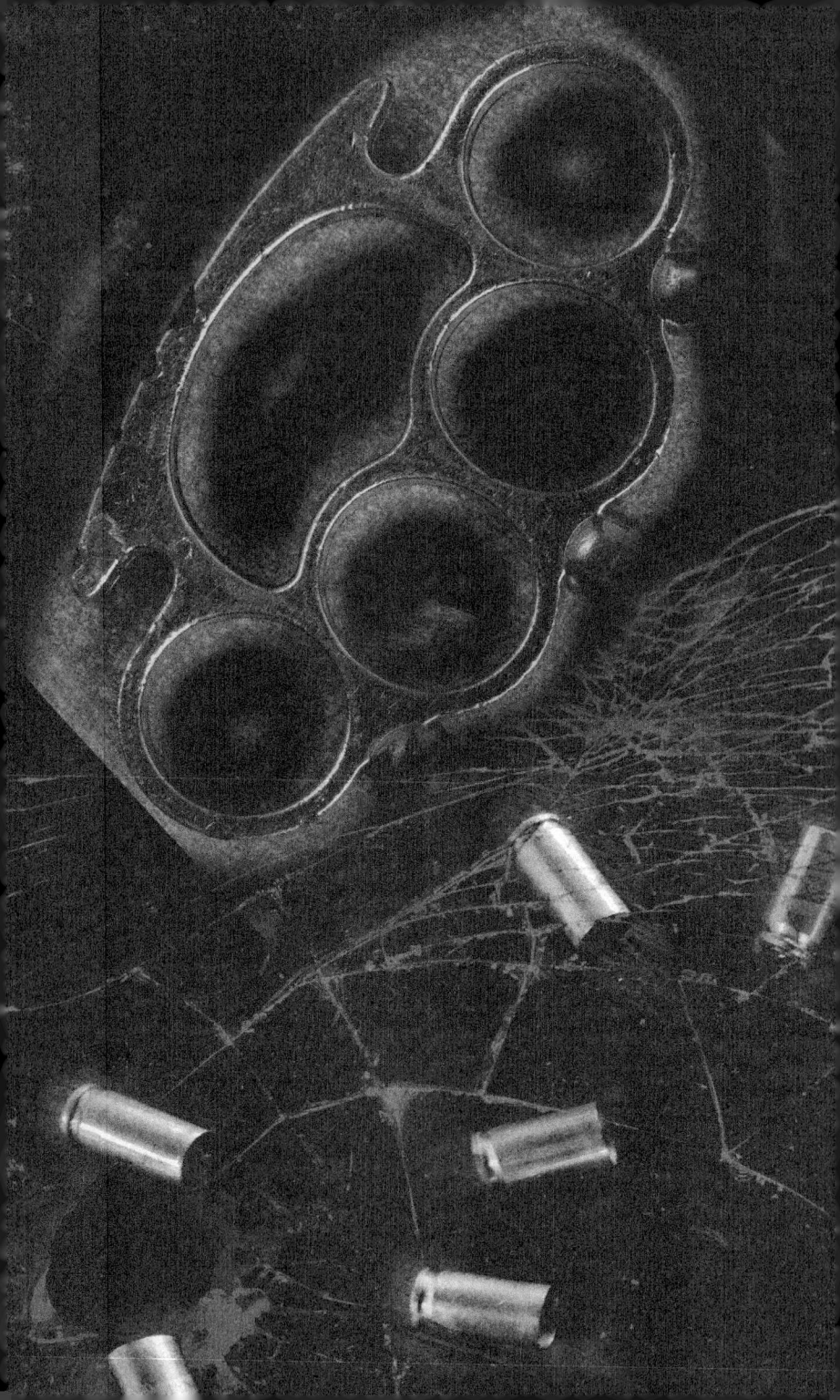

PLAYLIST

Got Me Started — *Troye Sivan*
Diet Pepsi — *Addison Rae*
Beggin' — *Maneskin*
The Loneliest — *Maneskin*
Figure You Out — *VOILA*
Petals — *VOILA*
Drinking With Cupid — *VOILA*
Bad Habits — *Ed Sheeran*
Until the Day I Die — *Story of the Year*
Novocaine — *Stellar*
Mercy — *Bad Omens*
Lose Control — *Teddy Swims*
Guys My Age — *Hey Violet*
Give Me Your Love — *Chris Grey*
Under the Influence — *Chris Brown*
Wherever I Go — *One Republic*
Timeless — *The Weeknd & Playboi Carti*
Use Me — *PVRIS (ft. 070 Shake)*
Church — *Chase Atlantic*

TRIGGER WARNINGS

Hello reader,

I write dark stories that can be disturbing to some. My books are not for the faint of heart, and my characters, many times, are not redeemable. This book contains dark themes to include graphic sex scenes, degradation, drunk sex, spanking, breath play, safe word, torture, kidnapping, and death of a parent. I may be missing some triggers, so instead, consider this a blanket trigger warning.

I trust you know your triggers before proceeding and always remember to take care of your mental health.

For more things Shae Ruby,
visit **authorshaeruby.com**

PROLOGUE
EMILIANO

My hands shake in anticipation as Luca opens the front door of the dingy apartment, and my nose scrunches at the coppery smell of blood in the air. I can practically taste it, and I swallow hard. We're here because we got a tip that Amanda, my soldier's wife, was the rat who gave up one of our warehouses, and it was stormed by the police shortly after. We came here to kill her, but it seems that's been taken care of.

I stand at the entrance, shutting the door behind me, and close my eyes. A million thoughts run through my head, mainly that there's a child in this house, and I need to find him and get him out of here. Then I'll deal with Elio. He can no longer be a part of us. Traitors don't survive.

La Cosa Nostra.

I may not be in charge yet, but I'm my father's right hand, and that counts for something. As the oldest of five, I know I'll be Don one day, and I have to prove that I have what it takes. Papà would be proud right now if he knew what I was doing, but I don't brag or talk about every job I do unless he's the one who gives it to me.

"Elio is here," Luca says, and I smile tightly. My soldier is loyal, and he goes everywhere with me.

"Where is the child?" I ask Elio with a sigh, hating that

Elio made everything so fucking messy. He knows better than to do that, and now I'll have to kill him. Murdering a mother in cold blood in front of her child—really? I thought he had more tact than that, but I've been mistaken about a lot of things lately. I thought he was one of the most loyal soldiers I've ever had, but if his wife was a rat, then so is he, in my book. His fate is now sealed.

No mercy.

Elio points down the hallway, and I follow Luca as we look in both bedrooms. The smell of blood gets stronger, and a whimper fills my ears.

"He's here." Luca points past the mangled body of the once-beautiful woman, and there, in the middle of blood and brains, sits a small child rocking back and forth. My heart squeezes in my chest at the sight, but I will my face to stay blank. I fucking hate when children get involved. They're too innocent for this world.

I nod, making my way toward the kid. He's shaking like a leaf, and with his black hair and big blue eyes, he reminds me of my child I left at home. There's no way I can walk away right now. It would make me scum. None of this is his fault.

I sit down on my haunches in front of him, my suit suddenly making me feel cramped, and his blue eyes widen. They're so light they look almost transparent, almost as if it's a trick of the light that they look blue in the first place. Pasting a smile on my face for his sake, I stretch out my hand.

"You're Cole, right?" I ask him in Italian, knowing he has learned to speak it. Elio taught him some; that much is obvious by the way he nods. I know his stepfather was hoping for him to follow in his footsteps, and if I'm being honest, after tonight he will have no choice. I'm not leaving him behind to open his mouth to anyone or go to the cops. But I can't kill him. Children are off limits, and just thinking of him going into the system makes me sick.

"Yes." He nods, looking at my outstretched hand with apprehension. "Elio taught me some Italian. He said he would make a man out of me, whatever that means."

I grin and whisper, "I'm Emiliano." *I'm Emiliano.* "You—"

"I know," he whispers back, and my hand almost falls to my side, but he takes it instead. "I know who you are."

I nod slowly, hoping my slow movements will calm him down slightly. He needs to go in the car before I finish Elio once and for all. "I need to get you out of here."

Cole's eyes shift toward his mother, and I see his eyes widen once more at the view. She's face down on the floor, a puddle of thick blood around her head. I can see her head has a hole in it.

He shudders, then turns to the side and throws up, letting go of my hand abruptly as his body heaves. He tenses, puking wave after wave on his hands and knees. I don't look away; instead, I wait patiently for him to be done. If he's going to be in this life, he'll have to get used to the sight. Although it would be cruel, even for me, to expect that of him right now. Once he's done, he wipes his mouth with the back of his hand.

"Look away," he says, choked up, tears running down his cheeks.

"A man never looks away," I reply, hoping it'll be the one thing he learns today. A visible shiver wracks his body, and I sigh. "Come on, Cole. We need to get out of here."

He nods, taking my hand, and I look at Luca expectantly. He meets my eyes and nods once, taking Cole from me and taking him to the SUV parked out back. I walk out of the small bedroom and down the hallway to where Elio sits on the couch. He's not bound or forced, and for that I'll make this quick.

He wears a mask of resignation.

"I'm not a rat." He sighs, and I believe him. Doesn't change what I have to do. "I didn't know about her."

I nod at him, taking my gun out of my side holster, and sliding a silencer in place. "You didn't have to kill her in front of him."

"He should see what happens when you open your mouth."

"He's just a child," I growl. "Children are off limits."

Elio's eyes widen at my tone, and he nods once. "And for that, I'm sorry."

"That kid is probably scarred for life." I sigh, bringing my weapon to his forehead. He presses against it, and I'm grateful he's making this easy. He'll die with dignity. "Thank you for your service, Elio."

He looks into my eyes until the very last moment, and I pull the trigger without an ounce of emotion.

A man never looks away.

Maybe I am a monster after all.

His body slumps back against the couch, brain matter and blood splatters decorate the white wall behind his head. He looks almost as fucked up as his wife, and I can't help but feel a deep sense of satisfaction at that fact. Almost like I'm avenging the child in my vehicle. I shouldn't care that much, but I've already decided Luca is going to take him in. The least I can do is make him see what I do for people who are loyal to me.

I make my way out back and to the SUV, holstering my gun before I'm visible. I made sure to be careful with the doorknob as I closed the door behind me. The last thing I need is for fingerprints to be traced back to me. Or Luca. He doesn't deserve that, and I need him by my side.

Luca stands by the driver's door, keeping watch, and I walk directly to him. "I need you to take him in," I tell him, and his eyes widen. "Do this for me, please. We can't afford to let him go."

He nods slowly, his eyes still wide. He looks terrified. "I don't know the first thing about kids, boss."

"I'm sure you can figure it out," I reply, suddenly feeling desperate. "Please."

"Alright, I'll take him in."

"Let's take him to the penthouse." I sigh, running a hand down my face. "I think he should meet Matteo. It would be good for him."

"And then?" he asks shakily.

"Then he goes home with you," I reply, and he nods.

Cole stares at me wide-eyed as I get in, scooting all the way until he's plastered against the side of the door on the other end of the vehicle. I look at him patiently, a soft smile on my face. I hope it reassures him, and sure enough, he relaxes slightly.

"Did you kill him?" he asks me, a hopeful shimmer in his eyes.

I nod. "Yes."

"Good."

I face forward for the rest of the ride, not saying anything to that, and when we finally pull up to the parking garage of my penthouse, I open the door and slip out quietly. He waits in the car, and Luca goes around and gets him.

The walk to the elevator is silent, and Cole doesn't look at me once. He's still visibly shaking, and a pang fills my gut. There's probably nothing I can do for him right now, but he'll have Luca now, and that's reassuring. I know he'd never let anything happen to him. He'll do right by him.

Once in the penthouse, the sound of cartoons greets us. Maria is in the kitchen fixing dinner, and Matteo, my five-year-old, is sitting on the white sectional couch with a bowl of chocolate ice cream. His face is dirty with it, and I smirk. When I look over at Cole, his eyes are wide with fear.

"Matteo, what did I say about eating ice cream on my couch?" I ask him gently, and he grins.

"You said not to do it." He shrugs. "But I want to watch this."

"Give me," I tell him as I close the distance between us, and he hands me the bowl with a pout. "I want you to meet someone."

Cole runs behind me and hides, and I grab his arm and tug him ever so gently to my side. His eyes are wide, and when I look at Matteo, so are his. But then a smile fills his face.

"Papà?" Matteo grins. "Is he staying with us?"

I shake my head. "He'll be with Luca." I look between them, and Cole tenses. "Matteo, this is Cole." I turn toward Cole, whose eyes are wide. "Cole, this is my son, Matteo."

Cole gulps and says nothing, but Matteo is not deterred in the slightest.

"Papà, he can have my ice cream." He grins at Cole. "Quick before it melts!"

I shake my head. "He needs dinner first. You know the rules."

"Yeah, yeah." Matteo shakes his head. "Cole, do you want to go look at my toys?"

Cole's eyes light up, and he nods rapidly. Matteo gets up from the couch and offers his pudgy little hand to Cole. He looks at it for a brief second before taking it in his, and they run off to Matteo's room together. I follow closely, watching as my son sits Cole down on his bed, raising his hands in the air as if trying not to spook him. But Cole smiles widely, clearly at ease, and I rub my chest when Matteo gives him a hug.

Cole breaks down.

"Papà says men don't cry," he whispers, "but I won't tell."

I swallow the lump in my throat and turn away, suddenly feeling like I'm intruding. But I don't go far because this moment is tugging at my heartstrings and allowing me to see a side of my son I don't often get to.

"My mama is dead."

"So is mine," Matteo says to Cole. "I'll take care of you. You have me now."

Tears sting the backs of my eyes, but I refuse to let them fall. If only he knew.

"But you're younger than me," Cole says incredulously, as if the notion of my son taking care of him is absurd. "How will you take care of me?"

"I'll take care of your heart." I shake my head, hating how much their conversation is affecting me, yet I can't seem to walk away. "And I know how to fight."

"Teach me?" Cole asks him.

"How do I know you won't use it against me?" my son replies, and I grin.

"I'll take care of you too," Cole says softly, and I look back at them.

They're on the bed, holding each other tightly. I find the will to walk away, knowing deep down that I made the right choice. They'll take care of each other now.

They'll be best friends.

CHAPTER 1
COLE

18 YEARS OLD

The silence is deafening as I wait in the warehouse with my soldiers for the shipment of coke to come in. They're late, and I don't tolerate tardiness. Matteo stands next to me in the shadows, passing me his cigarette, and I take a deep pull. The smoke fills my lungs, and I instantly relax.

Emiliano has me taking care of this. He usually alternates between Matteo and I, but he said I should have backup just in case something happens. I wonder if he's fucking psychic, because they've never been this late before. A shiver runs down my spine as a vehicle comes into view, and my soldiers shift from one foot to the other.

"Those aren't our people, boss," they tell me, and I narrow my eyes on the vehicle, trying to make out who the fuck it could be through the tinted windows. "Fuck, get down!"

In our confusion, we failed to see the other vehicles pulling up behind the blacked-out SUV. Now, shots are being fired, and we're dropping to the ground like flies. I look around at the five men on the ground—my men—*dead*. Anger boils my blood as I try to step away from the shadows, but Matteo grabs my arm.

"No," he growls. I look at him as he shakes his head. His dark gaze finds mine, and I hold it. "We aren't dying tonight."

"So we stay in the shadows like fucking cowards?" I snap. "I think the fuck not."

Matteo sighs, getting his gun out, and so do I. Our men shoot down multiple Russians across from us, but they continue to go down. Until it's just Matteo and I, with our weapons drawn, pointed right at Andrey Sokolov.

Andrey is the Russian Mafia heir, and he'll be Pakhan one day. I'd love to kill him, but I know I need the go-ahead from Emiliano before I put his entire empire at risk. Me killing Andrey would be an act of war, much deserved, but an act of war, nonetheless. I wonder if that's what he's doing though, declaring it for both of us. He is on our turf, after all. Killing our men.

"Are you two pussies going to shoot, or what?" Andrey grins, blond hair shining as he gets closer. "Italian scum." His accent is thick as he speaks, and he spits on the ground as he walks right toward us.

Matteo places a hand on my shoulder and squeezes, but I keep my eyes trained ahead, looking right at the motherfucker headed our way.

"No, Cole," he whispers. "You're—" Matteo says in Italian.

"English, fuckers." Andrey grins as he gets close enough that my weapon is pressed against his chest. "I want to understand your last words."

"Last words?" I scoff. "We are Made Men."

"You can't kill us without starting a war," Matteo says, and Andrey falters for a moment, stepping away from my gun. "And you know that."

Andrey nods, taking steps back with his gun trained on Matteo. A shiver runs down my spine as I see him pull the trigger, and the sound of the weapon going off makes my ears ring. I turn toward Matteo, who hits the ground immediately, and I feel the blood draining from my face. Dropping to my knees, I immediately press my hand to the gunshot wound, making him cry out.

Looking back, I see Andrey retreating with a grin on his face. I know that if I take my hand off Matteo's chest, he'll bleed out.

I put pressure on the wound with one hand, using the other to take my cell phone out of my back pocket. Then I dial Emiliano. He picks up on the very first ring, and I hear his heavy breathing in my ear. I close my eyes momentarily, trying not to look at Matteo.

"I'm sorry," I whisper.

"Why?" he asks slowly. "Why the fuck are you sorry, Cole?"

"I need the doc," I say in a rush, looking down at Matteo's pale and sweaty face. I press the phone to my ear with my shoulder and slap him as he begins to close his eyes. The blood coming out of his wound seeps through my fingers, and I almost gag. I don't have a weak stomach, but this is my best friend in the entire world. If he dies... I'll burn the fucking world down. "Matteo has been shot."

"Fuck!" Emiliano growls, the sound of a car starting in the background almost as loud as his shout. "Where the hell are you?"

"Warehouse five."

"Be there in ten with the doc."

"He doesn't have ten minutes, Emiliano," I say through gritted teeth, and more blood rushes out of Matteo's wound. "You're tired, aren't you? Open your fucking eyes!" I yell at Matteo, and his eyes roll to the back of his head. "*Shit.*"

"I don't give a fuck how tired he is!" Em yells, and I can hear tires screeching. "Keep him awake."

"Hurry the fuck up," I snap. "That fucking Russian is going to pay."

"Who?"

"Andrey Sokolov." And mark my words, he's going to die. Even if it's the last thing I ever do. "He's the one who shot Matteo."

"This is war," he growls, then hangs up.

I drop my phone to the ground, taking off my shirt one-handed and pressing it to Matteo's chest. His face is white as a sheet, his dark brown eyes looking up at the ceiling, a grimace on his face. But then his eyes connect with mine, and my heart begins to pound in my ears just as I feel his slow down.

"Cole…" Matteo whispers, and I shake my head rapidly. His hand wraps around my wrist, and he squeezes me roughly. "I love you, baby.."

I love you.

My heart trips and skips three beats, and my jaw drops. "Matteo—"

"No, let me fucking say it," he growls, and I hear a car pulling up. Probably Emiliano and the doctor, but I don't dare take my eyes off Matteo. "If I'm gonna die, I'm going to tell you how I fucking feel."

I gulp but nod.

"I love you," he whispers, as if his voice is suddenly giving out. "Since the moment I met you. I've loved you. And if I make it out of this—"

"You will," I growl.

"—I want to be together."

I gulp. "Matteo."

"Fuck that," he snaps. "If I'm going to die, the least you can do is lie to my face."

"I don't have to lie," I whisper. "I *do* love you."

Just not as much as you love me.

I look over at Emiliano as he runs over to us, and our eyes connect. My stomach flutters, and a fire rages in my chest. It's fucking scary what being in his vicinity does to me.

His deep brown gaze falters between Matteo and me, but his face is blank, devoid of any emotion. He doesn't want to scare my best friend. Or maybe it's both of us. He's always protecting us.

And I'm sick of it.

I don't need protection. I just need *him*.

But even I know he would never give me a chance.

It's freezing outside as I douse the Russians' auction house in gasoline. My breaths come out in pants by the time I'm done, little puffs of white that remind me to get some fucking gloves next time. I can barely feel my fingertips. It's December in New York, after all. I don't even know how I was able to take off my sweatshirt a few days ago when Matteo was shot. I guess the adrenaline kept me from feeling cold.

Matteo is thankfully alright now, but it was a close call. Our doctor was able to patch him up enough to get him to a hospital, and now he's still there with guards watching him around the clock. I haven't been able to bring myself to go see him. After his fucking love confession, I don't even know how to act around him. He said it in the heat of the moment—on the brink of death. Surely he didn't mean it. At least that's what I keep telling myself in order to survive because the alternative—breaking his heart—is too painful to even think about.

The only problem is that my heart belongs to Emiliano

Colombo, no matter how many times I try to convince myself that it will never happen. That he will never see me the way I see him. But my mind is just as delusional as my heart, constantly whispering, *what if*?

What if it did happen?

What if he suddenly sees me for who I am?

For what I can offer him?

He's not the kind of man who falls in love. Hasn't been in love probably ever—or maybe since he was with Matteo's piece of shit mother. Over the years, he's had one night stands. That much I do know, considering he brought someone to the penthouse a couple of months ago. I was staying with Matteo, which isn't out of the ordinary for us, and I went to the kitchen to get a drink. I heard them fucking, and that's when I realized I'm in love with him. The rage I felt in my chest as I listened to the sounds he was making stunned me. I couldn't believe he was making those sounds for anyone but me, even if that's the most delusional thing I've ever thought. Gay marriage is no longer frowned upon in the mafia, yet I doubt Emiliano would ever want me. But he already has an heir, so why does it matter who he's with? It doesn't. Still, it doesn't make a difference.

I'm completely fucked. Pining after a man who will never be mine. I don't know if I'll ever be brave enough to tell him how I feel, anyway. His rejection might kill me. He's completely in the dark about my feelings since I'm all business as usual, never letting my guard down or losing my composure. The last thing I need is for him to figure it out and treat me differently. Or talk to me like I'm still a child. Even though he's only fifteen years older than me, which isn't that much in my opinion. He's in his mid-thirties.

I light the match, throwing it on the ground on top of the gasoline, and take a step back as flames roar to life. It brings a grin to my face, but just as I turn around, there's a man in a suit drawing his weapon at me. My nostrils flare in my attempt to keep my composure. But my hands begin to shake and sweat. No matter what, I can't tell him why I'm trying to burn this place down—that much I know. I won't die a traitor. That's probably my fate in prison. The inmates will be chomping at the bit to get to me.

Fuck.

"Hands behind your head," the man says softly, and suddenly, the guys in the house begin to scream. Probably from being burned alive. "Hurry the fuck up."

I do as I'm told, placing my hands behind my head.

"Turn around."

I do it too, turning slowly toward the house. At least if I go down, they go down too. It's revenge for Matteo. "I need a phone call."

"Oh, you know your rights?" I hear the smirk in his voice. "Who are you going to call, Cole?"

Wait, how the fuck does he know my name? I frown, my lips tipping down. "Can you just tell me my rights like you're supposed to?"

"Gladly."

The agent proceeds to tell me my rights, cuffing me and shoving me into his undercover vehicle. The firefighters and ambulance show up immediately, and I tense. Motherfucker probably called them as I was pouring the gasoline. Just how long did he watch me for? How long was I unaware?

The ride to the station is short, and after being processed and put in a cell, I spend some time contemplating my life choices. What the fuck have I done? Arson is probably a few years in prison, right? Fucking hell, I messed up. Well, that's putting it lightly. If no one else kills me first, Emiliano sure will. But I can't think about it. I did what had to be done.

"Time for that phone call," a cop says, and I nod. "You have five minutes."

I get up and follow him out of the holding cell, hurrying toward the phone. I dial Emiliano's number—which I shouldn't be doing—and he answers on the second ring. He knows something is wrong.

"Hey," I say softly. "It's me." I pause at the silence on his side. "I'm booked."

"Fuck no," Emiliano growls. "What the fuck did you do?"

"Arson."

"What the fuck were you thinking?" he snaps, and I flinch. "You're going to prison, you know that right?"

"I did it for us," I tell him through gritted teeth. "Take care of Matteo."

"Cole—"

"Don't Cole me," I reply, taking a deep breath. "I did what had to be done."

"You're right," he whispers. "I'll get the best lawyer."

"Thanks, Em."

He sucks in a sharp breath. I've never called him that before, though I've wanted to. "Let me know if you need anything."

"I will," I reassure him. "Gotta go."

"Talk soon," Emiliano grunts, and I hang up without another word.

At the end of the day, I know I did what needed to be done. No matter the consequences, I avenged Matteo. An eye for an eye. I know Andrey didn't die, considering the firefighters got there quickly, but hopefully, he's at least badly burned. Hurt. Fucked up. Beyond recognizable.

It's the least he deserves for fucking with my best friend.

CHAPTER 2
COLE

21 YEARS OLD

Thirty-eight months in prison for grand arson, and today is the day I got released. Emiliano didn't come visit me once. Matteo came weekly. It shouldn't piss me off this much. I know he has to protect himself. He is Don now, but underneath it all, I'm more upset than angry. I just can't show how much he hurt me, or I'll be showing all my cards. No, I need to keep my feelings to myself. It's not the time to show weakness, not yet. But it is time to claim what's mine. And Emiliano Colombo will be mine, if it's the last thing I do.

I wish I could love Matteo the way I know he loves me. And the truth is, maybe once upon a time, I did. But now I realize it must have been puppy love because it doesn't compare to what I feel for his father. I feel a burning need for Emiliano. I'm fucking obsessed with him, and even after all these years, I haven't been able to kick it. He's like a drug I'm being tempted with, and I just know one hit will make it all better. The problem is that even I know one hit will never be enough. I want to own him. I want *him* to own *me*, too. Which is why I need to know when to make my move. And it can't be right now.

The problem is that Matteo and I have been each other's firsts for a lot of things. First kiss, first fuck. I knew his feelings for me—deep down, I did—and I encouraged it. And now I have to deal with the consequences. I don't know why I did it. Maybe because at the time I thought I had feelings for him, too. I'm not a piece of shit. I can't say I regret it now, because I could never regret him, but I do feel like an asshole for leading him on. I've always leaned on him like a goddamn crutch. Even while I was in prison, he was the only light in my life. I've known what he wants from me, and I really wish I could give it to him. But I just can't. I don't know how to let him down easy. The one thing in life that I would never want is to ruin our friendship.

Matteo nurtured me. He was patient and kind. He taught me what love is. He's the one who held my hand and let me cry in his arms. I just wish there was something I could do to repay him. Instead, now I'm going to break his heart, and it fucking guts me.

Matteo looks at me from the driver's seat with a glint in his eye, and my stomach drops. What is he thinking about? What is he planning?

"Papà is at the club tonight," he tells me with a grin. "We can get stupid drunk. I think you need it after all these years."

I nod and grin right back at him, because that does sound good. It sounds like exactly what I need. "You're not even old enough to buy alcohol." I chuckle. "How did you get it?"

"You act like I'm a fucking baby, Cole. I'm only one year younger than you, fucker." He laughs, pushing my shoulder playfully, keeping his other hand on the steering wheel. "I'm drinking my dad's liquor. You in or what?"

"He's going to fucking murder us," I reply. "That shit is top shelf."

"Nah." He shakes his head. "I think he'll understand. We're drowning our sorrows."

"And what sorrows do you even have?" I question, raising an eyebrow at him. But he's not looking at me anymore, eyes focused on the road instead of me.

"Missing you," he says nonchalantly, like he's not stabbing me in the chest with his every word. "It's been over three years, babe."

Fuck.

"I missed you too, Matty."

"Fucking hell." He laughs. "I'm way too old for that damn nickname."

"Never too old," I say with a smirk. "But yeah. Let's drown our sorrows. I need a drink and a joint."

"Nothing has ever sounded better." He grins, and it feels like he won't stop smiling. It feels good to be missed by someone. I wonder if Em—

"My room or yours? We can't drink in the living room. Just in case my dad comes home."

Oh, yeah. I'm moving in with them now that I'm out of prison. I guess I could've gone back to Luca's house, but it's better this way. I want to be close to Emiliano, and this is the best excuse. Getting back on my feet.

I roll my eyes. "If your dad gets home, you'll deal with him."

He tenses. "I'd rather not."

"Fine." I sigh. "Your room."

He looks at me, a triumphant smile on his face, then turns his head forward once more. Before long, we're pulling into the parking garage of the penthouse. I'm not sure why he still lives with Emiliano. His dad owns the building, so he could easily get his own apartment. Hell, I might even get my own apartment soon. Then again, living with Emiliano sounds better. Torturing him might be just what the doctor ordered. It'll help me feel better for sure. Just imagining his face as I walk around in my boxers makes me hard.

We get out of the car and walk to the elevator, entering the penthouse. Matteo quickly snatches a bottle of whiskey from the kitchen cabinet, and we go to his room. It smells like him, and the scent makes my heart beat just a little faster. It's always been comforting, and suddenly I wonder if I'm making the right choice by not being with him. Then again, I know I always fuck up. It's what I do.

He grabs a joint from his nightstand, lighting it, and taking a long hit. I laugh when he coughs and he passes it to me. I take a hit too, my head feeling light and fuzzy immediately. God, it's been such a long time. I'm going to be fucked up if I finish it with him. But maybe that's exactly what I need.

We sit on his bed, and he passes me the open whiskey bottle. I drink straight from the source, then pass it to him. We trade the joint for the whiskey, back and forth until we finish it. Before I know it, half the bottle is gone, and my head is spinning. I can tell we're both fucked up.

I lie down, my head hitting the pillow, and he puts the bottle on the nightstand. Matteo comes right to me, lying down next to me and facing me. He gets closer and closer until our foreheads are touching, and I suck in a sharp breath. His eyes are full of pain as his knuckles brush over my cheek, and maybe I'm touch starved, but my entire body lights up like fireworks. This isn't good.

"Beautiful.," he whispers, his lips brushing against mine. I close my eyes, unable to look at him. "One kiss."

And I don't know why I can never fucking deny him, because I nod and press my lips to his. The first press of our lips is lightning to my cock, and he rubs against it with his hand. I know he can feel how hard I am, and when he shoves his tongue between my lips roughly, we moan in unison.

"One night," I whisper, and he nods eagerly.

Matteo pushes me onto my back, then grabs a bottle of

lube from under his pillow. "Did you fuck anyone while you were in there?"

I immediately shake my head. "Fuck no."

"Good," he whispers. "I want to go bare."

I pause.

He's the only one who I've ever gone bare with. Hell, he's the only person I've ever kissed. So why am I hesitating?

"Unless you don't want to." He rears back, looking into my eyes. "It's whatever you want."

It's our last time, so I nod. "Fuck me bare."

I'm probably going to regret it. It's way too intimate.

Matteo takes off his clothes quickly, showing me golden skin and endless abs. A sculpted chest and tan nipples. His thick cock, curved slightly to the right. I know he's going to feel amazing, and my cock twitches in anticipation. I sit up and pull my shirt off, and he unbuttons my jeans, pulling them off roughly along with my underwear until we're both naked. He takes me in, and I wonder what he sees. But then he grins, and I know he likes it. Me.

"You're so fucking sexy, baby." Matteo groans, spreading my legs wide and staring. "Look at that pretty little hole. I'm going to fill it with my cum. Do you want that, Cole?"

I whimper, "Yes."

The truth is, I haven't had sex in so long that I'm all keyed up. I don't want to stop. I need this. I need him. Even if it's the last time I let it happen, for both of our sakes.

"But first, I'm gonna swallow yours."

He gets down on his belly between my legs, then licks the head of my cock. I tense and groan, and he sucks me between his lips and to the back of his throat. He swallows around me like a goddamn pro, and suddenly I wonder who he's been fucking. But I quickly get it out of my head. I want to focus on him. On this moment.

I hear Matteo uncap the lube, and suddenly cold, wet

fingers are pressed to my entrance. I relax and bear down, welcoming him into my body. The burn is blinding, and I take a deep breath in through my nose.

"Relax for me, baby," Matteo says. "If you can't take my fingers, how are you supposed to take my cock?"

"I'll take it," I say through gritted teeth, welcoming the burn and bearing down further. His fingers slip in, one after the other, until two are filling me. "Suck my cock, Matteo. Suck it or you don't get to come. I'll leave this room while you're fucking aching for me."

"Talk dirty to me." He smirks, then takes my cock back down his throat and crooks his fingers inside of me.

I see stars.

My vision turns fuzzy around the edges as he rubs against my prostate and simultaneously swallows around me. I grab his hair, tightening my fingers around the strands, and pull him closer to me until his nose is brushing against the neatly trimmed hair at the base of my cock. He inhales sharply, unabashedly smelling me, and I groan.

"*Fuck*, Matteo," I curse. "You really know how to take a cock down your throat. Are you going to be a good boy for me and let me fuck your face?"

"Mhm," he moans, and I plant my feet onto the mattress and begin to thrust up into his mouth.

I hear him gag, and my balls rise up toward my body as he continues to finger my ass. "That's it, Matty. Choke on my cock."

Matteo's free hand grips my hip for dear life as I fuck his face with wild abandon, and he swallows greedily as I come down his throat. He thrusts a third finger into me, crooking all of them, and my orgasm feels like it goes on for fucking ever. Once I'm done coming down his throat, he pulls away from me and removes his fingers from my ass.

"My turn." He grins, coating his cock with lube, and

pressing it to my entrance. "Fuck, Cole." Matteo grits his teeth as he sinks into me slowly. "Your ass is choking me. You're going to kill me."

I smirk. "It'll be a good death."

"The best," he agrees, then slams the rest of the way in.

My back arches off the bed as he steals the breath from me, and he shoves my legs toward my chest. Matteo pulls back slowly, then snaps his hips forward roughly, passing over my prostate with every single thrust. It lights me up from the inside out, and suddenly my cock is hard all over again.

"Look at you," he whispers. "Hard for me again. Do you like my cock in your tight ass, Cole? Do you like when your best friend fucks you?"

"Y-yes," I whisper back. "Fuck me harder."

Matteo spreads my legs, and I wrap them around his waist. He leans down until his torso is pressed against my cock, and with every thrust, it feels like I'm in heaven. I grab the back of his neck and pull him toward me for a kiss, thrusting my tongue into his mouth until he sucks on it. It's like he has a direct line to my cock, and when he slips his hand between our bodies and begins to jerk me off, I moan loudly.

"That's it, Cole," he groans. "Come for me. Come again."

I come with a shout, spurting rope after rope of cum all over myself and him. A moment later, I feel his cock twitch in my ass, and I clench around him. He hisses and moans, then I feel his cum filling me to bursting. I feel it seeping out of my ass, and I grin.

"Fucking hell, Matty." I smirk, slightly out of breath. "You still got it."

"I know, baby." He smirks right back, then pulls out of me slowly. I whimper.

Thankfully, there's a bathroom in his room, and he goes

and gets a wet rag to clean me up with. I'm thankful he always takes care of me, but the gesture is way too fucking intimate. I can't think about it too much though and as he gets back in bed next to me, I close my eyes.

Then the world goes black.

CHAPTER 3
EMILIANO

I slam the pots and the pans loudly on purpose before selecting the one I need. Maybe if I make a lot of noise, the boys will wake up. I doubt it though. If the missing bottle of whiskey from the top cabinet is any indication, they got fucked up last night. Not that I blame them. Cole spent a little over three years in prison, the least I can do is turn a blind eye to it.

The bacon, eggs, and pancake mix sit on the kitchen counter, waiting for me to cook them. But I don't really know if I should get started. Matteo's room is right next to the kitchen, so he's probably bound to wake up soon, but part of me wants to wait until they're both awake so we can all enjoy the meal. Maybe I can just wake them up when the food is done.

I should technically be in the office right now, selling more homes, but I wanted to be here for them today since it's the first time I'll see Cole since he got released. I didn't want to intrude on my son's moment with him, which is why I didn't tag along. I've known Matteo has been in love with Cole since the moment his brown eyes lit up all those years ago when I first brought Cole home. It was all solidified when he got shot by the Sokolov kid and had a mental breakdown when he knew Cole was locked up. He went batshit crazy, so much so that he almost went behind my back to kill Andrey. The only reason he didn't do it is because I told him he couldn't be here for his best friend if he was dead. His need for Cole won out.

Matteo also went to visit Cole weekly, about three hours away for the past three years. They called each other and wrote fucking letters. If that's not love then I don't know what is. They're probably in a relationship I don't even know about.

The sound of a door opening draws my attention to the hallway. I go to the edge of the kitchen just to see Cole slipping out of Matteo's room—completely naked. My entire body warms at the sight of his tight ass, and I frown. What the fuck?

I clear my throat.

"What are you doing?" I ask slowly, softly.

Cole startles, jumping and turning toward me. I keep my eyes trained on his face. His cheeks turn red, his crystalline blue eyes looking clear as ever, yet wide as saucers.

"Going to my room," he replies, taking a tentative step toward me. I know he's doing it so Matteo doesn't wake up, but I take a step back all the same. His eyes roam my body, focusing on my crotch. He raises an eyebrow at me. "Unless you don't want me to."

What the fuck is that supposed to mean?

I rear back. "Go get dressed."

"No."

"No?" I growl. "No one tells me no, Cole."

"Well, I am," he snaps. "You didn't visit me for years, and now you want to tell me what to do? This isn't work related. I'll do whatever the fuck I want."

There's anger in his voice—but I can tell he's also hurt, even if he's trying not to show it. I breathe in deeply as I try to keep my composure, but it's fleeting. "You will go to your room and put some fucking clothes on."

"And if I don't?"

"Then I'll make you," I growl.

Cole raises an eyebrow and smirks, and when I look down, his cock is hard. It's pale and long, with a pink head and a fat vein running along the length of the shaft. My mouth waters, and I look away. Why the fuck am I having this reaction to him? Why am I getting hard?

"I thought you were going to make me," he spits, and I narrow my eyes at his face. I refuse to look down again. It seems to be exactly what he wants. "Which is it?"

I close the distance between us, grabbing his hair and yanking him toward the room like a dog on a leash. He hisses, and the sound goes straight to my dick. What the hell is he doing to me? I've never been with a man, but right now, it looks more appealing by the second.

Letting go of him, I let Cole step away from me and go to his dresser, where he begins to take a pair of boxer briefs out. I watch him as he slips them on, the fabric catching under his perfect ass, and he bends over slightly to put them on. I get a view of his hole and his balls, and my mouth goes dry.

He doesn't turn to face me. Thank God for that. My hard cock would give me away immediately, and by the way he was looking at it earlier, I know he's paying close attention.

I don't want him, though.

I don't.

I'm just fucking glitching right now.

"Why didn't you visit me?" Cole asks, his voice small. "*Why?*"

"You know why, Cole," I reply. "I'm Don now. I can't put everything at risk. I—"

"I'm not important." He nods, and my stomach drops. Is that what he thinks? "Got it."

"Fuck!" I yell, throwing my arms up in the air and pacing

in frustration. "That's not what I'm trying to say, and you know it."

"Go fuck youself," Cole spits, turning toward me with wild eyes.

I close the distance between us quickly. "I fuck myself every once in a while, yes." I get close to him until we're sharing breath, then I wrap my hand around his throat tightly and slam him against the wall. He's so goddamn disrespectful. "But mostly I go to Luna's."

His eyes flare with a rage I have never seen from him, but then he smirks. His face turns red the longer I hold on to him, and he closes his eyes. Before I can pull away, though, he grabs my ass and presses me against his hard cock. I'm ashamed to admit that mine is just as hard. I don't know what the fuck he's doing to me—

Cole bites his bottom lip as he looks up at me, only about three inches shorter than my six-five. He's not a small man, and he's muscular, too. But right here, in my grasp, he looks almost delicate. Like I could dominate him. Like he'd let me. Would he?

I shake my head.

I shouldn't be having these thoughts.

He's Matteo's.

But Cole is looking at me like he's the predator and I'm his prey, and that just won't do. If anyone is doing the hunting here, it's me. I'm nobody's fucking bunny. I'm the goddamn wolf.

I lean in until our foreheads are touching, and Cole grips my wrist tightly, digging his blunt fingernails into my skin. I ease up on my grip, and he begins to cough violently. Yet he doesn't make a move to walk away from me; instead, he stays against the wall once he recovers from the fit. His blue eyes are blood-shot as he looks into mine, and he swallows hard, his Adam's apple bobbing.

"Let go," I whisper through gritted teeth, and Cole narrows his eyes at me, being stubborn as hell and not letting go of my ass. "Or do you need to be taught a lesson?"

"Maybe I do." He raises his chin defiantly, and my cock twitches.

I *really* need to get that under control.

I'm sure he felt it though, because a wide grin stretches his pretty face. His black hair falls over his forehead, and I push it back gently. Too fucking gently. "Did you fuck him?"

"No," he says, and relief fills me at his answer. "He fucked me."

My nostrils flare as white-hot anger flows through my veins, but I can't let it show. I don't even know the damn reason behind it. They have the right to do whatever the hell they want.

"Does that bother you, Emiliano?" Cole raises an eyebrow, seeing right through me. "That your son had his big cock in my ass? I wonder why that is…"

"It doesn't," I lie through gritted teeth, then clear my throat. "I'm fine."

"Sure." He smirks. "Whatever you have to tell yourself. But I see the way you look at me, even if you don't want to admit it to yourself."

"Oh?" I laugh. "And how do I look at you?"

"Like you want to eat me," he replies, looking smug as fuck. "I see it plain as day."

"You're wrong." He can't be right. "This conversation is over."

"As it should be," he snaps. "Matty is up."

Matty.

He's called him that since they were little kids, and Matteo will kill anyone else who uses the stupid nickname. It would be cute if it didn't show how close they really are. I have to figure out how to keep my eyes off him. I can't afford to have my son see how I look at the love of his life. The way I've *never* looked at him before.

I take three long steps back, giving each other some much needed space. Just as I do it, Matteo knocks on the door. He comes in when we're silently staring at each other and looks between us, frowning at whatever it is he sees.

"What's going on, Dad?" Matteo asks me, his voice low and growly, as if he's ready to defend Cole. It irritates the fuck out of me.

"You and Cole stole my whiskey." I sigh. It's the first thing that came to my mind; the only thing that I know could be a good reason to be pissed off. "It was my favorite."

"I'll buy you a new one," Cole says, a smirk on his face. I look over at Matteo and he's smiling at his best friend like a lovesick fool. I suddenly feel sick to my stomach. "Right, Matty?"

Matteo rolls his eyes. "Again with the fucking nickname." He huffs. "When will you fucking stop?"

"Never," Cole replies immediately. "You're stuck with it."

"Alright, boys." I sigh, interrupting them. Cole tenses at my words, and I frown. What the fuck did I say now? "I'm gonna make breakfast. Eggs and pancakes okay?"

"Perfect," Matteo says.

I look at Cole expectantly, and he nods as well. Matteo exits the room ahead of us, and I turn back toward Cole. I don't know why I do it—except I know he's got something he needs to get off his chest.

"I'm not a fucking boy," he growls, stepping up to me and getting in my face. "I'm a fucking man now. Want me to show you?"

I run a hand down my face, because what the hell does he even mean by that? I don't exactly want to know. I don't even want to think about it. "No need." I nod. "I got you, Cole."

"No, you don't," he replies with conviction. "You ain't got shit."

I roll my eyes and turn around, leaving him behind. He's being a pain in my ass, and I'll go right back to ignoring him if that's what it takes for him to chill out. Except this is Cole, and he doesn't enjoy being ignored. He loves to be the center of attention at all times. He wants me focused on him and him alone. Well, guess what? It's not going to happen.

Leaving his room, I make my way back to the kitchen where Matteo is sitting at the island, just for the bedroom door to slam shut. The walls rattle from the force of it, and I sigh.

"What the fuck crawled up his ass?" I ask Matteo, and he smirks. It reminds me of what Cole said to me. *No, he fucked me.* "You know what, never mind."

Matteo laughs, and I tense.

But I just turn to the stove and begin to cook, busying myself before I have a goddamn aneurysm. Because fuck Cole.

And fuck this shit.

CHAPTER 4
COLE

The Pink Pony Club looks different from the last time I saw it. It looks upscale now, with a bigger dance floor and an upstairs VIP area. The bouncers are everywhere, and the bar is packed with bartenders. You can just tell they have a good business. There are probably hundreds of people crammed in here, grinding to the beat of some new hip-hop song I don't recognize.

This is one of Emiliano's many legitimate businesses. He also has a brothel, a restaurant, and his most lucrative yet—a real estate company. His brothers help at that company, Colombo Real Estate, while also getting their hands dirty with drugs and weapons, among other things. I will say that before I went to prison he was trusting me and Matteo with more jobs, and I know Matteo took over while I was gone. But I'm ready to get back into it. I'm ready to get my hands dirty once more. Maybe it's in my blood—or maybe it's how he raised me. The expectations he set for me. I knew from the moment he took me in and made me family that I'd be a Made Man.

I'm upstairs with Matteo in the VIP area, sitting side by side on one of the couches. He's talking my ear off about God knows what, but I can't seem to pay attention. Instead, my mind is on Emiliano and yesterday morning. The way he slammed me against the wall and choked me—I loved it. I can't believe his cock was hard for me. He can say whatever he wants, but his body can't lie to me. He wants me too. His jealousy when I said Matteo fucked me proved that. I just need to find a way to make him give in to me. It's going to be difficult since I know he knows about Matteo's feelings for me.

If I'm being honest, I know it's probably the worst betrayal if I pursue Matteo's dad after everything we've done together. I just can't bring myself to ignore my feelings for Emiliano, though. It's going to make me the worst friend, and I honestly wouldn't blame Matteo if he tried to kill us both. I have faith he will come around eventually though. He'll be heartbroken, but eventually, he'll move on. He has to.

My phone buzzes in my back pocket, and I take it out to look at the new text message. It's from Emiliano.

> **EMILIANO**
> Come to my office. We need to talk.

I smirk and put my phone down, not bothering to reply. I'm not here on business. I'm here to spend time with my friend, and if Em doesn't plan on fucking me right on his desk, then I want nothing to do with him. And knowing him, he's not going to do that. I'm going to be left longing after him for the rest of my life. He's too loyal.

Matteo looks at me. "Who was that?"

"Your dad." I shrug. "Asking me to go to his office. He probably saw us on the cameras."

"So go." He frowns. "He'll be pissed if you don't."

"Fuck him." I roll my eyes and Matteo laughs. I guess a stint in prison has made me rebellious. Or just plain stupid. "I'm not here for business. He can wait."

"You're being stupid," he says with a sigh. "You know he'll have your ass right?"

"So let him have my ass." I shrug as if I don't care. I'd let him have my ass in more ways than one, anyway. "And I'm not being stupid, you little shit. I'm being brave."

"Sure." He chuckles. "Don't be a dick, though. He'll make you pay for it."

I sigh. He's probably right. The only problem is that I don't really seem to care about it much right now. Maybe I want to rile him up. Get a reaction out of him. It might be my only chance for a while. Except just as I lean back on the couch and get comfortable, spreading my legs, and throwing my arm up over Matteo, a bouncer shows up. He's walking right toward me with purpose, and I tense.

"The boss wants to see you," he says loudly, "now."

"Who the fuck does he think he is?" I mutter to Matteo. "Fuck this."

Matteo just smirks and slaps my ass as I get up, and when I look back at him, he winks. I should probably have a conversation with him soon to let him know it was the last time. That we can't keep doing that. I know it'll break him, but I can't find a way to let him down easy.

I turn around with a frown and follow the bouncer downstairs. He leads me to Emiliano's office even though I could've found it on my own, and knocks on the door. Em shouts to come in, and I open the door and close it behind me. He looks at me with a fire in his eyes that I want to stoke, but I'm glued to the door, my back against it. If he wants me, he can come here.

"When I call, you answer," he snarls, his white teeth showing like a rabid dog. I look him up and down, appreciating the way his body looks in a suit. Broad shoulders and thick arms filling it perfectly. His face is tight with anger, his jaw pulsing, but I can't bring myself to care. Instead, I admire his beautiful features: strong jaw, narrow nose, eyes the color of honey. I bet they'd look gorgeous dilated for me.

"You didn't call." I shrug. "You texted me. I figured it wasn't that important, and I'm not here for work."

"You will be at my disposal any time I call," Em says through gritted teeth, getting up from his chair and striding quickly toward me. "If I call you at one in the morning, you come to me."

I smirk. "Those are hoe hours." *Booty call hours.* "Are you going to invite me into your bed, Emiliano?"

"Don't say my name like that."

"Like what?" I ask innocently.

"Growling it like that."

"Why not?" A smile tugs at my lips, widening when he's close enough that our shoes touch. "Does it turn you on?"

"Nothing about you turns me on," he snaps. "Get it through your head."

"That's a lie, and we both know it," I tell him, grabbing him by his suit jacket and turning him around, slamming his back against the door. His breath whooshes out of him, and I smile in satisfaction, locking the door for good measure. "I bet your cock is hard for me right now, Em." His eyes widen, then narrow at the nickname. Three years ago, I would've never dared to talk to him like this. Maybe I am brave after all, or maybe I just don't give a fuck about anything. "Should we test that?"

"N-no."

"Is the big bad boss stuttering?" I chuckle, and his neck turns red. "What, baby? You can't get your words out?"

"Fuck off, Cole," he growls, putting his hands on my chest, yet not pushing me away.

"I don't think you want me to." I raise my chin in defiance, trying not to look so small, and look right into his brown eyes. "I think—I think you'd like to fuck me. Right, Emiliano?"

"You're either drunk or just plain stupid." He shakes his head, but when I press my hand against the front of his slacks, he whimpers. He fucking *whimpers* for me. I rub the palm of my hand over his hard cock, then unfasten his belt. "Fuck, wait."

"No waiting," I say through gritted teeth. "I've waited long enough."

"I'm not—" He sighs. "I can't. We can't."

"And why the fuck not?" I ask him, raising an eyebrow.

"I like women."

"So?"

"*Only* women."

"Beg to differ." I grin and can see the struggle he's going through right on his face, in his eyes. "Look how hard you are for me."

"Fuck." He groans when I rub the palm of my hand over his dick. "I—*fuck*. Yes."

I grin, unbuttoning his pants and shoving my hand in them. Trimmed hair meets my fingertips, and my cock throbs against the confines of my skinny jeans. I shove my hand in deeper, and he doesn't stop me, instead he stays still. I hold my breath as my hand meets silky, smooth skin, his hard cock warm in my grasp. He's fucking huge, way bigger than Matteo, and now I wonder what it'd feel like to ride his cock.

"I bet you'd feel like heaven in my ass," I whisper. "Do you want to try it, Em? Wanna put your cock inside of me? Or do you want to play just the tip?"

I grip his cock harder, jerking him faster, and he moans. "F-fuck."

"Why aren't you pushing me away?" I ask with narrowed eyes.

"Make me come," he says, then grabs the back of my head

and pulls me toward him until we're sharing breath. Our lips brush, and I swear I'm about to come in my fucking pants. "Or get the fuck out."

I don't give him time to say anything else; instead, I slam my lips to his. The way he sucks on my bottom lip has fire licking down my spine, and I thrust my tongue between his lips, not waiting for permission. He sucks on it, and my knees almost buckle. I swipe my finger over his slit, then up to use his pre-cum as lube, and goddamn he's leaking for me. He moans when I go faster, but I don't really want to let him come. He's been an asshole to me. I honestly don't think he deserves it.

"You're so fucking wet for me, Em." I groan, wanting to continue, but willing myself to be strong. I have a point to prove here. "How bad do you want to come?"

"Fuck, Cole," Emiliano says, snapping his hips forward with purpose. His skin is burning hot, and I want to drop to my knees and take his cock down my throat. I want him to use me, abuse me. "So bad."

"Beg for it," I whisper, and he tenses.

His nostrils flare.

"Now, Emiliano."

He doesn't; instead, he narrows his eyes at me. "A Don never begs."

I take my hand out of his pants. "Then I'll see myself out." I shrug. "Let me know when you're ready to come." My fingers have pre-cum on them, and I lick them all. "Mmmm. You taste so fucking good. Are you sure you want me to go?"

Emiliano's chest heaves, but he pushes me away and side steps me, walking back toward his desk. Disappointment fills me, but I can't be too upset. He's the one who doesn't get to come, and I finally have him right where I want him. He can't even deny how he feels anymore. He *showed* me.

"I need you to go to the docks for a shipment." He's back

to business as usual, and I force myself to keep a blank face. Not show any emotions. But it's hard. My cock is throbbing to the beat of my heart, and my hands long to wrap my fingers in the black strands of his hair and shove him to his knees. He will be on his knees for me one day. That's a fucking promise.

"For?" I raise an eyebrow.

"Guns."

"Consider it done," I say, then turn around and unlock the door, wrapping my hand around the doorknob.

"Oh, Cole?" he asks softly. "This never happened."

I smirk. "Sorry boss, but it did."

Making my way back through the throng of people shouldn't be this hard, but the place is filled to the brim. I look up, searching for Matteo, but he's no longer there. He's either dancing with someone or he left me behind.

Fucker.

I can't complain, though. I finally have Emiliano Colombo exactly where I want him, and now I'm never going to let him go.

No matter what he says.

He's *mine*.

CHAPTER 5
EMILIANO

Last night was never supposed to happen, but it fucking did, and now I don't know what to do with myself or the way I feel. I should've never let Cole push me into losing control. Just what is it about him that clouds my judgment? How the hell do I forget all about my son when Cole is in my vicinity? It never used to be this way before he went to prison, but now it's as if he has a leash wrapped around my neck, and he keeps tugging me along. It's starting to piss me off. I'm no one's fucking dog.

Yet, when his hand was wrapped around my cock, I forgot all about that. Hell, I was about to beg, but when he suggested it, I snapped back to reality. The problem is, for just one split second, he made me want to get on my knees for him. And that's dangerous. I can't want him that way. When I fall in love with someone, I consume them. I become crazed and obsessed. There's no way I could do that with the only person in this world who is off limits to me. He's Matteo's, and I have no right to take him away. But I just can't help but notice him now. I never had before. But for the first time ever, I'm seeing him as a man.

I'm noticing how handsome and fucking sexy he looks in those skinny jeans and leather jacket. So unlike me in every way. I wear suits, whereas he dresses down. Where I mostly keep my hair slicked back with gel, he lets his fall over his forehead. Where I'm more reserved until I'm pushed to my limits, he definitely takes what he wants when he wants it. And now he has me in his sights. I'm not stupid. I know he's not going to give up until he gets what he wants. The problem is that once I have him, it'll all be over for him. I'll be a rabid dog who doesn't want to let go. I'll be starved for a bite of his flesh. I already am. Which is why I have to stay as far from him as humanly possible, while still living under the same roof.

How the hell do I even do that?

Just the thought of seeing him around Matteo is making my blood boil with jealousy—which makes absolutely no sense. Cole's not mine, never has been, and never will be. I have to remember how insolent he is, and yet that's half of the reason why it feels so fucking good to give into him. Even if I know I'll have to push him away every single time. But that split second of weakness will get me through until the next time he comes back for more.

Fuck.

There should not be a next time.

I can not lose control. If it weren't for all the sacrifices he's made for this family, I'd have taught him a lesson or two by now for being a disrespectful little shit. Instead, my cock is getting hard over taunting words and a little thrill.

There's a knock at the door, three to be exact, before it opens and all four of my brothers stroll in like they own my office. Luca, my right-hand man and soldier, strolls in right along with them. His eyes are wide, and his hands are shaking. I roll my eyes and shake my head at him. He can be so paranoid.

"It's fine, Luca." I sigh. "These fuckers were gonna find a way to get past you, anyway."

He nods once. "Sir." And disappears from the room.

My brothers all take a seat across from me, making themselves at home, and I lean back in my chair. The high rise I own for Colombo Real Estate is huge, and my office overlooks Manhattan. The floor to ceiling windows are a dream, and sometimes I stay late just to watch the sunset over the New York City skyline. This place is my home, and even the hustle and bustle of the city and all of its noise, has provided comfort to me for decades.

I look at my brothers. Giovanni is facing Lorenzo in his chair, showing me his side profile. Lorenzo, in turn, faces him too, and they're having some kind of unspoken conversation, because suddenly they both turn toward me. Then there's Alessandro, the craziest one of us, who is facing me head-on and waiting for me to speak. We're closest out of all my brothers, and he has to know something is up, considering I haven't left this office all day. Antonio—Tony—our youngest, clears his throat and raises a single eyebrow at me, daring me to speak.

Giovanni and Lorenzo are closest in age, and they somehow almost look like twins even though they're not— they're eleven months apart. Antonio follows closely behind, with being only two years younger than Lorenzo. They're all still in their twenties, and Alessandro is thirty-four to my thirty-six. Which is probably why I'm closer to him than anyone else. Yet when it comes down to it, we all have each other's backs. No questions asked.

"Do you bitches need something?" I ask them all, looking from one face to the next, then focusing on Tony. His bright green eyes shine with mirth, as if there's something he knows that I don't. "What?" I snap.

"Nothing." Tony silently laughs, his body shaking with it. "I just never thought I'd see the day."

"What day?" I frown.

Giovanni chuckles, and I give him my attention now. "The day you became obsessed with someone again."

"What the fuck are you talking about?" I snap. "I'm not obsessed with anyone."

"Bullshit." Lorenzo chimes in. "You've been here all day without letting anyone in. You're not answering your phone, and you look like you want to punch someone."

"And that somehow means I'm obsessed with someone?" I frown.

"Did someone die?" Alessandro asks with a smirk, leaning back in his chair and spreading his legs as he gets comfortable. His hazel eyes narrow. "Or are you dying?"

"No." I shake my head. "But—"

"No buts," Tony says, interrupting me. "Tell us what's really happening."

I sigh, getting up from my chair and beginning to pace. Their eyes follow me to the windows, where I overlook the city and completely avoid their gazes. I don't know how they're going to react to what I'm about to say, but it can't be good.

"Well?" Alessandro presses, and I huff.

"I fucked up," I say slowly, my shoulders rising with tension towards my ears. "And I don't know what to do."

"Fucked up how?" Tony asks.

"Do we need to cut up someone into little pieces, then bury them?" Giovanni asks.

"Can I use my golf club?" Lorenzo asks, and I just know I'm going to get a headache.

They continue to rapid-fire questions at me, and I dutifully ignore them all. If they want to know what's going on, they'll shut the fuck up. Or Alessandro will make them.

"*Quiet*," Alessandro growls, and I grin.

He's so predictable.

Alessandro needs to be in control at all times. It's probably one of the many traits we share. The only difference is that while I'm calm and collected, level-headed even, he's batshit crazy. He doesn't know when to rein himself in and I have to keep reminding him. Maybe that's why he craves control so much. He's definitely out of it.

"Now," Alessandro begins calmly, "what were you saying?"

I turn to face him. "I royally fucked up, Alex."

"How?"

"I—" I shake my head. "I—"

"Yes?" Lorenzo smirks, and I narrow my eyes at him.

"Cole came on to me," I blurt out, and they collectively gasp. Everyone except for Alessandro.

"No." Alessandro shakes his head. "You can't."

"Don't you think I know that?" I snap. "I didn't plan this."

"Matty loves him," Giovanni whispers, and I bristle.

"Don't call him that," I growl. "You know he hates it."

"Do you hate it too now?" he asks with a smirk. "It's Cole's cute nickname for him."

The truth is, I hate everything about this. About him. I wish he hadn't moved in after prison. My life would be so much easier. "No," is all I say.

"Emiliano," Alessandro says gently, "he's off limits."

"He's Matteo's," Tony says, raising his hands in defeat when I look at him.

"What?" Giovanni chuckles. "Don't kill him—he's not wrong."

"You think I don't know that? I feel like shit. Plus, I never looked at him this way until now," I say, feeling the need to clarify. "And I've always been into women. *Only* women. This is... fuck, this is confusing me."

"We know." Alessandro clasps his hands in front of him. "It's not even about the age gap, though. Matteo will kill you."

"Fuck!" I yell, rubbing a hand down my face. "I fucking know it. But I can't keep him away—we *live* together. He came out of my son's room fucking naked the other morning."

"Naked?" Alessandro asks with a raised eyebrow.

"Oh, they're *fucking* fucking," Lorenzo says with a laugh, and if looks could kill, he'd be six feet under. Probably cut into tiny little pieces from my knife. "Shit—my bad."

"Tell me," Giovanni asks with a smirk, "how did that make you feel?"

"I wanted to kill my own son," I growl.

"Oh, he has it bad, ladies." Lorenzo grins.

"I'm not a lady," Alessandro grumbles. "What are you going to do?"

"I can't kick him out." I sigh, "So instead I'm here. And I'll stay here as much as possible until he either moves out or forgets about his little obsession with me."

"Well, at least we know you're not freaking out because he's a guy," Lorenzo says with a shrug. "I thought that would be more of a deal breaker for you."

I shake my head. I've never been into men before. Sure, I can acknowledge when someone is attractive, but that's about it. Cole, on the other hand, has my body doing all kinds of crazy things. Like popping boners in my office at the mere thought of his hand on my cock again.

I'm so fucked.

"That's not even the important thing right now," I tell him, hoping he'll drop it. I'll process my sexuality on my own time. "Or the worst part."

"Wait, it gets worse?" Tony raises an eyebrow.

I close my eyes and breathe in deeply, trying not to strangle each and every one of them. "He wants me bad," I say through gritted teeth. "He treats me like—"

"Like?" Alessandro asks.

"Like he's in charge." I sigh, going back to my desk and sitting down on my chair. "He's not going to stop until I give in."

"*Did* you give in yet?" Giovanni asks.

Yet?

I bristle, even though I know he's technically right. "Kind of," I tell him, remembering Cole's calloused hand wrapped around my cock. It felt heavenly. If I had the chance to do it again, I would. In a heartbeat.

Alessandro sighs. "Be reasonable."

"You don't even know the meaning of that word," I snap. "You and your crazy ass."

"Don't get him started," Giovanni says, and I roll my eyes.

"He'll cut you again, Emiliano," Lorenzo reminds me.

"Can you just leave?" I ask them. "I'm probably staying here tonight."

"Why?" Alessandro narrows his eyes at me. "You could be balls deep in *him*."

My jaw drops, and I can hear my brothers snickering. All of them except Alessandro, who, in turn, is as serious as ever. "What the fuck, Alessandro! I won't do that. You're supposed to talk me out of it."

"Am I?" he asks, tapping his chin with his forefinger. "We both know you don't listen to shit we say. You're like one of those girls constantly asking her best friends for advice, just to go back to her ex and fuck him anyway."

"After she's been cheated on," Lorenzo says.

"Repeatedly," Giovanni adds.

"I get it," I say through gritted teeth. "But I'm not going to do it—again."

My brothers laugh at me, and a shiver runs down my spine. I could kill them all right about now and feel nothing but a deep sense of satisfaction. They're really pissing me off.

Just not more than Cole already has.

CHAPTER 6
COLE

It's been forty-eight hours since I last saw Emiliano, and I know he's actively avoiding me. He went as far as staying the night somewhere else, and he better be careful who he spends his nights with—they might end up dead in the Hudson River. I'm almost ashamed to admit that I waited for him on the couch all night. I did it under the guise of spending time with Matteo, and we watched rom-coms until we both fell asleep. Like the good old days. I'm not ashamed to admit those are my favorite. I missed doing the simple things when I was in prison, and I'm going to make up for it however I can.

Speaking of Matteo, I'm no closer to telling him we're done than I was yesterday. Somehow, I feel guilty, and it's not a good time. Ten out of ten would not recommend fucking your best friend then falling in love with their dad. It's a recipe for disaster, and I know the time is coming when I'll have to come clean. It's inevitable. But I don't want to drop that bomb on him unless Emiliano and I actually get together. There's no reason to break Matteo's heart further if Em and I aren't going anywhere. Which will most likely be the case here. I know he wants me, but he's not going to let himself have me. He'll feel too guilty. He needs to take what he wants more often, but I know he's not going to do it at the expense of his son's happiness. Fuck him for being such a good dad.

Maybe I should move out. It would probably be best for me. I bet Emiliano would have a damn field day and celebrate until the end of time. Finally, his tormentor is out of his hair. But it's not that simple. I don't want to leave him alone, which means that I won't. No matter how much he begs the universe for me to give up, I won't. Not unless he marries someone else or kills me. And if it's the former, I'll just kill her too. Then he'll wish I was really dead—and he'll probably make it happen too.

Worth it.

"They're here," Matteo says, pointing toward the men at the docks. We're sticking to the shadows, just as always, in case there's unwanted company. Unfortunately for us, this is neutral territory. "Let's go."

I nod, stubbing out my cigarette, and he makes a face. He doesn't like it when I smoke. Says it'll kill me someday. The way I see it, I probably won't make it to thirty. Not with the way I work for Emiliano. I'm bound to get killed or end up back in prison sooner than I'd like. And I know if I go back to that place, I'll go fucking insane.

Matteo snaps his fingers in front of my face, effectively breaking me out of my thoughts, and I narrow my eyes at him. "Do that again, and I'll break all your fingers."

"Talk dirty to me." He winks, then goes ahead of me.

I was supposed to do this job alone. After all, Emiliano demanded I do it. But Matteo wanted to spend time with me and wouldn't take no for an answer when I told him I'd be busy with this. He said we could spend some time together afterwards, and it sounded like the perfect time to break the news to him, so I said yes.

My arm shoots out, halting him in place, and I narrow my eyes at the sight in front of us. There, about two hundred feet in front of us, stands Maxim, the Bratva's Pakhan. You'd think he'd send someone here to do the dirty work, but no, here he stands in all of his glory. Vulnerable and ready to be killed.

"Don't," Matty says through gritted teeth. "Don't fuck this up."

"Matty—" I sigh. "He's right fucking there."

"Don't start a war," Matteo growls. "You already got even with Andrey."

"Look at me," I snap, and he does. His brown eyes gaze into mine, and I grab his face roughly. "He almost killed you. We'll *never* be even."

"You're so fucking dramatic, babe," he mumbles, and I roll my eyes. "Always defending my honor."

"Keep your eyes peeled," I tell him, ignoring his sweet nickname. I don't have time to let him down easily right now. "They're fishy as hell."

"Is that...?" Matteo squints, and I follow his gaze. Sure enough, it's our client making deals with the Bratva. "What the fuck?"

"Goddamned double-dippers," I whisper.

We stay back though, especially since our men are in the parking lot, and observe them from a distance. It seems they're trading drugs, probably opioids, by the look of it. They load all the product into a van, then take off.

Matteo and I quickly make our way to our client, who looks like he's seen a ghost. I don't know why he's so damn surprised; we're right on time. As always. We're known for our punctuality, Matteo and I. We'd never mess up a deal. Except for maybe now. I'm tempted to pull out my gun and take care of our little problem.

Matteo seems to know exactly where my head is and whispers, "Don't do it, Cole. My dad will have our fucking heads. We'll do this the right way and ignore it for tonight. I'm sure he'll find a way to punish this motherfucker."

Fucking fine.

"Hey there, Armando," I say with a cheerful lilt to my voice. His eyes widen, and I pretend as if I didn't see anything. "Here for our merchandise."

"O-of course," he replies, looking like he's three seconds from pissing his pants. He looks terrified, as he should be. No one fucks with the Cosa Nostra. No one fucks with Emiliano either. "They're right here."

I text Luca, Emiliano's right-hand man and the person who raised me, and they bring the van around. Matteo and I watch as our guys load everything up and Armando backs up, his hands raised in defeat.

"I'm not going to kill you." I smile. "*Yet.*"

Armando swallows hard, looking absolutely terrified.

"You realize we have to tell my father about this, right?" Matteo asks Armando, but it's rhetorical.

Armando doesn't speak; instead, there's a wet spot on the front of his jeans.

"Matteo, he just fucking pissed himself." I throw my head back and laugh. "Oh, shit. This is too good."

"Nasty." Matteo grimaces. "You scared?"

Armando is still quiet.

"Cat got your tongue?" I ask him, my eyes narrowed on the wet spot. It's now going down his legs. "Never mind. Don't speak."

"Here's what's going to happen—" Matteo starts, and I interrupt.

"We're going to walk away. And you're not going to sleep tonight—or any night until we come back for you. And we will." I smile sweetly at the man. "Do you understand?" I ask him in Spanish.

He nods, and I feel Matteo's gaze on my face.

Armando runs away, going to the parking lot, and

disappears quickly. I smirk, then look at my best friend, who's still staring at me.

"Since when do you speak Spanish?" he asks, his mouth ajar.

"I speak French too." I wink. "And Italian."

"What the fuck, Cole?"

"*What*?" I laugh. "I had a lot of free time."

"Prison treated you well?" he asks, and I nod.

"Yeah, you could say that." I shrug. "I learned a lot."

"Well, don't let the Don find out," he says. "He might take all the jobs away from me."

I chuckle. "You can tag along any time. You know that."

We get in Matteo's car, the sweetest 1967 convertible Mustang. It's his baby. Classic cars have always been his thing. I slide my hand over the passenger side door, and he grunts. I know he doesn't like smudges on the black paint, so I just smirk. I can't deny the thing is a beauty though. A shiny black body with black rims. Red leather seats. And he also switched out the stereo so he could have Bluetooth. It's a dream car for sure.

"Don't bust a nut on my seats," Matteo mutters as we get in, and I laugh.

"Chill the fuck out," I say to him, and he narrows his eyes at me. "I would never do that to Cherry." Yeah, he named his car. *Weirdo*.

"For some reason, I don't believe you." But he grins at me. "Wanna go to Giovanni's?"

Giovanni's is another legitimate business the Colombo's run. Specifically, Giovanni Colombo's restaurant. It's five-star dining on crack. Only the best of the best can get reservations.

"What?" I ask in confusion. "They're closed."

"They're never closed for me," he says with a smile. "Plus, I made reservations for us."

My stomach drops.

"Uh," I stutter. *Is this a date?* "I don't—"

"Come on, Cole." His jaw pulses. "Can't a man have a meal with his best friend?"

I instantly relax. I know he can read me better than an open book. So, I just nod and smile. "Fine."

"Just fine?" he asks, but he's smiling as he pulls out of the parking lot.

"Yes, Matty. I'll eat with you."

"When you say it like that—" He looks at me with a glint in his eyes. "It sounds dirty."

I sigh. "Everything I say sounds dirty."

"Touché."

We pull up to Giovanni's about forty minutes later. It's dead, but the lights are still on. Matteo parks the car, and we get out. He lets himself in, and I trail closely behind him. As soon as we make it to the hostess, she grins and directs us to our table.

"We've been waiting for you," she says to Matteo, a little too friendly, in my opinion. But he just looks her up and down and smiles. "Right this way."

This is good, right? Maybe if he has eyes for someone else, he won't be so heartbroken when I tell him how I feel.

"Sorry, Chiara." He grins. "We got held up."

"Oh, it's never a problem, Mr. Colombo."

"Matteo." His grin stays firmly in place, and I look between them.

We walk through the restaurant until we make it to our table. Low lighting greets us, setting a romantic mood, and there are lit candles on the table. White tablecloths adorn the square tables as far as the eye can see, and it looks slightly different from the last time I came. It looks fancier. Even their uniforms are more formal. The Colombo brothers have clearly been busy building their empire. They've renovated everything.

I pull out my chair and sit down, and Matteo takes the seat across from mine. He looks at me expectantly, and I clear my throat.

"This is nice," I tell him, and his answering smile almost takes my breath away. I wish I could've fallen in love with him. We'd be perfect together. "Thanks for bringing me."

He waves a hand. "You like?"

"Yeah," I reply, looking around. "Shit's fancier than I remember."

"Mostly everything is." He smiles. "They've been busy."

"I can tell."

"What's up, Cole?" He frowns, looking right into my eyes. I flinch. "What aren't you telling me?"

Fuck.

He can always read me.

"Nothing—"

"Tell me." He sighs. "I don't want things to be weird between us. I promise we can get through anything—you should know that by now."

But, can we?

"I think—" I take in a deep breath. "I think we should stay friends. *Only* friends."

Matteo's emotions flit right in front of me. Surprise, disappointment, and lastly, a sadness I can't ignore. He's not hiding it. "Why?" He clears his throat. "Did you meet someone new?"

"No." I shake my head. "Nothing like that."

I'm just in love with your dad.

Fuck me.

He nods slowly. "Alright."

"I'm sorry," I say, tears burning the back of my eyes when I see one trail down his face. He wipes it away roughly and quickly, as if it never happened. I know I hurt him, and it's breaking my heart. I rub at the sore spot in the middle of my chest as if it'll make it better. "I do love you."

"Just not like I love you." It's not a question, and I don't insult him by denying it.

I nod. "I'm sorry."

"Stop saying that, Cole." He sighs. "We'll be fine."

Fuck, I hope so.

I have to believe it though.

I don't know what I'd do without him.

CHAPTER 7
COLE

Matteo isn't speaking to me. Seems like we can't get through just *anything* after all. Deep down, I knew that, but it had to be done. I know he's hurt, and with good reason, but I'm really hoping he'll come around. Thankfully, I've been able to avoid him as much as possible. The tension between us was threatening to suffocate me, and I've been able to dodge him for the past two days just fine. If it weren't for Emiliano calling this meeting, I'd be back in my room, holed up again. Instead, I'm with Matteo, entering Giovanni's.

One thing about the Colombo brothers is that they have an office in every one of their businesses, legitimate or not. The Pink Pony Club has Emiliano's office, where he spends a lot of his time, but it also hosts a basement that serves as a torture room. We do a lot of work at our warehouses, but sometimes Em likes to get creative. When it's not a spur-of-the-moment thing, he takes them there. If you're lucky enough to know about the club's dungeon, then that means you're either close to the Colombo brothers or you're about to die. There's no in-between.

Giovanni's, on the other hand, has private rooms reserved for people they're doing business with. They play poker and chat, drink the top shelf shit, and make deals. Which is where we're headed right now. To one of those rooms. If there's one thing I know about this meeting, it is that all the brothers will be there. I have to make sure to keep my eyes to myself as much as possible. I don't need anyone suspecting I have a thing for Emiliano. Not when they wouldn't hesitate to tell Matteo. I'm trying to save my friendship with him, not sabotage it even more. Though I know that if it came down to it, I'd choose Emiliano over Matteo each and every day.

What the fuck does that say about me?

I'm a traitor, even I can acknowledge that. I'm trading someone who has been there for me through thick and thin for a man who will barely even look at me. Who would never see something permanent with me. I'm just a game to him, possibly a good time, but that's about it. And it guts me.

The first time I realized that I was in love with Emiliano was when I was eighteen. After I heard him fucking someone at the penthouse, I began to follow him to Luna's Den—the brothel—weekly. I entered the room. Emiliano didn't bother locking the door, giving anyone access to watch. He didn't even realize it was me. He didn't look.

I still question whether he has a kink I'm missing or if it was just a coincidence. The problem was that when I saw the blonde bitch on her hands and knees for him; I was a changed man. My stomach flipped, my heart squeezed in my chest, and my eyes stung with tears. Not only was I jealous, but I had this deep feeling of betrayal that I couldn't work out. He didn't owe me anything—I knew that. Yet my heart wasn't getting the memo. It wasn't until that moment that I realized I was obsessed. Crazed. I wanted to *possess* him.

To this day, I can admit it wasn't my finest moment, but I stood there and stared as Emiliano pounded into her pussy. I'm one hundred percent gay, so I couldn't appreciate her body, but his was absolute perfection. I still wish I could've seen his cock. Watching it go in and out of her wasn't enough, and it left an ache in my chest to think about him with someone else. An ache I still fucking feel.

I still feel too much for him. An uncontrollable longing I can't kick. I'm mad with love and pent-up lust for him. I'm fucking *hungry*.

All I feel is famine.

"Are you going to get out of my car, Cole?" Matteo mutters, exasperation clear in his voice. "They're waiting for us."

"My bad," I mumble, opening the car door and not waiting for him.

My strides are hurried as I close the distance between me and the restaurant doors. The ache in my chest is almost unbearable as I hear Matty's footsteps close behind me, and I take a deep breath to keep myself in check. I knew this was going to be hard; I just didn't think it would be *this* damn hard. I didn't think he'd stop speaking to me. I was a goddamn fool.

Opening the door, I'm greeted by the warm air in the restaurant. The hostess is impeccably dressed, with black dress pants and a white long-sleeve button-up. I look over at her name tag and smile.

"Hello, Giulia," I say softly, looking right into her blue eyes. "Di Milano."

Di Milano is the code word to go to the back, and as soon as she realizes what's happening, her eyes widen. She schools her features quickly, though. A-plus for effort. Giulia nods and lets us through, not bothering to guide us. You either know where you're going, or you shouldn't be here in the first place.

I make my way to the back, going through a hallway next to the kitchen and opening the first door on the left. I don't bother knocking because I know they're expecting us. We're—

"You're late," Emiliano growls as soon as we go inside. I close the door and lock it, trying to keep a semblance of privacy. We don't need any interruptions right now. "Matteo." He nods, then completely ignores my presence.

My nostrils flare with anger, and I huff. The air is suddenly too thick to breathe, and when I look around, there are six pairs of eyes on me, including Matty's. Everyone's but Emiliano's. Great—now *everyone* knows something is going on. Just how long will I be able to hide this *thing* from my best friend? Surely he's going to figure it out all on his own if I don't tell him. There's not one subtle bone in my body.

Emiliano's back is turned to me, and I use that opportunity to sit on the worn black leather couch. I look around, taking in the poker tables and couches lining the walls. When I face forward once more, everyone's eyes are still on me.

"Is there something on my fucking face?" I snap, and Alessandro begins to laugh. "What the hell is so funny?"

"Nothing—" Lorenzo snickers. "It's all good."

It feels like there's an inside joke going around, and I'm on the outs of it. Probably because it's about me. My eyes narrow on each one of them, and they all smile innocently at me. Oh, yeah, it's definitely about me.

"Stop it," Emiliano growls, looking at his brothers one by one. I watch as they straighten and lose their smirks. It's somewhat satisfying. If only he'd fucking look at me now. "We're here to talk about the Sinaloa Cartel."

I nod, and he finally looks at me. "Armando didn't deny working with the Bratva," I say, and he nods slowly too. "Not that he could—the Pakhan was there."

Emiliano frowns at that. "He didn't get Andrey to do it?"

"Maybe he's scared I'll finish the job," I tell him with a smirk.

"Will you?" Giovanni asks. "Finish the job?"

I look over at Matteo, and we make eye contact. His eyes slowly widen, and he shakes his head. "No," he says. "He won't. He's not my knight in shining armor."

I hear the unsaid words though.

"Not anymore?" Lorenzo asks, but I'm tired of playing games with all of them.

I sigh. "Who's gonna kill Armando?" I focus on Emiliano's face, willing him to make eye contact with me, but he won't. And it pisses me off. I had him at my mercy barely a few days ago, and now he wants to act as if I don't even exist. "*Emiliano.*"

At the sound of his name coming from my lips, he does look at me. His eyes narrow. "You do it, Cole."

I smile triumphantly. "Where do you want me to ship his body parts?"

Emiliano rolls his eyes. "This needs to be a clean kill." *The fuck it does.* "You'll shoot him at the docks and leave his body there. It'll send the message we need."

"Fuck that." I throw my hands up in the air. "He needs to be tortured at least a little. We can't be seen as weak."

"Cole," Em growls. "You'll do as I say."

"No." I raise my chin defiantly.

"Out," Emiliano snaps, and I get up from the couch to do just that. Except that just as my hand wraps around the doorknob, I'm yanked back. "Everyone but Cole."

My back hits the front of Emiliano, and the breath whooshes out of my lungs. I clear my throat.

Matteo narrows his eyes at his dad, practically growling as he looks between us. "Why does he need to stay?" he asks, and Emiliano stiffens.

"Because I said so," Emiliano says through gritted teeth. "Now go, Matteo. I'm not going to repeat myself."

Matty looks into my eyes with a deep frown, but I nod. He turns away and walks out of the room right along with everyone else. The moment the door clicks shut behind them, I tense. Emiliano strides toward the door quickly and locks it. The sound is final, like a period at the end of a sentence.

At least we're alone now.

"If you wanted to spend time with me, all you had to do was ask," I taunt.

"You're such a fucking brat," Emiliano spits, invading my space and tangling one hand in my hair. I wince when he pulls at the strands and tilts my head up. The eye contact is heady. "Why can't you just keep your mouth shut?"

"What fun is that?"

"You're a pain in my ass," he scoffs, but doesn't let me go. "Are you trying to piss me off?"

"No." I try to shake my head, but it's painful. His fingers grip me tightly. "I just think you're wrong."

"About?" Emiliano asks, raising one eyebrow at me.

"Armando," I say through gritted teeth when he yanks my head back even more, the angle painful on the back of my neck. His spare hand comes to my hip, and he grips it tightly, pulling me closer. My cock hardens—very inopportune timing, if I do say so myself. "He needs to die a painful death. Teach everyone a lesson. No one fucks with the Colombo's."

There's a moment of silence on Emiliano's end, and when he licks his lips, wetting his bottom one, my cock throbs. My eyes focus on his mouth, and a smile tilts his lips. We're in some kind of stand-off. I won't budge, and he won't either. But he should know I always get what I want.

"You don't come in here and give the orders, Cole," Em says, his eyes focused on my lips. A shiver runs down my spine, and I shudder in his arms. "You're not in control."

I grin, which makes him frown. "You want to see how much better I am at taking control?" He shakes his head. "No?"

"*No.*"

"What if I want to show you, anyway?" I ask him, and he smirks.

Instead of replying, Emiliano lets go of me. I stumble back a step, righting myself quickly. He unbuckles his belt and unbuttons his suit pants, dragging them down under his ass until just his cock and balls are visible. My mouth waters at the sight, and if I'm not careful, there will be drool dripping down my chin soon.

His cock is thick and long, uncut. His tan skin makes the wide blue vein running along the top of his shaft stand out, and I want to run my tongue over it. The head of his cock is wide and a deep shade of red. I want to put him out of his misery already. I want to give him everything he's ever wanted. I want to show him I'm the best fuck he'll ever have. And if the stars align for us, I'll give him my heart on a silver platter.

"The only one in control here is me." He grins, taking his length in his hand and lazily stroking it.

My breath stalls in my lungs at the sight, and I long to reach out and touch him. I want to be bratty again and defy him, but the thought of his cock down my throat has those ideas dying a quick death. I want to be the reason he breaks apart tonight.

And I always get what I want.

CHAPTER 8
EMILIANO

I continue to stroke myself languidly, lazily, as Cole's wide eyes stay on my cock. He seems surprised, probably not expecting me to whip it out with no warning. But I'm tired of his shit. He wants to be a brat and talk back? I'll stuff his mouth until he can't.

Cole's lips are parted as his chest rises and falls with heavy breaths. His eyes travel back up to my face, searching for something in my eyes, then bites his bottom lip. I take a step closer toward him, tugging it free from his teeth, and he sucks in a sharp breath. He closes the space between us further, until his front is plastered to mine, making me drop my hand away from my cock. His shirt rubs against my length, the friction against the head of it making the breath stutter in my lungs.

"Touch me," I whisper.

He grabs the back of my neck, bringing my lips to his, and I groan. The first press of our lips makes my stomach flip. He wraps a hand around my cock, his thumb spreading pre-cum over my slit, and fire licks down my spine. My knees turn wobbly from the pleasure when he strokes me, and I bite his bottom lip until I taste blood. Cole gasps, then grins against my lips.

"You like that?" he asks, his hand speeding up. "Such a

perfect cock, Emiliano." A shiver runs down my spine at his praise, and I feel my dick twitch. "I want it down my throat."

Without warning, Cole lets go of me. I make a sound of displeasure at the back of my throat before I realize he's dropped to his knees in front of me. He looks up at me with a devilish smirk, and when I try to wrap a hand around myself, he slaps it away.

"Mine," he breathes. He says it low enough that I'm not even sure if I heard him right, but then he repeats it. "Fuck. You're gonna be mine whether you like it or not."

My cock jumps at his words. I'm about to tell him to get on with it, but then he wraps his hands around my body and squeezes my ass, burying his nose against the trimmed hair at the base of my cock. He inhales sharply and groans. I almost feel self-conscious, but then his tongue runs up my shaft, and I forget how to breathe. He's barely done anything and I'm already grasping at the threads of my sanity. I can tell he's going to ruin me for anybody else, and I don't want to let him. But I also don't want to stop him. Not right now.

Just one time.

He licks the head of my cock, lapping at the pre-cum, then takes me in his mouth, wrapping his lips around me and suctioning with his cheeks roughly. My eyes roll to the back of my head as his tongue goes under my foreskin, and I moan. He makes a little sound that I can't decipher, but before I can make sense of it, he takes me to the back of his throat and swallows me down.

"You're such a fucking whore, Cole," I say with a groan, and when he squeezes my balls roughly, I try my best to not blow. "Are you my little whore?"

He pulls away from me, and I immediately miss the wet heat of his mouth.

"Are you gonna talk slutty to me, baby?" Cole asks me, the pet name going right to my balls. Even now, he's being a fucking brat. Part of me fucking eats it right up. I enjoy putting him in his place. "Who knew you had it in you."

I grab my cock and slap him in the face condescendingly, and there's a fire in his eyes telling me I'm going to pay for it. *Bring it on.* His hands drop to his sides, and he licks his lips.

"Do you want this cock down your throat again, Cole?" I ask him softly. He leans forward and drags his tongue over the head of my cock once more, and my vision blurs as pleasure skates down my spine. "Want me to come in your mouth?"

"Do it." He nods. "I'm fucking desperate for it."

"How bad do you want it?" I smirk, wrapping a hand around my cock and pressing it against his lips. "Hmm?"

"*Please*," he whispers. "Give me your cock."

"Practically begging for it," I whisper back. "Open up. I'm going to fuck your face now—and you're going to take it like the good boy you are, aren't you?"

"I am a good boy." He grins, but I just shake my head. "*Your* good boy."

I hum, loving the sound of him being mine. And he is, even if it's just for right now. He wraps his lips around me once more, taking me to the back of his throat, and I grip the strands of hair at the back of his head tightly. He groans, the vibration traveling right to my balls, and I throw my head back in pleasure right as I snap my hips forward. Cole gags as I hit the back of his throat, and I begin to fuck his face, thrusting in and out of it like he's a toy. He wraps his hands around the backs of my legs, squeezing, digging his nails into me.

"What?" I taunt. "You can't take it?" He looks up at me, defiance in his eyes, and I moan. "Tap my leg if it's too much."

But even now I know he's not going to do it. He's going to

ride this out even if I kill him. He's a stubborn motherfucker —and I'm loving every second of it.

He sucks my cock like it's his full-time job, and my eyes roll to the back of my head once more. I continue to thrust into his mouth with wild abandon, and when my spine begins to tingle and my balls draw up into my body, I begin to shake.

"You look so good on your knees for me, my prince." I groan, looking right into his wide eyes. I don't know where the nickname came from—probably the heat of the moment—but I can't take it back now. "If I knew this was going to shut you the fuck up, I would've done it the last time you came onto me."

Cole moans around my cock, as if he loves the idea, and I watch as he unbuttons his jeans and whips his cock out. I don't have a good view of it, but he's suddenly stroking himself quickly. His eyes close in pleasure, and I tighten my hold in his hair until he opens them once more.

"I want you to look at me when I come," I demand, my cock twitching. "That's it, Cole." I moan. "So." *Thrust.* "Fucking." *Thrust.* "Good." *Thrust.*

I come with a growl, spilling down his throat, and my knees almost buckle from the pleasure. He moans, and his hand falters right as he whimpers. The little sound almost makes me hard again, and I breathe in deeply as I withdraw from his reddened lips. He looks disheveled. His hair is a mess, and I smile at the thought of me making him this way.

I want to see how he looks freshly fucked.

Cole stands up, putting his cock away before I can look at it, and disappointment fills me. But then he's on his feet, getting in my face. I try to take a step back, but he grabs the back of my head with one hand and swipes his fingers over my lips. I taste the cum on them, groaning.

"Open up, Em," he says with a grin. I shake my head. "Come on, don't make me force it on you."

I narrow my eyes defiantly and shake my head once more but then do as he said. He shoves two fingers down my throat, and I gag, but he goes even deeper.

"Suck." He grins. "*Now.*"

So fucking demanding.

But I suck, loving the way he tastes. I hum as he pulls his fingers out, and he takes a step back. I never thought I'd love this with a man, but he's different.

"You call me a whore," he says with a raised eyebrow. "But you're a dirty fucking slut too, Emiliano. You love my cum, don't you?"

"Yes," I whisper.

"Don't worry." He groans, looking down at me as I pull my pants back up. "There's more where that came from."

I'm quiet as we straighten our clothes. The one thing I don't need is for people to know what just happened in this room. But a small part of me wishes everyone knew too. Though I know that's not possible for us. I have to be okay with this being a one-time thing. Yet the thought of Cole being with someone else makes me murderous.

Cole walks toward the door, looking like he's about to leave. I don't know what I was expecting, but him walking away without so much as a kiss goodbye wasn't it. *Wait, what?* What the fuck is wrong with me right now? His hand wraps around the doorknob, and I clear my throat. He looks back at me expectantly, raising one eyebrow.

"Torture him," I tell him, raising my chin. His eyes light up, and I love I put that look on his face. "Send the message."

"Consider it done."

I smile tightly, nodding once. I wish he'd come back and demand things from me. Demand I make him mine for good. Taunt me some more. Tease me. Fucking anything but him walking away as if this never happened. But as he opens the door and shuts it behind himself, I'm left staring after him.

I'm so fucked.

My stomach churns with guilt as soon as he's out of sight. I shouldn't have done that, shouldn't have allowed him to push me off the edge of the very tall cliff. He's temptation personified, and I need to learn to stay the fuck away. Matteo has to come first—*always*. So, as much as I want Cole, I can't let myself have him. Not now.

Not ever.

CHAPTER 9
COLE

Leaving Emiliano behind earlier was possibly one of the hardest things I've ever done in my life, but the alternative terrified me. What if he kicked me out as if it meant nothing? No, I wasn't going to put myself in that situation. I wouldn't be able to handle it. Maybe I am a sensitive bitch when it comes to him, but I can't help it. This is so much more than sex with him. He has to know that.

My throat is still sore from earlier, but I'm not mad about it. The way he used me was a turn-on. Even my wildest fantasies could never compare to the real thing. Having his cock in my mouth was a dream all on its own, but the way he talked to me... I thought that would never come true. He has me wrapped around his finger, and I need to ask myself if this is the best idea. My dick really loves the thought of fooling around with Emiliano, but a much more possessive part of me doesn't want to be another one of his conquests. A notch on his bedpost. No, I want to be so much more than that. I want to be his. I want him to be mine. I want him to belong to me—mind, body, and soul. Because he *owns* me. And I know if I ever allow him into my body, I'll lose all the restraint I possess. Which is already close to being none.

Damn him for making me feel this way.

Emiliano and I are a match to gasoline, and if allowed,

we'd blaze through everything in our paths. He's just as possessive as I am. He might not say it, but his eyes did all the talking today. He claimed me in that room, and I let him, giving him scraps of myself that I don't easily hand over. I gave him my lips, and with my eyes, I offered him my heart. Except I know that's a horrible idea. Giving myself over to a man who has mixed feelings about me on the best days. And on the worst days? He wants nothing to do with me.

Not that I think I conveyed my emotions clearly enough. He seemed to be completely oblivious to what I was trying to tell him with my eyes. The way I offered myself to him—I never do that. Maybe he brushed it off, ignored it. I'm not entirely sure anymore. On the other hand, it's possible he knew. He looked longingly after me as I opened that door, and it made me weak in the knees. I almost stayed. Almost begged him to give me a few more minutes with him before popping our bubble. Instead, he gave me a reward for being his good boy. I can't say I'm upset, though. Not when I get to torture the motherfucker in front of me.

Emiliano gave me full permission to do as I please, and I plan to use that to my advantage. Tonight, I'm getting the blood lust under control. *Just one more taste.*

Ever since my mother was beaten to death in front of me, I've had problems. But doesn't everyone? Mine just seem to be a little more severe than most. I enjoy killing, and if I close my eyes just right, I can almost picture myself killing my stepfather. If only I'd had that pleasure. But no, Emiliano took care of it just like he always takes care of me. So now I want to return the favor and take care of him for a change.

I'm here on my own tonight. Matteo still won't talk to me, and I've been avoiding the hurt look in his eyes as much as humanly possible. Except he's taking this to new levels and going as far as not coming home at night. He hasn't been home in *three* days. It's a bit extreme, in my opinion. Who is he even with, anyway? The fact that I don't know bothers me. We used to tell each other everything. Well—not everything, I guess. I'm definitely a hypocrite because there's no way in hell I'd tell him about my obsession with his father. I know I wouldn't live to tell the tale. Matty would murder me with his own two hands. And thinking about how he loves to strangle people for fun, well, it doesn't sound very appealing. Not unless a cock is inside of me when it happens. It won't be his, though. The last time really was the last time.

The door to the basement opens just as I sit on a chair next to Armando. Strobe lights filter in and so does the booming music. Every beat of the bass is a throb to my balls, and as I watch Emiliano come down the set of stairs that lead to me, I wonder what it would take to convince him to kill Armando and fuck in his blood. For science, of course. I'm not a freak or anything. Okay, maybe a little.

His light gray suit is pressed and wrinkle-free, the color bringing out his olive skin tone, and his honey brown eyes fix on my face as he descends the steps. He doesn't interrupt or speak to me; instead, he goes to the far wall and leans against it, watching silently. Assessing me, probably. If I didn't know any better, I'd think he's trying to gauge my level of crazy right about now. But even he doesn't know just how demented I am.

"You fucked up," I say softly to Armando. "So, what to do with you now?" I tap my chin with my finger. "Oh! I know. You get to meet Ally."

Armando whimpers. "Who the fuck is Ally?"

Emiliano snorts, covering it up with a cough, and I grin. He can say whatever he wants, but even I know he enjoys my level of crazy. It matches his.

I present my scalpel to him, dangling it right in front of his face, and he begins to shake his head quickly. So fast I'm sure he's about to snap his own damn neck. Which I won't let him.

Where's the fun in that? I grab his face with one hand, squeezing his cheeks together, and he stays eerily still. He looks like a goddamn opossum playing dead. As if I could forget about him and move on.

"That won't work." I roll my eyes, not irritated in the slightest. Any day I get to do this is a good day in my book. "Your fate is sealed, fucker. Which one of your fingers would you miss the most?" I ask in Spanish.

Armando whimpers again, shaking his head as he pleads for me to just kill him. Emiliano chokes from behind me, and when I look at him, one of his eyebrows is raised.

"Since when do you speak Spanish?" he asks me, curiosity lacing his voice.

"Prison." I shrug. "Comes in handy nowadays."

Emiliano hums, striding slowly toward me. "Tell me something." This time, I tilt my head to the side, questioning him. "Anything at all."

I want to ask him why. What does he get out of this? Except I know it's the perfect opportunity to pounce. Maybe if I tell him how I feel…

"I love you to the moon and back." I whisper.

Armando chokes, but Emiliano's eyes stay steady on mine. His breathing turns ragged, and he closes the distance between us. Before I can even blink again, he's dragged me out of my chair and hauled me toward his body by my black t-shirt. Our chests collide, my breath whooshing out of me, but I stay stock still as his lips come to the shell of my ear. The contact makes me shiver, and when his hand comes to my lower back to push me against him, my body lights up with want and ardent need.

"You shouldn't say things you don't mean," Emiliano whispers against my ear.

"I don't lie," I say through gritted teeth.

"Careful, my prince." I suck in a sharp breath at the pet name. "Or I'll think you're mine and ruin your fucking life."

"Ruin me then," I taunt. "Unless you're okay with someone else taking your place."

Emiliano's hand shifts to the back of my neck, and I look into the dark depths of his eyes defiantly. Something seems to snap inside of him because the look in those dark orbs could only be described as feral.

Bingo.

My eyes follow the movement of his tongue as it wets his bottom lip, and it takes everything inside of me not to propel myself forward and close the small distance between us. It's an act of defiance against the universe, rejecting the gravitational pull between us. But I do it anyway, planting my feet firmly on the ground and refusing to move.

His hand on the back of my neck tightens impossibly more, and he says, "I think you know what will happen if you test that theory."

I shake my head. "Enlighten me."

"There will be rivers of blood flowing through New York City—and possibly even innocent lives will be on your hands."

"It's a good thing I don't have a conscience," I tell him. "Do you?"

Something like pain flashes in his eyes, and he lets go of me, taking a healthy step back. I immediately miss the warmth of his body pressed up against mine, and it takes a monumental amount of strength to not follow after him. This pain has a first and last name—and I can't hold it against him. Matteo Colombo might just be the end of us. Maybe we are doomed with no hope for a future. Maybe I've just been delusional, believing I could change Emiliano's mind.

Maybe, maybe, maybe.

I'm sick of not knowing.

Emiliano goes back to his place against the wall, and I take that as the dismissal I know it is. My place is next to Armando, anyway. He needs to die and soon. I'm already anxious to get it over with. I usually enjoy drawing it out, but I don't feel like being in Em's vicinity right now. I feel naked under his gaze. Exposed. Raw. I told him I love him, and he dismissed me. And that stings like a bitch.

I sigh, taking my gun out, and press it against Armando's forehead. His eyes widen in fear, and his teeth begin to rattle as he gets the shakes. At least he's still looking at me. At least he's not crying. I can appreciate that.

"Do you know why you're dying today?" I ask him, and he tries to nod, but I shove the gun deeper into his forehead.

"I do."

"Then you should've known better than to double-cross The Colombo's." My finger dances along the trigger, the gun already loaded, and I tense in anticipation of the recoil.

"Maybe you should be more worried about what is going on in your warehouses," Armando says, his bottom lip quivering. I raise an eyebrow at him, as if saying *go on*. He takes the hint. "There's going to be a bust tonight."

I frown. "And how do you know that?"

"People talk." Armando shrugs, and I lower my weapon and put it back in its holster. "You have cops on your payroll, right?"

"Obviously."

"One of them is working with the Russians." His voice is shaky as he says it, like he's just now realizing that if I take pity on him—which I definitely won't—they'll just swoop in and kill him themselves. It's tempting to let him live. But I'm getting bored already. The only thing making this interesting is that I need a—

"Give me a name." I grin, letting the crazy out. I'm so sick of these fuckers crossing us. "Now."

"I don't have one."

I raise an eyebrow, and his breathing turns shallow. "You sure about that?" I ask calmly. More than I really feel. But sometimes, I can be in control. Only on special occasions. This seems to be one of those. I also don't want to lose my shit in front of Emiliano. That's the last thing I need.

Armando shakes his head and says nothing.

I appraise him for one long moment, looking at the way he's tied to the chair, hands bound in front of him instead of behind. I don't question it. Mostly because it's convenient for me right now. I grab my scalpel, then his hand, gripping it roughly so he has no choice but to stay still. Emiliano's eyes are still on me, burning a brand over my skin, but I ignore him as best as I can. Instead, I slide the scalpel under Armando's fingernail and rip it clean off.

He screams.

"I can't hear you," I taunt. "What was that?"

I cup a hand over my ear as he begins to cry in earnest. "Officer Sean Murphy."

I draw out my gun once more, pointing it right at his head for the second time tonight. "Now, that wasn't so hard, was it?"

I pull the trigger, watching as brain matter splatters out of the back of his head. It rains down onto the concrete, and I sigh in contentment, holstering my weapon once more. I'm about to step out of the basement when Emiliano's phone begins to ring, and he halts me with his hand.

"What happened?" Emiliano mutters under his breath, and I watch with bated breath. *"Fuck."*

Silence.

"He's dead," he says, and I relax.

This I can deal with.

He needs another kill tonight? I'm his man. Anything else? I'm fucking out. I can only take so much pain and rejection for one day. I'm not putting myself in that situation again tonight.

"The police invaded warehouse five," Emiliano speaks softly, locking his cellphone. "I need you."

I need you.

How many times have I dreamed of those words coming from his lips? A million—possibly more. And yet, when it comes down to it, we don't need each other in the same way.

I huff. "Let's go get that dirty ass cop."

I'm giving him an out, and he takes it. "You seemed bored with Armando."

"I was." I nod. "Make the next one more interesting."

Emiliano throws his head back and laughs, and I can't help the small chuckle that leaves me. "You're crazy."

"You have no idea," I mutter, running a hand down my face as we ascend the steps that lead out of the basement and back to the club.

"I think I do."

He doesn't.

But I don't correct him anymore.

Let him find out for himself.

CHAPTER 10
EMILIANO

Cole and I have been stuck in the basement together for the past five hours, torturing the dirty cop. Technically, I'm not stuck here. I could've left hours ago. After all, he knows exactly what he's doing and doesn't need assistance. Especially not from me. But he looks so tired with his droopy eyes and the frown on his face. I can't help but wonder if I'm the one who made him this way. Because I'm an asshole. He told me he loved me, and I rejected him. I couldn't help it, though. How can he just expect for us to be together when my son matters too? His feelings matter. I can't just pretend he doesn't exist and take whatever I want. What kind of father would I be?

It still doesn't stop me from wanting Cole, though. Wanting him is an acute ache in the middle of my chest—this incessant longing that I can't turn off. And fuck, I really want to turn it off right about now.

I watch as Cole takes his sharp scalpel and cuts off the tip of another one of the cop's fingers. This is number three. Which means something is wrong with Cole. He's laying it on thicker than usual. Maybe it's got nothing to do with me, or maybe it has everything to do with me, but he looks like he's going to fall over from exhaustion at any moment.

Cole looks my way, holding his scalpel up in offering, and

I shake my head. I use all my strength to keep myself from floating over to him. Refusing to gravitate toward him like my body is screaming to. But my body doesn't know what's best for me, so instead, I use my brain to stay put.

He's speaking Italian to the cop, who probably doesn't understand one word coming out of his mouth, which means he's becoming unhinged with every passing minute. I need to put a stop to this and take Cole home. He needs to sleep this off. I haven't seen him this way since Matteo was shot.

"Stop!" I growl when Cole slices off the next fingertip. He tenses at my words, dropping his scalpel onto the small table he requested earlier. The cop isn't even screaming anymore. He's passed out cold. "Kill him."

"No," Cole snaps, refusing my demand to kill the cop. "I'm not done yet."

"The fuck you're not." I get closer to him, and a desperate part of me wants to close the distance between us completely and take him in my arms. "You're done when I say you're done."

Cole throws his head back and laughs. "That's rich coming from you," he grits out, and I raise an eyebrow.

"You sound a little crazy, Cole—"

"Oh, you think this is crazy?" He chuckles, the sound deep and growly. It lights up my insides, even though I know it shouldn't. "You haven't seen shit."

"I've seen enough." I sigh. "Come on, let's just get out of here."

"No." Cole's shoulders slump, and I know he's probably about to give in. "He has to die."

I pull out my gun, cock it, aim, and shoot the man in the head before Cole can even speak again. He gasps and turns around stiffly, eyes narrowed on my face.

I shrug. "We're done here."

"So, that's it?" he growls. "You just call the shots, and I have to do whatever the fuck you want?"

I chuckle, but it holds no humor. I'm trying to be gentle with him; instead, he's being a dick. I know he's upset with me but now is not the time to deal with it. "I'm Don, Cole. You've never had a problem following orders before. What's so different now?"

"I've swallowed your cum—that's what's different." I narrow my eyes on him as he stalks closer. But even now, I see how drained he is. The fight is leaving him soon.

"Plenty of people have done that." I look right into his clear-blue eyes as I say it. "If they can get over it, then so can you."

"Give me a name." He grins, and I can see how that would be a horrible idea. They'd probably end up at the bottom of the Hudson River.

"Fuck off," I tell him. "Don't be a dick and let's go home."

"I'm not going anywhere with *you*," he replies, raising his chin defiantly. "I'm going upstairs. Don't expect me to come home tonight."

I. See. *Red*.

Yet I take in a shaky breath and try to keep my wits about me. Somehow, I manage it. "Oh?" I chuckle, grabbing onto his arm and tugging him toward me. "And where will you go then?"

"Doesn't matter," Cole mutters.

"You can't leave like this." I try to get through to him, but even I see how futile that is. "You're tired."

"Nothing a dick in my ass can't fix."

My eyes blur with anger for a brief moment, and he looks triumphant. Like my jealousy brings him happiness. "Fuck—"

"Anyone's dick will do," he whispers. "Just not yours."

A stab to the gut would've been more pleasant than those

words, but I know I deserve them. I've been an asshole, and the only thing I care about right now is getting him home safe. Which is why I nod and grip his arm harder, all but dragging him up the stairs.

The sound of the music intensifies as we open the door to the basement, and Cole immediately tries to give me the slip. Except I'm onto him, and now I have two bouncers redirecting both of us to the back entrance, where my driver is waiting for us in the blacked-out SUV.

We drag Cole into the vehicle, and I instantly relax when he lies back against the seat. His eyes close, and his lips part as the softest of snores come from him. He's covered in blood, his entire face red, and when I look down, I can make out his shredded knuckles in the darkness.

He acted like a fucking madman tonight, torturing the guy for hours on end—for the fun of it. Maybe that's an exaggeration, though. He's clearly angry at me and needed to take it out on someone, and I can understand that. I'm not judging him. I'm just a bit concerned—

"Em," Cole grunts, his bloody hand coming to rest on my thigh. He squeezes painfully, then lets go suddenly, as if it never even happened. Before I can say anything to him, his breathing evens out and he's snoring softly once more.

The ride back to the penthouse is silent, and I keep my eyes on him the entire time. He looks so innocent in his sleep.

I shake my head at that thought.

There's not one innocent bone in Cole's body. Not anymore. His mother's death snuffed that out. He never talks about it, and even in the past he never mentioned her to me, only Matteo. But I know it's affected him—I'm just not sure the extent of the damage yet.

Speaking of Matteo, he hasn't been home in days. I was able to reach him a few hours ago to ask when he was coming back, to which he said that he didn't know. Apparently, Cole and him are not speaking because Cole said it would be better to remain friends. Matteo is absolutely gutted, and I can't blame him. After all the years he spent wishing and hoping for more, this has to be a slap in the face. And knowing I may have something to do with it is a stab in the back to my own child. I fucked up—and I continue to fuck up. I just don't know how to stop doing it anymore.

I *ache* for Cole, and I'm not above begging for relief anymore.

Finally, we pull up to the parking garage, and Luca drops us off near the elevators. I assist Cole with getting out, holding him up as he takes tentative steps, and we get in. The ride up is short, and we're jolted when we get to the top, making Cole almost fall on his face. Before that can happen, the doors open and I rush him inside the penthouse.

"Matteo—" he groans.

"Not home," I say softly, redirecting him toward my room. "You need to get cleaned up."

"I can do that just fine by myself," Cole says, his eyes finally open all the way, though it's clear that it's taking him some effort. "Just take me to my room."

"No." I shake my head, continuing to pull him toward my room. "You need a First Aid kit, and a shower."

Cole fights me, but I haul him harder, until I've shut the bedroom door behind us and locked it. The sound of his panting is loud in the darkness as I walk us through the bedroom, then turn on the bathroom light and practically shove him into it. He doesn't fight me anymore, instead he sits on top of the closed toilet lid as I rummage under my bathroom sink for the supplies I need. I usually keep a kit under here for myself. I just never know when I might need it, and our doctor might not always be available. Though I pay him a generous amount of money to be at our disposal.

I spend the next few minutes cleaning up Cole's knuckles.

They're red and swollen, the skin shredded, and he winces and inhales sharply at the contact. It should make me feel bad; instead, I'm rougher with him.

"Fuck, take it easy," he whines. "It fucking hurts."

"Don't be a little bitch now." I grin, and he huffs. "You didn't even feel it when you fucked up that man's face."

"The adrenaline is gone, you asshole," Cole mutters, and I roll my eyes. "I can shower now."

I nod, going to the shower and turning it on, then check the spray for the temperature. I wait until it's warm, then begin to strip down to my underwear. Cole watches me intently, then shakes his head quickly.

"I can do it alone," he tells me, though he's slumped on the toilet seat, exhaustion weighing him down. "I'll be quick."

"And let you break your neck?" I chuckle. "No fucking chance."

"Has anyone ever told you you're dramatic?" he asks as he looks into my eyes, and my brows kiss my hairline. "Because you are."

"Cry me a fucking river, Cole." I sigh. "Just get in while you do it."

"Fine," he growls, pulling off his shirt one-handed. Possibly one of the sexiest things I've ever seen him do. "What's your plan, though? You gonna wash me? Tuck me in, Daddy?"

"Brat," I mutter, watching him take off the rest of his clothes until he stands before me, naked.

My breath catches in my throat as I take him in. He has two tattoo sleeves. His right arm is more visible than his left as he makes his way to me, and I halt him to take a better look. There's a skull on his upper arm that's surrounded by roses and other flowers. Then his forearm has a woman with horns on her head, hollow white eyes, and skulls surrounding her body. There's another tattoo on his hand all the way down to his fingers, too.

"Like them?" he murmurs.

"They look good on you," I admit.

My hand reaches up toward his hair, pushing it away from his bloody face, and he sucks in a sharp breath. Before I can do something stupid like fuck him in front of the mirror, I grab his arm and direct him right to the shower spray. He winces when the water hits his hands, but other than that, he goes about rinsing off his face and hair of all the blood.

I grab the shampoo when he takes a step back from under the spray, then lather his hair with it, making sure to get all the blood. I massage his scalp with my fingertips, and he throws his head back with a groan. We don't say anything at all, but actions definitely speak louder than words.

Cole rinses his hair as I grab the body wash, then I begin to wash his neck from behind, his shoulders, his back. I pause when I get to the two dimples right above his ass, and he chuckles.

"Lower," he tells me, and I breathe in deeply. "Touch me."

I shake my head, even though he can't see me, but wash the firm globes, then kneel to wash his legs. He turns around as I'm on my knees, and when his cock bobs in front of my face, I lick my lips. So fucking pretty. I want to taste him, but I also don't know what I'm doing. And then it dawns on me—I don't want to disappoint him. I'm good at everything I do, but this is uncharted territory.

So I look down and begin to lather his legs, detouring from his cock on the way up, and then wash his torso without making eye contact. It's hard to keep my eyes off his face, but I do it anyway. He's not having it though, gripping my jaw roughly and forcing me to look into those eyes. Eyes as clear-blue as the lakes in Canada. That's what they remind me of. The Rocky Mountains. Glaciers, too. So beautiful.

"Wash my cock, Em," he growls. Before I can refuse him again, he grabs my wrist and directs my hand to his dick. I grab it out of instinct, then stroke it with the soap. He's not as thick as I am, or as long, but he still has a nice cock. "*God.*"

I let go. "That's enough."

He bites his bottom lip, and it shouldn't be as sexy as it is, but fuck, it turns me on. My cock throbs, weighing heavily between my thighs, and when Cole reaches out to touch me, I slap his hand away. He smirks as he washes the rest of the soap off, then trades places with me.

I keep my movements quick and clinical, trying—no, *needing*—to get out of here as soon as possible. If I'm not careful, Cole will end up with his hands against the wall as I fuck him until he can't stand anymore. He needs rest. I can't do that.

Cole steps out of the shower just as I begin to rinse my body, and he dries quickly, disappearing from the bathroom without another word. The disappointment almost brings me to my knees, but it's probably for the best.

By the time I get out of the shower, I'm exhausted and ready for bed. I dry quickly, then make my way out of the bathroom. Except there lies Cole, in my bed, tucked in. He's not on my side of the bed, and I wonder how he figured out where I sleep. As I get closer, I realize he's asleep, snoring softly. I should wake him. I should tell him to leave my room. I should kick him out to his own bed. But lately, I haven't been doing the things I should.

And I don't think I want to start now.

CHAPTER 11
COLE

Emiliano's body is hot against my back, his arm draped over my waist. We're both naked. When I got in this bed, I expected him to wake me up and kick me out, but I'm glad he didn't. Instead, he got in with me and stayed on the other side for as long as he could. Always fighting the gravitational pull between us. But as if the universe has other plans for us, he always ends up at my side.

Earlier was surreal. I never expected him to bring me to his room, much less take care of me. His gentle hands on my body stoked a fire inside of me, and I don't know how to put it out. I burn with the need to make him mine. I ache with the need to *keep* him. And I don't know how to put out the embers. I know it's a pipe dream, hoping for him to fall in love with me and not care about the odds stacked against us, but damn it, the hope fluttering in my chest every time he looks at me is hard to snuff out. I can see the desire in his eyes. The same need that I have for him reflected back at me.

I snuggle in closer to him, burying my face into the pillow, and inhale deeply. It smells like him, and I hope I smell like him, too. I can feel his dick thickening against my ass, and he groans as he grips my hip. I shouldn't tempt him. I should stay still and hope he lets me stay here until morning, but I just can't help myself. I want to *devour* him. So I do the only thing I can think of and rub my ass against his erection.

"Cole," Em growls, and it goes straight to my cock, hardening it to the point of pain. "Stop."

"Why?" I breathe, grabbing his hand as he tries to pull away from me. I direct it to my cock, and he wraps his hand around it without hesitation. No matter what he says, he can't deny how much he—"Don't you want me?"

Emiliano's harsh pants are loud against the shell of my ear, and he buries his nose in the crook of my neck and inhales deeply. I stay still for him, letting him do whatever he wants, but he doesn't move either. Just holds my cock in his hand and smells me. I should be freaking out right now; instead, I'm curious. Why isn't he doing anything?

"Please don't make me betray him," he whispers. "I'll never forgive myself."

"Just one night, Em," I plead, begging for anything he can give me. Even if it's not sex. I just want him to hold me for the night and not let go. I want to have something to remember him by when I'm feeling lonely. When I feel hopeless. When life doesn't go my way, as usual. "Tonight."

"Don't you get it?" He lets go of me, and I miss the warmth of his hand immediately. "It would make me a monster."

"So let's be monsters together," I tell him, flipping over to face him.

Emiliano hasn't moved, still on his side, facing me now. He grabs something from under the pillow, and his bedside lamp clicks on. I look into his deep brown eyes, at the pain in them, and my breath hitches. I know I shouldn't be pushing him, but I'm selfish. I want him. So fucking much. I'm willing to hurt, maim, and kill to get him. This isn't some passing infatuation. I live and breathe for him. He *owns* me.

He doesn't reply, instead continuing to stare into my eyes

with a frown that I want to smooth out. I lean in, completely obliterating the distance between us as I press my lips to his. The kiss turns heated quickly, my tongue brushing against the seam of his lips forcefully until he grants me entrance. And then my hands wander over his body with no true direction. First, I palm his pecs, then rub my hand over his muscular arm, gripping his bicep. After that, I drag my hand from his arm and down his back, all the way to his ass and grab him roughly.

I'm drunk with lust, unable to do anything but feel as I thrust my tongue deep into Em's mouth. Before I know it, I'm pushing him onto his back and straddling him. Looking up, I reach toward his nightstand and grab the bottle of lube on it, putting it on the bed next to me.

As my legs straddle Emiliano's hips, I look down at his hard cock, which is resting against his abs and leaking pre-cum. He looks up at me through his lashes, his bottom lip trapped between his teeth, and I swear on all that is holy, I've never seen a more erotic sight in my life.

"Fuck, Cole," Emiliano grunts when I grab his cock and grip it tightly. I hold it against mine, then wrap my hand around both of us and stroke slowly. He hisses, "*F-fuck.*"

"You haven't felt anything yet, Em," I whisper, tightening my hand even more and stroking faster. "I'm gonna ride your cock so fucking good."

Emiliano's back arches off the bed, and his harsh breaths are loud between us. He doesn't speak, only feels, and for that, I'm grateful. I don't want his words to ruin this right now.

I let go of us, and his cock slaps against his abs. My mouth waters at the sight of him. He's never been with a man before, so I grab the lube and begin to prep myself, stuffing two fingers inside of me. He looks between my legs in confusion, and I raise an eyebrow.

"What are you doing?" he growls.

"Stretching myself." I smirk.

"Why the fuck?" He narrows his eyes at me, and I raise up on my knees a little higher so he can see, but instead, he snakes his hand under me and edges a finger against mine. "This ass is mine, Cole. Let me in it."

He rubs the lube against my rim, then stuffs his finger inside of me along with mine. The breath whooshes out of my lungs at how full I feel, and I scissor my fingers to continue to stretch myself.

"Like this," I tell him, crooking my fingers until I find my prostate. When his finger brushes against it too, I whine long and loud. "That's the spot."

"Hmmm," Em murmurs. "Pull your fingers out."

I do as he says, and we both withdraw our fingers from my body. He grabs the lube and squirts some onto his fingers, then stuffs three inside of me without warning. I try to get away from the sting, but his free hand grips my hip tightly, holding me in place.

Em crooks all three of his fingers, finding my prostate after a few passes, and I moan. This man is going to be the fucking death of me, and I don't mind it one bit. He doesn't stop, not even when my cock begins to leak like a faucet, or when I wrap a hand around it and stroke myself at a feverish pace.

"You're gonna make me come," I groan, my entire body lighting up every time he pegs my prostate with his fingers. As if my words trigger my orgasm, my spine begins to tingle, and my balls draw up. But it's as if I'm waiting for his permission, dangling over the edge of the precipice. "Fuck, Em. I don't want to come yet. I want your cock in my ass."

"Who said you can't have both?" Emiliano asks me, his eyes flashing with lust. "I'll make you come a hundred times before I fuck you if I want to."

His words trigger my release, and I paint his chest and abs

with my cum. The territorial side of me sings at the sight of it, and I know he can tell when he smirks. My chest heaves as he pulls his fingers out of me slowly, and I immediately wish for them back.

"Lick me clean, pretty boy," Emiliano says softly, and I immediately drop down to lick his chest and abs. "That's it. Such a fucking slut for me, aren't you?"

"Yes," I moan, inspecting his skin, making sure I got it all.

Before he can say another word, I get the lube and slather his cock with it, then lift up and press it to my entrance. His thick length stretches me, dancing on the edge of pain, but I don't let it deter me. Instead, I take a deep breath and lower myself onto him until my ass meets his balls, taking him all the way. Emiliano hisses, then grits his teeth.

"Holy shit," he groans, and I lift and slam down harshly. His eyes roll to the back of his head. "Tight." I grin. "Too fucking tight."

"You're not gonna come already, are you?" I taunt, and his eyes meet mine, anger swirling in those pretty brown irises. "I'm not fucking done with you yet."

Emiliano's jaw tics as I roll my hips and grind against him, then change the pace and bounce up and down on him. He seems to like that best, if his moans are any indication, and I grab the headboard with one hand and wrap my other one around his throat, squeezing it tightly. His face turns red quickly, his eyes bulging out in surprise, and I smirk.

"You like that, don't you?" I taunt. "When I take control?"

He shakes his head, and I tighten my grip on him until his lips part on a silent moan. I go faster, not letting go of him, and I feel his cock harden even more inside of me. I know he's about to come, so I ease up on his neck.

"Don't you dare fucking come," I groan, then slap his cheek. If looks could kill, I'd be six feet under.

Emiliano pulls me up and off him, shoving me face-first

into the bed in a move I don't see coming. He wraps a hand around my waist roughly and pulls until my ass is up in the air, then he stuffs his cock inside of me once more. His thrusts are hard and punishing, and he spanks my ass so hard I see stars. My cock hardens to the point of pain, and he spanks me again, this time harder, and I whimper.

"That's the little sound I want to hear." He growls, "Submit to me."

"*Never*," I lie. "You'll have to fucking make me."

Emiliano grips my hips tightly, fucking in and out of me slower, and when I look over my shoulder at him, I see he's mesmerized looking at his cock thrusting in and out of my hole. His lips are parted in pleasure, and when I push back, he grits his teeth. It's the most beautiful thing I've ever seen, and I imprint it into my memory like a tattoo.

"I'm going to stuff you so full of my cum that there's no mistaking who you belong to," Em growls. "And then I'm going to eat it out of your tight little asshole."

My stomach flutters with butterflies at his words, and then he speeds up once more, brushing my prostate with every thrust. "Oh, *God*," I moan.

"Don't call out to him, my prince." Emiliano moans loudly. "He's not going to fucking save you from me."

"I don't need saving," I say as I wrap a hand around my cock and begin to jerk myself off. "I just need you."

"*Please*," he begs, the word full of aching. "Don't talk about your feelings. Not when I can't promise you anything."

My heart squeezes in my chest at those words. "Lie to me, Em," I moan, my balls drawing up for the second time tonight. My spine begins to tingle, and I know I'm about to come, even through the heartache. "Tell me I'm the only one for you."

"You're the only one for me," Emiliano says softly, and for

a split moment, he sounds honest too. "Now come for me, Cole. I *need* to come."

I push back against his cock, all the while jerking myself faster, until I'm spilling my cum onto his sheets. His hands tighten around my hips, and he fucks into me at a furious pace, then he stills, filling me up. I feel his cock jerking inside of me as his orgasm washes over him, and my eyes sting. Fucking hell, get it together, Cole. Don't you dare fucking cry right now.

Em pulls out of me swiftly, and I fall forward onto the bed, my chest meeting the mattress. I'm sticky with cum, but I ignore it. Rough hands pull my cheeks apart, and then his breath is on me. He licks me tentatively, then groans.

"Push my cum out for me, Cole," he tells me, and I do it. He licks it, rimming me and eating it out of me. "Fuck, I could eat you all day."

"Do it," I groan, loving his possessiveness.

He leans back in, licking me once more, and I close my eyes to the feeling of his tongue thrusting into my ass. Once he deems me clean, he pulls away. But when I look back, his face is blank, and his body is stiff. As if—

"Get out," he growls.

"W-what?" I stutter, confused. I get up, kneeling on the bed, staring at him wide-eyed. "But—"

Emiliano grabs my hair roughly and pulls me off the bed, my scalp screaming in pain. I shake him off, pushing him away, and he stumbles back. "I said—get out," he repeats.

"Why?" I ask him slowly.

"This was a mistake," he replies, and my heart falls all the way down to my ass. "It won't happen again."

"You think I'm a fucking mistake?" My voice shakes with the question, and I'm so afraid of the answer that I don't know why I asked in the first place. My eyes sting, and then a tear trails down my cheek. I wipe it quickly, but he saw it.

Emotions run through his eyes, but they're fleeting, and I can't decipher them. What I don't expect is his silence.

It stings more than words.

"Fuck you," I snarl, walking quickly toward the door.

My hand wraps around the doorknob and I swing it open so hard it bangs against the wall. I'm halfway down the hallway when he speaks again.

"Wait—" Em says, but I don't wait. I high-tail it to my room. Before I can close the door on him, he slaps his hand on it and shoves it open. "Matteo is in love with you. This is a betrayal!"

I laugh, and it sounds manic. "Fuck Matteo and fuck you too," I spit. "Stop fucking leading me on. I'm not your toy."

Pain flashes in Emiliano's eyes, but then he nods.

And as if he couldn't twist the knife in my chest any more than he already has, he walks away without another word. And that gaping hole in my chest? It bleeds and bleeds until I'm sure my life force is draining from me.

I'm too weak for him.

But no more.

I'm fucking done.

CHAPTER 12
EMILIANO

The alarm rings on my phone, showing me it's seven in the evening. Fuck, I slept through the day, but in my defense, I tossed and turned until the sun was already out. I know I did the wrong thing with Cole, just like I know I need to apologize to him. I should've never said he was a mistake. Especially not after the moment we shared. But damn it, I was freaking the fuck out. The thought of losing Matteo was like a weight in my chest, and I could barely breathe at the possibility of it. I'm not delusional. I know that if I do this—give Cole a real shot—Matteo will disown me as his father. I will be out of his life for good, and I can't bear the thought of losing him. I just also can't bear the thought of Cole walking out of my life either.

Getting out of bed, I go to the bathroom and brush my teeth. My skin is clear of any marks from Cole, no evidence of our night together left behind. And I hate it, yet also feel relieved. My bed is a different story though. The sheets are crumpled and cum-stained, and my pillows smell just like him—like coconut. It's odd that he'd smell tropical, but it also suits him at the same time.

I stand in front of my bedroom door, take a deep breath, and open it slowly. The house is eerily quiet. Matteo has clearly not come back yet. I walk down the hallway toward

Cole's room, just to stop in my tracks. His bedroom door is open, and when I get closer, I see there are bags and a suitcase on his bed. I don't care if it's an invasion of privacy. I head over to his dresser and closet, just to find all his stuff is packed up.

My stomach sinks, and it feels like I have to throw up.

I fucked up—*really* fucked up—and I need to find him. But where the hell would he go right now? I can't call Matteo either. He'd be suspicious and definitely ask why Cole and I are fighting. He'd forget all about his hurt feelings and confront Cole as well, and knowing him, he'd probably spill his guts to my son out of spite. But he wouldn't, would he? I'm not even sure anymore.

My phone begins to ring, startling me, and I run back to my room in hopes it's Cole. I'm disappointed when I see it's my brother Alessandro instead. I think about not answering. I think about hiding out in my room until Cole gets back and tries to leave me, but something tells me it might be an important call.

"Hello?" I mutter. "This better be good, Alex."

"I'll forgive you just this once, Emiliano." My brother sighs, and I can imagine him pinching the bridge of his nose. He always does it when he uses this tone of voice. "The Russians are on our territory. We just picked up two of them."

"*What?*" I bark, suddenly even more worried about Cole. If they find him, they're probably going to want payback for Andrey. I can't let them take him. "Find them all. Whatever it takes."

"Yes, brother." Alessandro sighs again. "I'm on it."

Alessandro hangs up, and I lower my cell phone from my ear. I don't know where Cole could be right now, but I know where I want to be. In that basement, torturing the motherfuckers who dared to step into my territory. And maybe, just maybe, get information from them. It all depends on how loyal they are. But my methods have made many men sing for me.

An hour later, I'm standing in the basement of The Pink Pony Club. My brothers are all with me, standing against a wall and watching the two men tied up in the middle of the room. Their hands are bound behind the chairs, a rope tied around each other's torsos. For a split moment, I want to kill them and get it over with. But then I remember Cole, and I know I need to figure out why they're here. Except I'm not all there. My head is definitely elsewhere.

I pace in front of them, and if I could wear a hole into the concrete, I definitely would've by now. My brothers all have their eyes on me, most of them with a curious look in their eyes. All except Alessandro, who seems to be more suspicious than curious. He can probably read me better than the rest of them. We've always been inseparable, which means not much gets past him. It's hard for me to lie to him and even harder to keep things from him.

"Emiliano," Alessandro snaps, and I look at him. His mouth is set in a tight line, his eyes searching my face for what I imagine are answers. "What the fuck is going on?"

"They're probably here for Cole," I explain. "As revenge for what happened to Andrey now that he's out of prison."

My brother nods slowly.

I turn toward the Russians. "Isn't that right?"

One of them doesn't even look at me, keeping his eyes on the ground. It honestly pisses me off. The utter disrespect. The other guy, however, looks right into my eyes defiantly, and I realize it'll be fun to break them.

"I asked a question," I tell them. "And I expect an answer."

The brave one looks right into my eyes and spits on the floor. "Italian scum."

I laugh, a full belly laugh. "Oh, you're definitely the brave one, aren't you? I'll enjoy breaking you the most."

"Cole is actually here, Emiliano," Giovanni says, and I look at him, my heart beating faster. "Do you think he'd like to do the honors?"

"No," I reply quickly, and Alessandro frowns.

"What aren't you telling us?" he asks. "What's wrong with you?"

I sigh. "It's complicated."

"We have all night," Lorenzo says, and I want to throttle him. They may have all night, but now that I know Cole is here, I definitely do not have all night. They'll be lucky if I stick around for another ten minutes. I need to lay eyes on him. "Spill."

"I don't want to talk about it," I snap.

"Well, you're going to," Tony says with a smile. It pisses me off even more that he's smiling, like he already knows the answer to Alessandro's question. "We do have all night."

"Fine," I growl. "Cole and I had sex."

The room is so silent you could hear a pin drop. My brothers are all wide-eyed, and if the situation weren't so serious, it would be comical. I'd be laughing my ass off. Except nothing about this is funny. Cole hates me and now he's in danger, and something tells me I can't do anything about it. He wants nothing to do with me if the suitcase and bags on his bed are any indication.

Alessandro is the first to speak up. "What the fuck were you thinking?"

"I wasn't," I reply dryly. "Clearly."

"Okay," Giovanni says, "so you had sex with him. What's the big deal?"

"Other than the obvious?" I frown. "Maybe the fact that I told him it was a mistake."

"Ouch." Lorenzo looks at me with a sympathetic look in

his eyes, and I want to punch him in the face until he doesn't pity me anymore.

"Yeah, *that*," Tony chimes in.

I love my brothers, but sometimes I wish they weren't so overbearing. I want to lick my wounds in peace and in private. I don't want to expose myself to them, but I know they're just trying to help me.

"Want me to get him for you?" Giovanni asks.

"No." I shake my head. "If you do that, he'll run away. His bags are already packed on his bed."

"Double fuck," Lorenzo says, pity in his eyes yet again.

"If you keep looking at me with pity, I'm going to fucking stab you," I say to him, and he grins.

"Bring it on, old man." He grins. "I got moves."

"Not for long," I mutter.

Alessandro steps away from the wall, coming to my side. He keeps his eyes on our captives, but he talks to me in a low voice.

"I got this," he murmurs. "Go get your boy."

"He's not mine," I tell him. "And he's *not* a *boy*."

Alessandro smirks, pushing me toward the door, and I stumble back a couple of steps. Before I can speak, Giovanni hums.

"I texted the bouncers," he says. "They'll get him from the VIP area. He's a little occupied."

"Occupied?" I ask through gritted teeth.

"Yeah." He smirks. "He's on some guy's lap."

Oh, hell no. How fucking dare he? My cock was inside him just a few hours ago. That just won't do. "Get answers," I tell Alessandro, then make my way up the stairs.

The music is booming when I step back into the club, and I fully expect the bouncers to bring Cole to me. Except when they knock on the door, they're empty-handed.

"Where the hell is he?" I snap.

"He gave us the slip," John says. "Went out the back."

I nod, getting up from my chair and going to the back of the club. I open the door, because these fuckers are incompetent as hell, and slip out. I text Alessandro to let him know where I am and that I need him. It's not smart for me to be out here alone in an alley. And when I hear the sound of fists connecting with flesh, I know I've made the right choice.

I make my way toward the sound, and there, behind the dumpsters, I can make out three guys beating someone. I take out my knife with my heart in my throat, somehow sensing Cole's presence. One of the men speaks in Russian, and I step forward quietly.

"Hey, fucker!" I yell, and all three turn around, momentarily distracted. It's long enough of a distraction that Cole takes his scalpel out and stabs one of them in the neck with it. The man goes down, and I smirk. "Coming here wasn't a good idea," I tell them.

They whirl on Cole, but now he's ready, and I've seen him take down more than one man before. I walk closer, debating if I should shoot them, but they're too close to Cole, so it's not an option. Then my brothers step out of the club, whistling a tune, and the Russians freeze.

Yeah, fuckers.

This was a bad idea.

CHAPTER 13
COLE

The Russians freeze as soon as they hear the tune coming from Alessandro, and I take my opportunity for what it is and punch one of the guys in the throat. I hear footsteps headed my way, and then there's a gun pressed to the guy's head. The other guy in front of me stays still, barely breathing, as Emiliano pulls the trigger.

"Fuck," The remaining Russian grits out. "Fuck, fuck, *fuck*."

"You shouldn't have come here," I tell him, stepping forward with my scalpel and slicing his neck from one end to the other before he can react to my words.

Emiliano looks at me with a smile on his lips, and for just a split second, I smile back. That is, until I remember what he said to me last night, and I narrow my eyes on him instead. His eyes widen, probably realizing I'm still angry, and he offers me his hand. I look at it, then walk past him.

"Cole!" Emiliano yells after me. "There are clothes for you in my office."

I laugh, stopping in my tracks right in front of the doors that lead back inside the club. "And how did you manage that?"

"Don't ask," he replies. "You need to clean up."

I nod, not arguing for once. I just sliced someone's throat, and I feel his blood all over my face and clothes. I need a shower. Thankfully, Emiliano's office has one. Not that I want to go in there right now, but it feels like I have no choice. The men hit my body and not my face. My ribs hurt—they're definitely bruised—but it's nothing I can't handle. Prison was fun in the way that I was always getting into fights.

Alessandro pulls out his cell phone, calling a clean-up crew, and before Emiliano can get another word in, I slip through the door. I make it all the way to his office without anyone seeing or stopping me, and for that, I'm grateful. I'm also glad I have some clothes to change into because I plan on going back to the dance floor, whether or not Emiliano wants me to.

His office smells like him—vanilla and spice—and I breathe it in greedily. Who knew I'd be such a junkie for the man, but the truth is, one hit only made my addiction worse. Now I know what it's like to be with him; the memories will haunt me for the rest of my life. It doesn't change the fact that I need to hate him, though. In order to protect my heart, I need to stay the hell away from the man. Otherwise, I won't survive.

As soon as I get back to the penthouse, I'm leaving. He said we're a mistake, and Matteo won't come home because I'm there. So it only makes sense to leave. I've already looked for an apartment out of his building, away from him. I don't want him to be able to keep tabs on me. I want him going crazy, out of his mind, wondering what I'm doing every day. Who I'm fucking. What trouble I'm getting into. Or maybe he doesn't give a fuck and I'm delusional. We are a mistake, after all.

I strip out of my bloody clothes, leaving them on the bathroom floor for Emiliano to pick up. I won't do him any favors; in fact, I'm going to do everything in my power to piss him off the way he's pissed me off. I will get a reaction from him if it's the last thing I do.

Turning on the shower, I wait until it's hot, then get in. I make quick work of washing up, getting every nook and cranny. Even going as far as washing under my blunt fingernails. I wash my hair and face thoroughly, then hear the door creaking open. I tense. Fuck, I forgot to lock the damn thing.

The glass door makes the image slightly distorted, but I can tell it's Emiliano. He's looking down at the clothes on the ground, and I smirk even though I can't see his face. He comes in and closes the door though, and I see him place the clothes on top of the sink's vanity. He's quiet, but soon enough, the water starts to get cold, and I shut it off.

I grab the towel and begin to dry myself, just for the glass door to swing open. Emiliano scowls at me, a move that shouldn't make him look this attractive, and I look away. Focusing on drying myself, I bend over and get my legs and feet. He sucks in a sharp breath, but I ignore it as I wrap the towel around my waist. Except there's no way out of the shower with him standing in the way.

"I'm not talking to you," I say simply, hoping he will move, even knowing he won't. He's a stubborn motherfucker. "Move."

We lock eyes, and his mouth is set in a tight line. "You will hear me out."

"Is this the Don or Emiliano speaking?" I ask him sarcastically, and he huffs.

"This is the man who fucked you last night until you couldn't move."

I laugh loudly, my whole body shaking with it. "Fuck off, Emiliano. You don't get to remind me of that."

"For as long as I live, I won't let you forget about it," he growls, stepping forward and wrapping a hand around my hair, yanking back roughly. I grimace at the pain, and he seems to love that, if the wild look in his eyes is any indication. "It's going to haunt you for the rest of your miserable life—*I* will haunt you."

The problem is that he's not wrong. He's so close to my reality that I wish I could put myself out of my misery and slit his fucking throat already. But I can't, because deep down I know I will always care for him. I'll always be in love with him, and that doesn't bode well. "I've already forgotten," I lie.

"You're not leaving me," he says through gritted teeth, and the image of my suitcase and bags on my bed flashes through my mind. I smirk. "You'll go home and unpack right now."

"No, *Daddy*," I purr, knowing he hates it when I call him that. "I will do no such thing."

His grip on my hair tightens, but I give him no reaction. That seems to piss him off. He steps into the shower, shoes and all, and slams me against the tiled wall. "You'll do as I say."

"Or what?" I raise an eyebrow. "You gonna spank me?"

Before I can process what's happening, my cheek is pressed against the wall, and the towel is pooling around my feet. There's a loud crack, followed by pain, and my body jolts. He actually did it—he fucking *spanked* me.

I snarl, and he does it again—harder this time.

There's water running down my back and to my ass cheeks from not drying my hair, and it makes the sting even worse. He spreads the water, then spanks me harder than the last one. I'm panting and my traitorous cock is rock hard. I could come just from that.

"Safe word," he growls, and I frown. "What's your safe word? Otherwise, I won't stop until I'm satisfied."

A shiver runs down my spine as he soothes the tender skin of my ass cheek, and I groan, "Yes."

"Yes is your safe word?" he asks with a smirk. "That's depraved, even for you, Cole."

I'm silent.

"Tell me, my prince," he says softly, and I tense at the pet name. He shouldn't call me that when it means nothing to him. "Do you get off on me forcing myself on you?"

Again, I don't say anything, but I do whimper when his hand unexpectedly cracks against my skin once more.

"No?" he asks, and I look at him over my shoulder. He's soothing the sting once more, but even I know I'm going to bruise. I probably won't be able to sit down for at least a few days. "Let's try again. Do you like it when I hurt you?"

His hand comes down on my ass yet again, but I've lost count of how many times he's spanked me. All I know is that my skin feels raw. "No," I lie.

"Tell me to stop," he groans, his cheeks flushed, his bottom lip between his teeth as he spanks me once more. "Tell me, Cole."

"No," I moan, and this time, when he spanks me, my dick jumps.

"You're making my cock so fucking hard," he groans, spreading my cheeks. He leans in, licking my rim, and I stand up on my tiptoes. "Where are you going, Cole? There's nowhere you can run to that I won't find you."

His breath is against my hole, and I close my eyes when his tongue comes back to it. He prods roughly until his tongue slips inside, and I moan loudly. I vaguely remember how fucking angry I am at him, yet I'm not strong enough to put a stop to this either. I'm fucked up.

Emiliano pulls away. "Do you think you can take four more?" he asks me, his voice soft, like he doesn't want to spook me.

I nod.

"Do you think you can come from it?" He smirks, and I

look away as my face heats. "Do it, Cole. Paint the wall with it."

I wrap my hand around my cock, jerking it slowly as he squeezes my cheeks roughly, then lets go of them.

Crack.

My fist tightens around my cock, and I jack it off furiously.

Crack.

My balls rise and tighten.

Crack.

A shiver runs down my spine, and my cock thickens even more.

Crack.

I come with a shout, painting the wall just like he told me to.

Emiliano soothes my raw skin once more, then bends down and kisses it. It feels hot and swollen, and my body feels weak and heavy. My head is fuzzy, like I'm floating. He seems to sense it and helps me out of the shower. He opens the bathroom door, guiding me toward the couch across from his desk. He sits down, bringing me on top of him until I'm straddling his lap, and my breathing turns shallow.

What the hell is he doing?

He runs his fingertips over my back lightly, making me tremble at the sweet gesture, and I close my eyes and lay my head on his shoulder, refusing to look at him.

"I'm sorry," he whispers, and I frown. "I should've never said that to you. You're not a mistake—you're not."

Tears prick the back of my eyes, and I shudder in his arms, trying not to break down. I make a weak little sound at the back of my throat, and I fucking hate myself for it. For showing him weakness.

"Please forgive me," he says, and I shake my head. "Please, Cole, I didn't mean it."

Fuck, is he begging right now?

"It just—it just felt like I betrayed Matteo, you know?" he continues. "You're his big love, and how the fuck am I supposed to take that from him?"

I'm quiet, just letting him talk to himself.

"But it's no excuse for how I treated you." His arms wrap around me tightly, and a traitorous tear escapes and lands on his shirt, soaking it immediately. "I'm sorry." His voice breaks, "Please, Cole."

"I can't let you hurt me again," I tell him, voice shaking. "I refuse."

"I can't make you any promises," Emiliano says, and I suck in a sharp breath. "I don't know how to want you without feeling guilty."

I nod, but I don't know how to reply. The general consensus is that he won't let himself have me, and if I keep insisting, he's going to break me. And I'm afraid that if I let him, I won't be able to gather the pieces of my heart and put them back together after he's done with me.

I can't let that happen.

CHAPTER 14
EMILIANO

Cole hasn't looked at me once since we got in my vehicle, and there's a pit in my stomach that makes me feel nauseous. I should be happy that he's coming home with me, that he relented; instead, I'm worrying myself to death. Worrying about how he didn't fucking forgive me. Worrying about why the hell that's so important to me. Why I practically begged him. He said he can't trust me with his heart, not with those exact same words, but the same meaning still applies. And what does it say about me that I want him to trust me? How is that even fair to him when I don't know what I want?

Well, that's a lie.

I know I want *him*, but now it's a matter of whether I'm willing to betray my son. The most important person in my life. I grew up with Matteo; that's what it means to be a young single dad. We've been extremely close, and I know how he feels about Cole. How could I possibly do that to him? Cole isn't even trying to convince me; probably thinking he has no shot. But the truth is, I want him more by the second. Every time he's in my vicinity, this visceral fucking need grows inside of me. I'm *aching*, and I don't even know what I'm aching for.

All I know is that rationality is flying out the window. I'm angry at myself for wanting him. Angry at Cole for wanting me back. And lastly, pissed off at my son for loving the only person I've ever truly wanted. That's the problem, right? I'm trying to be a good dad—a good person—so I won't let myself have Cole. I'm a fucking martyr. Why can't I ever have something for just myself?

Cole is probably going to grab his stuff and leave me as soon as we make it back to the penthouse, which is exactly right about now, considering we're pulling into the garage parking lot. I tense, unwilling to let him walk away from me. I'll tie him to my fucking bed if I have to—if that's what it takes to keep him by my side.

I'll chain him to me.

Cole opens the car door before we're even parked all the way, rushing toward the elevators. I jog after him, and when he attempts to shut the door on me, I slip my foot into the crack and force the doors back open. His nostrils flare as he huffs through his nose, and I crowd him until his back hits the wall. It takes me back to the bathroom, when I spanked him, and my cock hardens. Worst timing ever too, if the narrowing of his eyes is any indication. He wants nothing to do with me now that the high of the moment has worn off.

"Cole," I whisper, a choked sound. "Don't do this."

Cole pushes me away, and I stumble back a step just as the elevator doors swing open at the penthouse level. He sidesteps me, walking down the hallway in a hurry, and I follow after him. I seem to be doing that a lot, and for a split second, I wonder what the hell he's doing to me. Is he fucking with me? What does he actually want?

Before he can reach his bedroom, I grab his arm and pull him towards my room. Then I slam the door and lock it for good measure. We face off against each other, our chests heaving in unison, and before I even know what I'm doing, I crowd him. My hand cups his jaw gently, and he looks away. That won't do.

Tightening my hand on his jaw, his eyes flash to mine. I know I'm hurting him, but I'm beyond caring. I need him. Right now, I need him more than I've ever needed anything or anyone. "Submit," I growl.

"No," he snarls, gritting his teeth.

I grab his hair tightly, then push on his shoulder roughly, shoving him down to his knees. He tries to get out of my grasp, but I just pull on his hair harder until he whimpers. And, fuck, the sound goes straight to my cock.

"Emiliano," he growls, but instead of answering, I let go of his hair and give his shoulders a firm push, causing him to land on his ass.

Cole looks at me with a fire in his eyes that should scare me; instead, it turns me on further. He wants to murder me, I can tell, and yet I'd still give him whatever he wanted. I'm at his fucking mercy, and he doesn't realize it.

"What the *fuck*—" he snaps, and I drop to my knees between his spread legs. I put my hands on his chest and push again until his back and head meet the carpet.

I unbutton his jeans and shove them down along with his boxer briefs until they're under his ass. His cock springs free, pretty and pink and fucking mouthwatering. I want to—"Let me suck you off."

"W-w-what?" Cole stutters.

"You fucking heard me," I breathe, lowering my face to his nipple and wrapping my lips around it. I lick it once more after letting go of it, then bite down on it. He groans, his back arching off the carpet. "I want your cock in my mouth. I want you to teach me what you like."

Cole's exhale is shaky, and I put us face to face. He looks

up at me with wide eyes, and I take him in. The black hair over his forehead. The chiseled jawline. His narrow, pierced nose. Beautiful, pouty lips. The bottom one slightly fuller than the top. Then his eyes—the color of a Canadian lake. Practically transparent. Barely blue. And I—I just get lost in those eyes.

"You're staring," Cole whispers.

"How could I not?" I breathe, brushing his hair off his forehead with one hand while supporting myself with the other. "You're beautiful."

His eyes turn watery, and he closes them immediately, not wanting to look weak in front of me. It doesn't bother me though, and when a tear slips out of the corner of his eye, I kiss it away. It's too fucking tender, this moment, and it's going to fucking crush me if he keeps it up.

"Please, Em," Cole whispers. "*Yes*."

I lean into him and kiss his lips softly, then tug on the bottom one with my teeth. He makes this soft little sound at the back of his throat, barely audible, and I bite down harder until I can taste the coppery sweetness of his blood in my mouth. I lick his lip for good measure, then bend down lower to suck on his neck. I know I shouldn't, not really, but it doesn't stop me from leaving a bruise behind. I'm feeling possessive of him after being in his body one fucking time. I don't even want to think about what will happen after tonight.

I go back to his nipple and bite it, and the groan that comes from him makes my balls throb. He really loves nipple play. *Noted*. My hands roam his body, caressing and groping as I make my way down to his abs, and I run my tongue over every line until my lips meet the head of his cock. I have two choices: I change my mind, or I take him in my mouth and hope I don't fuck it up. Choice two wins. My tongue laps up the pre-cum at the tip of Cole's dick, and then I suck the head into my mouth softly.

"Oh, fuck," Cole moans loudly, his hands coming to rest on the back of my head. "More tongue."

I twirl my tongue around the head as I suck him deeper into my mouth, then take half of him between my lips. His hands tighten in my hair, and he shoves me down his cock until the tip of my nose meets the trimmed hair at the base. I gag violently, and he chuckles.

"You wanna suck my cock, baby?" He groans when I hollow my cheeks on the way up. My stomach flips at the word *baby*, as if I've never been called that before. "You gonna take it all?"

I take him to the back of my throat once more, inhaling sharply when he holds me there.

"Swallow," he says, and I do it—with effort. I gag once more, and he lets me up a little, but not before tears spill from my eyes. "You're such a good boy for me, Em." My cock tingles at the praise, and I rub against the carpet, chasing friction. "You look so fucking pretty when you gag on my cock. Look at these tears, baby…"

"Mmm," I moan as he brings a thumb to my cheek and brushes away a tear, then licks it up. Who knew sucking his cock would get me this hot and bothered? *Goddamn*.

I tug on his balls lightly as he shoves his cock down my throat again, this time fucking my face. Tears spill down my cheeks, and he goes harder when two of my fingers find his taint and I rub it.

"Finger me," Cole demands. "Make me come."

I pull away from him, taking his pants and boxer briefs all the way off, then shove his legs apart until I get a good view of his hole. I spit on it repeatedly, then press a finger against the rim.

"Two," Cole says through gritted teeth. "Stretch me for your cock."

There's lube in my wallet, which is in my back pocket, but I don't make a move to pull it out. No, I want it to burn. I want to hurt him for wanting to leave me. I want to—

Cole grabs my hair once more and pulls me toward his cock, and I thrust two fingers into him. He mutters a curse, but I get to work quickly, bobbing my head up and down as I feel around for his prostate. Once I find it, I crook my fingers in a come here motion and suck him to the back of my throat.

A broken moan greets my ears, and I taste his pre-cum on my tongue. I continue pressing my fingers against his prostate, continuing to rub it, and he starts fucking my face to the rhythm of my fingers. His legs begin to tremble, his balls draw up—

"I'm gonna come in your mouth, baby." My stomach flips as if I'm on a rollercoaster ride, right before the drop, and I hum. "Swallow it."

With another thrust into my throat, he comes. His body shakes with it, his eyes locked with mine the entire time, and his lips parted. His chest heaves as he pants and moans, and I swallow everything he gives me until he turns soft between my lips. Then I let him go. I press my cheek to the inside of his thigh, trying to catch my breath, and he looks up at the ceiling. But I'm not done with him, so I kneel between his legs and begin to unbutton my pants. Our eyes meet, and his widen.

"You didn't think we were done, did you?" I smirk, and he shakes his head.

"I'm not—"

"I still need to come, Cole," I say patiently, knowing he's going to give in one way or another. "You're gonna make me come, aren't you?"

"No."

"That's not your safe word," I point out, and he looks at me with narrowed eyes. "Do you want me to stop?" I ask him. "Say yes."

His nostrils flare as he shakes his head, and I know right now, I fucking got him.

Right now, he's mine.

Even if it's only for a little while.

CHAPTER 15
COLE

My legs are spread as Emiliano takes his pants all the way off, then his shirt, until he's kneeling completely naked in front of me. He looks at me with hungry eyes, and they roam from my face to my spread legs. I focus on the way his tongue wets his bottom lip, and heat unfurls in my stomach. Fuck, my refractory period usually isn't this short, but I feel like I could come one more time for him. I can be a good boy—

"Flip over," Emiliano says softly, and I shake my head. "Hands and knees."

"No." I smirk, looking into his deep brown eyes. "If you're going to fuck me, you're going to face me. You're going to look into my eyes and come to terms with the fact that you want me so much, you're willing to fuck your whole life up."

Emiliano mutters a curse under his breath, averting his gaze. I know he feels guilty, but he's going to have to get over it. I won't forgive him until he does. To be honest, I shouldn't even be doing this without having a conversation, but when he offered to suck me off, well, I'm weak, what can I say? Now I do have to make him come. Tit for tat and all that.

He faces me once more, looking right into my eyes, mouth set in a tight line. "You want me to face you?" he asks me.

"You sure? Because if we do this, there's no going back, Cole. If we do this, I'm claiming you as mine."

I laugh loudly. "Yeah, okay, Emiliano." I raise an eyebrow. "It's just sex, isn't it? It doesn't have to be more than that. After all, I'm your biggest mistake." I shouldn't throw it back in his face after his apology, but he needs to know I haven't forgiven him.

Em narrows his eyes at me, grabbing my thighs and hauling me toward him. My back burns as the rug chafes my skin, and I groan. That's leaving a rash. He grabs the packet of lube from his wallet beside him, ripping it open with his teeth, and nothing should be that hot. Goddamn it. Why does everything he does have to turn me on? I hate that he affects me this much.

"Nothing with you is just sex, Cole," he tells me through gritted teeth, lubing his fingers up and thrusting two into my hole. "You know there's something between us. So show me. Show me what I'd be missing out on if I can't have you."

I snicker. "Oh, now you want me to show you?" Emiliano presses one of my thighs toward my chest, giving him easier access. "I thought you didn't want me."

"I do," Emiliano growls, crooking his fingers inside of me and making me see stars. My vision has white dots all over it as he does it again, and then he pulls out and thrusts three fingers in. He scissors his fingers as I squirm, and I hold my other leg toward my chest, the whore that I fucking am for him. "I want you so bad I can't see straight."

Those words shouldn't affect me as much as they do, but I can't help it. This is everything I've ever wanted from him. So why does it feel like he's going to change his mind come morning?

I don't say anything.

"I know you feel it too," Emiliano says softly, pulling his fingers out swiftly. He lubes up his cock, then presses it to my entrance unceremoniously. "You can't deny there's something between us."

"There's nothing," I reply. "You've made sure of that."

"Your body says otherwise." Emiliano punctuates his words with one deep thrust, not bothering to go slowly for me. He doesn't stop until he's bottomed out, and tears sting my eyes from the burn. He's fucking thick, and he's not giving me time to adjust as he pulls back out all the way to the tip and snaps his hips forward brutally. "Look at your cock getting hard for me again, you fucking slut."

I moan as he pegs my prostate, and his eyes light up like it's Christmas morning. "Tell me you love me," Emiliano demands. "Say it."

"No," I growl.

Emiliano wraps a hand around my throat tightly, uncaring that I didn't take a breath before he did it. My lungs deplete, and my chest burns. My eyes water as my mouth opens and closes like a fish out of water, and I feel myself getting dizzy. Just as my vision begins to go black, he lets go of me.

His hand meets my face in a hard slap, my head snapping to the side, and I taste blood at the corner of my lip. What the fuck? My eyes narrow to slits, but he just smirks at me as I choke on a deep breath.

Motherfucker.

"Say it, Cole." Emiliano leans in and bites my neck roughly, then bites my pec even harder. "I have no problem with getting it out of you one way or another."

I press my lips together so I don't say the three little words that sit on the tip of my tongue. Because I do want to tell him, more than anything. But I can't. He fucked up.

Emiliano pulls out, flipping me over, man-handling me before I can refuse, and he presses my face to the carpet and enters me once more. I support myself with my arms, arching my back for him so he can get a nice view of my ass, and he groans.

His hand comes to my hair, his fingers tightening in the strands, and he pulls my head back hard. My neck arches, aching in the best way, as he fucks in and out of me. With his other hand, he grips my hip tightly, and I know I'm going to bruise. But right now, I don't care. I know he's claiming me, and even if I won't admit it to him, my body is in fucking heaven.

"You're mine," Emiliano says, snapping his hips forward, avoiding my prostate, making me angry. "I don't care if you say you're not."

"Em," I growl. "*Please.* Make me come."

"Say you're mine." Emiliano lets go of my hair, shoving my head forward until my cheek meets the carpet, and he drags me back until that burns too. He rakes his fingernails down my back, and I know he's leaving marks from the sting. "Tell me."

"I—I can't."

Crack.

His hand meets my ass roughly, exactly where it's already bruising, and I shout in pain. Fuck. Yet my cock hardens even more, leaking pre-cum. "I can do this all night."

His hand comes down on my ass again, and I whimper.

"You say you want me to be yours." I groan as the tip of his cock grazes my prostate, not quite hitting it right. "But you don't know what that means for you."

Emiliano fucks me shallowly, frustrating me, but he doesn't say a word.

"I'm possessive," I tell him.

"So am I."

"I won't be a secret," I say, looking at him over my shoulder.

His eyes are already on my face. "I wouldn't ask that of you."

"I'll be your equal, or I will be nothing of yours."

"Yes, Cole," he breathes. "Any other requests?"

"I'll think of something," I breathe as he thrusts against my prostate just right. "Oh, fuck, right *there*."

"Here, Cole?" he asks, hitting it again and again. "You know what I want to hear."

"I—" My hand wraps around my cock, and I begin to stroke it furiously. "I'm yours."

"What. Else."

"Fuck." I breathe as his grip tightens on my hips. He pulls me back toward his chest, making me kneel in front of him to ride his cock. He sits back as my ass meets his lap, and he thrusts into me, topping from the bottom. It feels fucking heavenly, and my spine begins to tingle as I jerk myself once more. My cock is leaking, my balls drawing up, and I begin to shake. "I love you," I whisper, and Emiliano moans loudly.

"Yes, yes, *yes*," Em groans. "Like that. Come for me, Cole. I can't last."

After three more strokes, I come all over my fist and the carpet. Emiliano shoves me face first into the carpet once more, thrusting quickly and deeply, his hips snapping against my ass loudly, and he comes with a moan, flooding my ass. I can feel his cum as it leaks out, and he pulls out and stuffs it back into me.

"Mine," he tells me with conviction. "You're mine. This ass is mine, and so is your cock."

I whimper.

"From now on, you'll forget anyone existed before me." He drapes himself over my back, panting against the shell of my ear. "And that includes my fucking son."

"Yes," I breathe. "You're the only one for me."

"I'll be the last person to fuck this tight little hole."

My breath whooshes out of my lungs at that statement, and my stomach swoops.

"You wanted to be mine?" he asks me, but I know it's rhetorical. "Just know I take that very seriously. You'll belong to me for the rest of your life, then even in fucking death."

Fuck.

"I'm yours, baby," I whisper, and he kisses my temple.

Emiliano gets up, goes to the bathroom, and then comes out with a wet rag. It's warm as he presses it against my ass, cleaning me up. It's a sweet gesture, and he seems to enjoy taking care of me after sex. And yet… I don't know where we go from here. Do I go back to my room tonight? Am I staying here?

"Come shower," he says, breaking me out of my thoughts, and I realize the water is already running. "Before the water gets cold."

I nod, go to the bathroom, and get in the shower.

We make quick work of washing each other, and then Emiliano helps me dry off. I brush my teeth and use the bathroom, and then I just stand there in the middle of his room, a ship with no direction. What the hell do I do?

"Are you coming to bed?" Emiliano asks, and relief makes my shoulders sag. "What? Did you think I was letting you go tonight?"

"I don't know what to think."

"Get in bed, Cole." He sighs, "I'm tired."

I nod and get in bed next to him, and he turns off the lights with the remote on his nightstand. He snuggles closer to me, pulling me into his body, and my head meets his chest. Em sighs, and his breathing evens out, and before long, I'm closing my eyes too.

I don't know how long I sleep for, but when the soft light of morning slips in through the blinds, I get up, careful not to rouse Emiliano. I use the bathroom and put on my boxer briefs, then open the door quietly and shut it behind me.

I'll be honest, I wasn't expecting last night. I thought for sure we'd fuck and he'd send me off to my room, pretending it never happened. For a moment, I wondered if any of his words and declarations were true. If claiming me was just a heat of the moment thing. But he seems to have meant it, as evidenced by the way he kept me close all night. Not letting me get too far from him at any point. Even in his sleep, he sought me out.

The sex was hot. Hotter than anything I've ever experienced; then again, it was like that the last time too. I thought it was a fluke, but it turns out, I just love everything about the fucker. It also didn't escape my notice that he got those three words out of me, yet he didn't say them back. Does it matter? Something tells me it doesn't, that he cares. But a part of me craves those words right back.

The house is quiet as I make myself a cup of coffee, then put two sugars and creamer in it. I'm not usually a coffee drinker, but when I do, it needs to be sweet. I put the french vanilla creamer back in the fridge just as the elevator dings, and I tense, looking down at myself. I have bite marks on my body and nail marks down my back. God, I'm a fucking mess. I can't let Matteo see me like this.

I run to my room and put a shirt on, then go back to the kitchen as if nothing ever happened. Except Matteo is already sitting at the kitchen island, taking a sip of my coffee. He makes a disgusted face, and I smirk, rounding the island until I'm facing him.

"You always did like this nasty shit." He grimaces.

"Yeah, well, not all of us can drink it black," I reply, going to the stool next to his and sitting on it. My ass immediately throbs, and I shift in the seat until the pressure eases. "I'm sorry," I sigh. "I didn't mean to hurt you."

"I know," Matteo says, looking into my eyes. He looks sad, defeated, and I hate it. "But you're my friend, Cole. I don't want to lose you. I'll get over it."

If he only knew what I've been up to with his father, we would be having a different conversation. But I can't think of it right now. I don't want to hurt his feelings. So waiting to tell him is probably best. "I love you, Matty. I don't want to lose you either."

Matteo leans in and hugs me, and I close my eyes. I hear him breathe me in, and I hug him tighter, hoping he doesn't smell his dad on me. Fuck, I really didn't think this through. I try to pull away, but he holds me tighter.

A throat clears from behind us, and I tense. He feels it, and he frowns as he pulls away. Emiliano looks at me like he wants to throttle me, or kill me, or both, and I look away. How am I supposed to explain to him I don't want to give up Matteo? That he's my best friend, and I promised him forever, too?

"Hey, son," Emiliano says, pasting a fake smile on his face. Matty looks between us, trying to figure out what's going on. I pray he doesn't. "Are you here to stay?"

"Yeah," Matteo says, clearing his throat. "I'm sorry I left. It was immature. I should've taken it better, but I was hurt."

Emiliano's eyes flash with something that looks like guilt, but he masks it quickly. I wonder if Matteo saw it, but then he gets up from the chair and goes to his dad, hugging him tightly. There's a knot in my throat when he looks my way, his hand outstretched toward me.

"Group hug." He grins.

I get up too and join in the hug, but instead of Emiliano's arm wrapping around my shoulders, he wraps it around my waist and tugs me toward him. I suck in a sharp breath but hug Matteo all the same, hating this and loving it in equal measure.

SHAE RUBY

This feels like a betrayal.

CHAPTER 16
EMILIANO

I clear my throat, pulling away from the hug. Reluctantly, I let go of Cole and step away, giving them both space even though it's the last thing I want to do. I want to claim Cole, make Matteo understand I never meant to hurt him, and not hide anymore. But I know that's not possible right now. Instead, I have to watch Matteo look at Cole with hurt in his eyes, and Cole averts his gaze. I can tell he feels guilty, and fuck, I do, too. But I also feel angry about what I just walked in on, even though I know it's irrational.

Matteo looks between us, and suddenly, the air is too thick to breathe. As if he can sense the tension, he frowns. "I have to use the bathroom," he says under his breath, then walks away.

Cole's eyes remain on the ground as I get closer, and instead of getting aggressive with him and claiming him, I reach out and stroke my knuckles over his cheek. His eyes widen in surprise and he looks up at me, his bottom lip trapped between his teeth.

"Why are you out here in your underwear?" I whisper so Matteo doesn't hear us. "No one should be able to see you like this, Cole."

Cole jumps when I rub the heel of my palm against his

cock, and he whimpers. "Sorry." He shakes his head as if he's in a daze. "I wasn't expecting him."

No shit.

I'm glad Cole woke up when he did, or we'd all be having a different conversation; yet, it doesn't piss me off any less. "You don't tell him you love him."

"What?" Cole narrows his eyes at me.

"It means something different to him," I say through gritted teeth, and he rears back. "I won't have you leading him on."

"I wasn't—"

"I'm the only one you love, Cole," I snap, hating myself for saying it. Hating myself for feeling so fucking over the top and possessive of him already, but it doesn't stop me from continuing to speak. "*Me*. No one else."

"Are you—" Cole sputters. "Are you *jealous*?"

"Maybe I am." My nostrils flare. "So, what?"

"You're not my dad," he snaps back. "I'll tell my best friend I love him if I so please."

"Cole—" I growl.

Matteo's door swings open loudly, and I take a step back, away from Cole. Right before he can come out, I storm off, slamming my bedroom door behind me. There's a knock at the door a moment later, and I close my eyes and count to ten. I don't answer because I know it's Cole, and I also know we can't make a scene right now. It's better this way.

"Em," Cole says softly, and I close my eyes as I try to slow down my breathing. I shouldn't be this angry. Rationally, I know that. But the irrational part of my brain is the one taking the wheel right now, and I don't know how to stop it. "Please, baby. Let me in."

"No," I say softly. "Go be with Matteo."

"*Please.*"

Fucking hell.

I open the door just a crack and Cole slips in uninvited, shutting it behind him. Then he's on me, slamming his lips to mine in a kiss that could only be described as frenzied. His tongue thrusts into my mouth as he grabs my ass and rubs his hard cock against mine, causing me to groan. My hands travel down his back and to his firm ass, and I squeeze tightly.

"*Baby*," he murmurs. "Don't be mad."

I huff and stay silent, yet I can't stop touching him. My hands roam and then move back to his face. I cup his cheeks and bring my lips to his softly, a little too sweetly, but he closes his eyes like it's the best thing that's ever happened to him. And that's when it dawns on me. Cole is a gift from the heavens, and I'm just the mere mortal who gets to have a taste of the divine.

"I'm not mad," I whisper, soothing him with a hand on his back. "I'm just—fucking jealous, Cole. You're driving me crazy."

Cole smirks. "All I hear is that you want me."

I roll my eyes playfully and smile. "You know I do."

There's a knock at the door, and Cole takes a few healthy steps back. Matteo walks in without waiting for permission, but I guess, thankfully, he knocked first. And then he looks between us, gaze flicking rapidly. He seems confused, which I guess I can't blame him for. Cole has never been in my bedroom before while Matteo has been in the penthouse.

"What's going on, Dad?" Matteo asks, and my stomach clenches with fear. "Why's he in here?"

"Just have a job for him," I reply calmly, even though my heart is beating erratically, and it feels like I'm going to throw up.

"And it couldn't wait until you were out of the room?" He narrows his eyes at Cole, looking him over from top to bottom, eyes focused on his crotch. "Why are you still in your underwear?" Matteo asks Cole.

"Huh?" Cole plays dumb, looking down at himself. "Oh—that." He chuckles. "I didn't even realize it. My bad, Emiliano."

"It's fine," I sigh. "Why don't you guys put on a movie or something?" The one thing I don't want is for them to spend even more time together right now, but I can only ask for so much. That wouldn't be fair to either of them, and I'm not heartless. Just a jealous asshole, I guess. "I'll be back tonight."

Cole frowns, staring at me, and Matteo raises an eyebrow.

"What are we, five?" Matteo smirks, and I nod.

"Pretty much," I tell him, grabbing my clothes and going to the bathroom to get changed. "See you later."

"Bye, Dad."

I get changed quickly into a gray suit with a white button-down, no tie. All the while remembering every second of last night. Every shared breath, every thrust, every bite. Fuck, if it wasn't the hottest thing to ever happen to me. Sex with Cole is different from anything I've ever experienced. Maybe it's because he's a man and I've never been with one before, but it's been the best experience of my life. He's so responsive, so vocal, so perfectly made for me.

I can't get enough.

It's more than sex with him, though. I don't know what it is about him that draws me in the way he does, but I'm starting to develop feelings for him, and I don't know how to show him in a healthy way right now. All I know is that I need him viscerally, and he seems to need me just as much. I'll learn how to calm the fuck down, but right now I'm going crazy with want. Want for us to be normal. For me to be able to claim him in front of everyone. For us to have something more than hidden sex. And I don't know what to do about it.

I'm coming to terms with my relationship with Cole. I can want him—care for him—and it doesn't take away from the love I feel for my son. It doesn't mean I'm a bad dad or that I'm trying to hurt him—even if that's what I'll accomplish. It just means sometimes I want something for just myself, and even though I never know how to take what I want for fear that this life is too much for someone else, Cole is different. He's already part of this life. There's nothing I'd have to hide from him. I wouldn't have to protect him from the truth. We could just be. Which is why we're perfect for each other.

I just wish Matteo could understand. But I get that he believes Cole is the love of his life. I, on the other hand, don't believe that. I think he has loved Cole fiercely their entire lives, and maybe he's confusing that for being in love. Sex clouds judgment, after all. I'm not saying he doesn't have feelings for him, but I bet if he gave someone else a chance, he could fall in love.

At least I hope so.

An hour later, I'm standing in my office, pacing the length of it. My brothers are sitting on the couch and the spare armchairs. Alessandro is looking at me like I grew a second head, and the rest of my brothers are either smirking or frowning. Probably because they've never seen me like this over anyone I've been attached to. Can they really blame me, though? How am I supposed to proceed?

"Can you tell us what the hell is going on?" Alessandro finally speaks up, and I stop to glance at him before I continue my pacing. I bring my hands to my hair and yank on the strands and Giovanni chuckles, the asshole. "You're freaking us out."

"Yeah, brother," Giovanni says. "Do tell us what has your panties in a bunch."

"Sex is clouding your judgment, huh?" Lorenzo grins, and I stop in my tracks. "Uh, oh. Hit a nerve."

"Sure did." Tony smirks.

"Can you all just fucking stop?" I snap. "I'm trying to

think." It's a lie. I'm not trying to think about anything. I just need their advice and don't know how to ask for it.

"Spill, Emiliano," Alessandro sighs, clearly running out of patience. Out of all of us, he's the least playful. "I don't have all day."

"Oh?" I murmur. "Do you have someone you want to tell us about?"

"Can you just get on with it?" Giovanni asks, and I narrow my eyes at him.

"Wait, do *you* have someone you want to tell us about, too?" I raise an eyebrow.

Giovanni's face turns red, and he tenses but shakes his head, his lips in a tight line. "This is about you, not me."

"Fine." I sigh, stopping at my desk and leaning against it. I look out the floor to ceiling windows, the view of the city failing to calm me down. "I fucked Cole again."

"Again?" Giovanni chuckles. "I thought it was a one-time thing."

"Yeah, well, one thing led to another, and here we are," I snap, remembering last night. The way Cole was so fucking defiant, yet pliable in my arms, too. "It's more than sex, Gio."

Giovanni's eyebrows raise, and he leans back on the couch, getting comfortable. As if he's here for story time. "Is it now?"

"Yeah," I tell him. "But there's Matteo to think about, too. I don't know what to do."

"What are you saying, Emiliano?" Alessandro asks slowly. "Do you want to be in a relationship with him?"

I nod.

"That's a fucking terrible idea," Lorenzo says.

"What the fuck?" Giovanni grins.

Tony just stares.

"You're out of your fucking mind." Alessandro stands,

and now he's the one pacing the length of my office. "Do you know what this will do to your son?"

"You don't think I fucking know that?" I yell. "I just—I can't help how I fucking feel!"

"You know Emiliano has never been in a relationship," Giovanni tells Alessandro gently, trying to calm him down. "This is the first time he's wanted anyone, Alex. Let him live."

Alessandro sighs. "They'll use him against you."

"Who?" I frown.

"Everyone who finds out you have a weakness now," Alessandro tells me slowly, as if I'm stupid.

"I'll protect him," I reply. "I'll keep him safe."

"You can't," Giovanni points out. "He's a Made Man. He goes on runs, and you know he won't let you take that away from him."

I nod because I do know that. "I can't give him up," I say weakly.

"Then don't," Giovanni tells me gently. "We'll support you. Right?" he asks the rest of them.

Lorenzo nods.

Tony grins.

Alessandro grunts.

"He's mine," I declare. "And I take care of what's mine."

"How are you going to tell Matteo?" Alessandro asks me, point blank. "What will you do if he wants nothing to do with you?"

"Let me worry about that," I say softly because I don't have an answer for that. "And I don't know what I'll do."

Because the truth is, losing my son or Cole can equally gut me. I just don't know which feeling is worse. I've always been taught that your partner is the one you pick above everyone else, but it's hard for me. Do Cole and I even have a future?

For my sake, I hope we do.

CHAPTER 17
COLE

I fucked up and I know it.

It feels like there's nothing I can do to make it better right now, regardless of how gentle Emiliano was before he left the penthouse. I could tell he was angry with me, and even though I couldn't understand why at first, I think I see it now. I guess I would be angry too, if he were spending time with someone he's had sex with before me. But it's not the same. Matteo has been my best friend since I was six years old, and I don't know how to get Em to understand that he has nothing to worry about. That Matteo is not a threat. But even I know that's far-fetched. He's not going to listen to logic. The man is practically a caveman.

Earlier he was so jealous, as if he couldn't stand the thought of me being with someone else. It's a far cry from a few days ago when he said we were a mistake. I don't want to be hung up on that, but I can't deny it stung. It still does. He apologized, and I swear I'm moving forward, but he's giving me whiplash. The way he claimed me last night is still imprinted in my brain, and I just want to shout from the rooftops that he's mine and I'm his, but it would hurt the other most important person in my life. I don't want to do that, yet I also know it's inevitable. Eventually, if Emiliano really is serious about me, we will come out to everyone, and Matteo will be hurt.

I wonder how he will react. Will he stop talking to us? Move out and forget I ever existed? It scares the hell out of me. I don't want to be in his past. I want to be in his present and future. Where I've always been—where I know I belong. But something tells me he'll never forgive this. That our friendship will be over. Is it worth it? Losing someone so important to me because of great dick? Well—no. Emiliano is more than that, at least to me. It's the fact I don't know where he stands that worries me. One minute Emiliano is pushing me away, then the next one he wants me once more.

From now on, I'm going to wait until he seeks me out. I'm done chasing after him. Done looking desperate—done *feeling* desperate. He can be the one to feel that way over me. Maybe if I act indifferent, he'll feel crazy enough to claim me once more. I crave his attention. Being in his arms is like taking a hit of my favorite drug. I'm a junkie for him, and I'm already having withdrawals. But I'm probably delusional, and he won't seek me out. So what do I do if he doesn't? Do I just pretend nothing ever happened between us until he breaks for me once more? Fuck, I don't know how to do this. Playing hard to get with him will be the death of me. The thought alone makes me want to scream, which is why I'm here, at Luna's Den, to drown my sorrows.

Luna's Den is Emiliano's brothel, but I'm obviously not here for sex. My friend from high school, Amy, works here. I used to come visit her often before I went to prison, and I wanted to surprise her. I called ahead to find out what time she'd be busy, and her break starts right about now. The one thing I love about this place is that it has a bar and lounge area; it's all very sophisticated and high-end. You can just tell that only the richest men come here. I wonder what Amy gets paid for her services. It has to be a lot of money. Good for her.

"Look what the cat dragged in," Amy says, sounding excited. I look at her, bouncing on the balls of her feet, and get up from the barstool to hug her. I squeeze her tight. "Ah, baby bear. What are you doing here?"

"Oh, you know." I grin as I pull away, holding her at arm's length and looking her over once as if searching for injuries. All clear. "Here to see my favorite girl."

"Your favorite one, huh?" She smirks.

"Yeah, but don't let Emiliano hear us talk about it." I purse my lips. "He's a jealous motherfucker."

At this, she frowns. "What does he have to do with this?"

"I've been—I've been seeing him." Her eyes widen. "In secret."

"Oh, wow." Amy slaps my shoulder, then takes a seat at the barstool beside mine. I sit down too, waving down the bartender. "You're a bigger whore than I remember."

I smirk. "Only for him."

"Are you dick-whipped?" She touches her chest as if she's in shock, and I laugh.

"You could say that," I admit. "It's still new, but Ames, I've had feelings for him since before I went to prison. I guess I thought they'd be gone by now. But no such luck."

"Fuck," she murmurs, and when the bartender comes to greet us, he looks at Amy and grins. A little intimately, if I do say so myself. "Six shots of tequila, on me."

"Fuck no," I growl. "I got the tab."

"It's on the house." The bartender winks.

"And you call me a whore," I mumble.

Amy laughs loudly. "So he has a crush on me." She winks. "Gotta milk it sometimes."

"Slut." I grin, shoving her shoulder playfully. This is what I love about Amy. It's easy with her. And I never have to worry about her wanting more from me. She knows I'm one-hundred percent gay. I've always liked dick. Women have never once appealed to me, and she accepts that. "I've got some secrets to spill."

The bartender places the shots of tequila in front of us, smiling sweetly at Amy. She smiles back. "We're good for now, Jordan." She winks, and he blushes. "I'll call you for more shots soon."

"Fucking hell, Ames," I cackle. "Have mercy on him."

"Never." She chuckles. "Now spill the tea."

"I royally fucked up." I sigh, and she raises one eyebrow, encouraging me to continue. I take a shot and slam it down. I need alcohol for this conversation. She does the same, except she sucks on the lime after. I just take it straight. "I let Matteo fuck me the day he picked me up. For old time's sake."

"You *what?*" she sputters, and I take another shot, grimacing at the taste. "Old times?"

"Yeah." I sigh. "We used to fuck sometimes."

"How often?"

"Well, he was my first, and I was his. Then after that, it was only occasionally," I tell her, taking the last shot. She still has another one left, which she gulps down now. "Don't judge me."

"Never," she says, her serious face firmly in place. "I just have to wonder—how the fuck are you going to be with his dad when you two have history?"

"I—"

"He's going to fucking kill you," Amy groans, waving down the bartender again. She asks for six more shots, and before I know it, I'm buzzed. "He knows how to hold a grudge, Cole. I don't think you will make it through this together."

"Thanks for giving me hope," I sigh.

"I'm just being real with you." She grimaces, and she asks for more shots. "And you know I'm telling the truth."

"I know," I say sadly. "And the worst part is that I don't know where I stand with Emiliano."

"What do you mean?"

I take the next three shots, and then my head feels light and fuzzy. I have to focus really hard on my thoughts, and I wave down the bartender and ask for water. He smiles and nods. "He—he wants me, then doesn't. He's giving me whiplash."

"What the fuck?" she snaps. "Coley-boy. He can't even make up his mind and you're willing to risk it all?" I nod, and she shakes her head, a look of pity in her eyes. "Fucking hell."

"I know," I sigh, accepting the water from the bartender. My eyes prick with unshed tears, and she rubs my back in slow circles. "I don't know what the fuck to do. Matteo is really going to hate me."

"You have to choose, babe," she says softly. "Who's worth more to you?"

"I can't pick." I shake my head roughly, and it swims, making me dizzy. "Matteo will have to pick for all of us."

"And you think Emiliano will keep you?"

"I don't know." If I'm being honest, this all feels like a dream. A figment of my imagination. I kind of want to wake up already. At least I'd know what's real and what's not. "He said he would, but he's pissed at me right now."

"Why?" She frowns.

"I told Matteo I love him." I shrug, and she winces. "As a friend, was that wrong of me?"

"I wouldn't say it was wrong," she tells me gently, laying her hand on top of mine. I need the affection right now. I need someone to tell me everything's going to be okay. "But I can see why that would upset him. You've had sex with his son, and he wants you to be his. Maybe he sees Matteo as his competition. That has to be hard, Cole."

"I guess I never thought about it that way." I frown. "That makes sense."

"See? This is why you come to me." She smirks, and I roll my eyes. "I'm smart sometimes."

"You're smart all the time." I grin.

"Hey, sexy," a man drawls from behind us, and I tense. "Mind if we go upstairs?"

Amy tenses. "Sorry, I'm off shift," she says softly, trying to keep it professional. "But you can schedule an appointment at the front desk."

"Nah." He grins. "I think you can fit me in right now."

"I'm busy—"

"Hey, you heard her," I snap at the man, getting up from the barstool and facing him. "She said no."

"She's a fucking whore, bro." He shakes his head. "She should be available."

"Excuse me?" Amy exclaims, her bottom lip wobbling.

"Motherfucker," I growl. "Get the fuck out."

"Who the fuck are you?" He narrows his eyes. "I'll leave after I fuck her."

"She's mine," I lie. "Now back off."

"I don't think so." The guy's eyes are still narrowed, and before I know it, I'm throwing the first punch.

My hand throbs as it connects with his jaw, and I feel my knuckles splitting open. They'll probably need stitches this time. I'll be lucky if my hand isn't broken.

"Cole!" Amy yells. "Stop!"

I take a step back, listening to her, and the man turns around and punches me. The blow to my jaw makes me stumble back a step from the surprise, but it will probably only bruise.

"You hit like a bitch." I grin, taunting him.

"That's enough," The bar manager growls, holding the other man back. "You need to go," he tells the man. "And you." He points at me. "You're going to wait for Emiliano's driver. You're wasted."

Amy's eyes widen, and then... she smirks. "Oh, this should be good." She chuckles. "Let him believe I'm your girl."

"He'll kill us."

"No, he won't." She rolls her eyes as I go to sit at the bar again. "I make him a lot of money."

"Fine. He'll kill *me*," I tell her through gritted teeth. "I like my life."

"He's going to be so jealous when he hears about this fight, baby bear." She laughs. "He's going to fuck you so hard."

"You think so?" I ask with hope, and she laughs again. "I'm so easy," I groan.

"Yeah, you are."

My head suddenly spins, the alcohol catching up to me. "Oh, fuck, I don't feel so good."

"Don't you dare puke on me." She grins. "Let's go to the bathroom."

"Alright."

Amy grabs hold of my arm, and I get off the barstool carefully, stumbling as she all but drags me to the bathroom. I thank all my lucky stars that I have her, even though I know I'm fucked. As soon as Emiliano hears about this, he's going to flip out. If he hasn't already.

And I'm looking forward to it.

CHAPTER 18
EMILIANO

It's midnight, and neither Cole nor Matteo are home yet. Are they together? Did they go somewhere? Matteo texted me saying he would probably be home late or not at all tonight, but Cole hasn't given me an update. No signs of life. Not that he's required to; he doesn't owe me anything. Logically, I know that. But the other part of me wants him to do those things. Wants him to care enough about me to give me something. *Anything.* I want him to tell me what he's doing and who he's doing it with. Not because I demand it but because I'm important enough to him to keep me in the loop. And that's crazy. I'm living in some kind of fantasy land with rose-colored glasses and heart eyes. What the hell?

I still can't get the conversation with my brothers out of my mind though. The way they reacted, clearly thinking it was a bad idea even though they agreed to support me. Logically, I know this will more than likely blow up in my face. That I could potentially lose my son and never get him back. That I could lose Cole because of someone trying to get back at me for something. That I could be seen as weak now. But none of those reasons seem to snap me out of this little infatuation I seem to have with Cole.

I care deeply for him, and I can't seem to wrap my head

around that fact. If someone would've told me this a month ago, I'd be laughing my ass off and telling them they're insane. But here I am, not long since he's been released from prison, pining and begging and *longing*. For him, for anything he'll give. It's not purely sexual, even though I wish it were. It sure would make things easier for me. I wouldn't have to come out to Matteo, and everything would be alright. We'd move on after it was over, and no one would know about it. But that's not what's happening here. Not even close.

Instead, I'm thinking of the future with him by my side. As my partner. My equal. Am I crazy for that? Seeing a future with him? I know how he feels about me, and I know I could reciprocate those feelings. It's only a matter of time before I get there. I'm already feeling more, wanting more from him. It makes no sense, yet it does all the same. I just can't seem to get enough of him or stay away.

My phone vibrates on top of the couch cushion right next to me, and I inhale sharply at the name across the screen. It's the brothel. They only ever call me at this time for emergencies. I really don't need this right now. I don't want to have to leave the house to go put out a fire. I want to wait for Cole and get in bed with him. Hold him all night. Maybe fuck him a couple of times.

I sigh, answering the phone. "This is Emiliano."

"Yes, Mr. Colombo." The bar manager's voice comes through, and I frown. "Cole is here waiting for you to come get him."

I sit up quickly, making myself dizzy. "Why?" I ask with urgency. "What happened? Is he okay?"

"He's fine," the manager says, and I deflate, sitting back on the couch cushions once more. "He got into a fight with a client."

I pinch the bridge of my nose tightly because of course he did. "Why?"

"It'll be easier to watch than for me to explain." He sighs, and I nod, even though he can't see me. "I sent you the clips to your email."

"Much appreciated," I tell him. "I'll send my car for him. Make sure he doesn't go anywhere."

"I don't think he can," the man tells me, and I frown. "He's *really* wasted."

"Thanks again," I tell him, then hang up.

I immediately go to my email, clicking on the clips from tonight. It shows Cole and Amy meeting up at the bar, hugging, then sitting together. I can't hear what they're talking about, but Cole looks really happy, and Amy looks fucking cozy with him. She keeps putting her hand on top of his, leaning over into him, and just making him laugh in general. I don't like it one fucking bit.

A shiver runs down my spine, and I grit my teeth. They've been friends since high school, I know that. When she came to work at Luna's Den, it was due to Cole's recommendation. Since then, she's made me a lot of money. She's the most popular girl we have, and it won't bode well if I snap her little neck. I guess I'll have to wait for an explanation from Cole before I take matters into my own hands. I can be mature. I can be patient. Kind of.

The clip changes to a dark-haired man putting his hand on Amy's shoulder and her tensing up. Words are exchanged between her and the man, then the man and Cole. Then my man gets up from the barstool and throws the first punch. I can tell it hurts the stranger with the way he grimaces, and I grin. Cole has always been a fighter—always. He learned how to use his fists when he went to live with Luca. So why is it bothering me now? Is it because of the reason for the fight? Because it's over a woman?

Cole stays in place as the man rights himself, and then the man is punching Cole back. It's as if he doesn't even see it coming—he must be really drunk—but he barely stumbles back a step. And even though I can't make out what he tells the other man, I know Cole is trying to goad him. That is, until they're permanently separated by the bar manager. Amy looks guilty, yet relieved, all at the same time. It makes me want to throttle her. Why the hell is Cole losing his shit over her?

I text Luca, letting him know to go to the brothel and pick up Cole, giving explicit instructions to not make any stops or detours. To bring him back home to me immediately. If Luca suspects something is going on, he hasn't brought it up. He's discreet, loyal, and values his life. I can admire that about him. I'm also grateful because the thought of explaining to someone where I stand with Cole when I don't even know is nerve-wracking.

My hands begin to shake with my anxiety the longer I sit here, and I don't really know what I'm so stressed about. Or maybe stressed isn't the right word—scared is. I'm afraid this thing between Cole and I is over. What if he made up his mind and no longer wants to be with me? What if I'm putting my relationship with my son at risk for someone who isn't even sure of me? But no, Cole has been persistent. He's sure of me, I know it. Yet the thought of him changing his mind terrifies me.

I get up from the couch and begin to pace the length of the living room, going to the floor to ceiling windows and taking a peek out at the city. From this high up, it looks incredible. I don't get a lot of time to admire it though because the elevator suddenly dings and the doors open.

Cole stumbles in, swaying roughly from side to side, and even though I don't want to help him, I also don't want him to fall on his face. I walk quickly toward him, wrapping an arm around his waist and leading him to the couch. He plops down on it, and I stand in front of him, arms crossed over my chest. I wait for him to look at me, but he's so wasted he can barely keep his eyes open. It pisses me the fuck off. But I find myself sitting on the couch next to him, then pulling his head down to my lap.

Cole goes down easily, pressing his cheek to my thigh and closing his arctic blue eyes. I thread my fingers through the soft strands of his hair, loving the way it feels, and he sighs. What would Matteo think if he came in right now and saw us like this? Would he suspect us? Or would he think I'm just being nice to Cole? I kind of want him to show up and put us out of our misery. I don't want to lie or hide anymore. He's the only person left to figure this out, and it needs to happen already. My life would be so much easier if I didn't feel like a fucking traitor every minute of the day. I know I'd still be a traitor if Matteo knew, but at least I wouldn't have to hide it anymore. I could be a traitor out in the open.

My fingers get stuck on a knot in Cole's hair, and I gently loosen it and continue threading them through his hair. He hums, the vibration going up my legs, and I inhale sharply when he runs his hand over my thigh and rubs it.

"Baby," Cole hums. "I missed you."

"Sleep," I reply stiffly. "Then we'll talk."

"I'm horny," Cole grumbles, and I roll my eyes. "Help me."

"You're always horny," I remind him, even though I want to choke him out and demand an explanation for what just happened at Luna's Den. "Get some sleep."

"Only if you promise to fuck me later."

"I—" I shut my mouth. Will I fuck him later? It's a good question. I can't promise him anything. What if we break up because of this? What if he betrayed me? "Cole—"

But he's already snoring lightly, and my body deflates.

Thank God.

CHAPTER 19
COLE

I wake gradually, a headache looming in the distance, and realize my cheek is pressed to Emiliano's lap. His hand is resting on my head, and deep, steady breaths are coming from him. I stay very still, not wanting to move yet, not wanting to alert him I'm awake. I know this is going to be an argument, and I'm not looking forward to it. I know I shouldn't have initiated the fight, but the man really crossed a line. What kind of friend would I be if I let that slide?

Even so, I know Emiliano will more than likely be angry. What I did is not good for business, and he'll probably order me to steer clear of that establishment for a while. I can't blame him, and while it sucks, I can probably meet up with Amy outside of it. Plus, the fact I was drunk probably doesn't help my situation with him. He's always telling me to be in control—of my body, my emotions—and I definitely wasn't. At the very least, he'll be disappointed in me. I can't say I blame him. Although I still wouldn't change a thing.

Thankfully, I'm not drunk anymore. My head isn't spinning, and I don't feel like I'm going to be sick. I can also think clearly, which is great because I'm going to need every brain cell I possess for the conversation I'm about to have.

When I look at Emiliano over my shoulder, I see his eyes are closed, and he's deep in slumber. The lamp on the end table is on, illuminating the room in a soft glow, and I get up. He feels my absence immediately, opening his eyes as soon as my back hits the cushions.

Emiliano looks at me with narrowed eyes, running a hand down his face, and my lips tip down in a frown. He turns his body toward me, his eyes still narrowed, and purses his lips. I just know he's about to fight with me. I sigh.

"Get it out of your system," I tell him, flinching back when he moves toward me. He scoffs. "I can tell you're angry."

"Angry?" he asks, and I close my eyes briefly and breathe in. I don't want to fight with him right now, but I know it's inevitable. "No, Cole. I'm fucking *livid*."

"Why are you so pissed off at me?" I ask slowly. "I—"

"Are you fucking kidding me?" he snarls, baring his teeth, and I can admit he's intimidating. I don't think I've ever seen him this angry. And really? Over a little fight? I don't think it calls for *this*. "You fought with a customer."

"He touched Amy," I snap. "He called her a whore and said she should make time for him."

Emotions flit through Emiliano's eyes in quick succession, too fast for me to make out any of them. But he doesn't seem appeased by this. "And you just have to defend her honor?" he asks me, but it feels like it has some kind of hidden meaning I'm not aware of. "Cole, knight in fucking shining armor."

I snort at that, and he practically growls at me. "Well, I guess I am."

"Why, hmm?" he asks me. "Why are you so invested?"

"She's my friend," I say slowly. "I would've done it for Matteo, too."

Emiliano tenses at the mention of his son's name, and I know I've made a mistake. "Yeah, I just bet you would."

"What the fuck is your problem?" I snap, getting angry myself.

"YOU! You're my problem!" he yells.

My eyes sting without my permission, and I look away. I'm never good enough for him; that's what I've gathered so far. It doesn't matter what I do. I always seem to fuck things up between us. It's frustrating that I can never show him how much he means to me. Or I do, and it doesn't seem to matter, anyway.

"Wait—" Emiliano breathes. "Don't. Please."

I look at him, and he shakes his head quickly, but it's too late. A tear trails down my cheek, and he looks broken up over it.

"Don't cry," he says softly, grabbing me and placing me right on his lap, my legs straddling him. "I can't stand it."

"I'm never going to be good enough for you, am I?" I sniffle. "Never."

"W-what?" He seems genuinely confused, shaking his head again. "What the fuck are you talking about?"

I frown, wiping my tears with the back of my hand. I don't want to look weak in front of him, but he makes me vulnerable. "No," I growl. "Tell me why you're angry at me. I don't think it's because of the fight. It's not, huh? So tell me."

"Why was Amy all over you?" he blurts. "Why were you all over her?"

"We're just friends," I clarify.

"Friends don't act like that."

"Wait—" I search his honey brown eyes, darker because of the lighting. His nostrils flare as he looks at me. "Please tell me you don't think I like her like that."

"Do you?" he asks through gritted teeth.

"God, Em." I groan. "I'm *gay*. I'm not attracted to women."

Emiliano's eyes widen, and his hands come to rest on my hips, gripping me tightly. He looks like I just told him I have a second dick, and it makes me chuckle. I've never even been with a woman. The thought of entering a vagina has never appealed to me. *Ever.*

He's stunned to silence—clearly.

"I've never even been with a woman," I tell him, and his jaw drops. "The thought grosses me out."

"*What?*" His eyes widen in surprise. "Never?"

I shake my head. "It'll always be men for me."

He narrows his eyes at the way I word that, and he lets go of my hip and wraps his hand around my throat tightly. I can barely breathe, and it makes my cock kick in my jeans. Fuck. "It'll always be *me* for you."

"Y-yes," I gasp, barely able to get the words out. "Always."

"Let me clarify this for you, Cole," Emiliano says softly, leaning in and biting my lip. He cups my cheeks gently, then kisses the tip of my nose. "You're mine. I don't want to hear about anyone else before me because there will never be anyone after me. I fucking *own* you."

I nod quickly. "I'm yours."

"You'll always be good enough for me." My heart clenches in my chest at his words, and his hands tighten on my face. "You're perfect for me."

"Fuck, stop." My eyes sting again. "I—"

"No." He shakes his head. "You need to hear this."

I breathe in deeply, and he continues.

"I want you just the way you are," he whispers. "I *need* you just the way you are. And that's never going to change."

"Don't be jealous," I blurt out. "I only want you, Em. It's only going to ever be you. I—" I shake my head. "There's no one else for me."

Emiliano beams at that, and I can tell he's trying to hold back, but he can't. It makes butterflies dance in my stomach, and when he leans into me to kiss me, I close my eyes to savor the moment.

The first press of his lips against mine makes my stomach flutter. I suck on his bottom lip, tugging roughly on it, and then we alternate until he's doing it back to me. There's nothing gentle about this kiss, and when I shove my tongue past his lips, he moans. His hands travel down to my hips, and he rubs my ass over his hard cock.

We rut against each other for a while, my lips never leaving his, until it's necessary to come up for air. And then I get up and hook my fingers into his sweatpants, and Emiliano lifts his ass to help me out. I shuck his pants to the ground, trailing my fingers up his thick thighs, and Em spreads his legs to accommodate me between them. I get a prime view of his hole, and I wonder if he'd ever let me in it. Would he let me show him the wonders of a prostate orgasm? I don't know, but I sure as hell will try.

Emiliano looks at me with lust in his eyes, and I want to show him why I'm the one for him. Why he should keep me. I want to show him how good I can make him feel, but mostly, I want to show him how much I care for him. How much I love him. I think I could do that through sex. But it also makes me wonder if that's the only thing he wants me for—

"What are you thinking about?" Em whispers, brushing his thumb over my bottom lip. "Hmm?"

"Nothing." But I don't make eye contact, and we both know I'm lying through my teeth. I don't want to bare my insecurities to him though. So I lean in and lick his slit, then suck the head of his cock into my mouth.

Emiliano yanks me off him roughly. "I asked you a question."

"I—" I shake my head. "Do you only want me for sex?"

His eyes widen. "No." He brushes his knuckles over my cheekbone, then cups my face. "I don't."

I nod slowly. "Are you going to keep me a secret?"

"No," he replies, his fingers tightening. "We can tell Matteo whenever you want. My brothers already know."

My eyes widen. "They do?"

"Yes, Cole." His jaw clenches, and I suck in a sharp breath. "This means something to me."

"This means everything to me," I admit. "I wouldn't survive you breaking my heart, Em."

His eyes turn soft, and my heart flips. "I won't," he says with conviction. "I won't break your heart."

"Swear it," I breathe. "Give me your word."

His jaw clenches. "I give you my word."

The way he says it lets me know he's serious about it. I can tell he means it, and my body relaxes. I think about sucking his dick, but that's no longer going to do it for me. I need him to fuck me. I need him inside of me. Right fucking now.

"Come on," I tell him, getting up from between his legs and grabbing his sweatpants from the ground. I reach for him, and he grabs my hand, getting up from the couch. "Let's go to my room."

Emiliano squeezes my hand, and I halt, looking back at him. "Are you sure?"

"I'm sure." I smile softly at him. Trying to reassure him. "I want you to fuck me."

I lead him to my room and lock the door, the sound loud in the silence between us. Em stands there, ready to follow my lead, but I just go to my drawer and grab a bottle of lube and my thickest vibrator, then place them on the bed. Before he can ask me what I'm doing, I begin to shed my clothes, and I watch with a smirk as his cock twitches. He wraps a hand around it tightly, then begins to stroke slowly, and my mouth goes dry.

Yeah, I'm *really* going to enjoy this.

CHAPTER 20
EMILIANO

Cole's naked body is a work of art. He has tattoos all over—just like I do—but I'm intrigued anyway. Not for the first time, I wonder what all of the tattoos mean to him. Did he get them because they're pretty? Or because of something deeper?

He makes a deep sound at the back of his throat, breaking me out of my thoughts. His eyes are on my cock as I squeeze it tightly at the base, trying to keep myself from getting too excited. He smirks at me knowingly, and I grin, unable to deny that I *could* come just like this. From his eyes on me. I stroke myself slowly, my wrist twisting roughly, and Cole groans at the sight.

"Fuck," he breathes, climbing onto the bed and lying on his back. "You look so fucking sexy, Emiliano."

My breath stutters as he coats his fingers with lube and stuffs them in his ass, the groan that leaves him making my stomach clench, my abs bunch. I watch him scissor his fingers inside of himself, stretching. He's not seeking to pleasure himself right now; it's all very methodical, and I watch curiously until he pulls out. Except he just grabs the dildo immediately, pressing the tip to his entrance, then pushing it in until he's stuffed full.

My breath leaves me on a gasp as I watch him take the

dildo all the way in his ass, then pull it out to the tip and slam it back in. Cole moans long and loud, and then he presses a button on the base of it and the sound of vibration fills the room.

His hooded eyes meet mine from across the room, and I take a couple of steps away from the door until I'm suspended between want and need. Until I'm standing right between his spread legs. My hands push his bent knees toward his chest, and then I grab the fake cock and thrust it in deeper, harder. I do it at an angle, and he shouts, pre-cum dribbling from his cock. It's hot as fuck, and I want him in my mouth, but I also want my cock in his ass, and he seems to be stretched enough for me at this point.

"Perfect," I murmur, pulling at the dildo to take it out. Cole clenches around it and shakes his head quickly, halting my hand with his fingers wrapped around my wrist.

"No." He shakes his head again. "I want you to fuck me with it in."

I suck in a sharp breath, looking at Cole's pink little hole swallowing the dildo. There's no fucking way in hell he'll be taking two in his ass—there's just no way. "Cole—no."

"Don't be a pussy," Cole whispers. "It's my ass. I know what I can handle."

I stay still between his legs, watching as he takes over the dildo and begins to fuck himself with it once more. He moans and writhes underneath me; the sounds coming out of him making my cock drip steadily. I inhale shakily, grabbing the bottle of lube from the bed, and lather it onto my cock.

Cole and I make eye contact, and he scoots up on the bed, making room for me. His legs fall open all the way, and I focus on the way his hole unclenches around the toy. He's red and puffy around his rim, and I gulp as I press against it lightly.

"Relax," I murmur, bathing my fingers in lube. I press two

of them against the dildo, and they slip right into his ass. The dildo vibrates violently around me, he must have it on a high setting, and I crook my fingers around until he shouts once more, his cock jumping and leaking like a damn faucet. I know he's close. I can feel the way he's clenching. "Let my cock inside."

"Hurry," Cole begs, "I don't know if I can hold off."

"Don't you dare come yet," I say through gritted teeth as I withdraw my fingers and press my cock head against his entrance. "Not until I'm inside of you."

Cole nods, relaxing once more, and the head of my cock is suddenly cradled in the wet heat of his ass. It feels intense with the steady vibration as I slip the rest of the way in excruciatingly slowly, and when my hips meet his ass, I groan.

"Goddamn it." I breathe, "Are you trying to kill me?"

"It would be a great way to go." Cole smirks, his cheeks red, his hair sweaty. His legs tremble violently. "I'm so full, Em. So full. *Please* fuck me."

I withdraw almost to the tip, then thrust in alongside the dildo. I can feel the vibrations all the way up to my balls, and my eyes roll to the back of my head. I lean over Cole, and his legs wrap around my waist.

"You just like when I use this hole, don't you?" I smirk, bottoming out and thrusting back immediately. With every thrust, we creep toward the headboard. "You want me to abuse it?"

"F-f-fuck," Cole mutters, his ass clenching around my cock until my eyes cross. "Harder. *Faster*."

I fuck him faster, feeling my sanity slip from my grasp. His legs spread wider, no longer wrapped around my waist, and he plants his feet on the mattress and begins to fuck me back. I pound into him roughly, one of my hands on his hips, surely bruising him, the other supporting myself by his head.

His wide eyes are focused on mine as I impale him, and he bites his bottom lip until he draws blood. I lean in further and lick the sweet coppery essence of him from his chin, then suck his bottom lip into my mouth until he moans loudly. I feel his ass flutter, clenching around my length, and I moan. I fuck into him faster than I ever have, desperate to fill him up, and he's right there with me. *Always* right there with me.

"Everything about you does it for me, Cole," I whisper against the shell of his ear. "Your ass, your cock, *you*. You're just fucking perfect."

"Oh, God," Cole moans. "More."

"You want more, baby?" I ask him, and his eyes widen. "What do you want more of?" I ask with a harsh thrust. "My cock? My words?"

"If you call me baby again, I'm going to fucking come."

I smirk. "So come, baby." Cole shivers, and I feel the telltale signs of my impending release. My balls draw up, my spine tingling, and I breathe in deeply through my nose.

Before I can give him a chance to reply, I'm switching our position by pulling away from him and sitting back on my haunches, all the while keeping myself inside his body. Cole spreads his legs for me once more, giving me a prime view of my cock in his ass beside the dildo.

"Double stuffed," I mutter under my breath, panting roughly. "All for me, right, Cole?"

"Yes, yes, *yes*."

I grab onto his hips tightly, thrusting in and out of him at a feverish pace, and when his ass flutters around my cock and strings of cum begin to shoot out of his cock, I fill him up with a shout.

"Cole!" I yell, his name on my lips as I come. "Fuck."

"Oh, goddamn," Cole says under his breath as I stop. "*Again*."

I withdraw from his body slowly, trying to make sure I

don't hurt him, then take the dildo out, too. He's red and puffy, swollen, my cum leaking out of his ass. "You want to come again?" I whisper.

"*Please*, Em," Cole whispers back. "I'm begging you."

"More." I grin, thrusting two of my fingers into him slowly, then crooking them when I find his prostate. "Beg more."

Cole mutters a curse under his breath as I push against the little bundle of nerves, and his back arches off the bed. "Please, I'll do anything."

"*Anything*?" I smirk.

"Make me come."

I take his cock down my throat, somehow still hard, and crook my fingers inside of him once more. Once, twice, three times. He's panting and moaning now. Groaning and grunting. *Begging*. My cock twitches between my legs once more, hardening at the feel of his length poking the back of my throat.

I moan loudly with Cole's cock down my sore throat, and when I swallow, his fingers tangle tightly in my hair. His hips have a mind of their own as he seeks his release, and he groans loudly as he comes down my throat. I swallow every drop, savoring him, and instead of letting him pull out of my mouth, I lick at his softening cock.

Fuck, I'm obsessed with him.

My chest heaves as he pulls out of my mouth, and I crawl toward him. I lie down next to him and face him, staring intently at his face. There's a soft smile on his lips, and my stomach flutters. It's short-lived though, because suddenly there's a loud boom coming from behind us, and when I look back, Matteo is standing in the doorway; the door split in half.

"Fuck," Cole growls, and when I look at him, I see there's

a gun in his hands, pointed right at my son. He lowers it immediately. "What the fuck, Matty."

"*Me?*" Matteo laughs loudly, looking between me and Cole. "What the fuck? Are you fucking kidding me, Cole? My dad? You couldn't fuck *anyone* else?!"

Cole flinches.

"We're not just fucking," I blurt out, and Matteo's eyes land on me. "He's—"

"What do you mean, it's not just fucking?" Matteo's voice breaks, and he looks between us quickly. Searching for something—for lies, I realize. "What is it then?"

There's a moment of silence, but before I can reply, Matteo is shaking his head and looking away from us.

"No." Matteo shakes his head again. "He's mine, Dad. You know this. You've *known* this. How could you? How could you fucking do this to me—"

"I'm not yours, Matty," Cole says softly. "You know that. You *have* to know that—"

"Fuck you!" Matteo snarls, then looks in my direction. His eyes are wild, his body tense as he clenches and unclenches his fists. "How dare you fucking take him from me?!"

I take a deep breath and get up from the bed, standing across from my son. I open my arms in invitation, and I know he understands when the first punch lands across my jaw. I can take this. I can do this for him—for us. It's the only thing I can offer him right now. Maybe it'll help him feel better. Maybe—

Fuck.

My ears ring as I land on my back, and Matteo comes to straddle my hips. Cole shoves him off, getting in his face and screaming at him. My head spins as my jaw begins to throb, the ache strong and steady. And I just close my eyes for a moment.

What the fuck did I do?

Matteo is going to fucking hate me for the rest of my life. We should've told him instead of letting him find us like this. We should've—

"I hate you," Matteo yells, and I open my eyes. He gets up from the floor and begins to pace. "I'll never forgive this—*never.*"

"I know." I nod. "I'm sorry."

Matteo chuckles. "You can't take this back," he says.

"Cole is mine," I grunt, getting up from the ground, rubbing my jaw. "He's mine."

"Fuck you!" Matteo snarls again, stepping closer to me, and Cole tries to get between us. I shake my head.

"Get it off your chest." I sigh. "But it's not going to change a damn thing."

"I'm moving out," Matteo says slowly.

"Wouldn't expect anything less," I reply.

"We—" Matteo looks at Cole. "We're never getting through this one."

Cole's eyes well with tears, and they begin to trail down his cheeks. "Matty, please. *Please* don't do this."

Matteo looks broken, but this feels too much like begging on Cole's end, and I don't fucking like it.

"Please, Matty." Cole shakes his head, the rest of him shaking too. "I—love you. Please."

This time it's Matteo who shakes his head. "Are you in love with him?" he asks Cole, who freezes in place. He doesn't even breathe. "Are you in love with my dad?"

There's a beat of silence.

"Yes."

Matteo's eyes fill with tears now too, and he nods. "Then it's done."

"No!" Cole shouts as Matteo turns on his heel and goes to his room, slamming the door and locking it. Cole goes after him, slamming his hand repeatedly onto the wooden surface. "Please, open the door."

"Enough!" I growl. Cole's chest heaves as he stops, then looks at me. "Him or me."

Cole frowns.

"Choose, Cole," I say through gritted teeth. "You have to choose."

I watch as he runs his hands down his face, then looks right into my eyes and nods. "You," he says through a choked sob, and then he heads right back to his room.

I follow after him, trying to locate my clothes through the haze of panic in my brain. Until my phone rings, snapping me right out of it. "Hello?" I say as I pick up Giovanni's call.

"Brother," he says tightly, and I hear shouting in the background. My spine straightens. "Luna's Den has been burned down. A note left behind."

"Burned—" I stutter. "*What?*"

"A note was left behind," he repeats. "For Cole."

My stomach sinks. "What does it say?"

"An eye for an eye," Giovanni replies, and when I look over at Cole, his face is devoid of any color.

It seems the Russians really fucked up big time.

This is war now.

CHAPTER 21
COLE

It seems like all I do lately is fuck up. While I can't deny the sex earlier was mind-blowing, the best of my fucking life, it was definitely ruined by Matteo coming into the room and flipping out. Now he's missing. Moved out. Never to come back.

I'm not naive, I know he meant what he said. We'll never get through this. What I didn't expect was for Emiliano to stop me from trying to make it right. *Him or me*. Choosing gutted me, yet it was also the easiest decision I've ever made in my life. I don't regret it, but I am broken up over it. I'm suffering. Regardless of everything, Matteo is my best friend in the entire world. He's fucking irreplaceable, and he always will be. There's no lifetime in which he's not that for me, and I'm gutted, absolutely destroyed at the thought of never speaking to him again.

I know Emiliano probably thinks I have feelings for Matteo right about now, but it's not in the way he believes. Matty has been part of my life for over almost two decades. I was just a scared little boy when he took me in, nurturing me, healing me. He's the most selfless person I've ever met, and that's what gave me hope for the longest time. For years, really. Even before Emiliano and I got together, I dreamed of being in his arms. And a stupid part of me thought Matteo would come to accept us being together. But not like this. Not the way he found out. That had to be the most painful way he could've ever found out about us. And I know he'll never forgive me—us.

When he kicked down the door, I thought it was someone else. Him discovering us was the last thing on my mind, which is why I grabbed my gun from under my pillow and pointed it at him. But nothing could've prepared me for the sight before me. Him looking absolutely blind-sided by us, and how angry and destroyed he looked over it.

When he hit Emiliano, though, I snapped. Nobody touches him—no one. Not even him. Even though I know Emiliano welcomed it, I couldn't stop myself from intervening. And that seemed to piss off Matteo even more. Now, we're both broken beyond repair, but I still can't bring myself to regret Emiliano. I don't know what happens next, but I do hope that now we'll be out in the open. That this was the push Em needed to close the gap between us.

The vehicle comes to a stop in front of Luna's Den. Well, what's left of it, anyway. It's mostly ashes now. Emiliano's brothers are standing in front of the burned building along with Amy, and something in me snaps. Before I can get out, though, Em grabs my arm and halts me in place.

He looks tired, and there are bags under his eyes. It's late —three in the morning—and we should be in bed right about now. But something tells me we won't be sleeping tonight. We'll be doing damage control. Plus, I know he won't sleep a wink with what just happened. He'll probably just toss and turn, thinking of Matteo and everything he's lost today. I'll more than likely do the same, to be honest. It feels like in the blink of an eye, I've lost it all. Everything but him.

He is enough, though.

I just have to keep reminding myself that this is what I

wanted—what I've wanted for years—and it's finally coming true.

"Don't," Emiliano says softly. "Don't go out there and make a scene just because she's here."

I nod slowly. "Alright, Em."

He nods too now. "Let's get this over with."

I get out of the SUV and he does too, rounding it and grabbing my hand, tugging me toward his brothers. He links our fingers together, and my heart flips in my chest. They all look at us, but there's no surprise on their faces. Instead, they look relieved. Like they were waiting for this.

"Amy," I breathe, and she lunges herself at me. She's crying, and when she pulls away, I frown. "What's wrong?"

"They gave me a note, Cole." Her voice trembles. "And it was for you. They want you."

"I heard," I tell her. "It's all going to be okay."

"It happened right after you left," she whispers. "They knew you were here. Probably burned the place down because they thought you were in here."

Em's hand squeezes mine roughly, and I look over at him. His eyes are wide, and he looks scared.

"You're done wandering, Cole," he tells me. "From now on, you don't leave my side."

I huff. "I'm not a child, Emiliano. You can't keep me attached to your hip."

"Watch me," he says through gritted teeth. "You're mine, and I'll protect you at all costs. Don't make me handcuff you to my bed. I'll fucking do it."

Giovanni chuckles, then says, "Kinky."

Even Amy smirks, then winks at me. "He has a point, Cole," she murmurs. "You're not safe."

"I haven't been safe for years." I sigh. "I can handle myself."

"That's what you think," Alessandro says. "But this is war

now. And they'll do whatever it takes to win it. Now that they'll know they didn't get you in there, they'll do whatever it takes to get their revenge. Especially now that they struck first. They know we'll retaliate."

"Blood will flow like a river in New York City," Emiliano declares. "Nobody touches what's mine."

"Andrey needs to die," I tell them with a sigh, and Emiliano grunts his agreement. "It won't be over until that happens."

Alessandro shakes his head. "No fucking way. Then they'll really want your head."

"What do you suggest, then?" Emiliano asks.

"That we lay low," Alessandro replies.

"We're not laying low." Em laughs loudly. "They just burned down my business. Are you fucking kidding me, Alex?"

"It was just a suggestion." Alessandro sighs. "But you're too hot-headed."

"No." Emiliano shakes his head, and I look at Amy, who seems terrified. She's looking around at the wreckage. Probably wondering how she's going to survive now without a job. Fuck. "I've never been more level-headed in my life. I can see things clearly now. It's time for them to know who the fuck is in charge of this city."

"And that's us?" Tony asks.

Giovanni shoves him with a grin. "Of course it's us, dumbass."

Lorenzo is just quietly staring at all of us.

"The brothel will be rebuilt." Alessandro announces, and we all nod in unison. "The firefighters declared that gasoline was at play, so the insurance company should pay for it."

"I want it even bigger and better than the last one," Em says.

Alessandro grins. "I'll make sure of it, brother."

Emiliano sighs. "I need to get out of here." He rubs a hand down his face, and he looks about ten years older than his thirty-six right about now. "I'm exhausted. It's been a long night."

"Care to share?" Giovanni asks, frowning.

"Maybe after I've gotten some sleep," Em replies. "Matteo found out. That's all I'll say for now."

Amy gasps, gripping my arm tightly. I direct my attention back toward her, and her eyes are wide with what seems to be concern. "Are you okay?" she asks me.

"No." I shake my head. "But I'll have to be."

"Please let me know if there's anything I can do."

"Short of convincing him to forgive me, I don't think there's anything anyone can do," I tell her with honesty. "I fucked up big time."

"Tell me about it later?" She squeezes my arm once more, then lets go.

"Of course," I sigh. "I'll text you."

"Okay," she replies. "We'll meet soon?"

"Yeah," I say softly, then clear my throat. "Are you gonna be okay?"

"Yes," she replies instantly, but I don't believe her. But I'm also not going to call her out right in front of her boss. "I'll be fine."

"We'll talk soon," I tell her, and she nods, walking away from me and to an Uber waiting at the curb. I didn't even realize they were there.

The brothers talk about rebuilding the brothel, and what's next, for about thirty more minutes. I just stand here with Emiliano's hand in mine as he grips me tightly. Our fingers are still interlaced, and I can't help but think about how perfectly we fit together. No one's ever held my hand like this before, not romantically, at least. It's nice. It makes me feel like he cares about me. Like we're in this together.

"Ready to go?" he finally asks me, and I nod.

We go back to the vehicle, and the ride to the penthouse goes by quickly in complete silence. Emiliano looks out the window the entire time, and I can't see his face. I'm sure that's probably on purpose, but once we get home, he can't fucking avoid me. We have to talk about this.

When we finally make it to the penthouse, Emiliano gets out and leaves me behind. I run after him, suddenly feeling desperate. My chest constricts, and my hands start to shake. Is this it? Is he changing his mind? Is he choosing Matteo over me? In a way, I can't blame him if he is. I can't say I'll be understanding, but I fucking get it, too. It's his son.

"Emiliano!" I yell as he gets in the elevator, and I run in before he can shut the doors. "Don't do this."

"I just need time."

"Fuck that," I snap. "I lost him too, and I need you."

His eyes are sad, begging me to understand, but I can't. I need him too much. I need him to make this better—the ache in my chest that's about to take me the fuck out. I meant what I said; he's not the only one who lost him tonight. I fucking need him to hold me.

"Please," I whisper just as the elevator opens and the living room comes into view. "I *need* you."

But Emiliano just keeps walking, headed toward his room.

"Don't be a fucking coward!" I call after him. "It's us now. You and me."

He stops in place, and I follow after him until my front is to his back. I wrap my arms around his waist, tugging him closer to me until there's no space between us, then lay my head on his shoulder. He takes a shuddering breath, and I can feel him shaking in my arms. And then I realize he's crying. Suddenly, I'm holding him up. He's sagging against me, and we slide down to the floor. I hold him to me. This man, who's usually bigger than life, is broken now. He turns to straddle my lap, burying his face into the crook of my neck, and I just hold him.

Emiliano sobs into my neck, wetting my skin with his hot tears, and my eyes sting with my own. We hold each other and cry in earnest, our sobs filling the silence, and it's cathartic as we break together. Hopefully, I'll be enough for him. I swear to try to be. I'll do everything in my power to deserve him, whatever it takes.

I soothe him by rubbing circles over his back, and he shakes in my arms. I'm not sure how long we stay there for, but eventually, he gets up and holds out his hand for me. I take it, and he leads us to his bed. We don't bother with going to the bathroom or brushing our teeth. He can't seem to part from me, and I'm just fine with that.

We climb into bed together and I take my side, burying my face into the pillow and inhaling shakily. It smells like Emiliano, and it soothes my soul. He comes closer, throwing his arm over my waist and tugging me into his strong body. He's all hard muscles, all man. I can't fucking get enough of it, of him. I close my eyes and try to focus on breathing. I know I won't get any sleep, and he probably won't either, but at least we're together. At least I'm finally in his arms. Finally, truly his.

I'm right where I belong.

CHAPTER 22
EMILIANO

It's been three days since Matteo walked out of my life, and I've never felt so empty. The house is unbearably silent. The last time he was away like this was when Cole rejected him, but at least I knew he would come back, eventually. Now I know he won't. I went into his room earlier today to find it completely empty. He retrieved all of his belongings while Cole and I were at work, and I can't blame him for doing it while we were gone. We probably would've ganged up on him and not let him leave. I don't want him to be gone, but at the same time, I understand where he's coming from. Even if he'll never understand why I've done this.

I know I'm selfish, fucked up. I've done the unforgivable, but I *am* sorry. I can't regret it, though. Having Cole—it's everything I've ever wanted. A partner who understands every part of my life. Someone to hold me up when I'm down, and I've never been so low in my entire life. He's been there for me in every way I've needed him, and I've done the same for him. When he held me in that hallway while I was breaking down, I knew he was it for me. I have never in my life allowed myself to be vulnerable in front of anyone but my brothers. But with Cole, it felt right. Like he'd understand. And he did, breaking down along with me. He picked up my pieces afterwards and tried to put them back together. Those pieces are jagged still, but he's trying so hard, and I want to try for him too. I have to trust that the hardest thing I've ever done is the best decision of my life.

Maybe we're moving a little fast, but Cole has moved into my room. His room is now a guest room, and all of his belongings are now in our closet. Nothing has ever felt so right, and I want him to sleep in my arms every single night. He seems happy about it, even though there's a lingering sadness in his eyes. I know I put it there when I made him choose. Maybe Matteo would've changed his mind if Cole begged enough, but him begging anyone but me made me feel even more possessive of him. I couldn't stand him begging my son. Someone who has been inside of him. This ugly green thing crawled inside my body and took over—jealousy. I can't deny that's what I felt. Like I was competing for Cole's affections, and it made me fucking crazy.

What Cole and Matteo had bothers me. Not their friendship, but the physical aspect of it. It makes me feel like I've stolen something from my son, and yet Cole doesn't love him back. So, I know I'm not taking him away, not really. But tell that to Matteo, who believes Cole is it for him. I know with time he'll get over Cole, but I don't think he'll ever get over my betrayal. I know I deserve it, but fuck, he's my son. I wish he'd give me a chance to explain that Cole is it for me. That he could be the love of my life, and that I want to find out. That I want to give us a fair shot. And I can only hope it works out now. I'll do whatever it takes. I've lost too much over this. Which is why I can't lose him. I won't let it happen.

Luna's Den burning down opened my eyes to my feelings for Cole. When I heard of the death threat, I couldn't fucking think straight. The only thing running through my mind was that I couldn't lose him. That I'd give up my fucking life for his. I'm not a masochist, but the thought of living without him is too painful to bear, and I don't really want to dissect that right now. Is it possible to be in love with someone so quickly? I thought it was purely physical, but fuck, I was so wrong. I've felt the shift between us, and in my moments of weakness, I think of what if. What if I said those words to him? Would it be the end of the world for me? Would it kill me to be in love? A few weeks ago, I would've said yes without a doubt. But now I know the answer is no.

I don't know what name to give these feelings. All I know is that they make me feel warm inside. Like everything is going to be alright by his side. But they're dangerous—these feelings. Because I also feel desperation. To shield him from life. To make sure he doesn't get hurt. Which is why I've forbidden him from going anywhere without me. It's the smart choice, even if he can't see it right now. I know he's desperate to be independent, not caged again. But I can't let that happen until the Russians are taken care of. I lose control when I'm not next to him, and he won't be the reason they win this war. Over my dead fucking body.

I can't stop us from living our lives, though. Which is why, even if it's not perfect timing, I'm taking him out on a date. I've never dated before, but he deserves this. What I did before doesn't matter, though, because it's in the past. I can't help but think about the meaningless relationships I've had. The women that have come in and out of my life, a notch on my bedpost. Like a revolving door, they came and went. It's not like that with Cole.

There's something about him that makes me want to crawl under his skin and take residence there. I want to hold him hostage and never let go. If he lets me, that's exactly what I'll do. For the first time in a long time, I don't want to force things. I want them to progress naturally. I want him to be with me because he wants to. And he seems to feel exactly that way about me, too. Even if we rival each other in jealousy and possessiveness. He's a little over the top, just like me. I used to think that would end in disaster, but I don't anymore. We're two peas in a fucking pod.

Cole is sitting across from me, wearing a suit and looking fucking edible. His hair is slicked back, and his clear-blue eyes stare at me from across the table. There's a slight blush to his cheeks, bubblegum pink, and I smile at him. He's beautiful and all mine. All fucking mine. I can't help but reach out to him, and he grabs my tattooed hand over the table.

I decided to take him to Giovanni's, my brother's restaurant. It's five star dining, and Cole deserves the best of the best. The Italian food is amazing. Plus, it's also guaranteed to be safe. Nothing will happen to him here.

I look around, taking in the exposed brick walls, the low lighting. The tables with white tablecloths, candles separating us. It's all very romantic, and once upon a time this could've never been me. Now, it's different. I don't know what's come over me, but I want this. Candle lit dinners and weekend getaways. Maybe even a vacation with him. Who the fuck even am I anymore?

The waitress comes around with an expensive bottle of champagne, pouring us each a glass. Cole smiles at her, and for a brief moment, I want to claw her eyes out when she stares at him for a little too long. But then I remember he only has eyes for me. Hell, he risked his most important friendship for me. If that doesn't mean he cares, I don't know what does. Although I know how he feels. It's more than caring, and it makes me feel some type of way. It makes me fucking crazy to think that he's in love with me. It also scares me that I'll become clingy, because I've never been that person before.

Nicole, the waitress, walks away. I grab the champagne flute and hold it up, and Cole clinks his against mine. "Cheers," I say softly. "To us."

Cole's eyes sparkle in the dim lighting. "To us." He grins. "To forever."

That simple word makes my stomach flip. *Forever*. Am I ready for that? I have to be. I've given up everything I care about for him. The only person who matters to me over everyone else. Everyone else except for *Matteo*.

"Tell me something," I say to him, looking right into those glacial eyes.

He raises an eyebrow and smirks. "What do you want to know?"

"Anything," I reply, taking a sip of the champagne. He does the same. "Something I don't know."

"That's going to be hard, Em." He grins. "You practically know everything about me."

"Not everything." I smile fondly. I do know a lot, though. How he bites his lip when he's thinking hard. He runs his hands through his hair when he's frustrated, and his hands down his face when he's angry. He goes to sleep early and wakes up before the sun rises. I know all the little things. But do I know the things that matter? "Tell me about prison."

"I studied French and Spanish while I was in there." He bites his bottom lip as he thinks, and my heart does this weird little flutter at the sight. At the knowledge that I still know him. "I also earned a bachelor's degree in business administration."

"I didn't know that." I smile. "Maybe you can take over one of the businesses."

I don't even think as I say it. All I know is that he's sticking around, so it makes sense to give him something of mine. Something to keep him occupied, so he feels like he's worth something. He likes being busy, always has, and he seeks validation too. I can give that to him. I can give him anything and everything he needs.

Cole's eyes widen. "Really?"

"Yeah." I nod. "I'm burned out, anyway. It would make sense." I shrug, and his smile lights me up from the inside out. "Running the real estate business is a lot. Gio has the restaurant, and my other brothers had the brothel. But I still manage the club too, which is exhausting."

"What are you saying, Em?" His hands shake on the table, and I reach out and steady one of them.

"I'm saying, if you want to, you can take over the club," I tell him. "I want you to."

"Fuck." He looks away. "I don't know if I'm good enough, Em. What if—"

"Nonsense," I say softly, squeezing his hand once more. "I'll train you."

Cole nods. "Okay."

He looks slightly nervous, but he stares at me intently. Like he can't tear his eyes away from me. The feeling is mutual. My eyes focus on those pretty pink, pouty lips, and suddenly I really want to kiss him. But I don't. I stay rooted to my seat, trying to exercise some self-control. It's slipping through my fingers steadily. I'm losing myself in him. Losing control. But I also can't seem to want to stop, even if he makes a mess of me.

"You're staring," he whispers, smiling at me, his hand tightening in mine.

"You're beautiful," I breathe, and he grins.

Suddenly, there's a commotion. Gun shots ring out, and the man at the table next to ours collapses to the floor, a pool of blood quickly following. Cole throws himself on the ground and so do I, and I take out my gun and aim it at the man with the weapon. The Russian is walking toward us from the front of the restaurant, clearly on a mission. He shoots at me, a bullet ringing right past my ear. I shoot him in the head from a distance. But then more men appear, shooting more of the customers, and my hands begin to tremble.

Fucking hell.

Cole and I are shooting now, taking them down, but the damage is done. This will be on the news, will probably draw the FBI to us. I guess it's a good thing we have legitimate businesses.

The sirens are loud as the cops show up and the firefighters, along with multiple ambulances. The hostess must have called after we took the men down. I run a hand down my face, my breaths coming out in pants, and Cole gets closer to me. It soothes me immediately, his proximity, and I'm able to think more clearly.

I guess they were really serious about getting back at Cole. It's probably Andrey's doing, and I know he has to die. They all do. And then I'll make an alliance with the new Pakhan. It's the only thing that's going to save us.

Our only choice.

CHAPTER 23
COLE

Last night was absolutely insane. Never in a million years did I think the Russians would shoot up Giovanni's, but we're going to get back at them. All of them have to die. I also never thought Emiliano was the kind of man to take me out on a date. I thought for sure I'd have to give that dream up, but he surprised me. He keeps me guessing, always on my fucking toes. I don't know up from down when I'm around him, and that's dangerous. He really does make a mess of me.

Sitting in that restaurant across from him felt different. Like some switch flipped between us. He's acting differently, I can tell. It's as if Matteo leaving solidified our relationship for him, and now he's making plans for the future with me. He offered me the club, for fuck's sake. That's a huge deal. The biggest step he could possibly take. It's even bigger than a marriage proposal, in my opinion. Is that where we're headed? Fuck, I hope so.

Everyone knows whose I am, and while some looked surprised, the people who matter to us have been accepting. Everyone except for one. The most important person of them all. I have faith he'll come around eventually, though Emiliano sure doesn't. He doesn't have to say it out loud, but I can tell by the way he's resigned himself to this. I haven't though. I want Matteo to forgive us, to be part of our lives. Maybe that's delusional, to think he could ever turn the page and start over with both of us, but I have hope.

I have to hope, or I'll go into a deep depression. The thought of losing Matteo forever is enough to make getting out of bed every morning a struggle. If it weren't for Emiliano being here for me, I'd be lost. I wouldn't know what to do with myself. But he is here, lifting me up every morning. Making sure I brush my teeth and take a shower. Putting food in my belly. We haven't fucked since the night Matty left, and honestly, I can't blame him. I don't think I want to right now either. It's hard enough as it is. What if we fuck again and he comes home to talk? The thought makes me want to throw up. But I know eventually we'll have to go back to normal. And I know Matty—he wouldn't just show up uninvited anymore. Not after what he saw last time.

It couldn't have been easy to see us together—naked. Was he there the entire time? On the other side of the door? Listening to us? The thought doesn't disgust me. Instead, it destroys me. He probably didn't know what the hell he was listening to at first. It had to be hard, realizing that his dad was the one fucking me. Which is why I don't blame him for disappearing. He deserves time to process this situation—as much time as he needs. And who are we to determine how much time is enough for him? Just how much did we hurt him? I know it was a lot, but will he ever come around? Will I hold it against him if he doesn't?

Fuck.

Now we also have the Russians to worry about. I can admit that I fucked up by not killing Andrey back then, like I wanted to. Instead, I opened a whole can of worms by almost cooking him alive. He wants revenge, but I'm not going to let him have it.

I was untouchable in prison, unfortunately for him. I had

a reputation for slicing throats with a mere scalpel, and everyone was afraid of my collection of sharp objects. Not that I advertised them. People just happened to know. Probably my cellmate said something. He had a hard time keeping his mouth shut. It's a miracle we got along so well, but he kept to himself mostly, and so did I.

I'm obviously out of prison now, though, which means Andrey thinks I'm fair game. I have to show him he's mistaken. That if he doesn't stop, the only one dying will be him. I have so many ideas for how to kill him too, and if there's one thing I've learned the past few days is that killing him is non-negotiable. It *has* to happen. I also think the best way to start over is by killing them all. The Pakhan, his daughter, and Andrey. It's the only way we can secure a new alliance with the Russians, by letting new leaders rise. Then maybe, just maybe, we can come to an agreement.

Emiliano stirs next to me, tightening his arm around my waist and pulling me in. He presses his nose into the crook of my neck and inhales deeply, then rubs it up the length of my throat and to my jaw. My eyes are still closed, and I focus on how good his body feels wrapped around mine. *This* is what my dreams are made of. This is what I've craved. How the hell did I get so lucky? How is this my life?

"You awake?" Emiliano asks, his voice thick from sleep. My cock stirs at the sound, and I breathe in deeply.

"Yeah," I murmur. "Just thinking."

There's a beat of silence, as if he's scared of the answer, but he still asks, "About what?"

"Last night," I say with a sigh. "The Russians."

Emiliano seems to relax at my words, as if this war is easier to talk about than his son. I know that's the topic of conversation he's trying to avoid. And it probably is easier to talk about this. It just sucks. I can't be the only one who wants him back.

"What about them?" he asks, his hand roaming down to my naked hip and gripping it tightly.

"We need to get rid of them."

"Obviously," Emiliano says dryly.

I huff. "I mean, we need to get rid of the Pakhan, Andrey, and even Natasha."

He stiffens. "Why Natasha?" I pause at his tone of voice, then narrow my eyes. "She hasn't done anything."

"Neither did all the customers at Giovanni's last night, and they were still killed," I snap. "She's his sister. She's gotta go."

"No." Em shakes his head.

"Why the fuck not?" I ask him through gritted teeth, trying to turn over to face him, but he holds me tightly in place and doesn't let me. "Do you want her?"

"What?" Emiliano chuckles. "*No.*"

"Then tell me why."

"I just..." He trails off. "I want to do things differently."

"Innocents have already died," I remind him. "The time to do things differently is over. We need a new alliance if we want peace."

Em nods. "Everyone but her."

Her.

The Russian mafia princess.

"I can't agree to that," I sigh. "We're taking that house, and if she's in there, I won't hesitate, Em. I'll kill her."

Emiliano's hand tightens impossibly more, and I know my hip is going to bruise. "Can we talk about something else?" He buries his face into the crook of my neck once more and bites me. "No business in bed."

I chuckle. "What would you like to talk about?"

He seems to think for a second, then says, "I don't want to talk."

"No?" I smirk. "Then what would you like to do?"

Emiliano's hand shifts from my hip to my now hard cock, and he wraps it tightly around me, stroking slowly. I have the sudden urge to straddle him and jerk us off, but he pushes me onto my back before I can do it, and in a move I definitely don't anticipate, gets between my spread thighs.

"Lube," he grits out, and I reach under my pillow with a smirk and hand him to him. "Always ready, aren't you? Such a dirty fucking slut."

Em uncaps the lube and lathers his fingers, and I watch him as he presses two to my hole. My eyes close of their own accord, and I breathe in deeply as he breaches me. "Yes," I breathe. "Such a fucking slut just for you."

He hums, crooking his fingers until he finds my prostate. My back arches off the bed and a filthy whimper escapes my lips. I open my eyes to find him watching me, and when he does it again, I force myself to keep my eyes on him. I don't want to miss a second of this.

"Those. Fucking. Sounds," Emiliano growls. "So fucking sexy."

My cock leaks onto my abs, a string of pre-cum dribbling obscenely, and I moan when he continues to rub against my prostate. "Please, Em," I beg. "Please suck me off. I can't stand the torture."

Emiliano smirks, and then his warm breath hits the head of my cock. I gasp at the sensation. "I missed this tight little hole, baby," he whispers, and my stomach flips when he calls me that. He licks the head of my cock, sucking on it and twirling his tongue around it, devouring my pre-cum. He pulls away too quickly, and my cock throbs, my ass clenching around his fingers as I groan loudly. "Did you miss my tongue?"

I whimper.

"Look at how your ass is sucking my fingers in. Just

begging to be fucked." Oh, fucking hell. His mouth is going to be the end of me. "Are you going to beg me too, Cole?"

"Yes," I reply quickly, all too eager. "Please, Em. Please. I'm fucking *begging* you. Put your mouth on me. My cock hurts."

Emiliano chuckles, then he licks my slit, sucking my cock back into his mouth. I'm afraid this is going to be over quickly when he rubs over my prostate once more, and when my spine tingles, I breathe in deeply through my nose. But he's nothing if not persistent, and when he takes me to the back of his throat and swallows, I feel myself thicken even more.

He's relentless as he works me from both sides, and I begin to shake. Just like I predicted, it's over quickly. My balls draw up, my legs tremble violently, and when he crooks his fingers once more, I gasp loudly. He moans around my cock. "I'm gonna—"

He hums, and the vibration goes straight to my balls, and I shoot down his throat. It constricts around me, making my orgasm last longer than I thought was possible, and his fingers thrust in and out of my ass hard as he milks my cock.

"Fuck," I mutter as he pulls his fingers out, making me feel empty. "That was—"

"My turn." Em grins, wiping his mouth with the back of his hand, and suddenly he's straddling my chest. "Be a good boy and let me fuck your throat."

I nod enthusiastically, and he presses the head of his cock to my lips. I lick it, tasting his pre-cum, and moan. "Such a hot little mouth," Em says as he pushes his cock between my lips and immediately thrusts into the back of my throat. I breathe in sharply through my nose and swallow around him. "I want to come all over you," he gasps. "Going to fucking wreck you, Cole."

I moan again, and he fucks my throat once, twice, three times, before he pulls out and comes all over my face. I close my eyes, feeling rope after rope of cum hit my cheeks, my forehead, and even my hair.

"*Fuuuuck*," Emiliano shouts. "Fucking hell."

I smile softly at him, opening my eyes. He's looking down at me like I hung the moon, and my stomach flutters. Something squeezes in my chest at the sight of him over me, and he moves down to straddle my hips instead of my chest.

"So fucking filthy," I murmur, running my hand over his thigh. I look at his thick cock, half-hard between his legs, and my mouth waters. I could go again right now; instead, I stay still when he begins to rub his cum into my skin. "*God.*"

"You're so fucking beautiful," Emiliano whispers, and my eyes sting. "I could stare at you all day and never get tired."

I smile. "Do it, then."

"Let's get you in the shower," he says as he gets off me, and I miss the feeling of his warm body on top of mine as soon as it's gone. "Then we can eat some breakfast and watch a movie."

"So domestic." I grin.

"Get used to it." He winks, and I swear he needs to stop making my stomach do crazy shit. "You're going to be my husband one day."

My stomach fills with butterflies now, and my eyes widen. He chuckles at the sight, offering his hand to me from the side of the bed. He holds my hand all the way to the bathroom, then turns on the shower and tests the temperature. Once he deems it safe, he pushes me under the spray.

Emiliano washes me thoroughly, gently, and I relish in it. No one's ever made me feel so fucking cared for before. I didn't know it could be like this with him. Soft. Gentle. Slow. I crave these little moments now, and I think he does, too.

"I—" *I love you*—I almost say it. But I stop myself.

"You what?" he whispers against the shell of my ear, getting closer, plastering his wet front to my back.

"I want to be your husband." A different truth. "Just so you know."

"I know," he replies, running his hands up my chest, then palming my pecs. "And you're going to be. I swear it."

I nod slowly, but don't say anything.

"Never doubt me, Cole," Em says softly. "I always mean what I say."

Right now, I wish he'd say it back. I love you. But this is enough. It has to be, and I won't push him. He'll say it when he's ready. It doesn't change the fact that I feel it, though, that the words are always on the tip of my tongue.

I'll just hold them back for now.

CHAPTER 24
EMILIANO

We're sitting on the couch watching a romantic comedy that Cole picked, but I can't seem to pay attention. All I see is him. I can't tear my eyes away. His hair is still wet from our shower, and he's wearing nothing but his pink boxer briefs with little ducks on them. I smirk. Never in a million years would I have thought that he owned those.

I observe his face. He looks tired, rumpled. There are purple bags under his eyes, and I can't help but notice he barely has an appetite. I made him his favorite—scrambled eggs with cheese, pancakes, and bacon. And he still barely ate it. I know he's sad, and he has every reason to be, but the way this has affected him slightly bothers me. It's as if he's going through a goddamn break up. But isn't he? A friendship of almost two decades is broken beyond repair. So, can I really blame him? I don't know why it's affecting me this much. I feel it too—I'm walking through life like a zombie, barely functioning. The only one holding me up is Cole. So I guess we're mutually fucked up over this.

I can't help but think about how things have been between us, though. We just click. There's no other way to describe it. I also can't help but think about the fact that choosing him was the right decision. He's part of me now. I can't seem to tear him out of my chest. Matteo will come around eventually—he has to. Right? There's no way he'll stay away forever. He has an empire to inherit. He has responsibilities—which he has been neglecting.

As my assistant at the real estate firm, he has been absent. I've officially granted him an indefinite leave of absence, but I can't hold his job forever if I don't know where he is or if he's coming back. Where even is he? Where is he living? I know I could find out if I really wanted to, but I want to give him his space. Respect his privacy for once. After all, I know this is a lot to process. I also know I don't deserve his forgiveness.

I wish I wasn't falling for Cole, that this was all a dream, but this is no figment of my imagination. What I feel for him is real, tangible even. This is the most authentic relationship I've ever had, and it sure as fuck feels like it. I meant what I said to him earlier. One day, he's going to be my husband, and we're going to rule this city together. I wonder how fast is too fast. What is an acceptable timeline for an engagement? I have the urge to make him mine. Now. It's like an itch I can't scratch. Just like my growing feelings for him.

Speaking of my growing feelings, I don't know exactly how I feel for him anymore. All I know is that I'm quickly falling for him. I can tell by the way I've been acting around him. So fucking soft. Something I've never been before. He seems to love it, though. And I wish he'd say those words to me again. *I love you.* I thought he was going to say them earlier, but then he didn't. It's a shame. I would've said them back. I think that's what this is, anyway. The feeling in my chest every time I look at him. As if we're tethered and he's pulling my heart on a string toward him. Always to him. I'm powerless to stop it, and quite frankly, I don't want to anymore. I want to drown in him—in these feelings. Mostly because I know he'll save me. He won't let me fall without him. He's already right there with me.

Cole turns toward me, smiling softly when he realizes I'm looking at him, and my stomach flutters. What the hell is that about? Am I getting butterflies from a mere look? What is this, high school? Fuck, I'm in so deep that I can't see the light. Then again, I don't really want to.

"You're staring again, Em." Cole smirks. "Are you going to do that a lot?"

"It's because you're so pretty," I answer honestly. Well, almost. I can't tell him I was noticing how wrecked he looks right now. I have a feeling he doesn't want to talk about it with me, and I'm not going to push the topic. After all, I don't really want to talk about it with him either. "Come here."

Cole straddles my lap, and my cock hardens immediately between us when his ass meets my thighs. He looks down at it and grins, shaking his head, but makes no move to take care of the issue. Shame. "Is this how you want me?" he asks.

"Maybe." I breathe as he presses his forehead to mine, brushing his nose against mine. He tilts his head and brushes his lips over my own, and my stomach flips at the contact. I don't know why. It can't even be described as a kiss. "I want you in all the ways."

"Tell me more," he says against my lips. "I want to know."

"I want you on your back." I tell him softly. "With your legs over my shoulders. On your stomach, humping the mattress as I fuck you. I want you just like this, riding me, kissing me, driving me fucking crazy."

"That can all be arranged, Em."

Cole presses his soft lips to mine, and it feels like I'm floating on a cloud. I'm suddenly dizzy with want. I need him. Need to take him right fucking now. I flip us until he's on his back, and he wraps his legs around my waist as I suck on his bottom lip, then tug it between my teeth roughly. I can taste blood in my mouth as I soothe the sting, and he moans, rocking against me, rubbing his erection against my own.

He licks the seam of my lips, seeking entrance, and I grant it to him. Our tongues tangle, and we battle for dominance, stroking against each other eagerly. Cole ruts against me faster, frantically, and I hump him right back. Seeking relief, friction. I want to come again. I want him to come just like this. I speed up, grabbing his ass and rubbing him against me harder. Cole's moans and whines are loud in the silence of the house, and I feel myself cresting, almost falling. I'm right fucking there.

And then the elevator dings.

Fuck, fuck, *fuck*.

Cole and I still, and I feel my cock throb between my legs. When I hear chuckles and cheers, my eyes close in annoyance. Because, really? They couldn't fucking call in advance? I gave them the code for emergencies. I just know this is not a goddamn emergency. Cole whimpers under me, burying his face in the crook of my neck just as I turn my head to look at my brothers.

"Bravo," Giovanni says with a smirk, and I narrow my eyes on him. "Pretend we're not here. You should finish. Blue balls are no joke."

Fuck, don't I know it.

I'm tempted to take Cole to my room and finish us really quick, but those hopes are squashed when Alex opens his big ass mouth.

"Absolutely not," he mutters. "I will never be able to unsee it as is."

Cole's legs tighten around my waist, and I turn to face him. His cheeks are bright red, his eyes wide. He looks delicious. I want to fucking eat him, devour him.

"Go to the room and get dressed," I murmur against his ear. "We'll finish this later."

"Later?" He swallows hard, then shakes his head. "No, Em. I'm gonna go jack off."

"Don't you dare," I say through gritted teeth.

"What are you going to do about it?" he asks with a bratty tone of voice, and my nostrils flare. I want to throw him over my shoulder and show him. Instead, I stay rooted to the spot, feeling eyes on us. "Spank me?"

"Yeah, *Em*." Gio chuckles. "Are you going to spank him?"

"That's kind of hot," Lorenzo says, and they collectively laugh.

"Can he go get dressed?" Alessandro asks. "I kind of want to sit down. But the couch is tainted, isn't it?"

"Not yet," Cole mutters, pushing me off. "But it was about to be."

"Good thing we came in when we did," Alessandro mutters under his breath.

Cole gets up from the couch, his erection tenting his boxer briefs, and he doesn't bother to hide it. Just goes on about his life and heads to our bedroom.

"He's gifted," Gio says with a smirk, and I breathe in deeply through my nose, trying to get rid of my boner. Fucking hell. It's not working. "He has a big cock."

"Eyes off my man," I say through gritted teeth, finally getting a hold of myself. "Before you lose them."

"Oooh." Giovanni laughs. "He's got it bad."

"Are you in love with him, brother?" Lorenzo asks with wide eyes. "You are, aren't you?"

"None of your business," I snap. I know Cole lurks and listens to our conversations, and this is not how I want him to find out. I'll tell him on my own time—when I'm well and truly ready. It's a big step, saying I love you to someone. I want him to know I mean it. I need him to know that it's not a lie. "Ask me again at the office, and I just might tell you."

"Tell him what?" Cole asks, and I flush. He comes around to the couch, sitting next to me in gray sweatpants. I can see the outline of his dick even though he's wearing underwear, and I sigh.

"Nothing," I say quickly.

My brothers all chuckle.

"What are you all doing here?" I ask my brothers.

"Can't we want to spend time with our dearest brother?" Gio asks, and I raise an eyebrow at him.

"Did you come here to talk about your restaurant?" I ask him, and he rolls his eyes.

"Absolutely not." He huffs. "Business stays at the office."

"It never has before," I tell him. "Cole and I were busy, you know. The polite thing to do is come back later."

"Good thing we're not polite," Alessandro says, and this time it's me rolling my eyes.

My brothers all flop onto the couch next to Cole, and it's a wonder six grown men can fit on it. But I have an enormous couch for this specific reason. My brothers and I have always spent plenty of time together, and though I don't admit it very often, I love it. We're tight knit.

"Alright," I tell them, defeated.

"I know what we can talk about," Cole suddenly says, and I narrow my eyes at him. "I want to take the Russians' house."

Giovanni chuckles, and Alessandro narrows his eyes at Cole.

"I thought I said no business," Gio says lightly.

Cole huffs. "This is important."

"Go ahead, Cole," Alessandro says with enthusiasm, and I chuckle. He lives for this shit. Work is all he's ever cared about. He should really loosen up a little, maybe get some pussy. Or dick. I don't know exactly which way he leans toward if I'm being honest. He's never brought anyone home. Never even been in a relationship. "Tell us more."

"In order to end this war, we need a new alliance," Cole

says, and my brothers all nod. "We need to get rid of the ones in charge right now."

"We can agree with that," Alessandro says, looking right at Cole. "And how do you suggest we do that?"

"We get rid of the Pakhan, Andrey, and Natasha." All eyes swivel to me. All eyes except for Cole's. No. He's too busy watching my brothers watch my reaction. "What?" he asks.

"Oh, nothing," Alessandro says. "I just don't think Natasha should be part of it."

"And why the fuck not?" Cole snaps.

"She's innocent in all of this," Giovanni says softly. Placatingly. "She won't interfere."

"Why does everyone keep saying that?" Cole looks at me now, eyes narrowed on my face. But I remain stoic. Fort fucking Knox. "I'm sick of being kept in the dark, Emiliano. Tell me. Right fucking *now*."

"Oooh." Giovanni chuckles. "He called you Emiliano."

My brothers chuckle again. Everyone except Alessandro. The fucker is so grumpy.

"There's nothing to tell," Alex says in my defense, even though we both know it's not true. "She just shouldn't be punished for her brother's actions."

"Why the hell do you all care?" Cole asks slowly. "It's never been an issue before—ending everyone."

There's a collective silence.

"She's not fair game, Cole," I say through gritted teeth, getting irritated. He should be following directions, not defying me. "End of discussion."

"Fine," he snaps.

Cole gets up from the couch, going to our bedroom and slamming the door. I deflate, my shoulders lowering as I slump against the couch. I pinch the bridge of my nose, just to hear someone snickering. When I look up, it's Giovanni, because of course it is.

"And I thought Alex was grumpy." He grins. "You should check on him."

"Leave, please," I sigh, getting up from the couch and heading to our bedroom. "I don't want to find you all here when I come back out."

"Fineeeee," Gio mutters, and I hear the elevator open. "We'll leave. But this discussion isn't over."

I roll my eyes and take a step toward the bedroom, taking a deep breath. And then I go in. I need to fix this. Right fucking now. I don't want to fight with Cole. We should be happy right now. Together. All over each other.

No.

This won't do.

CHAPTER 25
COLE

I'm pacing the bedroom when Emiliano comes in, but I ignore him as he stands by the door, watching me. He looks regretful, but I don't care right now. He's not budging, and I want to know why. *Need* to know. Is there something going on between Natasha and him? Was there ever? The thoughts are plaguing me, and I can't let it go. I fucking can't. It feels like my suspicions are right and he just doesn't want to come clean. But why?

Emiliano walks toward me, stopping right in front of me, and I stand still and look at him. He's looking into my eyes, searching frantically, then runs a hand down his face. Frustration bleeds from his every pore. I can practically taste it, but I'm putting my foot down. I'm not going to give him any part of me until he tells me what the hell is going on. He's hiding something—I know him well enough to be able to tell. And it doesn't bode well with me. He doesn't trust me. Or he simply wants to keep me in the dark. I don't know which is worse.

"Come here," Em whispers, stepping toward me and closing the distance between us, even though he's the one who asked me to come to him. His hand wraps around the back of my neck, bringing our faces together until our foreheads are touching. "Please don't be mad at me."

"Too late," I mutter.

"*Baby*," he murmurs, and my stomach flips. "I can't stand this distance between us."

"Then tell me the truth."

"I can't," he says, and he sounds pained by it. "You have to trust me. You need to let this go."

I laugh, trying to pull away, but he just holds on to me tighter. "You want me to fucking trust you?!" Our eyes connect, his brown ones dilating as he stares at me, licking his lips. I definitely don't look down at them, and I most definitely don't have the urge to kiss him. "Give me one fucking reason why I should trust you."

"Because I—" He gulps. "When have I ever lied to you?"

"Right now." I huff. "You're lying by omission."

"Fuck," Emiliano says under his breath, leaning into me even more. Our noses bump and our lips brush. I have the urge to close my eyes, to eliminate the distance between us. Obliterate it. But I won't. "I'm sorry. I don't know what to do."

"How about you just tell me?" I ask him slowly. "How about you just fucking trust me?" My voice breaks, and I hate it. How weak I feel around him. How easily he can just take me apart. "How about you *trust* me?"

"I do trust you," he says with conviction. But I don't believe him, so I shake my head. "But this is bigger than me. This involves more than just me."

"Who, then?" I ask through gritted teeth. I'll take any answers.

Emiliano sighs. "I really can't tell you."

I nod, reaching back and peeling his fingers from my neck one by one. He makes a pained sound when I put distance between us, but I'm not going to cave. No matter how much I already miss his touch. How badly I crave it. "Then that's settled. Find me when you're ready to talk."

I take a step away from him, then another, and his eyes water. This is just as hard for me, but I breathe through the sting in my own eyes. I can't think too hard about this or I'll break down. Am I doing the right thing by shutting him out? By pushing him away? What if I fucked up? What if he's never ready to talk? To come clean? Fuck.

"Where are you going?" he asks as I go into our closet and begin to look for black clothes. "What are you doing?"

"I'm going to take out Andrey tonight," I reply, letting my clothes drop to the floor and replacing them quickly. He stares at me and takes a step forward, but I shake my head. "Maybe anyone else I can find."

Emiliano narrows his eyes. "I forbid you from taking Natasha."

I laugh loudly. "Is this the Don talking now?"

"Absolutely," he says through gritted teeth. "You will do as I say."

"Hmm." I nod. "Yes, sir," I say sarcastically.

"I fucking mean it, Cole," Emiliano snaps, and I shiver a little. I love when he bosses me around, when he uses his stern voice on me. But I can't be weak. So I ignore my body's reaction and attempt to move past him. He stops me, getting in front of me. Our chests brush against each other's, and he cups my cheeks roughly and pulls me into him. "Please, don't go yet. Let me make things right."

"No." I shake my head quickly, not wanting to have a change of heart.

Before I can wrench away from his grasp, he slams his lips to mine. I'm powerless to stop him, and I just melt into his embrace, my hands gripping his hips and pulling him into me. I'm falling apart right in front of him. He's fucking wrecking me. When he thrusts his tongue between my lips, I moan. He groans. His hands tighten on my face, and mine tighten on his hips.

Just as he begins to rut against me, I pull away roughly, putting some much needed distance between us. "This changes nothing," I say, walking past him and putting on my shoes. He lets me, standing back, his chest heaving.

Emiliano doesn't say anything as I exit our bedroom, and he doesn't chase after me. I can't deny that I feel disappointed. I don't know what I was expecting, really. Goddamn, I'm worse than a woman.

Shaking my head, I grab my car keys and get in the elevator, pushing the button to go down to the parking garage. It's going to be a long time before I can take care of this—taking Andrey. I have to wait until midnight probably, when it's dark out and no one will see. I'm not going alone either. I don't want to put myself in a vulnerable situation, considering there are guards at the house and Andrey fights dirty. I mean, so do I, but at least I know what to expect.

I text Luca, and he agrees to come with me, along with more men. We won't have issues. They'll be outnumbered, and I breathe a sigh of relief. Luca's quick agreement was probably from Emiliano telling him to come with me. Even when we're fighting, he's still trying to protect me. It shouldn't make me all warm inside, but I can't help it. I'm so far gone for this man.

Fourteen hours later, I'm strolling into Andrey's home. My men took care of the guards, and now Luca is standing by my side as we walk through the huge house. We're quick, yet quiet, and we have to go through the living room to make it to the stairs that lead to the bedrooms. Just as we're walking into the living room, I see Andrey sleeping on the couch, the television on at low volume. I smile, because this is just too fucking easy. Why are there no guards inside? Doesn't he know he's vulnerable? That he should sleep with one eye open? This is a fucking war, and he just made this the easiest kidnapping known to mankind.

I take the syringe out of my pocket and walk quickly toward him, Luca taking out his gun and pointing it right at Andrey's face. I stab his leg with the needle, unloading the thick liquid into him, and he wakes with a gasp. We make eye contact and his eyes widen like saucers, but just as he's about to scream, Luca shoves the gun against his temple. He immediately slumps against the couch once more, and I count to ten. Then he's out, his eyes closing, his body relaxing.

"Good," I mutter, and just as I'm about to go up the stairs to see who else we can take with us, Luca stops me with his hand on my arm.

"Don't," he says slowly. "He'll have your head."

I grin manically. "It'll be worth it."

"No." Luca sighs. "It won't be."

I deflate. "Fine."

From there, I lift Andrey, hoisting him over my shoulder and walking out of the house. Fucker is heavy, his dead weight making me struggle slightly, but then I'm tossing him into the back of the van. I can breathe again in relief, and Luca notices. He grins, and I grin back.

"This ends now," I say softly.

"Yes, it does," he replies as we get in and pull away from the house.

I can't help but notice that it was all too easy. He was too confident in his guards. Didn't even sleep with a gun next to him. But now I know what this is—when I kill Andrey, everything is going to fall apart. The war will get worse. The Pakhan will seek retribution, and I'll be targeted. Which means everyone needs to die. *Everyone*—if we have a chance of making it out of this and making new alliances. I don't know how we'll manage that, how we're going to achieve a new alliance with them, but I'm sure we'll figure it out. It can't be that fucking hard. In fact, I'm sure the Pakhan's brother will be thanking us for giving him the opportunity to rise in rank and become the leader.

I tie Andrey up, getting his hands and feet. After all, I don't know how long he'll be knocked out for. The time varies from person to person. Before long, we're pulling into the warehouse, but I'm exhausted, so I just delegate everything to Luca. I'll come back tomorrow after I've slept off my anger. When I'm not so emotionally fucked up.

Getting in my car, I drive on auto pilot. I barely remember how I made it home before pulling into my parking spot. I stay in the car for another five minutes, debating if I should go inside or get a hotel room. But the need to be close to him wins out. I'll just stay in my old room for tonight. So that's what I do, going up the elevator until I'm standing in the penthouse's living room. I toe off my shoes and place them in the coat closet, then tiptoe my way across the living room and to the hallway.

Once I'm in my room, I leave the door open, knowing if I try to close it, I'll alert Emiliano of my arrival. The last thing I want to do right now is deal with him. I take off all my clothes and slip into my bed, getting comfortable under the sheets. Just as I close my eyes, I feel the bed dip behind me. I freeze, my breath stuttering in my lungs.

Emiliano buries his face into the crook of my neck and inhales, plastering his front to my back and throwing his arm over my waist, pulling my body into his. I can't move, can't even breathe. He presses a soft kiss to my neck, his lips lingering, and I close my watering eyes to keep myself from breaking down. It's only been a few hours, and I fucking missed him. The heat of his body against mine. His hand in mine. His lips. Everything. I hate fighting with him. Can't he fucking see that? He's breaking me.

"Wherever you go, I'll chase you," Emiliano whispers against the shell of my ear, and I whimper. "You'll sleep in my fucking arms, or you won't sleep at all."

"You're crazy," I mutter under my breath, and he chuckles, his warm, minty breath hitting my cheek as he leans over me.

"For you," he says softly, and my stomach flutters. "You make me this way. Out of my fucking mind for you."

I'm silent, not knowing how to reply without showing him all my cards. I'm weak for him and he knows it. But being weak is one thing, and being a fucking pushover is another. I won't be that—not even for him.

Emiliano turns my face toward his and presses his lips to mine softly, a kiss that ends way too quickly. But I don't chase him, don't go back for seconds. He doesn't seem to be deterred by that though. Instead, he presses his nose to the back of my head and inhales deeply, groaning.

"I can't live without you, Cole." I blink furiously at his words, willing myself not to cry. I won't fucking do it. A tear definitely doesn't slip down my cheek. At all. "Please don't make me."

I want to say never. I want to reassure him. Instead, I close my eyes and snuggle deeper into his arms, letting sleep take me under.

It's better this way.

CHAPTER 26
EMILIANO

The sun streams in through the windows in an unfamiliar bedroom, and it takes me a moment to remember that it's Cole's. I meant what I said last night—*everything*. I can't fucking live without him anymore, and I want to come clean; I just can't. Not yet, at least. There's too much on the line, my son included. So I'll tell him soon. I'll reassure him as soon as he wakes up, and he'll have to understand. He'll have to give me some time to get my affairs in order. I need to have a conversation with Matteo.

I'm proud of Cole for not looking for Natasha. I know that was hard for him—especially considering he thinks there's something between us when there's not. He doesn't trust me when I say that, and there's probably nothing I can do until I tell him everything I've been keeping to myself for the past twenty years. It's hard for me though. It's probably going to be one of the hardest things I've done in my life, and Matteo will never forgive this either. So all in all, I won't get my son back, no matter what I do. I'm fucked.

When it comes to Cole, though, I know I can make things right. He loves me, and that has to count for something. He will forgive me, he will. And if he doesn't, I'll have to make him. He can't get rid of me now; he's fucking stuck. I told him forever—and I meant it. Cole is going to be my husband if it's the last thing I do. I'm thinking of a spring wedding. People might think it's too soon, but not for me. I already know he's mine until my last breath. Why the hell should I wait?

Is it crazy that I'm ready to propose? That I bought a ring and hid it in a suit pocket in the closet? I haven't even told him I love him, but I will. As soon as we make up, I'll do it. I refuse to sound like I'm manipulating him into forgiving me—so I'll have to wait whether I want to or not. But I do feel it. I do. This pinching sensation in my chest at the mere thought of losing him over something as stupid as Natasha is making me crazy. I can barely fucking breathe through it.

Cole stirs in my arms, tensing when he feels me spooning him. My arm is still over his waist, and I pull him into me when he tries to scoot away from me. I bury my face in the crook of his neck and inhale deeply, loving his coconut scent. It drives me fucking crazy. Who knew I'd like that? But fuck, I can't deny that I love it. Everything about him makes me wild.

"Em," Cole growls. "You have to let me go."

"Never," I growl back. He needs to understand he's fucking stuck with me. He can't go back on his word, not now, not ever. Nothing will keep me from him—he made me a promise of forever and he better fucking keep it. "You're mine."

Cole whimpers in my arms, and I smirk. He might try to act tough, but I know I have him. He's weak for me, the same way I'm weak for him. I trail my hand up his sculpted chest, then wrap it around his throat tightly. He lets out a gasp, and my cock hardens against his bare ass. He's such a fucking slut for me, pushing against me, rubbing himself against my erection. My cock slips between his ass cheeks, and I groan, tightening my hand even more. I let go suddenly, and he doesn't even cough. I wrap my hand around his cock and pump him slowly. He doesn't stop me; instead, he moans like the whore he is.

"You like that, don't you?" I whisper against the shell of his ear. I am going to ruin him for everyone else. I'm going to fucking wreck him. "Are you gonna come with just my hand wrapped around your cock?"

Cole moans, but then swats my hand away, flipping over until he's facing me. We look into each other's eyes, and I wonder what he sees. Can he see how much I love him? Does he realize it?

This time, he's the one who grabs my cock, lining the head of it with his. My foreskin goes over his tip, and I groan at the feeling of it. He wraps his hand tightly around it, fucking into it, and my eyes roll to the back of my head. It feels so *good*. Cole gets even closer until our lips are brushing, and moans.

"You like that, baby?" Cole asks softly, his hand tightening around us. "You haven't felt anything yet. Just wait until I come in it."

"Fuck," I whimper, and his pupils dilate. "How are you so perfect for me?"

"I was made for you." He groans, speeding up. My spine tingles with the telltale signs of my impending orgasm, and I press my forehead to his. "I was made to take your cock."

"Yes." I moan, and a second later I feel his cum explode onto the head of my cock. It lubes me up, and I fuck into his hand faster. It's so tight and wet. So good. "Fuck, baby. I—" I moan. "This is way too fucking good."

"Come for me, Emiliano," Cole demands. "I want your cum."

"Oh, fuck." I moan as my balls rise, and I explode.

"That's it," Cole murmurs, letting go of me when my cock stops twitching. "God, I'm so weak for you. It's not fair."

There's a mess between us, on Cole's hand, on the bed. Neither one of us goes to move instead, we just stare at each other. His pupils are blown, a thin ring of blue surrounding pitch black. I know he feels it, this thing between us. We're inevitable. After he left last night, I was desperate. It was so unlike me to fall to my knees and cry, but I did it. I thought for sure we were over. Fuck, I'll admit it to him if it makes him forgive me. I've never felt like this before.

"I know you're mad at me—"

"Mad is the understatement of the year, Emiliano," Cole says slowly. "What I feel transcends anger."

"Fuck, I'm so sorry," I whisper, looking into his eyes. "I'll do anything for your forgiveness."

"W-what?" Cole stutters.

"I'll tell you everything," I reply. "I have to talk to Matteo first. This involves him, and it wouldn't be fair if he's not the first one to find out."

Cole nods. "Promise you'll tell me?"

"I swear it," I say with conviction, and he smiles softly at me, then presses a kiss to my lips. It's soft, and it's over way too quickly. "Just please don't be mad at me. I can't stand it."

"Okay." Cole sighs, and I melt into the mattress with relief. "I forgive you."

I push him onto his back and get between his legs, uncaring of the mess between us, and press kisses to his face. He cups my cheeks, bringing my lips to his, and I close my eyes and enjoy the feeling of it. His lips are so soft, so pouty, so full. I can't get enough of this.

"We gotta go soon," Cole says against my mouth. "Andrey is waiting."

"I'm proud of you," I tell him, and he stiffens. "You listened, even though you didn't want to. You followed orders. Now I trust you can be by my side through all of this."

Cole grins. "Well, I almost fucked up." He shrugs. "But Luca made me see reason."

"He's a good one." I chuckle.

"Let's get up." Cole sighs, and I do too.

I want to stay in bed for the rest of the day, but I understand why we can't. We have the advantage right now. It won't be long until the Pakhan realizes his son is missing, and then he'll retaliate. We'll be ready for it, though, and I'll protect Cole at all costs.

After we've both showered and dressed, we're on our way to our hidden warehouse. A new one I just acquired. One the Russians don't even know about. I'm using it to my advantage while we still can, especially since I don't know how long we'll stay hidden for. Who knows if I can trust the men I employ. Some of them could turn on me if they're offered even a little more money. I can't buy their loyalty. Which is exactly why I've only revealed it to my most trusted men.

The ride there is silent, but it's comfortable. His hand grips my thigh the entire way, and I just stare at him. How can someone be so fucking perfect? His face is so symmetrical too, it's truly unfair. So handsome. I can't stand it. I want to look away, but I can't. He's absolutely riveting.

Once we pull up to the warehouse, Cole is the first one out of the SUV. He walks to the door with purpose, and the two guards step away from the door to let him through. They nod as I approach, and I nod back, chasing after Cole. It's dark in here, and Andrey is being kept in the back. Cole leads the way as if he's been here a hundred times, even though this is our first time walking these halls.

We make it to the back room quickly, and Cole laughs loudly at the sight of Andrey's fucked up face. It seems like my brothers already got started without us. Giovanni's hands hang by his sides, brass knuckles dripping blood. He loves those. Loves to fight with his hands. Cole, on the other hand, loves sharp objects. Saws and scalpels being his favorite.

"My turn," Cole murmurs, squeezing Giovanni's shoulder before taking a scalpel out of his pocket. I chuckle, and my brothers' heads swivel my way, their eyes wide. I'm not sure they've ever seen Cole in action before. Not like this. "I can't wait to fucking end you, you piece of shit," he says to Andrey, who just smiles.

"There's nothing you can do to me that will make me out my family."

Cole tilts his head to the side, assessing Andrey. "I'm sure there's plenty I could do."

Cole walks closer to Andrey, and the man whimpers weakly. He might not want to give up information, might even hold it all in and not give us shit, but the reality of it is that he's scared—as he should be. Cole isn't fucking around right now. Andrey is a dead man. Once the Pakhan finds out about this, he'll really put a target on Cole's head. I have to do whatever it takes to protect him. This is all a horrible idea, and I might regret it later, but the least I can do is give him closure. He *needs* this.

I blink, and Cole's scalpel is suddenly in Andrey's arm. He drags it through muscle, and it bleeds profusely. A guttural scream escapes Andrey, and I wince. Cole is pissed off, and when he's angry, he's unpredictable. You really don't want to be on his bad side.

He steps away from Andrey with a manic grin on his face, and Giovanni shivers beside me. Yeah, brother, Cole is just a tiny bit crazy, but I love that about him. I don't have to worry about breaking him. He can handle himself and this life. He can be my equal. We can do this together, and one way or another, we fucking will.

"Jesuuuuus," Giovanni mutters when Cole sticks his fingers into the tattered skin of Andrey's arm, making him scream. "That's disgusting."

"Just a little bit," Alessandro says with a grin, clearly

enjoying the show. "But this is entertaining, that's for sure. Cole has it in him, after all."

"We've always known that, though," Lorenzo says with a shake of his head. "He's kind of insane."

"I can hear you," Cole says, turning around to face us. There's a smirk on his face, and he looks unbothered by my brothers' monologue. "I'm right here."

"Well, you are crazy." Tony chuckles.

"Come here," I tell Cole, and he dutifully walks toward me until he's standing in front of me. His Vans are touching my very expensive loafers, and I smirk. We're so different from each other, but we work anyway. I grab the back of his head and kiss him softly, pressing my lips to his. He thrusts his tongue into my mouth, stroking languidly, like we don't have an audience. "God, I can't get enough of you."

"Same." Cole smirks, stepping away from me, going back to Andrey's side.

My brothers are staring at me with a grin; everyone but Alessandro, the grumpy bastard. He's never happy, I swear to God.

Cole crouches in front of Andrey, stabbing his leg and dragging the scalpel through muscle, away from the main artery. Andrey screams once more. "Here's how this is going to go," Cole tells Andrey. "I'm going to ask you some questions, and you're going to answer."

"Never," Andrey whispers.

"Where's the safe house?" Cole asks. The safe house is where the Pakhan and Natasha must be hiding by now. They're not going to stay at their headquarters when Andrey has been kidnapped from there. "I want to know."

We're met with silence except for a deep groan from Andrey. He's clearly in a lot of pain and bleeding profusely. He's not going to make it very long if Cole continues this little game.

"Where is it, Andrey?" Cole asks through gritted teeth.

"There are too many to count," Andrey whispers, clearly in pain.

"Then where is your father?" Cole asks him again.

"Not telling you that."

Cole smirks, stepping away. "Shame." He sighs. "I was going to kill you quickly, but it seems like you want to play for a while, and who am I to deny you?"

Andrey whimpers. "Fuck you."

Cole looks at me. "Have the doc stitch him up, babe." Oh, fuck. He's not playing games. "I'm not done with him."

I nod. "Consider it done."

He walks toward me, his hands bloody, and I've never seen him like this. Sexy. Uninhibited. I should've been present for more of his jobs. I'm regretting staying away right about now. This has been entertaining, to say the least.

Cole washes up in the sink behind me, then dries his hands. Once he's done, he walks toward me and grabs my hand, pulling me out of the warehouse until we're back in the SUV. He kisses my cheek and smiles, and my heart flutters in my chest. I want to say it. Those three little words, but I hold back.

This is not the time.

Not yet.

CHAPTER 27
COLE

Emiliano wanted to go back home, but I wanted to come to the Pink Pony Club. I need to burn some energy, and what better way to do it than getting fucked up and dancing? Maybe fuck around a little with him as well. Would he fuck me if I was drunk? If I begged him? God, I hope so. If not, then I guess the fucking will have to take place first.

I'm amped up after torturing Andrey. The motherfucker is a tomb, but I guess I can't force him to talk. Either way, he's a dead man. I'll figure out the safe house on my own if I need to. Well, safe houses, apparently. Plural. Which makes it even harder for us, especially since I have no idea where to get started. Did they leave New York City? How about New York in general? Wherever they are, we need to figure it out.

I also have to figure out what the hell Em needs to talk to Matteo about. What could Natasha possibly have to do with either of them? I don't have a fucking clue, and it's bothering me. I have to trust that he's going to tell me though. The hard part is going to be convincing Matteo to come around, even for an important conversation. Where could he be, anyway? I'm surprised Emiliano hasn't had him followed. I'm also surprised he's given him space and hasn't gone after him at all. It's so unlike Emiliano, but then again, what the fuck do I know? I agree with giving him space either way. He deserves to take his time trying to figure this out and come to terms with it.

The question is—will he ever come to terms with it, or is this how it all ends? I don't want to give up on him, but I made my bed, and now I have to lie in it. There's nothing I can do but wait for him to come around. And it kills me slowly every day. With every hour that passes, I miss him even more. It makes me wonder if I made a mistake by not telling him how I felt before. All those years he came to visit me in prison.

We finally pull up to the club, Luca parking in the back. We make it inside, the strobe lights almost blinding, the boom of the music vibrating through my body. I love this place. It makes me feel alive. Before Emiliano, I'd come here to pick up men. It was fairly easy, and the way I dress gave me a bit of anonymity. No one would ever suspect I'm involved with the Italian mafia. I mean, look at me. I look like a glorified emo boy. Not that it has ever stopped me.

Emiliano grabs my hand and pulls me through the club, dodging people left and right. Right to the bar, exactly where I want to be at the moment. He orders us three shots of tequila each, and we slam them back-to-back. After we've finished the last shot, we make eye contact. It's heady, and now I'm fucking horny and ready for him. Who knew a simple look could get me all hot and bothered?

"Wanna dance?" I ask Em, and he looks skeptical. "Come on. You know how to fuck, right?"

Em raises an eyebrow, and I smirk.

"It's just like fucking." I tell him, pulling him toward the throng of bodies moving to the beat of the music. "I'll show you."

I turn around, pressing my ass against Emiliano's groin, and grabbing his hands to place them at my hips. He grips me tightly as I start moving against him, his cock hardening against my ass. I smirk, knowing all too well what this is doing to him—to *us*. My cock is throbbing between my legs, and I'm ready to say fuck it all and take him upstairs and show him what I can really do. But I don't. Instead, I move sensually against him. We flow like water, move like we're fucking.

"I could come just like this, Cole," Emiliano tells me against the shell of my ear. "Is that what you want?"

I look at him over my shoulder with a grin. "No." Maybe this was a bad idea. Maybe I need to go upstairs with him. Right fucking *now*. "I want you to come in my ass. Want to feel you for days, baby."

Em's eyes flare with lust, and a shiver runs down my spine. I'm so fucking ready for him, and I know all I have to do is say the word and we'll be on the way to his office. Instead, I torture us for a bit longer. I rub my ass against his cock, and his hands tighten even more on my hips, surely bruising me, but I like when he's rough with me. I've come to realize that I love everything about this man.

Definitely dick-whipped.

I turn around, pressing my leg between his, and he's practically humping my thigh. "Take me upstairs." I tell him, and he grins, nodding.

"*Finally*," he says.

We make our way through the crowd and up the stairs in the back, not slowing down even when we reach his office. He pulls me quickly towards the bathroom, closing and locking the door for good measure. Then he's on me, pressing me against the door, slamming his lips to mine. He tastes like tequila, sin, and something so uniquely him that my head begins to spin with the lust I'm feeling. He sucks on my bottom lip roughly, tugging it slowly with his teeth, and I groan, reciprocating. When I'm done sucking on his lips, I thrust my tongue into his mouth languidly. It's at odds with the desperation I feel, but I also want to savor this moment.

Emiliano pulls away first, grabbing my hand and tugging me to the sink. He wraps a hand around the back of my neck, forcing me to look at us in the mirror, pressing his lips against the shell of my ear. His eyes flash and he smirks. I can feel his breath on my skin, and I shiver.

"Look at us, Cole," he whispers, and my cock twitches, hardening painfully. "I want to fuck you just like this."

I whimper. "Please." One simple sentence from him and I'm falling apart at the seams. I'm not above begging, never above begging. "I need you."

"So fucking greedy for my cock, aren't you?" He grins, pushing on my lower back until my ass is sticking out. I unbutton my jeans and lower my zipper, and it's loud in the silence between us. He bites his bottom lip as I push them down to my knees, showing him I'm not wearing any underwear. He looks down at my ass and grabs it with both hands, spreading me to look at my hole. "Fucking hell. You're so pretty."

"All for you," I breathe. "All yours."

Emiliano lowers his pants too, then reaches into the medicine cabinet and pulls out a bottle of lube. He slathers his fingers in the thick liquid and presses them to my hole. It's cold and I jump but then relax once he breaches me with one and then two fingers. Once he gets to three, I'm whining and pushing my ass back toward him as I fuck myself on his fingers. They brush against my prostate with every thrust, and my cock leaks profusely.

"Enough," Em groans. "I don't want you to come yet."

I pant as he withdraws his fingers from me, and then he's coating his cock with lube. He notches it at my entrance, then pushes in with one long thrust, bottoming out far too gently. I want to feel him. I want to be sore for days. I want to walk funny and not be able to sit the hell down.

"Harder," I demand. "Faster."

Em smirks as he looks at me, pushing on my lower back once more. I hug the sink now, my neck straining as I lift my head to keep eye contact with him. His hands grip my hips tightly, and he bites his bottom lip, then releases it. A bead of blood bubbles up, and I clench around him. It makes his eyes roll to the back of his head, and it makes me immensely proud that I have this effect on him. This much power over him.

"Tell me how much you love this, Cole," Emiliano says through gritted teeth, as if he's struggling not to come on the spot. "I want to hear you scream."

Emiliano bends his knees and changes the angle, pegging my prostate, and I begin to shake. He does it again and again, and my moans start getting out of control. "Em!" I moan loudly. "I love—I love this so much. Don't stop, please."

"Say my fucking name."

"Emiliano!" I scream as my spine tingles and my balls draw up. "I'm gonna—I'm gonna come."

"Hands free." He groans. "Don't touch your cock."

He pegs my prostate again, the head of his cock passing over it with every thrust at this angle, and I make eye contact with him. It pushes me over the edge, staring into those beautiful brown eyes, and my cock begins to spray cum everywhere. I shout as I come, knowing I can be as loud as I want, and his lips part.

"You." *Thrust.* "Are." *Thrust.* "Mine." *Thrust.*

"Yours!" I tell him.

I feel his cock twitch, and then, a second later, he's filling my ass. He stills, keeping his cock inside of me as he presses his front to my back and kisses the side of my head. He looks like he wants to say something; instead, he slowly pulls out of me, moving me away from the sink for a moment as he retrieves a washcloth and wets it with warm water. He cleans me up gently, and I suck in a sharp breath. Once I've put my jeans back on, I realize that I have cum all over my shirt. I smirk and shake my head, turning around to grab the washcloth from him so I can clean myself, but he shakes his head.

With my back to the sink, he presses me against it, crowding me. He kisses me softly, then breathes against my lips as his forehead meets mine. "I love you, Cole."

Fuck.

Surely I'm fucking delusional. It must be the sex talking. "W-what?"

"I said I love you," he reiterates, and my stomach flips. "And I mean it. I've wanted to tell you for a few days now, but I never found the right time."

"Fuck, Em. I love you too."

"I know you do, baby," he whispers.

I watch as he tucks his shirt back into his slacks and then pulls them back up, buttoning them. All the while, his eyes are on my face, as if he can't bear to not look at me. It makes my heart flutter in my chest, and I exhale loudly. I want to go home and get in bed with him, have his strong arms wrapped around me. I need him to hold me.

"Let's go home," Emiliano says softly, as if reading my mind, and I nod. "Wanna get something to eat?"

I smile. "Yeah, I'm starving."

Em opens the bathroom door and slips out, but then he stops short and extends his hand toward me, willing me to take it. And that's how we exit the club, hand in hand. I can't believe he told me he loves me.

It feels too good to be true.

CHAPTER 28
COLE

Emiliano and I have been in some kind of love bubble for the past two days, staying in bed together, fucking our lives away. I swear I've lived out most of my fantasies with him, and we've fucked in every position on my bucket list. It's been amazing, and I wouldn't trade the past couple of days for anything. Ever since he told me he loves me, he hasn't been holding back. He says it all the time now, and I can't get enough of it. But that also means I'm emotional and need to get my shit together. Especially now that we're headed to see Andrey.

I totally forgot about him the past few days that we've been holed up in the penthouse, but no more. We can't afford to let more time slip through our hands. He has to die, and he has to die *today*. Every second he's kept alive could be a second he gets rescued, and like hell am I going to let that happen. This ends now. This battle between him and I is over, and I'm the fucking victor. Now we have to get ready for the war. I know the Pakhan is going to retaliate if I kill his son. It's only a matter of time before it happens, and we have to be ready. There will be a price on my head.

Even though I know I'm in danger, it still won't stop me from doing what I have to do. Andrey fucked up all those years ago by shooting Matteo, and now it's time to finish what I started. After this, it's imperative that I find his family and end this once and for all. Like I've already told Emiliano, we need a new alliance. The Pakhan needs to die, and so does his precious Natasha. I will die on that fucking hill. Yet I know Emiliano will protect her from me, which means I won't be killing her. It's a damn shame too. I was willing to get creative with their deaths. It's been a long time since my blood lust was satisfied. The beast inside of me craves it, and who am I to deny him?

Killing Andrey will have to be enough for now, though, that much I do know. And then Em will want me to lie low for a while. This war is just getting started, and the threat of an eye for an eye will be carried out no matter the cost. So if I don't want them to have my head, I will unfortunately have to do what Emiliano asks of me. Even if it's completely unnatural for me to hide. But for him, I'd do just about anything.

Walking around in the dank warehouse, I circle Andrey's chair. We debated having him stand with chains around his wrists hanging from the ceiling, but in the end this won out because it'll be easier to make him suffer. He's not going to talk, that much is obvious, so whatever torture we inflict will be for fun. I have to say, I admire his resilience. He's looking worse for wear, and yet he hasn't said a fucking peep. While it's annoying, I have to give it to him. At least he's not a traitor. Although I probably would've killed him faster, showed him more mercy than I have, if he had given over any information.

Emiliano stands across from Andrey, fiddling with his gun, and in a moment of clarity, I realize I want to use one for the final blow. Put Andrey out of his misery. I don't want to keep drawing it out, in fact, I kind of want to be done with him. I've already tortured him plenty, slicing him up. He got stitched back up by the doctor, but I'd be surprised if the wounds weren't getting infected in this dirty tomb. And that's exactly what it is, though he won't be getting buried here.

Although I'm done with the torture, Emiliano seems to have one more trick up his sleeve, and he's circling Andrey like a shark scenting blood. He looks like a predator right now, and I have to give it to the Russian, he looks completely unphased. That is, until Emiliano steps up to him with a knife.

Andrey whimpers, and Emiliano grins, saying, "I'm going to ask you something, Andrey."

He looks defiantly up to Emiliano, raising an eyebrow. I smirk, because the fucker has some balls. Andrey nods at Em, daring him to continue.

"Do you know what happens to the fuckers who don't give me the information I ask for?"

Andrey's eyes don't even widen. He doesn't shake or piss himself. He's stoic. Raising one eyebrow, he shakes his head.

"I cut out their tongue for their insolence." Emiliano informs him matter-of-factly. "And then I dump their body in the river to drown."

At this, Andrey's eyes widen. I bet he doesn't want to die by drowning, and I can't fucking blame him. I'd be scared too. Drowning sounds like the worst possible way to go. If I was going to die, I'd want to go out with a bang. Quite literally. One shot between the eyes will do it, and though I don't beg, I'd probably ask for it nicely. Andrey is doing no such thing though, even though he is trembling. If he asked for it though, I'd give it to him.

"Cole," Emiliano says my name softly, and I go to his side. "Would you hand me the tools please?"

I nod, grabbing the tools needed to cut out Andrey's tongue. I grab the sharpest knife I can find, and that in itself is showing him mercy. Emiliano raises an eyebrow at me when I hand it over but doesn't say anything. He proceeds to stand right in front of Andrey, and he begins to shake at Em's proximity.

"Hold him steady for me," Emiliano demands, and I get behind Andrey to hold his head. "Now, Andrey. Don't be a fucking pussy and open your mouth for me."

Andrey shakes like a leaf now but does as he's told. Emiliano nods with a smile on his face. He takes the tools and holds Andrey's tongue out of his mouth, then slices it clean off with one swipe of his knife. A scream echoes in the warehouse, Andrey's, but then he goes still. I see blood running down to his lap when I peek over his shoulder, and Emiliano and I make eye contact.

"Can I kill him now?" I ask with a sigh. "I'm getting bored."

Emiliano nods slowly, and I pull out my gun from my hip holster. I cock it, loading it, then press it to Andrey's temple. He lets out a sharp exhale. "I'll make this quick, Andrey, since you so kindly did as you were told." Emiliano shakes his head with a smirk at my words. "One last shot for mercy."

I pull the trigger before Andrey can react, and he slumps forward. There's a moment of silence between us as I put the gun back in its holster, and Emiliano and I make eye contact. I know this is going to be a thing now, but I can't bring myself to care.

"A shot for mercy, huh?" Em grins. "Are you getting soft on me now?"

"Never." I huff. "I just didn't want to deal with him anymore."

"Mhmm," Em hums. "Let's get out of here, Cole. This place smells like shit."

Without further ado, we exit the warehouse and go back to the SUV. Now it's only a matter of time before the Russians figure out Andrey is dead, if they don't already suspect it. It's been three days since he was taken, and while they haven't come after me, I know they have to be plotting my death. Which is exactly why I don't fight Emiliano when he tells me he wants us to go home.

I can't believe I took pity on Andrey and shot him in the head. But honestly, after being so fucking loyal to his family, I figured he could die with honor and dignity. He may have shot my best friend, but he didn't kill him. Not for lack of trying, but still. Andrey was a fucking nuisance. A bug I wanted to squash with my shoe, and that's exactly what I got. I had the honor of breaking him just a little bit, and that's enough for me. No way am I going soft. Right?

We finally pull up to the penthouse, and Luca parks in our assigned spot. Emiliano seems to be in his head tonight, and I want to make him feel better. I bet now that it's over with Andrey, he's worried. I can't blame him. I have to convince him to locate Matteo—he's in danger. We have to warn him, maybe even put him in a safe house outside of New York. Preferably on the West Coast, as far away from this city as possible until it's over. I know none of this will end unless the Pakhan is dead—or if I am.

As we go up the elevator, a feeling of dread settles in my stomach, and I don't know why. But that question is answered when the door opens and there stands Matteo in the living room, looking worse for wear. He's wearing gray sweatpants and a light puffer jacket, and when he turns and makes eye contact with me, my breath whooshes out as if I've been punched in the gut.

"Matty," I whisper, and he closes his eyes as if he's in pain. Emiliano stiffens beside me, but I practically run to Matteo and envelop him in a tight hug. He lets me, even though his arms hang limply down his sides. He doesn't hug me back, and though I wish he would, I'll take anything he'll give me.

"I've fucking missed you. Please tell me you're back. Tell me you'll give me another chance."

Matteo shakes his head slowly, and my stomach drops. I pull away from the hug but kiss his cheek softly. He makes a pained sound in his throat, and my eyes sting with unshed tears. His aren't fairing any better when he opens his eyes, gazing into mine, and I know he's hurting just as badly as I am. Maybe even worse. Because while I lost him, he lost the two most important people in his life.

"Please," I whisper.

Matty reaches out to me, brushing a tear away from my cheek, and Emiliano clears his throat. We don't turn around though, no; we keep looking at each other. "Tell me it's not true."

My brows furrow.

"Tell me you didn't kill him," he whispers back, and my stomach flips. "Tell me there's not a target on our heads."

"Fuck, Matty, I can't."

He nods, dropping his hand from my cheek, and takes a step back. His eyes harden when he looks at his dad, and I feel like I'm going to throw up. I look back at Emiliano, who's staring at Matteo with cold eyes as well, and swallow hard. This is not going to end well. They're both jealous. I can see it plain as day.

"I'm here, Dad," Matteo practically spits. "What did you want to talk to me about?"

I look over at Emiliano, confused, but he doesn't look at me. Not for one second. He keeps his gaze trained on Matteo. "Cole," Emiliano says through gritted teeth. "Go to our room. I have to talk to my son."

Matteo flinches at the mention of *our* room, and another tear falls down my cheek. I fucked this all the way up, didn't I? He's never going to forgive me now. Fuck. I can't even blame him.

I do as I'm told, going to the bedroom, but not shutting the door all the way. Instead, I sit against the wall next to the door and try to listen in. If they're not going to tell me what they're talking about, then I'll have to take matters into my own hands.

Hopefully, Emiliano doesn't kill me for it.

CHAPTER 29
EMILIANO

Cole thinks I don't know that he didn't close the door, but I'm plenty aware. I'm letting him have this, though. Maybe it makes me a coward to let him listen in instead of facing him and telling him myself, but I just don't have it in me to do it. It's bad enough that I have to tell Matteo. He's going to hate me even more than he does now, and Cole might just jump on that bandwagon, too. Neither of them will be okay after this, I'm sure of it. I just hope that Cole's promises of forever stick or I'll have to chain him to the fucking bed and not let him leave. Matteo, on the other hand, might be more difficult to convince. He has a fucking back bone now, and he already hates me. So what's a little more hate, anyway? He's already never coming back.

"What did you want to talk about?" Matteo asks through gritted teeth. "I want to go home."

"And where is that, anyway?" I ask him calmly.

"Oh, you don't know?" Matteo chuckles. "I find that hard to believe."

"I have been letting you have the space that you need." I sigh, and Matteo grits his teeth. "But I do have one question."

"What?" Matteo growls.

"Will you be coming back to work?" I ask him, "I'm giving

you an extended leave of absence, but I do need my assistant."

"Cole can be your assistant," he snaps.

"I don't want Cole to be my assistant." Matteo's eyes flash at my words, and I see anger in them. But I also see pain—lots of it. "I want you."

"Too bad." Matteo shakes his head. "So fucking sad."

"What are you, five?" I snap back. "Be serious."

"Be fucking for real, Dad." Matteo's eyes narrow, and his nostrils flare with anger. "I don't think I'll be going back. But I'll let you know if I change my mind."

"And how long will you make me wait?"

"However long it fucking takes."

I deserve that. I know I do. It still makes me livid. How dare he talk to me like that? But I also have to understand he's not talking to the Don right now. He's talking to his dad. And as his dad, I need to try to be understanding. I broke his heart. I shattered it. I can't expect to be forgiven this quickly and without putting in the work.

"How about we meet once a week for dinner, just you and I?" I ask him slowly. "We can work this out."

"Absolutely not."

"What about therapy?" I ask him, and his eyes widen. "We can go to family therapy once a week."

"You'd do that?" His eyebrows clash as he frowns, but he recovers quickly.

"I'd do anything for you," I reply, but it sounds like a lie.

"Leave him." Matteo's bottom lip trembles. "Leave him and I'll come home."

"I can't." My voice breaks. "I love him. He's going to be my husband."

Matteo's eyes widen. "It's been five fucking minutes, Dad! You can't be serious."

"I'm always serious." I run a hand down my face in

frustration, and he watches me silently. "Come to therapy with me. We can fix this."

Matteo shakes his head. "I highly doubt that."

"We won't know until we try," I say with exasperation. I know why he's holding back, why he won't agree to it. But fuck, I'm trying. I want to do this—need to do this. I don't want to lose him.

"I'll think about it," he replies, and my body sags with relief. "Now, what did you ask me to come here for?"

"Can we sit?" I ask him, and he raises an eyebrow.

"I'd rather not."

"Please." I practically beg. "It's a long story, and we're going to be here a while."

Matteo nods, then sits on the sectional couch. I sit on the other end of it, giving him space. I don't know how he's going to react to this, but I wouldn't blame him if he punched me in the face again. Hell, I want to punch myself in the face for keeping this from him this long, but I didn't have a choice. Now that it's an all out war, though, I feel like he deserves to know.

"I can't sugarcoat this, Matteo." I sigh, and he tenses, raising an eyebrow as he stares me down. "Do you know about the Russian princess?"

"Natasha?" he asks, his brows furrow as if trying to figure out the next words coming out of my mouth. But he'll never guess them, no matter how hard he tries.

"Yes."

"I know about her, yes." He nods slowly. "What about her?"

I steel myself, my balled-up fists in my lap. "She's—" Matteo and I make eye contact. "She's your mother."

A myriad of emotions overcome his face in slow motion, but the most prevalent one is confusion. I can't blame him. I'm dropping this bomb on him without preparing him for it first, but would he really ever be ready to face this? I don't think he would be.

It's been twenty years since Natasha and I have spoken. She just handed him over and bolted. Her pregnancy wasn't a secret, but the father was—*is*. I've been a secret all along. That was her dad's request if I didn't want to put the baby up for adoption. I was to take him and never speak about the mother or who she was. He didn't want her marriage to another ally to be compromised, and that man turned a blind eye to her pregnancy, then married her a couple of months after she gave birth.

This is why I've kept it a secret all along. For Matteo's safety. I don't think Natasha would let anything happen to him at the hands of her father, but I also can't be sure. She's never shown any interest in him or getting to know him. Hell, she's never even contacted me to ask how he's doing. She disappeared as if we'd never happened, and maybe we didn't. It probably was all in my head. I didn't even get to be with her at all throughout her pregnancy. I was just a stranger, a one-night stand to her. A stupid decision. Though I could never regret it. It brought me Matteo.

I still don't know what to do about her, though, so this is me giving Matteo the chance to decide. Does he want to reach out to her and possibly get to know her? Would she be open to that? Would she reject him the same way she rejected me? I don't know, but something tells me that if Matteo reaches out, and she turns him down, I'll probably stab her in the neck my damn self. I can't let her die until he makes his choice, though, and if he wants her to be a part of his life, then I have to respect that.

Matteo makes a face as if he's tasted something sour, and then he shakes his head. "I don't believe you." He grits out. "I look nothing like her."

"You have her nose," I reply, trying to remember exactly

what she looks like. It's been years since I've laid eyes on her. "The texture of her hair. Her chin."

"Why the fuck would you tell me after all these years?" he asks me, brows furrowed. "Shouldn't you have told me this, I don't know, as soon as I was able to make sense of it?"

"I had a deal with the Russians." I sigh, running a hand down my face as he runs his hand through his hair. "I wasn't allowed to tell you, or anyone else, for that matter. But now we're at war—"

"Because of Cole," he mutters. "Fucking Cole."

"—and he wants to kill her."

Matteo tenses, our eyes clashing. "Who wants to kill her?"

"Cole." I sigh. "He wants to kill them all. So I have to know, Matteo. What will it be? Do you want her alive? Do you want to get to know her?"

"And if I do?"

"Then we will respect your decision and leave her alive." I tell him, and his shoulders almost reach his ears, he's so tense. He has to know I'd do this for him. "It will be up to her if she wants to talk to you, though."

"I'm assuming she's never wanted to?" he asks, his eyes welling up with tears.

"No, son." I shake my head, but I don't want to pity him, so I look away. "She hasn't."

Matteo clears his throat and nods. "She—" He takes a deep breath. "I don't know what to do."

"It's your choice."

"Can you at least tell me your story?" he asks me, and I hesitate. "How you met?"

"And then?" I ask him slowly.

"Then I'll make a decision."

I'll be honest, I really don't want to do this. I know he deserves the truth, but it'll hurt Cole, who is most definitely listening in. But I can't deny Matteo this. and I'll have to set my feelings aside for him.

"Okay." I take a deep breath. "I'll tell you everything."

Matteo nods, leaning back against the cushions and getting comfortable. As he should be, considering this is a long fucking story. He's silent, waiting for me, and I sigh yet again.

"It was almost twenty-one years ago when I met your mother…"

And then I proceed to tell him everything.

CHAPTER 30
EMILIANO

TWENTY YEARS AGO

My father always makes me come to these ridiculous events, which seems pointless at just sixteen years old, but he doesn't seem to think so. He tells me that every one of these events will teach me how to be Don one day, but if he knew I'm just paying attention to the girls, he'd have steam coming out of his ears. I'm supposed to be listening to the speakers and learning about donations; instead, I'm plotting with Alessandro. While I can't make many demands, I wanted to at least have my brother at my side tonight, and father made it happen. After lots of begging, but still.

Alex and I are sitting at one of the round tables across from the podium. It's dinner time, which means this fancy evening is just getting started. After, comes the dancing and even more drinks. Not that I'm supposed to be drinking, but I've been stealing them from tables when people walk away. Sue me, I don't regret a damn thing. I need the liquid courage to get through this stupid night. The way I see it, nothing good can come of it. I might just die from boredom. Is that a thing? Can I perish just from listening to one of the guest speakers? I don't know—and I don't want to find out.

The round tables are adorned with white tablecloths and champagne-colored runners, tall candlesticks in the middle as centerpieces. Expensive bubbly is being passed around on trays, and I grab one and chug it in one go before the server can notice that I'm underage. He flinches at the realization, and I raise an eyebrow. But he's too much of a coward and wants to keep his job, so he walks away quickly.

This party is pretentious as fuck, though. There's an open bar with only top-shelf liquor, an ice sculpture, and even a chocolate fountain. Servers are starting to bring out the main course, and while I'm starving, I've also noticed a really pretty girl at the table next to ours. She's sitting right next to Andrey Sokolov, who I'm assuming is her brother if their resemblance is anything to go by. I've personally never been into blondes before, but I can't deny she's beautiful. Pale blonde hair, almost silver, with equally light blue-gray eyes. She's fucking gorgeous, and while I wouldn't marry her for an alliance, maybe I can convince her to have some fun with me tonight.

"Don't even think about it," Alessandro murmurs, always the voice of reason. "She's spoken for."

"I don't want to marry her." I shrug with a grin, and Alex narrows his eyes on me. "What? I can't tap that?"

"*Tap?*" Alessandro huffs. "Who even says shit like that? And sure? How long will you last, though, two minutes?"

"Oh, hush." I roll my eyes, ignoring his bad mood. He's the grumpiest motherfucker I've ever met. Maybe he's the one who needs to get laid. But no, she's mine. I'm not offering her up to him. "I'll last long enough."

"She'll turn you down," Alessandro says with a grin, as if the thought brings him joy. "There's no way you're fucking her. It would be stupid on her end."

"And why would it be stupid?" I raise an eyebrow.

"You don't even know who you're dealing with, do you?" he asks, grin widening. "God, you're such a twat."

"I'm assuming she's the Pakhan's daughter." I snap my fingers repeatedly, trying to remember her name. "She's—"

"Natasha," Alex murmurs, "and she's *betrothed*."

"She's got a few more years, though, right?" I raise an eyebrow. "She doesn't look old enough to get married."

"Yet," Alex emphasizes. "She's seventeen."

"Oh, so one year older than me." I shrug nonchalantly. "Not a big deal, right? I'll fuck her once and that'll be the end of it."

"You act like she'll agree." He smirks. "As if she'll give you the time of day."

"She will." I look him dead in the eyes. "In about an hour she'll be in the bathroom with me, getting railed against the stall."

"*Okaaaaay*." Alessandro snorts. "That's very graphic."

"Don't doubt me, brother." I grin at him, and he rolls his eyes. "I always get what I want."

"Are you sure she's worth the trouble?" Alex asks, and I shake my head.

"No trouble." I sit back in my chair, spreading my legs and looking right at her. Natasha. "Only a good time."

"Sure," Alessandro says dryly. "Until she's not."

Natasha looks up from the table then, gorgeous eyes connecting with mine. She smirks, looking me up and down, and it takes everything in me to stay relaxed. My hands are clasped on the table, and Alessandro is still talking to me, but I don't hear him. I can't focus on anything but the thundering of blood in my ears and her eyes on mine. I need to talk to her, get things moving along. The night is almost over, and I'm practically Cinderella. I have until midnight.

"Do you think she'll want to dance?" I ask my brother. "That's a good way to woo her, right?"

"Why do you need to do that to fuck her?" he asks, brows furrowed.

"I'm not a fucking caveman." I laugh, and Natasha raises an eyebrow at me. "I have manners. And I can appreciate having to earn her time, too."

"Run along then, brother." Alessandro huffs, and I know he's annoyed. "Go woo her."

But just then, our food is placed in front of us. I spend the next hour making eyes at her and making small talk with my father. Shit I definitely don't want to be doing. Then, like the dutiful son that I am, I listen to the guest speakers and pay attention. Mostly because I know I'm being trained to be Don, and I don't want to disappoint. So I put in the effort, despite how I feel about it.

I check my watch, seeing that we still have a few hours until midnight, which is when the party is over. Everyone is finishing their five course meal, and they begin to get up to mingle or go to the dance floor. I take that as my cue to go to Natasha, giving my brother *the* look, and he rolls his eyes, but nods all the same. He understands what I meant by that one look, and I'm grateful I don't have to keep trying to convince him. He'll cover for me if needed.

Making my way to Natasha, I stop right beside her chair and lean down to whisper in her ear. "Can I have this dance?"

Natasha looks up at me, smirking. "What makes you think I want to dance?"

"Don't you?" I shrug nonchalantly, as if my heart isn't trying to beat out of my chest. She might just be way out of my league. "Just one dance, then I'll leave you alone."

She seems to contemplate my question, but then nods once, getting up from the chair. I grin victoriously, offering my arm up to her, and she loops hers through mine, holding on to my arm with a death grip.

I lead her to the dance floor, a slow song playing through

the speakers, and hold her close to me. We sway with the music, and she looks up at me with wide eyes.

"Who taught you how to dance like this?" she asks, slightly breathless.

"I've had lessons." I grin, and her eyes widen even more, as if she's surprised. But she looks impressed too. I can tell. "You like?"

Before she can reply, I spin her, and she lands with her hands on my chest. "It's definitely not what I expected."

"I love to surprise people."

"Consider me surprised," she replies with a flirty grin. "So, what's your name?"

"You're telling me you don't already know?" I ask, brows furrowed.

"I do, but the polite thing to do is introduce yourself." She looks into my eyes as she says it, her blue-gray ones sparkling. "I'm Natasha. Pleasure to meet you."

"I'm sure the pleasure will be all mine, Natasha." I smirk, and she raises an eyebrow. "I'm Emiliano."

"So, Emiliano," Natasha says slowly. "Why did you come up to me, anyway?"

"What, a guy can't ask for a dance?" Now it's my turn to raise an eyebrow. But she can see right through my bullshit. I bet she has a lie detector.

"And is that all you want?" She smirks, running a hand down my chest. "Or are you here for more?"

"It depends." I shrug. "Do you want more?"

"I could be convinced."

My stomach flips at those words, and I give her a soft smile before spinning her slowly once more. She looks surprised and impressed when she makes it back into my arms, and I thank my lucky stars for the stupid lessons I hated. Because right now they're coming in handy. I wonder if they'll come in handy in the future too, but my guess is yes.

Coming to these events has never appealed to me before, but if I get to see her again, I'll attend all of them with a smile. I bet my dad would find that suspicious, but as I look around, I don't see him anywhere. Alessandro is still sitting at our table, though, looking right at us with a scowl on his face. I give him a two-finger salute and continue to dance with Natasha.

"So, Tasha." I smile. "Tell me something about yourself."

"No." She shakes her head. "Tonight, I'm someone else."

"I can respect that," I reply seriously. "I can be someone else, too. For you."

"And who are you?" she asks me softly.

"Not Italian." I narrow my eyes on her face, wondering what she wants to hear. "Just a regular guy."

"I like that," she replies, her hand sliding to my lower back. "I'm not Russian either and definitely not engaged."

"Never engaged." I smirk.

"So what are you waiting for, Emiliano?" she asks. "Are we getting out of here, or what?"

"Bathroom?"

"Thought you'd never ask." She grins.

Natasha leads me off the dance floor and past the tables. We make a detour through a deserted hallway, and she takes me to a family bathroom that's hidden and I didn't even know existed. It makes me wonder how many times she's done this, but I shake it out of my mind right away. I don't really care.

We go into the bathroom and she locks the door behind us, taking off her dress and dropping it to the floor. She's not wearing a bra, her perky breasts on full display. Her rosy-pink nipples harden as she stares at me, and I close the distance between us quickly, slamming my lips to hers. I thrust my tongue into her mouth in a sloppy kiss, and she groans.

Turning her around, I make her face the mirror as I unbuckle my belt and unbutton my dress pants. She grabs onto the sink with a white-knuckled grip as she thrusts her ass towards me, and I take my wallet out of my back pocket and grab a condom. Tearing the foil with my teeth, I push my pants down under my ass and whip my dick out, then slide the condom on. I press my dick to her entrance, sliding inside of her slowly. My eyes roll to the back of my head as I bottom out, and she moans and stands on her tiptoes.

And so I fuck her.

It's equally the best and worst thing that's ever happened to me.

CHAPTER 31
COLE

I listen to Emiliano tell his story, equal parts grateful and pissed off. Grateful because I finally understand why he won't let Natasha die, and it's actually a respectable reason. It's not because he cares for her, it's because he cares for Matteo. I can respect that, even if it puts us in a difficult situation. How will she act if we let her live? Will she make our lives difficult? Compromise a future alliance? Will she complicate everything we're working hard to accomplish?

Something tells me the answer is yes, but there's nothing I can do about it. I know Emiliano will do everything in his power to protect her now, especially with Matteo on the edge of making a decision. A selfish part of me wishes he didn't give a shit—that he wasn't willing to meet his mother. She abandoned him after all, hasn't cared about his well-being or becoming a part of his life in the last twenty years. I know if she had, Em would've given her a chance.

I'm still angry, though. Mostly because Emiliano didn't have the decency to tell me himself. I know what this is. He knows I'm listening in, and he's taking the easy way out. He doesn't want to face me; he wants me to find out this way to avoid explaining himself. If he thinks I'm going to just let him get away with this, then he's sorely mistaken. I deserve to have this conversation with him. Emiliano will have to explain himself to me. It's what partners do. They communicate—and I'm not letting him off the hook.

Listening to the story of how he and Natasha met has been torture. Jealousy has always consumed me when it comes to Emiliano, but this is different. He actually has a child with the bitch, so she means *something* to him, even if he denies it. And listening to this proved that. He pursued her, yet what was I expecting? Of course he did. It shouldn't bother me. It was twenty fucking years ago. She can't mean that much to him if he hasn't made any effort to go after her. Besides, she's married now. He can't still be hung up on her. Right?

Fuck, the doubt that consumes me is all encompassing. I shouldn't feel this way—don't want to feel this way—but I can't help it. I'm doubting everything between us. Didn't he know this would happen if we didn't have a simple conversation? Why is he being a coward right now? It makes me want to storm out of this room and confront him, but I also know that if I do that, it will scare Matteo off. He'll see me and bolt, and I really want to know how this story ends. Mostly because I'm curious, and if he's not going to tell me himself, then I'm going to take advantage of this moment.

I focus intently on Emiliano's voice, and I can tell he's trying to keep his voice light because he doesn't want Matteo to flip out. He's trying to come off as soothing, but he's just pissing me off even more.

"You don't need the details of what happens next—I'm sure you can guess—but the most important part is that the condom broke."

My heart plummets to the floor, and I don't even know why. I mean, she had his baby, for fuck's sake. But why does it make me irrationally jealous that she had his cum inside of her? I knew that, logically, but hearing about it makes me bristle.

"I figured as much," Matteo says slowly. "Though I thought maybe you guys had unprotected sex."

"Never," Emiliano rushes to say.

"But you've had it with Cole?" Matteo asks, and it sounds like he's gritting his teeth. Forcing his words out.

"I don't want to talk about Cole." Em sighs, and I hold my breath. "I just need to know if you want Natasha in your life."

Matteo laughs, an ugly fucking sound, and my stomach drops. He hates us. Hates his dad. I can tell. "And what if I want to talk about him?"

"Then we can do it another time," Emiliano snaps. "When he's not listening."

"I don't give a fuck if he's listening!" Matteo shouts. "Why does it fucking matter, anyway? You're going to tell him everything I say."

"Not if you want to keep it between us."

"I don't care to keep anything between us," Matteo says. "He's dead to me."

"Don't say that—"

"Why not?" Matty chuckles, and I feel dead inside. "It's the truth."

"You don't mean it," Emiliano whispers, yet I can still hear it. The house is so silent. "You can't."

"Oh, but I do," he says slowly. "How does it feel to have my scraps, Dad? I had my cock in him first, so many fucking times. Do you really think he doesn't think about that? Me? Are you that fucking delusional?"

I flinch, then hear the slap from a mile away. Emiliano hit him. Oh, fuck, this isn't good.

"Shut the fuck up!" Emiliano growls. "Don't talk about him."

I hear flesh connecting with flesh, and I get up from my place on the floor and rush out to the living room. Matteo is shaking his hand out, and Emiliano is sprawled out on the couch. Not one to give up, he gets up quickly, rubbing at his jaw. I rush toward them, ready to go against Matteo, when he turns to me with sad eyes. It does something to my heart. I don't like seeing him this way, and I hate that we did this to him.

"It's true, right?" Matty asks me, and my heart breaks just a little more. "You still think about me?"

"Yes." I nod slowly, and Emiliano flinches. "But not in the way you want me to…"

"Then how?" Matteo asks, his voice breaking.

"I think of you as my best friend who's had my heart for forever," I whisper, "and how I want you back. But I don't think of you romantically, Matty. Not anymore."

"I fucking hate you," Matteo growls. "Both of you."

"I know." My eyes sting, and a tear trails down my face. Matty watches it as it trails down my neck and soaks my shirt. "I'm *so* sorry."

"But you don't take it back?" he asks, voice hoarse. "You won't leave him for me?"

I shake my head. "No, Matty. I can't."

"Let me guess." He chuckles. "You're going to say you're in love with him."

My bottom lip trembles as more tears trail down my face, but I nod. "I'm sorry."

"Stop fucking saying that!" he shouts. "It means nothing to me. Fuck your apologies, and fuck *you*, Cole!"

I flinch. "I deserve that."

"No, Cole," he says through gritted teeth. "You deserve worse."

Matteo looks between Emiliano and I, then trains his gaze on my face. He shakes his head and goes to the elevator without another word. He doesn't even say goodbye before leaving, unceremoniously hitting the button to close the door. Not that I planned on chasing him. He has to know that.

While I love him with all my heart, I have Emiliano to think of, and I don't want to put our relationship at risk. I can't—won't.

Emiliano sits on the couch, but I can't bring myself to do the same. Instead, I let myself crumble to the floor, my knees hitting the hardwood. Sobs wrack my body, and before I can process what's happening, Emiliano is suddenly by my side, enveloping me in his strong arms. I don't know how long I cry for, only that my body is exhausted by the end of it.

Matteo is never going to forgive me; that much is obvious now. I should've seen it before, and maybe I had, but I was definitely in denial. Selfishly, I thought that after everything we've been through, he'd find it in his heart to forgive me. But do I really deserve it? I don't think I do. I know I don't. It still doesn't stop me from hoping and praying that it happens one day. Even if it takes twenty years. I have to hold on to hope.

I straddle Emiliano against the couch, burying my face in the crook of his neck. I can't breathe in through my nose, and I wish I could smell him right now, let his scent soothe me. Instead, I settle for his warmth. He rubs soothing circles on my back, and I press a kiss to his throat. He needs comfort as badly as I do, if not more. I may be losing my best friend, but he's losing his son. The one person he's dedicated his whole life to. I know it can't be easy—and yet he chose me. Every day he's choosing me. I can't take that for granted. So, as much as it pains me to do so, I stand up on shaky legs and offer him my hand. He stands up too, and I lead him to the bedroom wordlessly.

Stripping Em's clothes and my own, I let them fall to the ground. We can clean them up later. Right now, I need to be in his arms. I need to seek comfort in the only way I know how. It feels wrong to push for more, so when we're finally lying down, I just let him spoon me and close my eyes—pretending to fall asleep. Eventually, Em's breathing slows down, deepening, and I know he fell asleep. I don't have the same luck, though. My eyes hurt from all the crying, yet I can't seem to stop. I can't breathe in through my nose still, and my pillow is soaked from my tears.

I snuggle closer to Emiliano until our bodies are plastered together. His skin is hot, and I know we're going to be sweating soon, but I can't bring myself to move away. This is the only place I feel safe right now. The only place where my pain is a little dulled. I don't want to think about it anymore; if I do, I'll keep crying. So this time, when I close my eyes, I let sleep take me under. I'll deal with the repercussions of today after I wake up. Until then, I let myself be held through the pain.

Emiliano will make the pain better.

He always does.

CHAPTER 32
COLE

It's been five days since Matteo came home and everything went to shit, and things have been tense between Emiliano and I. We ended up talking about Natasha and hashing things out, but the reason for the tension between us has been due to Matty. I have accepted his need to protect Natasha, even if I don't agree with it. Matteo has yet to come forward and tell us what he wants to do, not that I expect it anymore. Maybe he'll try to contact her on his own, though I don't think it's a good idea. What if she rejects him? Emiliano told me she's never wanted anything to do with Matty, and if she lets him down, if she disappoints him, I'll kill her myself, regardless of what Emiliano says. But for now, I won't defy him. It won't end well for me.

I have to have a good reason to slit her throat, and I'm hoping she'll give me one. Maybe that makes me vindictive, but I'm not excited by the prospect of Emiliano's past lover being near us. What if she reaches out to him? Will he entertain her? I bet if it had to do with Matteo, he would. It makes me irrationally jealous to think about it, and I know I need to fucking stop. I just can't. For whatever reason, I'm stuck on this.

Now that Andrey is dead, I'm staying hidden. Em doesn't want me to take any chances just in case they're watching and waiting—which we're sure they are. The Pakhan is probably going crazy, but they know this building is off limits, so they haven't tried it. *Yet*. I bet if they get desperate enough, they'll attack regardless of where I am or the repercussions of it. But I'm tired of being in the stupid penthouse. There's only so much I can do with my time. I've tried reading, watching movies, a new TV show, and even baking. None of that has made me feel better, especially because Emiliano has been going to work, leaving me alone. Not that I expected anything different. He has businesses to take care of. It's just that I'm going insane.

Emiliano comes home to me every night, though, insatiable as ever. He bends me over every chance he gets, has fucked me on every single surface of this house except for Matty's room. Occasionally, he fucks me slowly, on my back, while he looks into my eyes. It's intense, and it feels like I've transcended every single time. Making love to him has been a spiritual experience. It's probably the closest I'll ever be to God. I see heaven in his eyes every time he gazes into mine. He leaves me breathless, boneless. It's an out-of-body experience, as if I'm watching it happen, and I'll never tire of it.

Speaking of things I'll never get tired of, it's the way he takes care of me. I don't like to cook, so he brings me dinner every single night. After eating, he takes me to the shower and washes every part of me reverently. He treats me like I'll break under his hands, and for the first time in my life, it doesn't bother me. I feel cherished, loved, and it's jarring. I never thought we'd be here, but fuck, I wouldn't trade this for anything in the world.

I hope he meant what he said about me being his future husband, because I don't plan on going anywhere. He's stuck with me now, and he'll have to kill me if he wants me to leave his side. Not that I think he'll ever be strong enough to do that. I see what I do to him, and even though sometimes I have my doubts and irrational insecurities, I know he loves me. I can feel it in my bones. It's in the way he looks at me, in the way he touches me. With so much care and adoration I never thought he was capable of. Now that I've had it, I never want it to stop. Which is exactly why we're in this new penthouse, walking through it with the purpose of starting fresh.

I don't want to live in *his* penthouse anymore. It holds too many memories with Matteo—painful memories now. I think if Emiliano and I have any hope of making it, we can't live with the ghost of his son roaming our home. Besides, I want our home to be *ours*. I want to decorate it with him. Pick out the furniture. Start over from scratch. I want all our memories to be new, and I want them all to be good. I know that's probably unrealistic, but it's better than what we have right now.

This penthouse is gorgeous too, with its four bedrooms and four and a half bathrooms. The hardwood floors are a dark chocolate brown, giving the home a masculine vibe. There are floor to ceiling windows all throughout the living area and in every single bedroom. We would have a view of the New York City skyline and the Hudson River, and we'd be close to amenities such as fine dining and bars. I know it's a little way from his other businesses, but I don't want to be that close to them. He has drivers, he can deal with it. The kicker? This place is expensive. I knew Emiliano had money, but this is on a different level.

The realtor let us in on a little secret; the last bid was *six* million dollars for just the penthouse, and Emiliano wants to buy the entire building. It makes sense, as he owns the building where we currently live, and this is a new build, completely unoccupied. He'd be able to sell all the condos and make a profit. He'd probably be a fucking billionaire from it. Not that I don't think he already is, but money has never mattered to me when it comes to him. We could be poor, and I'd still be in love with him. He's irreplaceable.

When I told him I wanted to move, he didn't even hesitate. We've walked through six penthouses today, but I've seen the way his eyes absolutely sparkled as we walked through this one. This is *the* one.

"So, what do you think?" I ask him, and he grins. "You like it?"

"I love it, Cole," he replies softly, walking me through the primary bathroom. It's bigger than the others, with a shower and a porcelain claw-foot tub. I stare at every surface, especially the vanity and mirror, and he smirks knowingly. "Can't wait to fuck you right there." He tips his chin to the sink, and I grin.

"Where else are you going to fuck me, Em?"

"*Everywhere*," he grins. "Let's go back to Lily."

Lily is the realtor, and she's waiting patiently in the kitchen when we make it back to her. She grins widely, knowing she's going to make a hefty commission from us. Not only are we out-bidding the six million dollars, but he's also offering to buy the entire high-rise. When he makes his bid, her jaw drops, and she nods quickly.

"Mr. Sokolov won't be happy." She frowns. "I can't pass this up, though."

Emiliano stiffens at the mention of the Pakhan, and now he has a fire lit inside of him, I just know it. Before, he wanted this penthouse for us, but now it's a competition. He has to have it. I don't take it personally, though. After all, he's only given in because of what I want.

"Good." Em smiles tightly, and it doesn't reach his eyes. I know she can tell because she begins to shift on her feet. "I'd like to close on this as soon as possible."

Lily nods. "Of course. I'll get started today."

"I can pay cash today," Emiliano tells her, and her eyes widen. "Does that work for you, Lily?"

"Y-yes." She swallows hard. "Of course."

"I don't want to take my chances on another bid," he tells her patiently. "I want this finalized today."

"But—"

"No *buts*." He smiles. "I pay cash, and you draft the paperwork as soon as possible."

"Yes, sir."

Seemingly satisfied, Em nods, handing her a business card. "Here's my contact information. I expect to hear from you today."

"O-of course," she stammers.

With those parting words, we head out to the blacked-out SUV. The windows are bullet proof, thankfully, and for the first time ever, I'm thinking we probably need that. Getting into the vehicle, I scoot over to the far end and begin to buckle up, but Emiliano stops me with a hand on my arm. I look over at him and he smirks.

"Did you like the place?" he asks me, and I nod. "Good. We can move as soon as we close on it."

"I'm excited." I grin, meaning it.

"You know what I'm excited for right now?" Emiliano whispers. "Getting you to suck my cock."

My stomach flutters at his words, but I look back at our driver, who's keeping his eyes trained on the road. He knows Emiliano might just claw them out if he sees something he's not supposed to. So he keeps his gaze forward, and Em unbuttons his suit pants.

"Please, baby," Emiliano says softly. "I need you."

I nod, unable to speak for fear that my voice will shake. I've never had sex with anyone while having an audience, but he doesn't seem to mind it. In fact, he seems desperate, and I don't want to deny him.

I slide down to the floor and Em lowers his pants until they're under his ass and his cock bobs in front of my face. Getting between his legs, I watch as he strokes himself once, a bead of pre-cum leaking out of his slit. My mouth waters with the need to taste him, and I lean in. But he just slaps my face with his cock, and I gasp.

Emiliano smirks. "Are you gonna be a good boy and suck my cock?"

"I'm always a good boy," I lie, and he chuckles.

"You're a fucking brat," he whispers, then grabs my hair and presses the head of his cock to my lips. "Open."

I open my mouth, sticking my tongue out for him and looking into his eyes. He slips his cock into my mouth, my tongue gliding over the underside of it, and I wrap my lips around his length. His grip on my hair tightens as he groans, and he surprises me by shoving my head down until I'm choking on him. My nostrils flare as I inhale deeply and swallow around him, then bob my head up and down. I have one mission right now: make him come before we get back to the penthouse, and I'd say we have about five more minutes.

"That's it, Cole," Em growls, shoving my head down once more, then pulling me up by my hair. I have no choice but to let him. I'm just a puppet, and he controls all my strings. "You suck me so fucking good."

I moan around his cock, gagging on it on the way down. But I work through it anyway, not wanting to disappoint him. Keeping my eyes on him, I watch as he bites his fist in an attempt to keep quiet when I swallow around him once more. When I inhale deeply and take him all the way, he strokes my hair lovingly. My eyes sting with tears, and they trail down my face as my spit drips from the corners of my lips. It's fucking sloppy, and I feel it running down my chin. Emiliano seems to love it though, and when I swallow around him once more, then bob my head up and down quickly, he tenses.

"I'm gonna come," Em warns me. "Swallow it all, Cole. Take all of it down that pretty little throat. I want to hear you choking on it."

With that, he grabs my head with both hands and fucks my throat from the bottom. His cock spasms as he comes, and I end up choking a little, just like he wanted me to. By the time I come back up for air, I have cum and spit dripping down my chin, and Emiliano has a sated grin on his face as he leans back. I wipe my face with the back of my hand, and he tucks himself away, lifting his hips to pull his pants up.

"Missed a spot," he whispers, then grabs me by the hair and pulls me into him. He kisses me like he's dying, like his oxygen depends on me. "God, Cole, what are you doing to me?"

"Nothing you haven't done first." I smile softly up at him, and he nods.

And I can't deny that I feel so fucking loved.

So why does it feel like it's going to be taken from me?

CHAPTER 33
EMILIANO

It's been a few days since I bought the high-rise, and I have never competed for something like that in my life. The only reason I wanted to rush it was because I didn't want the realtor to let Sokolov know about my counter bid. Didn't want her to give him the chance to outbid me. The deal is done, yet I can't help but wonder what comes next. I need extra security here, just in case the Russians want to act stupid and get brave.

Aside from the bidding war, Cole and I are both very happy with our decision to buy the penthouse. It's perfect for us, and he was right, we need to live somewhere not tainted by memories of my son. I don't want to see the guest room and think about Matteo fucking Cole in there. I realize how fucked up it sounds that I'm the one fucking Cole now, but when Matteo said I got his sloppy seconds, I lost my goddamn mind. Cole is mine now, and I'll be damned if I let anyone talk badly about him, even if it's my own son.

Speaking of Matteo, I let him know that Cole and I were moving out of the penthouse and that he was welcome to keep it. He didn't want to, though, and I can't blame him for that. I wouldn't keep it either if I were him. I still offered it, it's the least I can fucking do. I'm still unaware of where he's living, seeing as he hasn't bought anything or rented under his name. I'm assuming he's in a hotel under someone else's name or he's living with a friend. Hopefully not couch surfing.

I get he doesn't want to live in one of the condos below my penthouse because he wants his pride to stay intact, but I also hope he's not homeless. That would just break me. He took all of his belongings with him, though, down to the last trinket on his dresser. So really, where would he put his things if he didn't have a place? I know I should stop worrying about it, but I can't help it. He's my son. I'll always see him as my baby no matter how grown he is. So why can't I do right by him? Why do I have to want Cole so fucking bad?

All I know is that Cole and I are inevitable. I don't just want him; I *need* him. He's the blood in my veins. The oxygen in my lungs. I feel like I'll die if I let him go. I wasn't kidding when I said he's mine forever. I won't let him go. Not now. Not ever. Over my dead fucking body. That man is *mine*. Which is why when he told me he wanted to start fresh, I couldn't deny him.

Today is move-in day. My penthouse is packed in a mountain of boxes, and we decided to get all new furniture, which will be delivered today, along with new appliances. Cole sold my furniture on Facebook Marketplace, and I've never felt older. Not that we needed the money, but he said throwing them away was a waste. I can't even argue with that.

Now here we are, moving boxes into our new place as Cole signs for our bedroom set delivery. The bed is upholstered because he said he wanted to sit up and read—like a little old man. Who even reads in bed at twenty-one years old? Apparently he does. And according to him, he's reading gay romance books. Said he's currently reading a monster romance where one of the main characters has two dicks. I laughed so hard my belly hurt.

I'm looking forward to making new memories with him here, and as Cole pulls the Christmas tree and ornaments out of boxes, I realize I've never done this with anyone before. It feels meaningful, intimate. Domestic, even. I've never had a partner before. For the past twenty years, nothing mattered but my son. This feels different. This matters.

Boxes are stacked in the dining room since we don't have a table yet, but the rug for the living room is in place now, so we can at least sit there since we also have no couch. Everything but our bed is supposed to be delivered tomorrow. Breakfast in bed doesn't sound half bad, though.

Cole comes up to me and gives me a sweet kiss, just a soft press of his lips against mine. I close my eyes and savor the moment, breathing in his coconut scent. I'll never tire of this. Never get over it. He hands me an ornament and smiles at me, his eyes twinkling, and I follow him over to the tree. He's already fluffed it and plugged in the lights, and I return his smile.

"I got us something," he tells me, pulling something out of his pocket. It's a wooden ornament, and when I flip it over, there's a picture of us with the words "Our First Christmas" engraved into the wood. I swallow the lump in my throat and look into his eyes. He seems unsure of himself in this moment. "Like it?"

"Love it," I reply without hesitation. "Love *you*."

A smile tips up his lips, and he gives me another kiss, there and gone quickly. "I know it's cheesy—" he begins.

"—romantic," I interrupt.

"But you better get used to it." He grins. "It's just the way I am."

"I can be romantic too," I say softly, brushing his hair away from his face.

"Prove it." He grins.

"I will." I wink. Sooner than he thinks.

I know we've only been together for about two months, but I don't want to keep waiting.

We put the ornaments up together, stopping occasionally to kiss, and it's more fun than I thought it would be. Mostly because of the look of concentration on his face when he's trying to figure out where to put the next ornament. We put ours up front and center, and I just know my brothers are going to give me so much shit over this. But I don't care. This is special to me. Cole is.

After we finish, Cole goes to the kitchen and makes us two mugs of hot chocolate from scratch. He's going all out with Christmas music at low volume in the background, and he's setting the mood more than he knows. I busy myself with lighting some candles, and when he hands me the mug of hot chocolate, I breathe in deeply to stave off my nerves. We take our time drinking it, and I can't lie, it tastes amazing. I've never been one for Christmas cheer, but I'm a changed man, it seems.

We finish our drinks and I get a bottle of champagne and two flutes and take them over to the rug, setting them down. I'm just about to sit too when Cole shakes his head and stands up, holding something behind his back. I raise an eyebrow, and he looks down at the champagne.

"Special occasion?" he asks softly, and I nod with a smile. "Come here, baby."

I close the distance between us, and he shows me what's behind him—mistletoe. It has to be the funniest and cutest thing he's ever done. I smirk, and he shakes his head.

"Better not laugh at me." He grins, putting the mistletoe above our heads.

"Never," I lie.

Instead of laughing, I lean in and kiss him, sucking his bottom lip into my mouth. The kiss turns heated, and soon enough I'm thrusting my tongue into his parted mouth. He meets me in the middle, stroking his with mine. But for the first time, maybe ever, he's submissive. We're not battling for dominance. He's letting me have this one. I'm not sure how that makes me feel.

Cole lets the mistletoe fall to the rug, then cups my face with both hands and continues to kiss me. My cock hardens, and I grab onto his hips, but don't act on it. We pull away to catch our breath, and when I drop down to one knee, Cole looks at me in confusion.

"Cole." I breathe, pulling out the ring from my back pocket. "I've always known you were put in my path for a reason, but I never could've imagined why. *You're* my reason. The reason I wake up in the mornings and get out of bed. The reason I keep going. You've shown me what it's like to love someone and be loved right back. I never knew it could be like this—effortless, and yet not. All I know is that I'm never letting you go. You're my oxygen, Cole, and without you, I'll suffocate. I'm never giving you up, *never*."

Cole's eyes fill with tears, and he's looking between me and the ring with parted lips.

"Will you marry me?" I ask him. "Will you be my husband and spend forever by my side?"

Cole drops to his knees in front of me. He looks at me with his wide blue eyes, and my stomach flutters. "Yes," he whispers. "It's us forever, Em."

I grin, slipping the ring onto his finger and slamming my lips to his once more. It's urgent, needy, and everything I knew it would be. I'm so glad I made this decision. So glad I took a chance on us.

Cole pushes me onto my back, unbuttoning my jeans and

pulling them down my legs along with my boxer briefs, then shucks off his clothes. He straddles me and grabs our bare cocks, giving them one firm stroke, and I groan.

And that's how we spend the rest of the night.

Making each other come over and over again.

CHAPTER 34
EMILIANO

It's been a week since Cole and I got engaged, and I've never been this happy in my entire life. I guess being in love for the first time will do that to you. Living in our new home is going well. We've had all of our furniture delivered, and we've unpacked most of our boxes. We're almost settled in, and everything feels right in my life right now.

Cole lights up the Christmas tree every single night as soon as it gets dark outside, and we watch a romantic comedy before bed without fail. I do it for him, because I think it's cute, even if I've never been a huge fan of them. But the thing is, I'd do anything for him. I think I've already proven it, but I feel the need to continue proving myself every single day.

According to him, he still can't believe I asked him to marry me. He had his doubts, I guess. I can't blame him for it, considering the situation. Especially the issues with Matteo. But I didn't take our relationship lightly, and when I promised him forever, I meant it. Asking him to be my husband felt right, no matter how soon it was. My brothers were all surprised. Well, everyone but Giovanni. He thought it was the funniest thing ever. Said I was dick-whipped and honestly I couldn't even deny it.

The least I can do is make Cole happy, considering we

both lost someone important to us because of our relationship. I never want to make him doubt if this was the right decision for him, so I'll do everything in my power to make sure he feels cherished and loved every single day of our lives.

The only thing putting a damper on my day was Matteo reaching out to me to let me know he is interested in meeting Natasha. He said he wants to be the one to reach out to her, though, and I don't know how to feel about that. I'm nervous, that much I do know. I don't think she wants to hear from him, and he's going to get hurt. But now I know nothing can happen to her, and I will protect her for him. Cole won't be too happy, but he'll understand. I think he's already resigned himself to that reality.

Matteo is also coming to the company's Christmas party tonight. Cole and I are already here, mingling, but my son is nowhere to be found so far. I don't know why he's coming anyway, don't know how I managed to convince him. I won't lie, I'm a little scared he'll make a scene when he sees Cole's ring, he's not above doing that. That's the last thing I need, though. I don't want my employees to know my personal life or just how messy it is. Though I bet they'd eat that shit up.

Speaking of my employees, everyone is enjoying themselves. We throw this party every single year, and we go all out with the plated style catering and even a dance floor. It's a formal event, black tie, and it never disappoints. This is the first year that Cole has come, and I'm excited to have him on my arm and introduce him as my fiancé.

I look around the room and take in the decorations, smiling to myself. Everything looks amazing. Long tables are lined up with about twenty guests each. Poinsettia garlands drape over the tables on top of the tablecloths, and they drag down to the floor. There are tapered candles setting the mood as well, and white peonies hanging from a chandelier above each table. Everything is breath-taking, and it makes me wonder what kind of wedding Cole wants.

Taking Cole out to the dance floor, we slow dance to *You Make it Easy* by Jason Aldean. We look into each other's eyes the entire time, tuning the rest of the world out, and I lean in and kiss him. It's languid, unhurried. Our lips meet in a familiar dance, and he wraps his arms around my neck as he sucks on my bottom lip. We keep the tongue to a minimum considering where we are, but it doesn't seem to bother him. I guess we can both be professional, about nine percent of the time.

We pull away from each other just to find Matteo staring at us, his eyes wide. I mutter a curse and turn to Cole, who's looking right at his best friend, too. He moves as if he's going to go talk to him, but I halt him with a hand on his arm. Announcing our engagement to him should be done by me. So I walk toward Matteo with purpose, and he narrows his eyes at me.

"Really, Dad?" Matteo asks lowly. "You invite me just to rub this in my face?"

"I need to talk to you." I tell him, and he raises an eyebrow. "It's about Cole."

"What more could you possibly have to say?"

"We're engaged," I reply, and his eyes widen once more. "I'm sorry—I just didn't want you to find out another way. I needed this to come from me."

"So it's that serious?" he asks, venom in his voice.

"Yes, it is." I sigh. "A spring wedding."

"Unbelievable," Matteo scoffs, and I flinch. "This is absolutely insane. You've barely even been with him."

"I know him, Matteo." I rebuke. "This is what I want—what we want. Does it matter that we've only been together a few months? Not to us. We both know what we want, and I don't want to play the long game."

"Wow." He chuckles. "Just when I thought I couldn't hate you more."

I flinch, and he smiles. "You can't mean that." I shake my head. "What can I do to make this better? Did you think about therapy?"

"I have." He nods slowly. "I just don't know if it'll help any."

"You can't know unless you try."

Matteo looks at me with tears in his eyes, and it breaks my heart. "I don't know, Dad. Okay? I'm not sure what I want to do."

"I can wait," I whisper to him as people get closer to us. "*Please.*"

"I want to talk to Cole," he replies, and my stomach drops. "Then I'll make a decision."

That leaves a sour taste in my mouth. Jealousy consumes me, and I know it's fucking irrational. What if he convinces Cole not to marry me? What if he steals him away from me? No. Cole wouldn't do that to me. Right?

"I'm going to talk to him," he tells me again. "Whether you want me to or not. We both know he wants to, and I need to hear it from him, Dad. I need closure."

"What kind of closure?" I narrow my eyes at him. "Don't you dare—"

"What?" He rolls his eyes. "Don't you dare kiss him? Fuck him?" I bristle, and he smiles. "Don't worry, Dad. He's a loyal guy. I'm sure he wouldn't do that."

I nod. "He is."

"But it won't stop me," Matteo tells me, and I swear my stomach bottoms out. It's about to fall out of my ass. "I need this, Dad. It's the only way I can move on."

"What a way to move on," I mutter. "Maybe this is a bad idea."

"Oh, now you want to change your mind?" His smile is

saccharine. I'm about five seconds tops from wringing his neck. "I thought you wanted me in your life."

"Not at the expense of my marriage, Matteo."

"You're not married yet." He shrugs. "He's free to make his own choices. And who knows, Dad? He might just pick me instead. I've seen the way he looks at me. Like he's fucking dying without me. If you think he doesn't have feelings for me anymore, then you're fucking delusional."

He's not wrong, and that's what kills me. Cole has been a mess without Matteo in his life, and it's made me wonder if his feelings went beyond friendship. I can't think about that too much. I fucking proposed. I asked him to spend the rest of his life with me, and he said yes. I have to trust that he loves me. That we're in this together. That something like Matteo begging him to come back won't break us. I have to trust that our relationship isn't fragile.

Even if it kills me.

"Do what you need to do," I reply grimly. "But after that, you're going to therapy with me, and we will fix this. You'll be a part of our lives again."

"I can't pretend nothing happened, Dad." He chuckles, but it holds no humor. "You can't expect me to do that. I'll make amends with you. I'll go to therapy with you. But being around Cole is too painful, and I don't know how long it'll take me to come around." A tear slips down his cheek and he wipes it angrily with the back of his hand. I know it bothers him to show me weakness. "He's the love of my life." His voice cracks. "You can't expect me to watch him live his life with...*you*."

I get it, I really, really do. I don't blame him. But it doesn't take away from the fact that it hurts so fucking bad. He's going to get closure from Cole and then abandon him, and it's going to destroy both of them. I don't want him to do this, but I don't know how to make it stop either.

"Don't leave him forever." I swallow past the knot in my throat. "He won't survive it."

"And I won't survive seeing him happy with someone who isn't me."

"You can be strong, Matteo." I sigh. "He's not. He watched his mother get beat to death. He lost everything and everyone. And who saved him?—"

"You did," he huffs. "You got him out of there. You brought him to *me*. You fucking did this."

"*You* saved him." I shake my head. "You're the one who took care of him."

"You stole him away." He looks away, and I can't help but agree with him, so I nod. I know I did that. I took him. And nothing will ever change that fact between us. "You stole the only good thing in my life."

"I—I'm *so* sorry, Matteo."

"Sorry isn't good enough," he says lowly, "I'm going to go talk to him now. Please give us some space."

I nod, but he doesn't even look at me before he walks away. He goes straight to Cole, who's standing at the edge of the dance floor, and when Matteo approaches him, a tear slips down his cheek. Matteo wipes it away with his thumb and grabs Cole's hand, and Cole accepts it, walking behind Matteo as he pulls him away from me.

My heart is in my throat as I watch them head outside, but I don't follow. I said I'd give them space, and I'm going to do it. Even if it's killing me inside. I walk toward the bathrooms, my pace hurried as I feel my face heat. I hope I don't make a fucking fool of myself by crying in front of my guests. I hate this. I hate this so fucking much. I'm going to lose him. I might lose them both. All I can do is hope that I'm enough for Cole. That he doesn't leave me. That he loves me just as much as I love him.

But what if he doesn't?

CHAPTER 35
COLE

Matteo leads me outside, his hand clasped tightly in mine, and my stomach drops. Emiliano is probably sick, and I think I'm going to be too. Nausea churns my stomach as Matty takes me to the side of the building, pushing me against the wall and caging me in. He looks angry, sad, fucking devastated. All the things I feel too. Angry because he left me. Sad because he's my person. Devastated because he's never coming back.

His nostrils flare at the same time as his eyes water, and I can tell he's trying not to cry. I reach out and cup his cheek, and he closes his eyes as if he's in pain. It makes me want to drop my hand, but I don't. I can tell he needs this.

"I'm *so* sorry, Matty," I whisper. "Please believe me."

"I believe you, baby," he whispers back, a tear trailing down his face. Mine stream down my own now, too. "But I can't help but hate you, too."

"Oh, God." I close my eyes. "I can't take it. Please don't say that."

"We have to be done, Cole."

"No, no." I shake my head quickly. "*Never*. I can't stay done with you. Please, Matty. You mean everything to me. Don't leave me."

"Oh, fuck." A breath shudders out of him, and he sobs. "Don't say that to me. Don't say it like you fucking love me."

"I do love you!" I growl. "Why can't you see that?!"

My stomach drops as he leans into me until we're sharing breath, and I have the sudden urge to push him away. But I don't. I let it happen. Oh, fuck. I did this.

"Tell me you're in love with me too and I'll leave you alone forever."

"I can't." I shake my head. "I don't want you to."

My entire body trembles with fear as Matteo swallows hard, and a lump forms in my throat. It feels like I'm going to pass out from how dizzy I am, and suddenly it's hard to breathe. He's going to leave, never to come back. No matter what I do or say, he's already made his decision.

"I know you're in love with me too, Cole," he whispers, and I shake my head, trying to deny it. I'll deny it until my dying fucking breath. It would ruin everything. It would ruin my relationship. It would ruin our chances of having a friendship, too, because at the end of the day, I've always wanted Emiliano more. There's no choice to make, no matter how much it guts me. "I see it in the way you're so fucking devastated. You love me." His voice shakes, and he slams his fist against the wall right near my head, causing me to jump. "Say it. Fucking admit it."

I close my eyes and take a deep breath. I can't say it. I can't do it.

"Tell me, baby."

I shake my head.

My bottom lip trembles as he takes a step forward until our shoes are meeting, and he tips my chin up with his forefinger. I open my eyes and see the pain in his. It feels like someone's taking a knife to my chest and stabbing me with it. I can't breathe.

Can't fucking breathe.

"Fucking. Say. It."

A sob escapes me, and I bite down on my bottom lip to keep the next one trapped in. I can't do this. I have to leave. But the way he's looking at me absolutely guts me. Like he'll die if I don't admit it. "I do, Matty. I do love you." Fuck me, I mean it, but it's not enough for us. "Fuck, please don't leave."

Matteo slams his lips to mine without warning, and I tighten my lips, not returning his kiss. He pries my jaw open with his fingers as he cups my face, and I gasp with pain as he slips his tongue into my mouth. Holy fuck. I have to stop this. I have to.

But I can't help but myself from whimpering into his lips. Fuck, I hate myself now. I'm a fucked up person. I hate everything about this. Yet I can't help but feel full for the first time since he left. My heart beats just a little faster as he strokes his tongue against mine, and I try to turn my face away from him. It's useless though. His grip on my jaw is tight.

I shove him back, tears in my eyes as I shake my head. My bottom lip trembles. "Matty—"

"No." He shakes his head. "We're over. This is over. I can't be around you anymore."

"Matty, please," I beg. "Don't do this!"

But he's walking away now, and my knees buckle as I hear him whisper, "Goodbye, Cole."

I slide down the wall, pulling my knees up to my chest and laying my head down. I sob until I can't breathe, and then I sob some more. I did this; I did it to myself. He told me if I admitted it, he'd walk away. Why did I have to say it? Why can't I be fucking strong? Oh my God. I ruined everything.

Getting up, I brush the dirt away from my pants. I need to go inside and splash water on my face. I need to compose myself. I need to go back to Emiliano—the love of my life. I need to come clean. I need to—

Suddenly, there are hands on my body, pulling me in one direction. I go to scream, but a cloth is draped over my mouth and nose in an instant, and I'm conscious long enough to see that I'm being led to a van on the side of the road.

The Russians.

I'm so fucked.

The smell of decay wakes me, and it's hard to rouse. My eyes are heavy and I can't open them. My tongue feels thick too, my mouth dry. I ache all over my body. Just where the fuck am I? My wrists hurt from the restraints, my shoulders too from my hands being pulled behind my back. I'm sitting on a chair, and it's fucking freezing in here. I wonder how long it'll be before they kill me. I can't alert them to being awake, so I keep my eyes closed and attempt to breathe evenly. I'm not sure how long I've been here, but I couldn't possibly have been unconscious for more than a few hours. Right? The idea of having been here longer than that is terrifying. Emiliano must be going crazy looking for me.

Maybe this is exactly what I deserve for fucking up. Maybe death is what I need. I fucked up *big* time. I didn't mean to—fuck, I didn't mean it. I also couldn't help but return Matteo's kiss just for one second. I knew deep down in my gut that it was the last one I'd ever have. That it was the last time I'd see him. I know now he's probably going to disappear on us, never to return. I don't even blame him.

I'm fucking devastated, and I'm not even the one who was betrayed. But I can't help but feel that way—betrayed and abandoned, as well. He left me. He did the one thing he swore he'd never do. What did I expect, anyway? I hurt him beyond repair. I just expected something different. I guess I thought he'd understand. That he would get it. That he'd want me to be happy. But it seems he only wants me to be happy by his side, and fuck, I wish I could be. Except, my feelings for Emiliano can't be ignored either. I'm stuck between a rock and a hard place.

Emiliano or Matteo.

Matteo or Emiliano.

At the end of the day, there's really no choice to make. Matteo has to be my past, to give Emiliano and I a chance at a future. That doesn't mean that I'm not hurting, that I'm not completely fucking eviscerated over my choices. In another life, Matteo could've been enough for me. I would've picked him. I wouldn't have been in love with his dad, too.

Too.

Because isn't that the truth? I'm in love with them both. And yet, the choice has already been made. If that means Matteo can't be part of my life anymore, then so be it. Maybe it's for the best. I don't know if I could handle him bringing someone else home. Sharing a life with someone who isn't me. Isn't that the most hypocritical thought I've ever had? But I never claimed to be perfect. No, I'm fucked up. *Clearly.*

A chair scrapes in front of me, and I tense, inhaling sharply. So much for pretending to be unconscious still. Fuck me sideways. They have to know now, and they probably do considering I feel eyes on me. It's like a brand searing my skin, and I wonder what they see. Do I look as broken as I feel? Are my eyes puffy? Is my face still blotchy from crying? Just how long did they watch me cry outside that stupid hotel? They probably think I'm a pussy, but they're about to find out just how strong I am. No matter what they say, what they do to me, I'll never talk. Never betray my family. Will never give up any secrets or vital information about Emiliano *or* his businesses. I'd rather die.

I hear a whoosh right before I feel the sting of a slap against my cheek, and my head rears to the side from the sheer force of it. I don't make a sound though, and when I open my eyes, I see that it's a pissed off Maxim Sokolov—the Pakhan. He's staring daggers at me, his eyes intently on my face. He's probably concocting plans right about now, trying to do the math in his head, trying to figure out what will break me down. Well, it's going to take a fucking calculus class to figure me out, and he looks stupid as fuck. Definitely can't do math.

"The prince awakes," Sokolov says with a smirk. "And he's been crying. How fucking sweet. Tell me, Cole. Are you heartbroken over Matteo? Father *and* son. I have to give it to you, you have balls."

I tense, the urge to flinch strong, but I don't dare move. I can't show any fucking weakness, and he's probably going to try to fuck with my head before he kills me. I can only hope it's quick, but I doubt it. I won't get the same treatment I gave his son. No, I'll definitely be worse off. Much, much worse. Not that I was too kind to Andrey, considering I did slice him up, but at least I had mercy on him in the end.

"There are pictures, you know," he says, and this time I look at him with narrowed eyes. He's got a smile on his face, and I want to punch it clean off. But I can't move, so there goes that. "I might just send them to your precious Emiliano. How do you think it'll make him feel? You kissing his son?"

"Fuck you," I spit, because there's not much else I can do. I probably deserve it, even though I'd like to come clean on my own. I know my time to do that has passed. That ship has definitely sailed. Far, far away from me. "Do what you need to do."

"Oh, I will." He smirks. "Dmitri," he growls, directing his attention to one of the guards. "Take his ring."

My stomach drops straight down to my ass, and I swallow hard. Fuck, I hoped I could at least keep that. Hoped I could die with a piece of Emiliano on me, but no, he's taking that away from me. He's taking everything away. Em will probably hate me after he sees the pictures. Probably won't come for me now, but I deserve it. What did I expect anyway? Fucking forgiveness? I was so, so wrong, and now I've lost them both.

"Send it to Emiliano Colombo."

I clench my fist, but Dmitri finds a pressure point easily, making me open my hand. He slides the ring off with a finality that I feel in my very bones. It's over. Emiliano and I are done.

I'm going to die here.

CHAPTER 36
EMILIANO

I've looked everywhere, fucking everywhere. I searched the entire hotel. All the restrooms. My old penthouse, our new one. I searched the club. Giovanni's. He's nowhere to be found. The only explanation is that he was taken by the Russians, and I know where most of their warehouses are, but not all of them. I wonder if he's even in New York anymore. Something tells me they're not being sloppy with this, and it makes me even more nervous. What if he's dead by the time I get to him? What if I lose him? Fuck, just the thought of it makes me sick. Weak in the knees. And isn't that what I already am?

I fall to my knees and pull at my hair, refusing to cry any more than I already have. I have to be strong right now. I need to think clearly so I can get Cole back. But it's hard to see past the pain. It's impossible to not feel my heart breaking, splintering, shattering the longer he's not by my side.

My brothers sit on the sectional couch that Cole picked, and I inhale sharply to keep my tears at bay. Everything reminds me of him. He decorated this entire fucking place. What will I do if I lose him forever? Fuck, I don't know if I can live without him anymore. I don't know if I want to.

There's a ding at the elevator, and when I look toward it,

there's no one in it. Just a box. So I go and retrieve it before the door closes. It almost does, but I push it open once more, feeling like this is significant somehow. Like this small box matters. For whatever reason, I can't fucking explain. I just know it in my bones. Maybe there's a clue inside of it. Maybe—

When I open the box, the first thing I see is a note and Cole's engagement ring. My stomach drops at the implication, and a sob almost breaks free. Alessandro comes to stand next to me, offering his support by laying a hand on my shoulder, and my eyes sting. I don't know how I can be strong like this.

Alessandro takes the box from me, shuffling stuff around, and his face pales. He grabs the note and begins to read it, but I can barely hear it over the thundering of my heart in my ears. I only catch bits and pieces of it. Every other sentence.

There's nothing you can do.
He's going to die.
Don't even try to look for him.
You'll never find him.
Look at the pictures.
I'd say I feel sorry for you, but I don't.

Alessandro gasps, and I see what he's holding. Pictures. His face pales further, and he tries to put them back in the box, but I just yank them away from him. I wish I hadn't—because there's the evidence that my son didn't respect my relationship. That he took what he wanted, and that Cole gave it to him.

"*I'm going to talk to him,*" he tells me again. "*Whether you want me to or not. We both know he wants to, and I need to hear it from him, Dad. I need closure.*"

"What kind of closure?" I narrow my eyes at him. "Don't you dare—"

"*What?*" *He rolls his eyes.* "*Don't you dare kiss him? Fuck* him?" I bristle, and he smiles. "Don't worry, Dad. He's a loyal guy. I'm sure he wouldn't do that."

I nod. "He is."

"But it won't stop me," Matteo tells me, and I swear my stomach bottoms out. It's about to fall out of my ass. "I need this, Dad. It's the only way I can move on."

I've never hated my son before, but I do now. I have this visceral fucking need to end him. It feels like we're enemies now, and maybe we are. There's no way we can come back from this. At least not on my end. He fucked me over. He—

But isn't that what I did to him in the first place? Maybe I need to get off my fucking high horse. But it's hard to do it when I'm hurting this bad. I still want to hate him, and maybe I really do. Should I hate Cole too? He betrayed me more than my son did. I always suspected he was in love with Matteo as well, but this just proved it. He looks pained. Like his world is ending with a simple kiss. I don't know how to feel about it, but it triggers my possessiveness. It makes me want to chain him to me and never let him leave my side. He's mine, damn it. My love. My world. My fucking *husband*.

Mine.

"I think we should call Matteo," Alessandro says softly, as if trying not to spook me. Like I'm a wild animal, and maybe I am. Right now, I feel like one. I'm feral. "He's clearly the last one who saw him."

"No fucking way," I growl. "He's dead to me."

"You don't mean that," Alex soothes, but I shake my head. Because right now, I really do mean it. "He's your son."

"He fucked me over."

"You fucked him over, too," he reminds me, and I look at him with narrowed eyes. "Don't forget that."

"Show me the pictures," Giovanni says, and I shake my head. "Why the fuck not?"

"They're mine," I growl. "I'm going to fucking burn them."

Alessandro pulls out his cell phone, then presses it to his ear. I see. Fucking. Red. I'm just about to tackle him when Giovanni is suddenly holding me back. No. No. *No*.

"Matteo," Alessandro murmurs. "Cole's been taken."

There's a moment of silence in the room, but I hear Matteo clearly. He's breaking down. He's devastated. He's coming. I don't want to fucking see him. I can't do it. I'll fucking kill him. It's too fresh.

Alessandro hangs up, raising his hands in defeat, and I'm just about to deck him when Lorenzo comes to my other side and both Gio and him hold me back.

"What the fuck do you think you're doing?!" I scream, and Alessandro flinches. At least he's a little scared. Good, because he's not getting out of this one. No fucking way. "I fucking hate him, Alex! He's not coming to my home. Fuck no!"

"He's your son!" Alessandro says through gritted teeth. "He loves his best friend. He'll help us find him. Maybe he saw something. Maybe—"

But I don't hear anything he's saying—still stuck on *he loves his best friend*. How can I not be stuck on it? He gives it a whole new meaning. He's in love with Cole. In love with the love of my life. And I can't fucking stand it. As soon as he gets here, I'm beating his ass. Mark my fucking words.

My brothers let me go just as Alessandro goes to the couch, putting some much-needed distance between us. He looks wary of me, and good, he should be scared. I feel all this rage inside of me, and I'm going to let it out one way or another.

I pace the living room, back and forth, in front of my brothers for what feels like hours. No one dares to speak. No one addresses the elephant in the room. Not when Alessandro went back to the couch to sit down, and not when I put the pictures on my coffee table for all of my brothers to see. They don't dare say anything negative about Cole, and for that, I'm grateful. Even if I'm hurt, even if I'm dying inside, I don't want anyone to speak ill of him. That's where I draw the line, and I think my brothers know that. Even Alessandro isn't talking shit about him. Maybe they know I'm a quick trigger right now. They should know it was a bad idea to bring Matteo here.

I look down at my watch just as the elevator dings, signaling the arrival of my son. I tense, and suddenly Alessandro is taking quick strides toward me, but it's too late. I bring my arm back and punch Matteo in the face, hearing the crunch of bone. I think I broke his nose. Fucking good. He definitely deserves it. Fucking asshole.

"What the fuck, Dad—" Matteo hisses, straightening up and looking into my eyes. But then he seems to realize that I know something, because he smiles. He *smiles*. Blood smears over his lips as he does. "I guess I deserve that. But I warned you in advance, dear ol' Dad. I don't play fair. I play to win."

"Fuck you," I growl, and Alex comes to my side and holds my arm. "You need to get out of my house."

"It's Cole's home, too." He shrugs. "And he'd want me here. I'm not going anywhere until we find him."

"Why now?" I chuckle. "You said you were done with him. What kind of sick fucking game are you playing?"

"I'm not playing anything," Matteo says through gritted teeth. "I'm not here to try to get him to be with me. I'm here because I can't abandon him now. I want him out of my life—but not dead. *Never* that."

I get it. I really do. But it still doesn't change how I feel—jealous, murderous. I want to wring his neck and fucking destroy him. The urge to do so is strong, and it scares me, because I've never felt this way before, and certainly not towards my kid. I don't want to feel this way anymore. Maybe I need to accept that I fucked up just as much he did. But it's not the same. He wasn't in a relationship with Cole. I am. And he disrespected it. Stepped all over it. He knows no fucking boundaries, and if he does, he certainly doesn't respect them.

Fuck.

I don't know how to do this. How am I supposed to play nice while feeling this way? I think it's nearly impossible, and I don't know if I have it in me to try.

"I know you don't want me here, but I can help. Just let me help." He sighs, running a hand down his face in frustration, smearing blood all over himself. "He has to be in a safe house. We just have to figure out where before they kill him."

"They aren't going to." I shake my head quickly. "They can't. I'll kill them all—"

Matteo's eyebrows rise toward his hairline, and he looks at me in disbelief. As if he can't fathom the words coming out of my mouth. I realize I sound insane. They're definitely going to kill him, and fast. We have to find him. We have to—

"It's going to be okay, Dad," Matteo whispers. "I'll do everything I can to help us find him. I'll reach out to Natasha. I'll find out."

"She probably doesn't know anything."

"That's doubtful." He rolls his eyes. "She probably knows every move he makes."

"And how are you going to contact her?" I ask him, my brows furrowing. "I don't think I need to tell you that you can't show up unannounced."

"I have her phone number," he replies, and my stomach does a weird little flip. Fear. That's what I'm feeling.

I'm scared he's going to prefer her over me now that I fucked up our relationship. That he'll go to her from now on.

That she'll be there for him in ways that I can't be anymore. But don't I deserve that? I did it to myself.

"Okay." I sigh, hating this situation. Yet I'd do anything to find him, even if it's thanks to Matteo. "Thank you."

"I'm not doing it for you." Matteo scoffs, and my nostrils flare. "I'm doing it for him."

"I bet you are," I mutter.

Matteo moves toward the elevator and presses the button, then turns to look at me. "I'll be in touch, Dad." I nod once and his lips purse. "Oh, and just so you know…he loves me, too."

And with those parting words, he gets in the elevator and leaves.

"Fuck!" I roar, ready to destroy the entire place, but I can't because everything belongs to Cole, and I can't do that to him. I fall to my knees and bury my face in my hands, then mutter, "Fuck," again for good measure.

I don't know if I can take this.

Don't know if I can handle it.

I just want him back.

Need him back.

CHAPTER 37
COLE

I'm not sure how long I've been here; all I know is that I'm aching all over my body. My hands are still tied behind my back, my wrists raw, my shoulders in pain. Just how long are they going to keep me here before they kill me? I wish they would just get it over with. Instead, they've left me alone to rot. I haven't eaten or drank any water either. Maybe that means I haven't been here that long. How long can I survive without those essential things? Then again, it's possible this is my torture. Lack of food and water. I sure as fuck feel hungry and parched. I also feel like I could murder all of them.

I wish I could say I can't believe they sent the pictures to Emiliano, but then again, yes, I can. Sokolov is a piece of shit, and he's hitting Em exactly where it hurts. I bet he's also hoping no one comes for me, that no one looks for me. After all, I've lost everyone who has ever mattered to me. Emiliano and Matteo. Both of them. Man, I really went and fucked up my entire life. I doubt they care about me anymore, and I sure as hell know they won't be coming for me now. Not after everything I've done.

Matteo hates me because I'm with his dad. Now, Emiliano hates me because Matteo and I kissed. Matty probably told him about what I said in a moment of weakness, and that makes me hate him, too. Even if it's just a little. Then again, I don't want to die with hate in my heart, so I'm letting it go. I'm going to remember all the good memories as the life is snuffed out of my eyes. And it's going to happen. Sooner or later, I'm going to die here. In a musty fucking warehouse that smells like dead people.

I wonder how many people have died here. Something tells me it's a lot. The smell alone makes me gag, so I'm mouth-breathing. The concrete floor is caked with dried blood, and there are chains hanging from the ceiling. It's like a little dungeon here. *Lucky me*. Then there are the guards. There's a table on the other side of the room with six chairs, and all of them are occupied. Two guards are standing inside by the door, and it makes me wonder how many more are around outside. This is a mini fortress, and even if Emiliano came for me, he probably wouldn't get past them. So there's that. Only one thought circulates my brain right now—I'm going to die here.

I'm. Going. To. Die.

I should feel more fear than I actually do, and I can't deny I'm a bit scared, but I've also resigned myself to my reality. The only hope I have is that they don't drag it out. I'm weak, but they won't break me, which means I shouldn't have any hope. They'll make me suffer. And as I see Sokolov come into the warehouse, the doors closing behind him quickly, my stomach tightens with renewed fear. Yet I keep my face blank, devoid of any emotion. I won't fucking show weakness.

"Cole." Sokolov grins, dragging a chair to sit across from me. I look into his icy blue eyes and almost shudder, but I suppress the urge to. "Always a pleasure."

I grin, hiding the pain I'm feeling, and clench my fists to try to regain feeling in my hands. "Wish I could say the same about you."

"And you won't be saying that after today, either." He

shrugs, completely unaffected. As he should be. I have no power here. "You see, we're going to play with you for a little bit. Get some information out of you. But you won't die today. No, that would be a mercy."

If he only knew, I did have mercy on his son. But I don't say anything, just nod slowly.

"Nothing to say?" he asks with a smirk.

"I won't give you information," I reply, trying to shrug but failing to do so as pain shoots to my shoulder. "You should know better than that."

"Always so stubborn." He tuts. "I'll break you soon enough."

Doubtful.

But I stay quiet. I don't feel like pissing him off right now, not when I know he's able to take it out on me. That feeling is solidified as one of his men drags a metal basin toward me. Sokolov takes a couple of steps back and lets his bodyguard place the nasty thing in front of me, then puts a hose inside of it and begins to fill it with water.

No.

Fuck.

I swear to God, I don't have the fucking energy for this. Maybe I'll just let them drown me. That could get me out of this shitty situation. Yeah, I think that's exactly what I'll do. Maybe if I inhale a lungful of water, I can put myself out of my misery. Then again, I know he won't make it that easy for me. He'll torture me for a while—really lay it on thick. I can't even be mad about it. I did this to myself, and I knew exactly what I was getting into when I killed Andrey. I was aware of the possibilities when I sliced him up, and I was aware of them when I shot him in the head. Deep down, I think I knew this day would come. I thought I'd feel ready—instead, all I feel is regret.

Regret that I didn't make better choices. Regret that I

didn't say *I love you* one last time. Just...*regret*. I look up toward the ceiling and try to regulate my breathing, as I hear the ominous whoosh of the water filling the basin I tell myself that it's all going to be okay. All I can hope for is that Emiliano doesn't hate me too much. But even I know that it's a far-fetched dream. I'll hang onto it, though. I'll take that dream to my shallow grave and bury myself with it. It's all I have left. A shred of hope.

"Chain him," Sokolov mutters, and my head snaps down, my chin to my chest.

My nostrils flare as I look around, watching as the man unsnaps the wrist restraints and opens them from the chains. Someone comes to me from behind, cutting off my zip ties from my wrists, and undoing the rope from my torso. I can breathe again—finally—but I try not to get too excited. I won't be breathing for long. Not now that the hose has stopped, and the basin is full, the water almost sloshing over.

The guard who untied me comes to my front, my hands falling forward, but I feel too weak to move them. I can't feel them, anyway. It's also too crowded here to try to get smart right now. No, I won't try anything. I'll just take my punishment like a man and die with honor. Which is why when they haul me up and out of the chair, I give my best attempt at walking. My knees buckle multiple times, but he just drags me toward the chains hanging from the ceiling, as if I'm not inconveniencing him in the slightest.

I stand upright as he snaps the wrist restraints on, and then I let go and let my body hang. My shoulders scream in pain, my hands tingling, but at least I feel something. Yet I bet I won't want to feel anything in a minute, if the whip Sokolov is holding is any indication. He paces circles around me, and when he's in front of me, he snaps the whip against his hand softly. I don't even flinch, and it bothers him. I've never been flogged before, and the thought of it is terrifying, but there's nothing I can do about it anymore, so I'm not going to sit here and cry.

"Here's how this is going to go," Sokolov says as he looks into my eyes. His icy blue orbs peer into my soul, and I wonder if he can taste my fear. Maybe he can, because he grins widely and nods. "I'm going to ask you some questions, and you're going to answer them. If you don't, I'll have to whip you."

"Might as well get started." I sigh. "I'm not telling you shit."

"Where is warehouse number seven?" he asks, his tone laced with curiosity. "And what do you store there?"

"I don't know," I lie.

Sokolov grins and comes around to my back, and I hear the crack of the whip before it lands on my skin. It's a deep burn, a different kind of pain, but I bite my bottom lip and keep my grunt in. I refuse to show weakness. I fucking refuse.

"Who's the accountant of The Pink Pony Club?" he asks.

"What the fuck don't you understand? I'm not going to talk," I say through gritted teeth, and he chuckles like it's the funniest thing he's ever heard.

"Very well," he whispers, and then I'm being flogged again.

And again.

And again.

He spends more time asking questions I refuse to answer, and before I know it, my back feels raw. I can feel the blood running down my skin, and when I hear the crack of the whip against my flesh once more, I flinch and stand up on my tiptoes. He laughs loudly and does it again, and I hold back a scream. My bottom lip is bloody and bruised, abused from biting on it, but I'm not going down without a fucking fight. Quite frankly, the pain from my mouth grounds me, and for a split second I can ignore the one on my back. But it's short-lived, because that pain is worse.

"You really are stubborn, aren't you?" He doesn't sound put out by my silence at all, but he finally stops. "What is it going to take for you to talk?"

"Me with no pulse," I reply with a grin. "Maybe I'll haunt you from my grave."

"Who said you'll have a grave?" He comes around to face me and grins. "No, Cole. You're going in the river where no one will ever find you. Not your precious Emiliano, or your dear Matty."

I frown at the mention of Matteo's nickname, suddenly wondering how he knows about it. He must sense the confusion, or maybe he sees it on my face, because his grin widens.

"I know everything about you," he says slowly. "I know your stepfather beat your mom to death, just like I know Emiliano killed him. This is common knowledge. It's no wonder you fell in love with *Matty*. He was the only one there for you, wasn't he?"

I'm quiet, but he's not wrong, and he knows it.

"Maybe I've been doing this all wrong." He sighs. "I'll have to take him and find out. Make him scream real pretty for me. What do you think?"

"Don't you dare fucking touch him," I say through gritted teeth.

"Possessive." Sokolov laughs, "I wonder how Emiliano feels about that."

I flinch, and he just laughs harder.

Anger bubbles up inside of me, and I stand on my toes again. I swear to God, if he comes any closer, I'll kick his face in. I don't give a fuck if I dislocate my shoulders in the process. It's over for me, anyway.

Pain shoots down my back as I move, and I wince. He sees

it and smiles, but then turns away from me, looking for something.

"You," he yells, pointing at a guard. "Let him down and take him to the water."

I begin to shake with fear. I can't help it.

My teeth begin to chatter, clacking together painfully, and when the guard lets me down and my skin pulls taut as my arms fall down to my sides, I have to blink away the tears in my eyes. Maybe if I cry under the water, they won't notice. Yeah, that's what I'll do. Right before I inhale it.

Goodbye, world.

It was a good run. But I'm tired now.

The urge to sob as the guard pushes me down to my knees in front of the basin is strong, but I inhale deeply and keep the tears at bay once more. Sokolov stands across from me, waiting patiently as the guard places my body over the lip of the basin, grabbing onto my hair roughly, and I don't even struggle. I just let it happen.

The fight has left my body.

"Are you sure you have no answers?" Sokolov asks once more.

"I'm sure," I say through gritted teeth, looking down into the murky water.

My head is pushed down into the water, my upper body following, and this time I let myself scream from the pain of the wounds on my back. My tears mix with the water, and I swallow some of it right before I'm yanked up, not being given the chance to try to drown myself.

Shame.

It's a fucking shame.

I cough and sputter as I break the surface once more, and Sokolov laughs. I hear the guards chuckling in the background too, and I close my eyes and inhale deeply right before I'm pushed under the water once more.

This time I make sure to inhale, letting water go deep into my lungs. But not without some regrets.

I'm sorry Em.
Sorry for everything.
Sorry for not being strong enough.

CHAPTER 38
EMILIANO

It's been exactly forty hours since Cole was taken, and I haven't slept a fucking wink. Matteo said that Natasha was going to give him the information on one condition—that she come to us in person to discuss it. At my penthouse. My fucking home. I almost called it off, almost told him to tell her to go fuck herself. I don't want her to know where I live, what my space looks like. I don't want her to see the life Cole and I have built, but I'm desperate. My strength is waning with every hour that passes, and something tells me that Cole is closer to death than he was yesterday. If he's not already dead.

I can't fucking stand it—the thoughts swirling through my mind the longer he's gone. I've never felt this weak in my entire life. But isn't that what love does to you? Makes you weak? Fucked up? It sure as hell is making me feel that way. What if Natasha is secretly against us? What if she tries to kill us? It's not like she's ever cared about Matteo. She has never reached out to try to get in contact with him. Has never even asked about how he's doing. She just…disappeared.

Here she is, though, on her way to my home, probably happy about the fact that I'm fucking falling apart at the seams. Matteo is pacing my living room, I'm standing near the elevator, and my brothers are just lounging on the couch like they own it. As if my life isn't falling apart. They're the picture of calm. I've considered that maybe they're doing this on purpose, to keep me calm, but it just pisses me off even more. I want them to share my pain, not appear nonchalant. But I know that's a big ask. They're probably pissed at him for hurting me. And I *am* hurt. Probably beyond repair.

I don't know what's going to happen to us once I rescue him. But I have to go get him. I can't just let him die. At the end of the day, he is the love of my life, even if I'm not his. I can't deny that I've already been mourning him. I've been in bed, unable to get up to shower or eat. I'm weak. I know I need to get my shit together now that Natasha is coming with information, but it's hard to do when it feels like my world is in shambles.

If it weren't for Alessandro staying with me this whole time, I don't know what I would've done. While he hasn't been able to force me to shower or shove the food he makes down my throat, he has been understanding and compassionate. He has treated me like he knows what it feels like to have his heart broken, and yet that can't be right. He has never had a partner before. Not anyone that I'm aware of. Yet he has sat with me on the couch with my head on his lap, fingers threading through my hair as he soothes me when I sob. It's almost like when we were children all over again. He was always the one taking care of me instead of the other way around. Sometimes I think he should've been the eldest. Should've been the head of this family. But I got stuck with something I've never wanted, and now here I am. With nothing left.

None of it matters. This empire doesn't matter to me, especially not if I can't share it with Cole. I used to think my businesses and Matteo were all I needed in my life. I wasn't happy, but I was content with it all. Resigned. But I was wrong—so very, very wrong. None of it makes sense without him anymore. Maybe I'll retire and move away. Cut my losses, take my money, and disappear. God knows it'll destroy me to see him with my son again, and isn't that what he wants? Fuck, that kiss was telling. He can deny it all he wants, but I saw it. My eyes have been opened. Not to mention what my son said to me.

He loves me too.

I should've known it wasn't one-sided. That he reciprocated Matteo's feelings. Now that I know...I can't forget about it. I don't know how to move on from it. Don't know how to live with this knowledge. All I can hope for is that he's alive and can be happy with whoever he chooses, even if it's not me.

My buzzer is loud, telling me Natasha is here, and just for the briefest of moments, I hesitate. I remember her twenty years ago and how beautiful and nice she was, but that image crumbled the moment she handed over our child. And now what? She wants to come play house? Fuck that and fuck her. But I can't deny that I need her. In this moment, I'll let go of my pride and worry about the end result. Getting Cole back. She has information; she told Matteo as much before he invited her here. So I'm going to shove my ego way down deep and give her a chance.

I let her in, and a moment later, she appears in my elevator. My brothers are quiet as she steps into the penthouse, and I look over at Matteo to see his reaction. His eyes are wide as he takes in his mother in the flesh, and she smiles softly at him. She looks almost the same, as if she's only aged a few years rather than two decades. Her white-blonde hair is loose down her back, styled with curls, and she's wearing a tan wool coat around her form, clad with stilettos. Some things never change.

Natasha seems completely unbothered by the fact that her father is going to die. In fact, she seems eager for it. Which I guess makes sense. She probably hasn't been treated well over the years. He forced her to marry some creep, for fuck's sake. A man older than her by thirty years, who she was engaged to since she was a fucking child. Disgusting. I thank my lucky stars that I don't have a daughter. I'd probably have a lot of men jumping at the chance of an arranged marriage.

Matteo walks toward her and engulfs her in a hug, her small form almost disappearing between his arms. She's tall but slender, and I can't deny that a lump forms in my throat at the sight. I don't know why I suddenly feel emotional, but if my son wants this—wants her in his life—then I have to be supportive. I guess she's not too bad if she's helping me get my fiancé back. Then again, maybe she's only helping us because Matteo loves Cole. Not because of me. Yeah, that would make more sense.

She pulls away from his hug and smiles up at him, then turns on her heel and faces me. Her smile widens, and she comes to me and gives me a hug, too. She smells like flowers, smells so wrong, but I hug her back because it feels like I have to. I've never hated her, not really. She gave me the best gift I could've ever asked for. My son.

"Natasha," I say softly as she pulls away from me. "Thanks for coming."

She nods. "Well, my son called me, and I couldn't say no."

I almost ask her when she's ever cared about him, but I bite my tongue until I taste blood. Now is not the time to question her. Now is the time to get information out of her. *Swallow your fucking pride.*

"Do you know where he is?" Matteo asks, and she turns toward all of us. "Did you find him?"

"Of course I did." She grins. "Or I wouldn't be here."

"And what do you get out of it?" I ask her, raising an eyebrow. "Why are you helping us?"

"Besides wanting to see him dead?" She frowns. "He's a piece of shit. It's time for someone new to take over."

"And who will that be?" I hope it's not her fucking husband, or I'll have to kill him too.

"My husband wants nothing to do with it. He's getting old." She shrugs, as if reading my mind. "My father's business partner will be taking over. He is younger, and my father has been training him for this since Andrey died."

"So, he basically knows nothing." I nod slowly. "Andrey only died a month ago."

"He's capable, and he's been working with my father for a very long time." She tells me, looking around the room at my brothers. "He's going to help us with his men, under one condition."

I stiffen at that. "What is it?"

"One of your brothers has to marry his son."

My brothers all burst out laughing; everyone but Alessandro. Instead, he narrows his eyes at her. She can't be fucking serious right now.

"You're joking," I chuckle, but she seems serious.

"Those are the terms for his help." Natasha shrugs. "His men can take down my father's men. Easily."

"We'll bring our own men, too," I tell her, and she nods.

"Good." She smiles. "Then what's it going to be?"

"*Fuck*," Alessandro mutters, and I look at him. He has a look of determination on his face. "I'll do it."

There's a moment of collective silence as everyone in the room turns to look at him, and Natasha's eyes crinkle in the corners as her smile turns into a grin.

"Good choice," she says, "He's young. Twenty-four. Really pretty."

"I don't care." Alessandro shrugs. "He's just a husband."

"No." She shakes her head. "There will be a contract. You will consummate the marriage, and you will be monogamous. Petrov doesn't play around. He will look after his son."

"Fine," Alex says through gritted teeth. "I accept the terms. Now, can we get on with it? I feel like bashing someone's head in."

"Very well." Natasha nods. "I'll tell you everything you need to know."

"Will you be coming with us?" I ask, genuinely curious. Will she face her father and tell him she was our mole? I really want to know.

"Yes." She nods once again. "I will be by your side."

I look over at Matteo and find him smiling at his mother, and I almost roll my eyes. But I can't even deny how relieved I feel she has information.

"He's not in a warehouse," Natasha starts. "He's in a safe house in upstate New York. He's secluded, and no one would know where he is, except father texted me to let me know he'd be there. He offered for me to go with him, and I declined. He didn't think anything of it. That was his first mistake."

I nod, urging her to continue with my hand.

"There are twenty guards. Ten of them surrounding the perimeter, and ten inside. We will need all the men we can get."

"Done," I reply. "I have one condition."

"I'm helping you, and you have conditions?" Natasha raises an eyebrow, but she seems amused instead of annoyed. "You've always been funny."

I ignore her comment. "I kill your father."

She thinks this over and nods. "Fine."

Well, that was easy. I definitely didn't expect that.

An hour later, I've gathered all my men and have them get into vehicles. Luca is driving me and my brothers, and we even pull up the third row seating for Matteo and Natasha. I want them to be protected with us. This vehicle has tinted and bullet-proof windows, and I've realized I can never be too careful. Who knows if she's tipped him off? What if Sokolov knows we're coming? What if this is all a trap? She has no reason to help us. None.

Except for Matteo.

Swallow your fucking pride.

We pulled up about two miles from the safe house, which is in the middle of nowhere, and now we're on foot wading through the woods. Thankfully, we're wearing snow gear, because we're knee-deep in white powder. I fucking hate the snow. But I'd do anything for Cole, so I suck it up and don't complain. I don't say a fucking word as I lead the way, with Luca at my side and Matteo right behind us. I look back and see Natasha is flanked by Petrov's men, and I let out a deep breath.

Fuck, I'm nervous. I can't help it. We're about to storm into a house with twenty men. One of us might die, and I can only hope it's not one of my brothers. At least if I die, I know Matteo will take care of Cole. I try not to think of that, though, mostly because it makes me murderous all over again, and my son has been helpful in helping us find him.

We're completely silent as we slowly make our way toward the house, the only sounds being loud breathing and the crunch of our boots in the snow. My feet are cold and cramping despite me having great boots, but I try to ignore it as best as I can. After about an hour of walking, we finally make it to the edge of the house. I can see the guards surrounding it, and a shiver runs down my spine. The trees are all dead with no leaves, so really, we barely have any cover. They'll notice us soon, which means we have to be ready.

"We need to split up," I whisper and look back, and Matteo nods slowly. "Some of us take the front, the others take the back. We can't let them escape."

"Done," Matteo whispers back.

My men and Matteo follow me through the woods and toward the side of the house, and Petrov's men go toward the back, along with Natasha. I don't focus on them anymore, though, instead we make our way out of the woods and toward the guards on the side of the house. I pull out my handgun with the silencer and shoot one of them in the head, and he falls over. The guy he was talking to is stunned into silence, and when he looks up at me, I shoot him too.

We stealthily press our bodies to the side of the house, and Luca leads the way. He's at the edge of the home and looks over, then nods. We storm the three guards, shooting them all. One of them doesn't die, and he shoots back until Luca is hit and slumps over.

Fuck.

No.

Not Luca.

I drag him to the side of the house and see he's been shot on his left shoulder, which is better than I thought, and he just shakes his head at me.

"Keep going," he says through gritted teeth. "I'll be fine."

I nod. "You," I say through gritted teeth, directing my attention to one of the men behind me. One of my men. "Stay with him. Protect him with your life. If he dies, I'll have your fucking head."

He nods quickly, then comes to Luca's side, standing beside him with his gun at his side. We hurry along, walking to the door, and I look back at my men. At Matteo. There's a look of determination in his eyes; they're cold and narrowed. His jaw is set, and I know he's as ready as he's going to get, but I ask anyway.

"Ready?" I search his face for signs of doubt, but there's nothing.

"Let's do this," he replies.

Just like that, I open the door to the house, and we're greeted with utter silence. There is no one here. Not one fucking soul. I look around the house and notice the living room first, but I barely glance at it. I'm a man on a mission, and I don't have the time to take it all in. I'm in search of something, anything, that will lead me to Cole. When I finally find a set of stairs that lead to the bottom of the house, I signal my men to halt.

There, at the bottom of the stairs, right in front of a door, are two guards. I shoot one in the chest, and he shoots back, missing me but getting one of my men. He falls to the ground with a loud thud, and I curse, shooting the other guard manning the door in the head this time.

Fucking hell.

They probably already heard us, and when I look back, I see Natasha beside Matteo and all of Petrov's men behind us. My brothers come to stand right behind me, and I lead the way down the steps. Once we make it to the bottom, I hold my breath and open the door. Loud music is blaring from some speakers, and I realize they probably don't even know we're here. So I hurry inside, my brothers flanking me, and we quickly begin to shoot.

I find Sokolov sitting on a chair right in front of Cole, who is hanging from the ceiling by chains clasped over his wrists. He stiffens when the shootout begins, but I don't have time to look back and see what's happening. No, I go directly to Sokolov, who's pulling out a gun from his holster and aiming it at me.

"I wouldn't do that if I were you," I say with a smile. "It won't end well."

"No, what won't end well is this." He gestures toward Cole. "Him."

"Kill him and I'll bury you alive," I reply through gritted teeth.

He grins. "Worth it."

Sokolov turns toward Cole, pointing the gun, and I shoot him in the head. Unfortunately, his gun goes off right before he falls to the ground, and I notice the bullet hole in Cole's right side of his chest. There's utter silence, and then Matteo screams. I run towards Cole, and his eyes widen as he looks at me.

"Em," he whispers. "*Em*."

"It's okay, Cole," I whisper, unclasping his hands from the chains, and he falls into me. I hold him up, barely. He's dead weight. "You're going to be okay."

But I realize that may not be true. He's bleeding profusely, bleeding all over me, and I yell for my brothers to get the car to us. Matteo and I carry Cole up the stairs and out of the house together, and once we're in the car, I press my hand to his wound with a blanket. He's freezing, his skin cold, and he's also shivering.

"Fuck, don't do this to me," Matteo says from the front seat, but Cole's in and out of consciousness, not aware of anything surrounding him. "Cole! Snap the fuck out of it!"

My nostrils flare as he talks to my man. My everything. But I don't snap at him; instead, I press a kiss to Cole's cheek. I turn his head slightly and lean in, whispering in his ear.

"You're so strong, baby." My throat tightens, and tears start welling in my eyes. I breathe through them. "You're going to make it out of this. Don't you dare fucking leave me. I *need* you."

My driver speeds up as I tell him we need to get to the

nearest hospital right fucking now. Matteo already spoke to one of the surgeons and offered him an astronomical amount of money to operate on Cole. We're paying for his discretion, and he agreed. The only thing Cole needs to do is hang on.

"Only a couple more miles, Cole," I say soothingly, pressing my hand harder against his wound, and he groans, his eyes rolling to the back of his head. He's still in and out, his face pale, sweat running down his temple. "Hang on for me. *Please*."

We finally pull up to the hospital, and Matteo and I jump out of the car. Suddenly, we're swarmed by nurses who put him on a stretcher quickly and lead him inside. We run after them, but we're led into a waiting room. I don't pay attention to anything except for one of the recliners, and I sit down with my face in my hands, letting myself finally break down.

He's probably not going to make it out of this.

He was shot in the chest.

He could fucking die.

I wouldn't be able to live with myself if he dies. It would be my fault. We were sloppy. We should've had a better plan. It's at this moment that I wish I hadn't killed Sokolov so quickly. I wish I could've made him suffer more than I did. The way he died was fucking merciful and painless. I fucking hate it. He deserved worse than that. Cole deserved more from me.

"You really do love him, don't you?" Matteo asks softly from his chair across the room.

I look up at him, making eye contact. "Yes."

He nods. "I can tell."

I take a deep breath and try to calm myself down, to no avail. What I'm about to say goes against everything I feel, but I can't be selfish right now. If Cole survives this, he'd be getting a second chance at life.

"What you said to me about him loving you…" I shake

my head, trying to snap out of it. "If he wants to be with you after this, I won't stand in the way. I'll let you have him."

Matteo shakes his head. "He didn't even notice me standing beside you, Dad," he says sadly. "He called for you. You're the one he wants."

My heart flutters in my chest, because yes, he did. In his weakest moment, he called for me. "I'm just letting you know, still."

"I appreciate that," he replies, "but he already chose you."

"I don't know, son." I shake my head. "Death can really put things into perspective. Maybe he changed his mind."

"I doubt it." He sighs, running a hand down his face. "He's yours, Dad."

"Will you come around, Matteo?" I ask, a lump forming in my throat. "Will you go to therapy with me?"

"Yes, I'll go to therapy with you."

I deflate, relief filling me to bursting. "Thank you. I won't let you down again."

"You can't ask for the world, though." And I know I can't. I really hurt him. "I don't think I can go to your wedding."

"I understand."

"Cole won't." He chuckles. "He's fucking stubborn. He'll want me there."

"I'll talk to him." I sigh. "If he even makes it out of this."

"Don't say that," Matteo snaps. "He has to make it out of this."

He does, doesn't he? I can't imagine a world without my Cole in it. I never saw him as more than my son's best friend, not until he got out of prison, but I can't deny I've always cared for him. And how couldn't I? He's... him. Cole lights up every room he enters. He's the life of the party.

And now? He's everything I could've ever asked for. He's everything I need. I love him so much, it's incapacitating. I can't even blame Matteo for loving him, too. What's not to love?

"You're right." I run a hand through my hair and lean back in my chair, closing my eyes. "He does have to make it out of this."

The nurse comes in right then, sitting across from us, and her face says it all. She doesn't have great news. Fuck.

My heart drops, my stomach flips, and I bite the inside of my cheek to keep from crying out. I have to be strong for Cole and for my son. I can't be the one to break down. Not right now. Not again.

"His heart stopped twice during surgery," she says, and my breath catches in my throat. "We were able to get it restarted, thankfully. He's almost done. They're just stitching him up right now. He'll be going to the ICU right after, and he'll recover there. Only one person will be able to stay with him."

I nod. "It will be me."

Matteo scoffs, but I don't give a fuck. Cole needs me, and he's with me. Until he wakes up and tells me he doesn't want me anymore, he's still mine. I really don't care what Matteo has to say about it.

I *can't* care.

All that matters is Cole.

CHAPTER 39
COLE

I open my eyes to find myself in a bright room with white walls. I blink repeatedly, trying to make sense of where I am. The last thing I remember is being in that place with Sokolov—what looked like a basement. I can still smell the death in that room, even though I'm clearly not there anymore. Can still feel the way he whipped me, the way I woke up with water coming out of my mouth and nose as they pumped my chest. I should've known they wouldn't have mercy on me and let me drown myself.

I turn my head to look around the room, just to notice Emiliano sitting at the side of the bed, his cheek resting on the firm mattress. There are purple bags under his eyes, and one of his hands is curled up in my blankets. I try to move and wince, the pain in my chest debilitating.

Sokolov shot me.

He fucking shot me.

I shouldn't even be surprised; he did tell me he was going to kill me, but I didn't think he'd have enough time to pull the trigger once Emiliano got to him. All I remember is the shot ringing out and the burning pain in my chest. Then everything went dark and fuzzy around the edges. I was so cold. So, so cold. But Emiliano was steadfast in his faith. He had faith in me. That I would pull through. I still remember the way he encouraged me in the car. I don't remember much else, but I'll always remember that.

I try to speak but wheeze instead. Fuck, my throat is so dry, and it hurts like a bitch. I close my eyes and take a deep breath, trying to swallow, but failing to do so. It takes me another minute to compose myself, to gather enough strength to try again.

"Em," I whisper, then try to clear my throat. He stirs, and I thread my fingers through his hair softly. He seems to like that, nuzzling closer to me, until he realizes what's going on and wakes with a start. My hand falls to the side as he sits straight up and looks at me with parted lips. "Water, please."

"*Cole.*"

I stare expectantly, and he snaps out of it, helping me with the cup. Fuck, I feel useless. I can't remember the last time I needed someone to help me this way. Maybe never.

Emiliano places the cup back on the side table after a few sips, and I try to sit up, which is a horrible idea. The wounds on my back pull tighter, and my chest is on fire. He seems to get the idea, though, and raises me to a sitting position with the button on the side. I sigh in relief as I finally get into the position I want to be in, but wince in pain when I try to move.

There's suddenly a knock at the door, and a nurse comes in with a bright smile. She looks way too happy to be here, something I'm definitely not, but I don't want to be grumpy with her, so I swallow down my comment and look over at Em. He's frowning as he looks at me, and I frown right back. Why is he so upset? Did something else happen? I grab his hand and hold it just as the nurse comes to the other side of the bed and checks the bags hanging from the hook.

Nurse Molly asks me if I'm in pain, which I obviously say yes to, and she scans the pain medication vial and asks for my name and date of birth. She goes through the motions rather quickly, and when she's finally done, she tells me to press the call light button if I need her. We're left alone a moment later, the silence suffocating, and I look at Emiliano's face. What I see almost breaks me. His face is red, his eyes watery as he looks at me. But there's so much pain in his eyes that I know it's not just about me being here. No, this is about Matteo.

I nod slowly, squeezing his hand once, and say, "I'm sorry."

"You hurt me," he says without hesitation. "You really fucking hurt me."

My eyes sting as I look at him, but I don't make excuses for myself. "I'm so sorry, Em. I made a mistake—"

"You love him, Cole." He shakes his head. "How is that a mistake?"

I shake my head too now. "What I feel for him will never be what I feel for you. I'm in love with you. I'll always choose *you*."

"But—"

"No," I plead, begging him to understand. "Please don't do this. Don't."

"I have to." His voice cracks. "You deserve the chance to be with him."

"I don't fucking want to be with him!" I yell, getting frustrated. "Can't you see it's always been you? It will always be you! I want to marry you. Please, don't leave me."

"Cole—"

"No. Please," I beg again. "Please, don't do this. If you leave me now, I won't survive it."

He's quiet, but his eyes don't stray from my face.

"If you leave me, it will all be for nothing." At this, a tear slips down his cheek. He wipes it angrily, as if it's offended him. "I won't be with him either way."

"Why not?" Emiliano asks, his frown deepening.

"I want to be with you," I reiterate. "I choose *you*. Always."

Emiliano makes a tortured sound at the back of his throat and drops his forehead to the mattress, his shoulders shaking. I thread my fingers through his hair and stroke it gently, hoping he can sense how much I love him from one act alone.

"It's you," I tell him again. "It will always only ever be you."

"Are you sure?" he asks me.

"Positive." I smile, and he must hear it in my voice because he lifts his head and looks at me. He looks defeated, and I fucking hate it. "Everything is going to be okay."

"Is the wedding still on?" he asks with a soft voice, and I grin.

"Yes, husband." And I can't fucking wait. "A spring wedding."

At this, he does smile. *Finally*. His tired eyes crinkle in the corners and my stomach flips as if I'm on a rollercoaster.

God, I really love him more than anything.

It's been a few days since we came home, and Emiliano has been watching my every move. I'm still weak and bed bound, but at least I'm in my own bed. While the hospital was accommodating, I was eager to get out of there. The only upside to being there was the pain medication, but our doc has me on the good shit, anyway. I'm still in a lot of pain, but it's dull now. One little detail no one told me about was that my back has over one hundred stitches on it. At least they're dissolvable. I'm still angry that Sokolov managed to mark me for the rest of my life, that he had the power to do so in the first place, but at least Emiliano doesn't seem repulsed by it. Instead, he's been fawning over me as if I can't do anything on my own. And maybe I really can't—but I wouldn't know since I haven't tried. He'll have to let me soon enough.

Another little detail I'm not particularly happy about is that I have to wait six weeks for sex, and knowing Emiliano, he'll force me to wait the full six weeks. He won't put me in danger, even if I want it so fucking bad. I've been so damn horny, and it doesn't help that he's looking absolutely edible. A little rugged with the beginnings of a beard, and I fucking love it. He looks like a fucking snack, and I definitely want to devour him. But apparently I won't be doing that.

I also heard that the reason for my rescue was thanks to Natasha, and here I wanted to kill her. I kind of still do. She's a shit mom, and Emiliano has been inside of her, which means I hate her on principle alone. But since she technically saved my life, I guess I'll have to be nice. For Matteo's sake. Not that he's around. I haven't seen him at all since the basement. It's probably delusional of me to think so, but I thought that after my near death experience, he'd come around to speak to me. And I don't know? Apologize for how we left things? I don't fucking know anymore. It hurts that he hasn't come to see me. Of all the people I wanted by my side during my recovery, he sits high on the list. Oh, who am I kidding? He sits at number two.

That's probably the only reason I've been texting him like crazy. He hasn't replied to any of my one hundred text messages, and it stings. I know the way things ended between us wasn't ideal, but I thought being on death's door would've brought him back to me. I just need him back in my life—as a friend. I have to tell him how I feel, and hope that he can forgive me and move on—by my side. I know that's probably far-fetched. It doesn't stop me from hoping, though. And hope is a dangerous thing.

Emiliano comes into the room with a frown on his face, and my eyebrows rise all the way to my hairline. I haven't seen him this upset since we were at the hospital, and I can't help but wonder—

"What's wrong?" I ask him, and he sighs, coming to sit next to me on the bed. I'm sitting up, which is hurting my back, and he looks at me with narrowed eyes.

"You should be lying down." Em dodges my question, and it doesn't go unnoticed.

I comply, if only to get information out of him and lie down. "Happy?" I grin.

"Much happier," he says dryly. "Someone's here to see you."

My heart begins to pound in my chest as I hear Matteo's name come from his lips, but I can barely hear anything else he's saying. My nostrils flare as I take in a deep breath, and my heart rate goes down slightly.

"I trust you, Cole," Emiliano says softly, a sad look in his eyes. "Don't make me regret it."

I shake my head quickly. "I won't."

He nods, then exits the room quickly, leaving the door open. I assume Matty is going to come in here now, and my heart begins to beat wildly in my chest all over again.

A few moments later, Matteo comes into the room, closing the door behind himself. My stomach flips when he walks closer to me, but he still stays a couple of feet away. There's a lump in my throat that I can't swallow past, and all I know is that I want this distance between us obliterated.

"Come here, Matty."

His eyes widen at the nickname, and he shakes his head. "I can't." But even as his voice breaks, he takes another step toward me, and then another, until I can touch him if I reach out.

"On the bed, please," I say softly, trying to convince him,

and he looks indecisive for all of a few seconds before he toes off his shoes and lies down next to me. I flip over and get closer, his head on Em's pillow as he turns his body to face me. He reaches out, about to touch my face, but then his hand drops to his side. I shake my head. "Don't."

"Don't what?"

"Don't treat me differently," I whisper. "Don't stop what you were going to do."

Matteo looks conflicted, but then he reaches out to brush some hair away from my forehead, and my eyes flutter closed at the contact. "You can't do that, Cole. Not anymore," he says.

"Do what?" I frown, confused.

"Act like you love when I touch you."

I nod, but still, I reach out and brush my knuckles over his cheek. "Why didn't you answer me?"

"I needed time." He shrugs. "I can't—" His voice breaks. "I can't just come every time you call. You chose him."

"That doesn't mean I don't want you in my life, Matty." My chest tightens as he searches my eyes, and he nods slowly. "I need you in my life."

"I don't know if I can be your friend, Cole." Matteo sighs. "I just—love you so much."

"I know." My voice cracks, too. "And I'm so fucking sorry."

"I know you are."

Matteo gets closer until we're sharing breath, then tilts his head up and kisses my forehead. I close my eyes at the contact.

"I don't want you out of my life," I tell him, and he stiffens. "Please. Just—please don't go."

"I don't know what to do, Cole," he replies with a frown. "I don't know how to stop feeling this way. I don't think I can watch you with my dad."

"I know." I nod quickly. "I'm an asshole for asking this of you. But it doesn't take away from the fact that I mean every word. I want you in my life, and I'm not giving up. I'm not giving *you* up."

Matteo nods too now. "Baby steps."

"I can agree to that," I say quickly, feeling hope bloom inside of me for the first time in so long. "Anything you want."

"I won't be coming to the wedding."

I sigh. "Alright."

"It can't be the way it used to be."

"Why the fuck not?" I snap, and he has the audacity to chuckle.

"I was too codependent on you, Cole."

"Okay." I can't help but agree, if only to keep him in my life. I'd do anything at this point. "I can agree to your terms."

"Great."

Matteo smiles at me, and his eyes light up in a way they haven't in a long time. I can't deny he looks like shit. Hair longer than usual, purple bags under his eyes, a permanent frown on his face, but he's beautiful. Inside and out. I've missed him so fucking much. So I just stare at him, hoping like hell we can be the friends we've always been, even if he said we won't be.

I'm holding onto hope, regardless.

CHAPTER 40
EMILIANO

SIX WEEKS LATER

I t's been six weeks since Cole came home from the hospital. Six weeks of worrying that he'd change his mind about me. Matteo hasn't been around since the last time he came to see Cole, and I'm kind of grateful for it. We've been going to family therapy once per week for the past month, and I know these things take time, but I thought I'd see a difference in his demeanor sooner. Turns out he still hates me. I don't blame him, I'd hate me, too. Sometimes I do hate myself for what I've done to him. But then I come home to Cole and I can't feel anything but happiness. I know I'm selfish, but I've never claimed to be anything else.

Today is the day Cole was physically cleared by the doctor to resume normal activities, which means he has expectations. I plan to meet every single one. I'm ready to fuck him into the mattress, and as he comes out of the bathroom completely naked, I can't help but admire him. He's beautiful. Golden skin on display for me, his half-hard cock hanging heavily between his legs. My mouth waters at the thought of what I want to do to him, and he smirks knowingly.

Cole walks toward me with purpose, climbing onto the

bed and straddling me. I hold his hips in a bruising grip, knowing I can be as rough as I want now. Though the thought isn't appealing today. No, I want nice and slow, gentle. I want him to remember this moment for the rest of his life. I want him to dream about it.

He grinds his ass over my cock, giving it life, and I harden immediately. I want inside him right now, but more than that, I want him down my throat. I want to smell him, taste him, feel him. I want it all with him. So I grab him by the hips and hoist him up until he's straddling my chest instead. His cock bobs in front of my face, the slippery crown touching my lips. I lick him, wanting a taste, and moan.

"Do you want my cock in your mouth, Em?" Cole asks me, a sultry tone to his voice, and I nod.

"Yes."

"Open for me," he demands, pressing the head of his cock between my lips. I open my mouth and let him in, sucking on the tip. "Fuck, you're way too good at that."

I beam, proud of myself for bringing him pleasure, and take him farther. I suction my cheeks and pull him to the back of my throat and breathe in deeply when he holds himself there. I gag violently, but he doesn't let up.

"Relax your throat for me." I do, and he goes deeper. "Such a good boy for me, aren't you, Em?" My stomach tightens at the praise, and I swallow around him. "So fucking good for me, baby."

Cole pulls back and thrusts back in, slightly shallow, or at least not all the way in my throat. I'm able to breathe through it, then begin to bob my head up and down to help him out a little. I reach between us to play with his taint, then slide a finger back to his hole, and he moans loudly. I can tell he's close from the way his cock thickens even more, from the way it twitches between my lips. I want him to break. I want him to let go.

I grab the lube next to me and coat my fingers with it, then bring them to his hole. Breaching him with one finger, I go deep and slow, taking my time. By the time I add a third finger, Cole is a panting, groaning mess. He's been fucking my mouth lazily, as if he has all fucking day, when in reality, I know he's been waiting for this.

I give him what he needs, crooking my fingers until I find his prostate, and he shoves his cock back down my throat with a powerful thrust. I gag, and no amount of breathing in through my nose makes it better, but when I pass over his prostate twice more, he comes down my throat with a low moan. It has to be the most erotic thing I've ever heard in my life.

"Yes, Em," Cole breathes, slowing down, his cock softening between my lips. "That was amazing."

I smile as he pulls out of my mouth, and he looks down at me with excitement. I have to say I'm pretty excited too. It's been an eternity since I've been inside of him, and I need it like I need air. Cole drops to the bed beside me and lies down with his head on his pillow, looking like a god. I'm ready to worship him, make him mine. I'm ready to watch this angel fall from grace.

Wiping my mouth with the back of my hand, I get up and kneel between his legs. He spreads them wide, giving me a nice view of his hole, and I swallow hard. I'm probably going to embarrass myself and come in five seconds, but I don't even care anymore.

I coat my cock with lube, then pull Cole down slightly by his thighs and spread them even more. I notch the tip at his entrance and push in slowly; the heat enveloping me, causing my eyes to roll to the back of my head.

"Fuck," I grunt, slowly feeding him inch by inch until I've bottomed out. "You feel like heaven."

Cole smirks, but when I pull back all the way to the tip

and slam my hips against his ass, he moans. I know it's hitting his prostate with every thrust, and I watch him harden right before my eyes. But this isn't how I want to do this today. I don't want to be hard and rough. I want soft and slow. I want to savor him. I want to remind him who he really belongs to—but gently.

I lower myself over him until we're sharing breath, then roll my hips gently. His legs wrap around my waist, squeezing as my hips meet his ass, and he moans loudly.

"Right there," Cole pants against my lips, and I look into his eyes. They're dilated, black swallowing blue, and my stomach flips. "Oh, God."

My forehead meets his as I close the distance between us and kiss him.

The first press of our lips makes butterflies take flight in my stomach, a whole swarm of them. They're going crazy, and I'm getting lightheaded. Cole slips his tongue between my lips, stroking, searching, teasing. My cock grows impossibly harder, and I feel his leaking between our bodies, the pre-cum sticky on my skin.

My moan echoes in the otherwise silent room, and Cole's legs tighten around my waist. I go a little faster, a little harder, desperation suddenly clawing at my insides. I need to come. I need it. I need to come inside of him. I want to mark him, prove that he's mine and only mine.

I pull away from him, pressing my lips to his throat, and suck hard. It's going to leave a bruise, and the thought of it only makes me hotter, makes me fuck him faster until we're sliding up the bed toward the headboard.

"Mmmm," I moan. "Fucking hell, baby. I'm gonna come. I can't take it anymore."

I angle my hips just right, and Cole's back arches off the bed. I know I hit the right spot, so I do it over and over again until my spine begins to tingle and my balls draw up. His cum bursts out of him in spurts, coating every inch of skin between us, and I lose my rhythm. A moment later, I'm coming inside of him, my cock jerking and filling him to the brim. I don't pull out yet, but I still feel the warmth of me leaking out of him around my dick.

"I can't believe you made me wait the full six weeks," Cole says with a gasp as I pull out of him slowly. "Fuck you for that."

I smirk and press a chaste kiss to his lips. "Yes, well, I didn't want you to get hurt."

"Do my feelings count?" He pouts and I chuckle. "Because if they do, then you failed miserably."

Shaking my head, I get off him and go to the bathroom, wetting a rag with warm water and coming back to clean him up. Just as I finish, there's a knock at the door, and we both jump.

"What the fuck…" I curse, opening the door slightly and peeking my head out.

"Are you fuckers finally done?" Alessandro snaps, clearly annoyed, and I roll my eyes.

"How long have you been here?" I ask him.

"Long enough," he says through gritted teeth. "Now get dressed. We have matters to discuss."

I can't imagine what we would possibly need to discuss on a Friday night at ten, but he's either annoyed, or really believes it's urgent. I nod and close the door, grabbing my sweatpants and a t-shirt, and get dressed quickly. Cole is still on the bed, his cock resting against his thigh. He looks worn out and peaceful, and I lean down to kiss him.

"Go to sleep, baby," I whisper, kissing his pierced nose. "I'll be right back."

"Fine," he groans. "But hurry up. I need my cuddles."

I chuckle. "I'll hurry."

With that, I turn off the light and head out of the room, closing the door behind me. My brothers are all sitting on my couch, everyone except for Alex, who's pacing my living room. I can tell something is wrong. I just can't imagine what it is.

"What's going on?" I ask slowly, carefully.

As soon as those words are out of my mouth, Alessandro is turning toward me with narrowed eyes. He huffs like a bull, and I raise an eyebrow at him. But he just turns around and begins to pace once more. I turn to the rest of my brothers, but they just shake their heads at me.

"What—" I begin, but I'm interrupted.

"If you ask me that one more time, I'll kill you," Alessandro snaps and I snort. I want to dare him, to come up with some witty retort, but I swallow it down. This seems serious for him. "Or him."

I frown. "Who's him?"

"Nikolay Petrov," Alessandro growls, as if it should be obvious to me. "I want to murder him in cold blood and throw him in the river."

I raise an eyebrow at him. "You don't even know him."

"Oh, I've met him," Alessandro says through gritted teeth. "I want out."

"Out?" I laugh. "You know that's not possible. You *will* be marrying him."

"No fucking way." He shakes his head vehemently.

"And why the fuck not?" I snap, not sure if I'm curious or annoyed. Probably a bit of both. He knows he can't get out of this, and yet here he is, interrupting my Friday night with Cole. I pretty much fucked him to sleep, and I should be by his side right about now. "Hurry up, I want to go to bed."

"Can you stop thinking about dick for just one minute?" Alex snaps. "This is important."

I take a deep breath and nod. "What's wrong?"

"He's too happy for me," Alex begins, and at this, we all laugh. "Fuck all of you—it's true. He's like a ball of fucking sunshine."

"And he's a twink," Giovanni supplies. "A really hot one at that."

"A twink?" I ask, and he grins. Though Alessandro's frown just deepens. "What?"

"I'll show you a picture." Gio waggles his brows. "I think Cole will really like him."

I narrow my eyes at him. "Like, platonically?"

"Obviously." Giovanni rolls his eyes. "Cole is a total bottom, and so is Nikolay, so there will be nothing to worry about on that front."

"So, what's the issue, Alex?" I raise an eyebrow as he looks at me. "No one is going up your ass. I'd say that's a win."

"A win is a win," Gio agrees. "Come, take a look."

He pulls out his phone and searches for his name on Instagram, just to show it to us. A guy with white-blond hair and sky-blue eyes stares back at the screen—half naked. I raise an eyebrow at Giovanni, and he just smirks. I wonder if that's why Alessandro is about to blow.

"He has an Only Fans." Gio waggles his eyebrows. "He doesn't collaborate, though. Just has solo content."

"Well, that's another win, I'd say." I smirk at Alex, who looks about thirty seconds away from slitting my throat. I laugh. "So your husband is a porn star, and a twink, and a ball of sunshine. Sounds fun."

"Yeah, Alex." Gio smirks, and the rest of my brothers chuckle. "What's not to love?"

"We're supposed to be monogamous," Alex says through gritted teeth.

"And you will be." Gio rolls his eyes, and I can't lie, this is pretty amusing.

"Why are you stalking my husband?" Alessandro growls, and we all raise our eyebrows. Our collective laughter is so loud I wouldn't be surprised if Cole got out of bed for this. "Fuck you all."

"So what else?" I ask with a sigh. "What's the deal breaker?"

"He's fucking crazy," Alessandro says to me, eyes wide. "He wants us to solidify our engagement with a blood pact."

I raise an eyebrow. "Kinky."

"Said that's how it's done in Russia." He sighs, running a hand down his face.

"He's fucking with you," Gio tells him, and I smirk.

"He called it a crimson pact." Alessandro rolls his eyes.

"I think you should do it," I tell Alessandro with a shrug. "Appease him. An act of good faith."

"And what? Give in to his every demand?" Alessandro narrows his eyes to slits, and I nod. "You don't do that for Cole."

"You don't know that." I grin. "I do anything he wants."

"Difference is you're dick-whipped, and I have a clear head," Alex says.

"Not for long, I bet." Gio laughs, and I join in. "How much do you all want to bet Nikolay is going to seduce him?"

We go around placing our bets, and all the while Alessandro looks like he's going to blow up. But he doesn't. Instead, he grins.

"I'm going to enjoy proving you all wrong. I'm *straight*." he says calmly, as if that matters. It doesn't. I've been right where he is now. "There will be no seducing. I hate him already."

"Why?" I ask him.

"He's the enemy," Alex says with exasperation. "On principle."

I roll my eyes. "Not anymore. Now, he's an ally."

Alex scowls at this and heads for the elevator. "I'm not doing this stupid crimson pact with him!"

"Oh, yes, you are," I call after him.

He gets in the elevator, and I just grin.

He's so doing it.

CHAPTER 41
EMILIANO

Alessandro fought against the crimson pact as much as he could, but in the end, Nikolay won. They exchanged cuts on the palm of their hands and mixed their blood together. It was all very old-school, just for Nikolay to smirk when it was all done and over with. I have a sneaking suspicion that it was all a big joke, that he's somehow making fun of Alex, but I can't help but think it's hilarious. I should be defending my brother, but this is the man he's marrying. He should probably get ready. It feels like there's going to be a war between them, and I don't know who's going to come out the winner.

My brother is clearly a jealous man. He hasn't outright said it, but he hasn't had to. I think Nikolay will be using that against him, especially because Alex doesn't know any self-control. He flips out and shows all his cards, and Nikolay seems to be very calculating and methodical. He's a plotter, I can tell, and right now, he's plotting how to make Alessandro's life miserable. It makes me want to welcome him into the family even more. Someone needs to get my brother to loosen up before he pulls a muscle. He doesn't understand the concept.

We're sitting at Giovanni's for a private dinner after hours. The windows and walls are finally fixed from that shootout, and everything is back as it should be. Business is back to usual, thankfully. We didn't lose any customers even after the news was everywhere. And it was—annoyingly so. Unfortunately, or maybe fortunately, we were too busy with Cole being kidnapped to give a damn.

There is a long table in the back of the restaurant for large parties, which we are now occupying. It's me, Cole, my brothers, and Nikolay. Though we're also waiting for Matteo, who hasn't been around since Cole came home six weeks ago. I don't find it odd though, all things considered.

My brothers keep the conversation going, everyone except Alessandro, who is sulking. Nikolay has the biggest smile on his face, as if my brother's unhappiness brings him joy. I chuckle, raising an eyebrow at Nikolay, and he smirks knowingly. Yeah, he's definitely a plotter.

His hand goes under the table, and Alessandro jumps, clearly startled. "Keep your hands to yourself, devil, before I cut them off," Alex practically growls.

"Oh, husband." Nikolay grins. "Then who's going to touch your cock?"

I choke on my water and Cole laughs out loud. Nikolay is nothing if not entertaining. That's for fucking sure. The rest of my brothers turn to watch the show as well, the table falling silent.

"I have a hand—actually, I have two of them."

"Not as good as mine." Nikolay grins. "Though if you insist, at least I'll make some content for you. So you can perform." Giovanni howls at this, and I snicker. "And you *can* perform, right?"

"I perform just fine," Alessandro says through gritted teeth.

"Oh, goodie," Nikolay says, a dreamy expression on his face. "We'll have to see about that."

"I guess we will," Alex snaps. "Enough talk about our sex life, please."

"*Impending* sex life," Giovanni says with a smirk. "Let us know all about it, Nikolay."

"Oh, trust that I will be filing formal complaints," he replies, and all of us laugh.

"Shoot me now," Alex begs me. "Please, Emiliano. I'll do anything."

"No way." I grin. "I want to see what happens next."

"Do we need popcorn?" Gio asks, then shakes his head. "Never mind—we definitely need popcorn."

"So, do you plan on quitting your Only Fans after you get married?" Cole asks, purposely stoking the fire.

Giovanni looks at Nikolay expectantly, and Alessandro scowls, looking at him too.

"Absolutely not." Nikolay grins. "I love what I do."

"You won't need the money, Nikolay." Alessandro frowns. "You can quit."

"Oh, you sweet summer child." Nikolay cups Alessandro's face, looking up at him with fake adoration, and Alex's eyes widen for just a split second before he schools his features. "I've never needed the money. I just like doing it."

"You will stop," Alessandro growls, and Nikolay shakes his head. "You will. I won't allow this to continue. You're my husband."

"So possessive." Nikolay laughs, diverting his gaze away from my brother and looking at the rest of us. "Is he the only one, or does it run in the family?"

"It's in our blood," I say, grinning.

"I love it." Nikolay sighs. "But sorry, Daddy. I'm not easily convinced."

"Don't call me daddy," Alessandro snaps.

"Why not?" Nikolay pouts. "You're ten years older than me."

"Not old enough to be your daddy." Alex sighs. "Let's drop this conversation, please, for the love of God."

"God has nothing to do with this, *Daddy*." Nikolay grins, and Alex scowls. I'm convinced it will be his permanent facial expression for the foreseeable future. "I don't believe in him."

"What do you believe in?" Cole asks, clearly curious.

Nikolay winks. "Love."

Giovanni coughs and laughs. "Oh, fuck. This is too good."

"My sweet, sweet husband will fall in love with me." Nikolay sighs, cupping Alex's face with both hands. And Alex lets him. Oh, shit. "I'll be manifesting it."

"Like witchcraft?" Alessandro asks, clearly worried.

"Just like that, husband." Nikolay grins, pulling Alessandro down and kissing him soundly. Alex stiffens, ripping Nikolay away from him. Sweet Nik isn't deterred in the slightest, not even missing a beat. He just grins again. "I'll be casting spells on you. I'll have you know I have an altar."

"Of course you do." Alex frowns, prying Nikolay's hands from his face finger by finger. "Fucking hippie."

"Oh, you haven't seen anything yet." Nikolay pats Alessandro's face condescendingly.

"And I don't want to." Alex rolls his eyes. "I think I'll just let you live in the condo by yourself. I'll live in a hotel for all I care."

Nikolay pouts, clearly put out. "No way. I need dick every single day, and we'll be monogamous."

Alex sighs, looking heavenward. "Please, God. I've never asked for anything before. But now I'm begging for mercy."

"You'll be begging me too." Nikolay winks.

We all laugh again, and Cole squeezes my thigh under the table. When I look at him, he seems… *happy*. His eyes are sparkling, and he has a wide smile on his face. It's the first time in a long time since I've seen him this way. He has been sad ever since we brought him back from that basement, and

I've hated every second of it. He has nightmares now, too. Not every night, but often enough that I'm worried about him. I've recommended my therapist to him, but he's refused. I need him to get better, though. I'll definitely be pestering him until he gives in.

It's then that the little bell by the front door chimes, signaling Matteo's arrival. Cole tenses beside me, looking away. But not before I see the pain on his face. Nikolay seems to notice it too, because he frowns for the first time. The seat across from us has an empty space for Matteo, and I fear Cole won't be able to handle seeing him. He schools his features though, but everyone looks at him, anyway.

All the air seems to be sucked out of the room as soon as Matteo comes into view... with a man beside him. A man who looks older than my son by at least five years, and I narrow my eyes. Matteo looks at me and smiles, though, a genuine smile, and I'm forced to relax. Mostly because he hasn't smiled at me in months.

"Hi, everyone. I need to make space for one more." Matteo smiles, not daring to look at Cole. I can tell it's on purpose. Doesn't even acknowledge him. I look down to see Cole's hands fisted in his lap.

My brothers all shift their seats and silverware, making space for one more. Matteo just grabs a chair from another table, placing it next to his chair, and they sit down. The man has dirty blond hair and green eyes, and I can't deny he's attractive. He has this sophisticated look about him. He's wearing a black turtleneck shirt with black dress pants and a tan wool coat that reaches past his knees. He looks at Matteo with star-struck eyes. As he should. My son is a catch.

Matteo turns his face and whispers something in the guy's ear, and the man blushes a crimson shade. Everyone has fallen silent, waiting expectantly for introductions, and I clear my throat. At this, my son looks back at me and grins.

"Everyone, this is Hudson." He looks at Hudson once more, and the man looks at me. "My husband."

I choke on my spit, then raise an eyebrow at him. But he just smiles. "Husband?"

Cole clears his throat and asks, "Since when?"

"Since almost two months ago." He smiles softly at Cole, but there's a flash of something in his eyes. I can't tell what it is. But it feels a lot like he's being vengeful. As if he married this poor fucking man to spite Cole. "Sorry, I didn't tell you all. It was a quick thing."

"I can tell," I say slowly. "Where did you get married?"

"Vegas." He shrugs, as if that's the most normal thing to say. Was he fucking drunk when he got married? "Don't worry, Dad. I had my wits about me."

"Just how quick was this?" I ask with a frown. "Matteo?"

"We met when I moved out. Got married right before Cole —" He stops himself. "Had that…accident."

"Before the Christmas party?" Cole asks tightly, and Matteo nods slowly. "Hmmm." Cole hums, but this time he doesn't look broken up about it.

"So tell me, Hudson." I smile. "How old are you?"

"Thirty-two." Hudson smiles back, placing his hand palm up on the table. Matteo holds it, his wedding band glinting in the low lighting.

I freeze. My son just turned twenty-one about a week ago, not that he spent it with us. Fuck. He didn't even bring up Hudson in therapy. I should feel offended, and maybe I do, to a certain degree, but I also understand.

"And what do you do?" I ask him. "Do you have a career?"

I mean, of course he does. He's dressed nicely. He clearly has money, but he just smiles politely, as if he's been expecting this interrogation.

"I'm a surgeon," he says, and Matteo looks at him with a

soft smile, squeezing his hand. As if he's encouraging him to speak. "And I teach at NYU."

"Fancy," Giovanni supplies, and I nod. "He's a catch."

"And tell us, Hudson." I smile back. "Do you know about the family *business*?"

Matteo looks at me, his eyes flashing with defiance. He's trying to convey something, and I'm catching on quickly that Hudson has no idea about the Cosa Nostra. His eyes beg me to shut the fuck up.

At this, Hudson nods. "I know about the real estate company. It's hard not to know about it."

I nod and smile. "Yeah, the biggest one in the city. Matteo should probably come back to work soon."

At this, Hudson frowns. "I don't mind taking care of him until he's ready."

That tells me he knows something about what happened between us. Though I shouldn't be surprised, they *are* married. I just wonder if he knows about Cole. He doesn't seem to, considering he didn't even bat an eye when my man got up and left. He seemed completely unperturbed. Clearly ignorant. Oh, yeah. Matteo hasn't told him about his love life. That much is clear.

"Fair enough." I sigh. "I just need my assistant back soon." I wink, and Matteo stiffens. Hudson seems to sense it because he turns his face and presses a kiss to Matteo's lips. My son relaxes instantly.

"I'll be back soon, Dad," Matteo says, looking at me once more. "After my honeymoon."

"Honeymoon, huh?" I grin. "When is it?"

"Soon," he replies with a smile. "It will be after your wedding, though."

"You're coming?" I frown.

"Of course I'm coming," he says softly. "I'm Cole's best man."

Everyone turns to look at him, and I stiffen. What the fuck? He told Cole he couldn't do it, and now he wants to?

Cole looks up at Matteo, his eyes wide, but doesn't say anything. Instead, he reaches over and grabs my hand, squeezing tightly. We make eye contact, and he shakes his head slightly, and I know it means this is the first time he's heard of it as well.

"You're best friends, right?" Hudson asks, and Matteo nods. "Since childhood?"

Cole smiles at Hudson, and it seems like a genuine smile. "Yes, since Matty was five years old."

"You'll have to tell me all of his embarrassing stories," Hudson tells Cole, whose smile broadens even more.

"I'd love to," Cole says, then proceeds to tell Hudson all about him and Matteo growing up together.

And right now, all I can think about is how lucky I am to have all my family here.

Together.

Hopefully forever.

EPILOGUE
COLE

It's my wedding day.

Time has passed in a blur the past three months, and now we're here. I can't even believe it. Four and a half months ago, everything was hopeless. I didn't even think I'd make it out of that basement alive, and now I'm about to walk down the aisle to my husband. I'm about to promise him forever and always—and I've never been happier. I'm finally where I've wanted to be for years. By his side, permanently. We're going to be unstoppable together. We already are.

We picked everything for the ceremony and the reception together. The same way we do everything else. He didn't even suggest I do it all on my own, which I'm grateful for. I wanted him to be a part of it. It's his wedding too, after all. Nothing, absolutely nothing, could taint today. I know it's about to be the best day of my life.

Matteo has already left me in the groom's suite to join his father at the altar—as my best man. Alessandro is Emiliano's best man, and so they're all waiting for me to walk down the aisle right about now. The wedding planner ushers me outside toward the back of the cabin, and when my shoes meet the grass, everything goes quiet in my head. I'm at peace, finally, exactly where I'm supposed to be.

The pianist begins to play as soon as he sees me, and

everyone turns their heads to look at me. It's beautiful here, with white chairs lined up in rows. White petals are strewn about on the grass, and it's simple but elegant. We opted for a small ceremony with just close friends and family. We're getting married in Washington State to avoid any interruptions from enemy gangs or anything we could be unprepared for. We're determined for this day to be special.

I walk down the aisle slowly, my focus solely on Emiliano, and he grins at me. I can see the tears streaming down his face already, and it triggers my own. Fuck, I knew I'd be emotional, but I'm a mess. He wipes his eyes and face right as I get to him, and he gives me a soft smile that reaches his eyes. They crinkle at the corners, and it makes my heart burst in my chest. I hold his hands, and we turn our bodies to the side.

"We are gathered here today to join Emiliano and Cole on the most special day of their lives. Today, we will see them bind themselves and their lives to each other—for all eternity."

The officiant talks a little more about our love, how strong it is, how much we've overcome. It brings a smile to my face, and before long, it's my turn to say my vows.

"Emiliano." I breathe in through my nose to stop myself from sobbing. "I take you today to be my husband. I promise to always choose you, forever and always. I'll love you fiercely until the day that I die, and even in the afterlife. I will always find you, in this life and the next. You will always be mine."

Emiliano's eyes widen and he sniffles. Tears stream down his face as he looks at me, and his eyes dip to my lips as if he wants to kiss me already. I grin and squeeze his hands, reminding him it's his turn to say his vows.

"Cole." Emiliano clears his throat. "I promise to always fight for you and love you unconditionally for the rest of my life. You are my one and only, and that will never change. I'll love you until my dying breath, and even after that."

The officiant grins. "I declare you husbands." I look at Emiliano expectantly, dropping his hands and stepping closer to him. We cup each other's cheeks and gaze into each other's eyes. "You may kiss now."

This kiss is different from any other we've shared. It feels more meaningful.

The first press of our lips I feel in my chest. It's as if he has a direct line to my heart, and when I part my lips and let him stroke his tongue along mine, my heart squeezes in my chest.

This.

This is what I had been waiting for all my life. This is what I had been yearning for. This love.

It's everything.

He is.

WHAT'S NEXT?

Thank you from the bottom of my heart for reading Shot For Mercy! Please don't forget to review if you enjoyed the book. Reviews are so important to indie authors like me. I am forever grateful for your support!

If you'd like to be part of the community and talk about the book, join the Facebook Group, Ruby's Darklings.

Stalk me:

My website is **authorshaeruby.com**

Sign up for my newsletter at **authorshaeruby.com**

Follow me on Facebook at **Facebook.com/authorshaeruby**

Join my Reader Group at
Facebook.com/groups/rubysdarkling

ACKNOWLEDGMENTS

This is the moment I get to thank everyone for everything they've done for me, so without further ado, here we go!

To my readers, first and foremost. I want to thank each and every one of you for being here and supporting me. I could not do this without you.

To my husband, Conner, I love you forever and always. Thank you for everything.

To my mother, thank you for always supporting me and loving me. I love you.

To my dad, thank you for listening to my craziness. I love you.

To Erin, my girl. I love you soooo much. Thank you for being by my side. You complete me.

To N.J. Weeks, I love you! Our daily talks keep me going, bestie.

To Slasher, thank you for nurturing my crazy ideas and helping me bring them to life! I'm so grateful for you! I love you!

To Quirky Circe, thank you for always being here and designing the most beautiful covers and interiors!

To Angie, thank you for always believing in me! I am so grateful to have you by my side. I love you!

To Michelle Lancaster, choosing an image was the easiest thing I've ever done. You are so talented!

To my beta readers—Ellie and Jay. Thank you for sticking by my side! I love you both!

To Ellie, I'm so grateful to have you in my life!! Here's to many more years and a lot more books.

To Jay, my ride or die, thank you for sticking by me all these years. And for your help with the dedication. You saved my life. I love you!!!

To Marinka, our friendship is so special to me, and it keeps me going! I love you so much. Thank you for always being here for me.

To my Street Team, you guys are AMAZING!! Thank you for all your help. Wow, I really couldn't do this without every single one of you.

Lastly, I want to thank my social media followers both on Instagram and TikTok, my Facebook page, and my Readers Group. None of this would be possible without you spreading the word about my books!

All of you mean everything to me.

With love,
Shae Ruby

ABOUT SHAE RUBY

**Author of dark romance & toxic love.
Sometimes diverse.**

International Bestselling Author in five different countries, Shae Ruby spends her time writing (mostly queer) books that make you *feel*.

Her stories come from deep within her bleeding heart, and she lets the drops flow into her words.

Shae Ruby is represented by Lunar Literary Agency.
For all subsidiary rights, please contact Angie Ojeda-Hazen:
angie@lunarliteraryagency.com

MORE BY SHAE RUBY

THE BROKEN SERIES:

Shattered Hearts (MF)

Battered Souls (Love Triangle)

Tattered Bodies (MFM)

HEATHENS SERIES:

Unhallowed (MMF)

Unholy (MM) — *Releasing Spring 2025*

LA FAMIGLIA COLOMBO SERIES:

Shot For Mercy (MM)

Crimson Pact (MM) — *Coming Summer 2025*

STANDALONES:

Bloody Tainted Lies (MF)

Stay With Me (MF)

Antidote (MM)

Cross My Heart (MM)

Printed in Dunstable, United Kingdom